W9-AFP-265

THE 87TH PRECINCT NOVELS OF ED MCBAIN

ICE

ED McBAIN

MYSTERY

THE BEST MYSTERIES OF ALL TIME

THE BEST MYSTERIES OF ALL TIME

ICE

ImPress is an imprint of The Reader's Digest Association, Inc.,
Bedford Road, Pleasantville, New York 10570.

McBain, Ed, 1926–
Ice/Ed McBain.
    p. cm—(The best mysteries of all time)
ISBN 0-7621-8889-8
1. 87th Precinct (Imaginary place)—Fiction. 2. Police—United
States—Fiction. I. Title. II. Series.
    PS3515.U585I37 2003
    813'.54--dc21
                                    2002155128

PRINTED IN THE UNITED STATES OF AMERICA

The city in these pages is imaginary.
The people, the places are all fictitious.
Only the police routine is based on established
investigatory technique.

ONE

IT WAS still snowing hard when she came out of the theater.

The snow, wind driven, struck her face sharply as she stepped into the alley and closed the stage door behind her. She glanced upward, shaking her head as though reprimanding God, and grimaced at the myriad tiny darts of white swirling in the reflected glow of the hooded light hanging over the door. Reflexively, she lifted the collar of her coat and then yanked the muffler from around her throat and draped it over her head like a scarf. Holding the ends together just under her chin, she began walking toward the street at the end of the alley.

In this city, there were only two good seasons, and even they were sometimes lousy. Winter and summer, you could forget entirely; they were either too hot or too cold. Like *this* winter, which had started in November instead of when it was supposed to. London was worse, she supposed. No, London was better. Well, at least London was dependable; London was *always* lousy. Well, that wasn't quite true, either. She could remember days, when she was living there—ah, those lovely balmy summer days, strolling up Piccadilly, blond pony tail swishing behind her, nineteen years old then and worlds ahead to conquer. Summertime in London.

The snow underfoot was at least a foot deep.

Luckily, she had decided to put on boots before leaving her apartment for the performance tonight, not because she was expecting snow—the snow hadn't begun until sometime after the curtain went up—but only because it was so damn *cold*. The boots afforded at least some protection. They were shin-high, her blue jeans and leg warmers tucked into them, her long gray cavalry officer's coat coming almost to their leather tops. There wasn't a taxicab in sight. Naturally. This city. She had lingered too long in the dressing room, leisurely cold-creaming off her makeup, getting out of the silver-spangled costume all the dancers wore for the finale, and then into her sweater, jeans, socks, leg warmers, and boots. She'd made her big mistake in listening so long to Molly. Molly was having trouble with her husband again. Molly's husband was an unemployed actor who seemed to hold her responsible for having landed a part in a hit musical while *he* was still running around town auditioning. Never mind that Molly's weekly salary paid the rent and put food on the table. Never mind that Molly, like *all* the gypsies in the show, busted her ass doing complicated routines six nights a week, not to mention Wednesday and Saturday matinees. Molly's husband kept railing at her, and in the dressing room Molly kept repeating his angry tirades, and it was all you could do to get out of there by eleven if you weren't careful. It was twenty past eleven now; Molly had gone on *forever*.

All the cabs had been snatched up by audiences pouring out into the night when the shows broke all up and down the street. She could either walk north to Lassiter and hope to catch an uptown bus on the corner there, or she could walk south to the Stem and then four blocks east to the subway station, where she could catch an uptown train. The avenue bordering the theater on the north was perhaps the roughest in the entire city, thronged with hookers and pimps at all hours of the day, but especially after dark. Besides, with this snow, would the buses be running on schedule? No, the subway would be best.

When she reached the brightly lighted Stem, however, she was surprised to find that it was still crowded with people, despite the rotten weather. She stood on the street corner for a moment, debating whether it wouldn't be simpler just to *walk* home. She lived only ten blocks from the theater. If she took the subway, it meant walking the four blocks to the station, and then another block to her apartment building when she got off the train. Besides, would the subway be safer than the Stem at this hour of the night?

She decided to walk.

She walked with a dancer's peculiarly duck-footed waddle. She had been a dancer ever since she was nine—sixteen years now—including four years of study at the Sadler's Wells in London. She had been living then with an oboe player, a young man who could never understand why dancers looked so graceful onstage and so oddly awkward off. Walking duck-footedly, but briskly, she smiled at the memory and thought again of London and longed idiotically for the wet and gloomy winters there—winters *without* the stubborn cold that held this city in its icy grip for months on end. This was February. Spring was only a bit more than a month away. But where was it? She paced herself as if she were doing a routine, head ducked against the wind and the snow, so many strides to the corner, so many strides to the corner after that, pause there for the traffic light—*five* six seven eight—striding out again, the tails of her gray coat flapping in the wind, the snow swirling around her, the blinking lights on the rooftop billboards flashing palely through the fierce sharp flakes.

It was ten minutes to midnight when she reached her own corner.

She turned left at the familiar phone booth, banked with snow now, and began walking toward her building in the middle of the block.

In this city, the neighborhoods changed rapidly. Ten blocks farther downtown, it would have been extremely dangerous to stand on a street corner waiting for a bus at this time of night. But here, only half a mile uptown from the theater, the block between the Stem and Lassiter was a safe, secluded enclave of juxtaposed brownstones, high rises, and small shops. Her own building was midway between the two avenues. The shops, at this hour, were shuttered and dark. She passed the streetlamp two buildings down from her own and was approaching her own building when the man stepped out of the shadowed doorway to the service entrance.

Her head was still ducked against the blinding snow; at first, she only *sensed* his presence. She stopped. He was holding a gun in his hand. She knew only sudden lurching terror. She opened her mouth to scream, or to plead, or to shout for help, but the gun exploded, and she felt a searing sensation below her left breast, and then she fell over backward onto the sidewalk, into the snow, blood bubbling from the wound and soaking the gray cavalry officer's coat.

He stood over her.

He glanced briefly over his shoulder.

He leveled the pistol at her head then and fired two shots directly into her face.

THE girl lay wet and gray and red against the white snow.

The snow was still falling. A patrol car was angled in against the curb, its blinking red dome lights flashing red onto the red-stained snow around the girl. Two detectives from Midtown East stood looking down at the dead girl. Behind them, the two patrolmen who'd first responded to the call were putting up wooden police barricades and cardboard CRIME SCENE placards. One of the detectives was named Henry Levine, and he had been working for the police department since he was twenty-one. He was now forty-six. He looked down at the dead girl's shattered face without blinking. His partner was twenty-eight years old. He had been a cop for six years and had only recently been promoted to Detective/Third Grade. The plastic-encased card clipped to the lapel of his overcoat identified him as Ralph Coombes. In the color photograph behind the plastic, he looked like a teenager.

"I never saw anything like this in my life," he said.

"Yeah," Levine said.

"Did you?"

"Yeah," Levine said. He looked over his shoulder to where the two patrolmen were working on the barricades. One of the wooden crossplanks refused to seat itself properly on the sawhorses. The patrolmen were swearing.

"You gonna be all night there?" Levine asked.

"This thing don't fit right," one of the patrolmen said.

"Her face all blown away," Coombes said, shaking his head.

"Leave it alone," Levine said to the patrolmen. "Come here a minute, willya?"

The heavier of the two patrolmen left the stubborn plank to his partner. He walked over through the snow and put his hands on his hips.

"Who reported it?" Levine asked.

"Guy coming home from work. Lives there in the same building."

"What's his name?"

"I didn't get his name. Frank!" he called to his partner. "You get that guy's name?"

"What guy?" his partner yelled back. He had finally managed to get the crossplank seated on the sawhorses. Dusting off his gloves, he walked to where the other patrolman, his hands still on his hips, was standing with Levine. "What guy you talking about?" he asked.

"The guy who called it in," Levine said.

"Yeah, I got it here in my pad, just a second." He took off one glove and began leafing through his pad. "I can't find it," he said. "What the hell did I do with it?"

"But he lives in the girl's building, huh?" Levine said, sighing.

"Yeah."

"And he's the one who called nine-one-one?"

"Yeah. Whyn't you go ask him yourself? He's inside there with the Homicide dicks."

Levine looked surprised. "Homicide's here already?"

"Got here before you did."

"How come?"

"They were cruising, picked up the ten-twenty-nine on the squawk box."

"Come on," Levine said to his partner.

The two Homicide detectives were standing in the lobby of the building with a man wearing a plaid mackinaw and a blue watch cap. The man was tall and thin, and he looked frightened. The two Homicide detectives were burly and broad, and they looked self-assured. They framed the thin frightened man like belligerent bookends.

"What time was this?" one of the Homicide detectives asked. His name was Monoghan.

"About twelve-thirty," the man said.

"Half-past midnight?" the other Homicide detective asked. His name was Monroe.

"Yes, sir."

"How'd you happen to find her?" Monoghan asked.

"I was coming home from work. From the subway."

"You live in this building?" Monroe asked.

"Yes, sir."

"And you were walking home?" Monoghan asked.

"From the subway?" Monroe asked.

"Yes, sir."

"What kind of work do you do, you're getting home so late?"

"I'm a bank guard," the man said.

"You get home this time every night?" Monoghan asked.

"Half-past midnight?" Monroe asked.

"Yes, sir. I'm relieved at twelve. It takes me a half hour to get home by subway. The subway station's a block away. I always walk home from the subway."

"And that's when you found the girl?" Monoghan asked.

"Walking home from the subway?" Monroe asked.

"Yes, sir."

"Look who's here," Monoghan said, spotting Levine as he came toward them.

Monroe looked at his watch. "What took you so long, Henry?"

"We were on a coffee break," Levine said, deadpan. "Didn't want to rush it."

"Who's this?" Monoghan asked.

"My partner. Ralph Coombes."

"You look a little green around the gills, Coombes," Monroe said.

"A little Irish around the gills," Monoghan said.

"You sure you two guys'll be able to handle this without your mamas here to wipe your asses?" Monroe said.

"At least the cops in Midtown East *have* mamas," Levine said.

"Oh, hilarious," Monoghan said.

"Sidesplitting," Monroe said.

"This here's Dominick Bonaccio," Monoghan said. "Man who found the body. He was coming home from work."

"From the subway station," Monroe said.

"Right, Bonaccio?" Monoghan said.

"Yes, sir," Bonaccio said. He looked even more frightened now that two other detectives had joined them.

"You think you can take over now?" Monoghan asked Levine.

"The squeal's officially yours, am I right?"

"That's right," Levine said.

"Better call your mamas first," Monroe said.

"Tell 'em you're gonna be freezin' your asses off tonight," Monoghan said, and laughed.

"You feel like pizza?" Monroe asked him.

"I thought Chink's," Monoghan said. "Okay, you guys, it's yours. Keep us informed. In triplicate, if you don't mind."

"We'll keep you informed," Levine said.

The Homicide detectives nodded. First Monoghan nodded and then Monroe nodded. They looked at each other, looked at the two detectives from Midtown East, looked at Bonaccio, and then looked at each other again.

"Okay, pizza," Monoghan said, and both cops walked out of the building.

"Choke on it," Levine said under his breath.

Coombes already had his notebook in his hand.

"Do you know who the girl is?" Levine asked Bonaccio.

"Yes, sir."

"How come? Her face is gone."

"I recognize the coat, sir."

"Uh-huh," Levine said.

"It's a new coat. I met her in the elevator on the day she bought it. She told me she got it in a thrift shop."

"Uh-huh," Levine said.

Coombes was writing.

"What's her name?" Levine said.

"Sally. I don't know her last name."

"Lives here in the building, huh?"

"Yes, sir. Third floor. She always gets on and off the elevator on the third floor."

"Would you know what apartment?"

"No, sir, I'm sorry."

Levine sighed. "What apartment do *you* live in, sir?"

"Six-B."

"Okay, go to sleep. We'll get in touch with you if we need you. Would you know where the super's apartment is?"

"On the ground floor, sir. Near the elevator."

"Okay, thanks a lot. Come on," he said to Coombes.

The rest was routine.

They awakened the superintendent of the building and elicited from him the information that the dead girl's name was Sally Anderson. They waited for the assistant M.E. to pronounce the girl officially dead, and then they waited while the Crime Unit boys took their pictures and their prints. They went through the dead girl's shoulder bag after everyone else was through with her. They found an address book, a tube of lipstick, a small packet of Kleenex tissues, an eyebrow pencil, two sticks of gum, and a wallet containing several photographs, twenty-three dollars in fives and singles, and a card identifying her as a member of Actors Equity. The ambulance carted her off to the morgue while they were making their drawings of the crime scene.

It was not until later that morning that Detective Steve Carella and the 87th Precinct were drawn into the case.

TWO

WELL, there it is, Carella thought. Same old precinct. Hasn't changed a bit since I first started working here, probably won't change even after I'm dead and gone. Same rotten precinct.

He was walking uptown from the subway kiosk on Grover Avenue, approaching the station house from the west. He normally drove to work, but the streets in Riverhead hadn't yet been plowed when he'd awakened this morning, and he figured the subway would be faster. As it was, a switch had frozen shut somewhere on the track just before the train plunged underground at Lindblad Avenue, and he'd had to wait with another hundred shivering passengers until the trouble on the line was cleared. It was now almost 9:00 a.m. Carella was an hour and fifteen minutes late.

It was bitterly cold. He could understand how a switch could freeze in this weather; his *own* switch felt shrunken and limp in his trousers, even though he was wearing long woolen underwear. Just before Christmas, his wife had suggested that what he needed was a willy-warmer. He had never heard it called a willy before. He asked her where she'd picked up the expression. She said her uncle had always called her cousin's wee apparatus a willy. That figured. She had been Theodora Franklin before he'd married her, four-fifths Irish with (as she was fond of saying) a fifth of Scotch thrown in. So naturally her cousin owned a "wee apparatus," and naturally her uncle called it a "willy," and naturally she'd suggested just before Christmas that what a nice Italian boy like Carella could use in his stocking on Christmas morning was a nice mink willy-warmer. Carella told her he already *had* a willy-warmer, and it was better than mink. Teddy blushed.

He climbed the steps leading to the front door of the station house. A pair of green globes flanked the wooden entrance doors, the numerals 87 painted on each in white. The doorknob on the one operable door was the original brass one that had been installed when the building was new, sometime shortly after the turn of the century. It was polished bright by constant hand-rubbings, like the toes of a bronze saint in St. Peter's Cathedral. Carella grasped the knob, and twisted it, and opened the door, and stepped into the huge ground-floor muster room that was always colder than anyplace else in the building. This morning, compared with the glacier outside, it felt almost cozy.

The high muster desk was on the right side of the cavernous room, looking almost like a judge's altar of justice except for the waist-high brass railing before it and Sergeant Dave Murchison behind it, framed on one side by a sign that requested all visitors to stop and state their business and on the other by an open ledger that held the records—in the process known as "booking"—of the various and sundry criminals who passed this way, day and night. Murchison wasn't booking anyone at the moment. Murchison was drinking a cup of coffee. He held the mug in thick fingers, the steam rising in a cloud around his jowly face. Murchison was a man in his fifties, somewhat stout, bundled now in a worn blue cardigan sweater that made him look chubbier than he actually was and that, besides, was nonregulation. He looked up as Carella passed the desk.

"Half a day today?" he asked.

"Morning, Dave," Carella said. "How's it going?"

"Quiet down *here*," Murchison said, "but wait till you get upstairs."

"So what else is new?" Carella said, and sighed heavily, and walked for perhaps the ten-thousandth time past the inconspicuous and dirty white sign nailed to the wall, its black lettering announcing DETECTIVE DIVISION, its pointing, crudely drawn hand signaling any visitors to take the steps up to the second floor. The stairs leading up were metal and narrow and scrupulously clean. They went up for a total of sixteen risers, then turned back on themselves and continued on up for another sixteen risers, and there he was, automatically turning to the right in the dimly lighted corridor. He opened the first of the doors labeled with a LOCKERS sign, went directly to his own locker in the row second closest to the door, twisted the dial on the combination lock, opened the locker door, and hung up his coat and his muffler. He debated taking off the long johns. No, on a day like today, the squadroom would be cold.

He went out of the locker room and started down the corridor, passing a wooden bench on his left and wondering for the thousandth time who had carved the initials C.J. in a heart on one arm of the bench, passing a backless bench on the right and set into a narrow alcove before the sealed doors of what had once been an elevator shaft, passing a door also on the right and marked MEN'S LAVATORY and a door on his left over which a small sign read CLERICAL. The detective squadroom was at the end of the corridor.

He saw first the familiar slatted wooden rail divider. Beyond that, he saw desks and telephones, and a bulletin board with various photographs and notices on it, and a hanging light globe, and beyond that more desks and the grilled windows that opened on the front of the building. He couldn't see very much that went on beyond the railing on his right because two huge metal filing cabinets blocked the desks on that side of the room. But the sounds coming from beyond the cabinets told him the place was a zoo this morning.

Detective Richard Genero's portable radio, sitting on the corner of his desk in miniaturized Japanese splendor, blasted a rock tune into the already dissonant din. Genero's little symphony meant that the lieutenant wasn't in yet. Without a by-your-leave, Carella went directly to Genero's desk and turned off the radio. It helped, but not much. The sounds in this squadroom were as much a part of his working day as were the look and the feel of it. He sometimes felt he was more at home in this scarred and flaking, resonating apple-green room than he was in his own living room.

Everyone on the squad thought Carella looked short when he wore a turtleneck. He was not short. He was close to six feet tall, with the wide shoulders, narrow hips, and sinewy movements of a natural athlete—which he was not. His eyes, brown and slanted slightly downward, gave his face a somewhat Oriental look that prompted the squadroom wags to claim he was distantly related to Takashi Fujiwara, the only Japanese-American detective on the squad. Tack told them it was true; he and Carella *were*, in fact, cousins—a blatant lie. But Tack was very young, and he admired Carella a great deal and was really fonder of him than he was of his no-good *real* cousins. Carella knew how to say "Good morning" in Japanese. Whenever Tack came into the squadroom—morning, noon, or night—Carella said, "Oh-hi-oh." Tack answered, "Hello, cousin."

Carella was wearing a turtleneck shirt under his sports jacket that Saturday morning. The first thing Meyer Meyer said to him was, "Those things make you look short."

"They keep me warm," Carella said.

"Is it better to be warm or tall?" Meyer asked philosophically, and went back to his typing.

He did not, even under normal circumstances, enjoy typing. Today, because of the very pregnant lady across the room who was shouting Spanish obscenities at the world in general and at Detective Cotton Hawes and an appreciative chorus of early-morning drunks in particular, Meyer found it even more difficult to concentrate on the keyboard in front of him. Patiently, doggedly, he kept typing, while across the room the pregnant lady was loudly questioning Cotton Hawes's legitimacy.

Meyer's patience was an acquired skill, nurtured over the years until it had reached a finely honed edge of perfection. He had certainly not been born patient. He had, however, been born with all the attributes that would later make a life of patience an absolute necessity if he were to survive. Meyer's father had been a very comical man. At the *briss*, the classic circumcision ceremony, Meyer's father made his announcement. The announcement concerned the name of his new offspring. The boy was to be called Meyer Meyer. The old man thought this was exceedingly humorous. The *moile* didn't think it was so humorous. When he heard the announcement, his hand almost slipped. In that moment, he almost deprived Meyer of something more than a normal name. Fortunately, Meyer Meyer emerged unscathed.

But being an Orthodox Jew in a predominantly gentile neighborhood can be trying even if your name isn't Meyer Meyer. As with all things, something had to give. Meyer Meyer had begun losing his hair when he was still rather young. He was now completely bald, a burly man with china blue eyes, slightly taller than Carella—even when Carella *wasn't* wearing a turtleneck. He was smoking a cigar as he typed, and wishing he could have a cigarette. He had begun smoking cigars on Father's Day last year when his daughter presented him with an expensive box in an attempt to break his cigarette habit. He still sneaked a cigarette every now and then, but he was determined to quit entirely and irrevocably. On a day like today, with the squadroom erupting so early in the morning, he found his patience a bit strained, his determination somewhat undermined.

Across the room, the pregnant lady—in a mixture of streetwise English and hooker's Spanish—yelled, "So how comes, *pendego*, you kippin me here when I couldn't make even a *blind* man happy in my condition?"

Her condition was imminent. Perhaps that was why the four drunks in the detention cage in the corner of the room found her so comical. Or perhaps it was because she was wearing nothing but a half-slip under her black cloth coat. The coat was unbuttoned, and the pregnant lady's belly ballooned over the elastic waistband of the peach-colored slip. Above that, her naked breasts, swollen with the threat of parturition, bobbed indignantly and rather perkily in time to her words, which the drunks found hilarious.

"Tell me, *hijo de la gran puta*," she said grandly to Hawes, grinning at the detention cage, pleased with her receptive audience and playing to the house, "would *you* pay for somebody looks like me?" and here she grabbed both frisky breasts and squeezed them in her hands, the nipples popping between her index and middle fingers. "Would you? Hah?"

"Yes!" one of the drunks in the cage shouted.

"The arresting officer says you propositioned him," Hawes said wearily.

"So where *is* this arresting officer, hah?" the woman asked.

"Yeah, where *is* he?" one of the drunks in the cage shouted.

"Down the hall," Hawes said.

The arresting officer was Genero. Genero was a horse's ass. Nobody in his right mind would have arrested a pregnant hooker. Nobody in his right mind would have filled the detention cage with drunks at nine o'clock on a Saturday morning. There would be stale vomit in the cage tonight, when the citizenry began howling and the cage was *really* needed. Genero had first brought in the drunks, one at a time, and then he had brought in

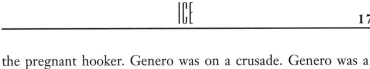

the pregnant hooker. Genero was on a crusade. Genero was a one-man Moral Majority. Which, perhaps, the *real* Moral Majority was as well.

"Sit down and shut up," Hawes said to the hooker.

"No, keep *standin'*," one of the drunks in the cage yelled.

"Turn this way, honey!" another one yelled. "Let's see 'em one more time!"

"*Muy linda, verdad?*" the hooker said, and showed her breasts to the drunks again.

Hawes shook his head. In a squadroom where fairness was an unspoken credo, it rankled that Genero had dragged in a pregnant hooker. He could be forgiven the cageful of drunks—*maybe*—but a pregnant hooker? Even Hawes's father would have looked the other way, and Jeremiah Hawes had been an extremely religious person, a man who'd felt that Cotton Mather was the greatest of the Puritan priests, a man who'd named his own son in honor of the colonial God-seeker who'd hunted witches with the worst of them. Hawes's father had chalked off the Salem witch trials as the personal petty revenges of a town feeding on its own ingrown fears, thereby exonerating Cotton Mather and the role the priest had played in bringing the delusion to its fever pitch. Would his father, if he were still alive, have similarly excused Genero for his zeal? Hawes doubted it.

The woman came back to his desk.

"So what you say?" she said.

"About what?"

"You let me walk, okay?"

"I can't," Hawes said.

"I got somethin' in the oven juss now," the woman said, and spread her hands wide on her belly. "But I pay you back later, okay? When this is all finish, okay?" She winked at him. "Come on, let me walk," she said. "You very cute, you know? We have a nice time together later, okay?"

"Cute?" one of the drunks in the cage yelled, insulted. "*Jesus,* lady!"

"He's *very* cute, this little *muchacho,*" the woman said, and chucked Hawes under the chin as though he were a cuddly little ten-year-old dumpling. He was, in fact, six feet two inches tall, and he weighed an even two hundred pounds now that he wasn't watching his diet too closely, and he had somewhat unnervingly clear blue eyes and flaming red hair with a white streak over the left temple—the result of a peculiar accident while he was still working as a Detective/Third out of the 30th Precinct downtown. He had responded to a 1021, a Burglary Past, and the victim had been a hysterical woman who came screaming out of her apartment to greet him, and the super of the building had come running up with a knife when he spotted Hawes, mistaking Hawes for the burglar, who was already eighteen blocks away, and lunging at him with the knife and putting a big gash on his head. The doctors shaved the hair to get at the cut, and when it grew back, it grew in white—which had been the exact color of Hawes's terror.

The streak in his hair had accounted for a great many different reactions from a great many different women—but none of them had ever thought he was "cute." Looking at the pregnant hooker's naked breasts and appraising eyes, he began to think that maybe he *was* cute, after all. He also began to think that it wouldn't be such a bad idea to let her walk and to take her up later on her fine proposition. She was a good-looking woman in her mid-thirties, he guessed, who carried her coming infant like a barrage balloon, but who had a good slender body otherwise, with long strong legs and very nice breasts indeed, swollen to bursting now and being flaunted with deliberate coercive intent as she sashayed past Hawes's desk, back and forth, back and forth, black coat open, belly and breasts billowing like the mainsail and jibsail of an oceangoing schooner. The drunks began to applaud.

If he *did* let her walk, of course, Genero would bring departmental charges or do something else stupid. Hawes was pondering the inequity of having to work with someone like Genero when Hal Willis pushed through the slatted rail divider, dragging behind him two people handcuffed to each other. Hawes couldn't tell whether the people were boys or girls because they were both wearing designer jeans and woolen ski masks. The drunks in the cage cheered again, this time in greeting to the masked couple. Willis took a bow, spotted the pregnant hooker with the open coat, said, "Close your coat, lady. You'll freeze those sweet little darlings to death," and then said, "Come in, gentlemen," to the two people in the designer jeans and the ski masks. "Hello, Steve," he said to Carella. "It's starting early today, isn't it? Who's that in the cage? The Mormon Tabernacle Choir?"

The drunks found this almost as amusing as they found the pregnant hooker. The drunks were having the time of their lives. First a topless floor show and now a stand-up comic with two guys in funny costumes. The drunks *never* wanted to leave this place.

"What've you got?" Carella asked.

"Two masked bandits," Willis said, and turned to them. "Sit down, boys," he said. "You won't believe this," he said to Carella, and then he turned to where Meyer was typing and said, "You won't believe this, Meyer."

"*What* won't I believe?" Meyer asked, and his words seemed to command the immediate respect of everyone in the squadroom, as though—like a superb ringmaster—he had cracked a whip to call attention to the morning's star performers, diminutive Hal Willis and the two masked men. The pregnant hooker turned to look at them, and even closed her coat so that her *own* star performers would not detract from the action in the main ring. The drunks put their faces close to the meshed steel of the detention cage as if they were death-row inmates in a B-movie, watching a fellow prisoner walk that Long Last Mile. Hawes looked, Carella looked, Meyer looked, everybody looked.

Willis, never one to shun the limelight, upstaged the two masked and manacled bandits and said, "I was heading in to work, you know? Snow tires in the trunk 'cause I planned to have them put on at the garage on Ainsley and Third, okay? So I stop there, and I tell the mechanic to put on the tires for me—don't ask why I waited till February, okay? The *Farmer's Almanac* said it was gonna be a harsh winter. So he starts jackin' up the car, and I take the key to the men's room, and I go out to take a leak—excuse me, lady."

"*De nada,*" the pregnant hooker said.

"And when I come back, these two guys are standin' there with cannons in their hands and yelling at the mechanic, who already crapped his pants, to open the safe. The mechanic is babbling he hasn't got the combination, and *these* two heroes here are yelling that he'd better *find* the combination fast or they'll blow his god-damn brains out, excuse me, lady. That's when I come out of the can zipping up my fly."

"What happened?" one of the drunks asked breathlessly and with sincere interest. This was really turning into a *marvelous* morning! First the topless dancer, then the stand-up comic, who was now becoming a very fine dramatic actor with a good sense of timing and a wonderful supporting cast of actors in masks as in the Japanese traditional No theater.

"Do I need an attempted armed robbery at nine in the morning?" Willis asked the cageful of drunks. "Do I need an armed robbery at *any* time of day?" he asked the pregnant hooker. "I stop in a garage to get my tires changed and to take a leak, and I run into *these* two punks."

"So what'd you *do?*" the drunk insisted. The suspense was unbearable, and all this talk about taking a leak was making *him* want to pee, too.

"I almost ran out of there," Willis said. "What would you have done?" he asked Hawes. "You're zipping up your fly, and suddenly there are two punks with forty-fives in their hands?"

"I'd have run," Hawes said, and nodded solemnly.

"Of *course*," Willis said. "Any cop in his right *mind* would've run."

"I'd have run, too," Carella said, nodding.

"Me, too," Meyer said.

"No question," Willis said.

He was beginning to enjoy this. He was hoping the drunk would ask him again about what had happened back there at the garage. Like any good actor, he was beginning to thrive on audience feedback. At five feet eight inches tall, Willis had minimally cleared the height requirement for policemen in this city—at least when *he* had joined the force. Things had changed since; there were now uniformed cops, and even some detectives, who resembled fire hydrants more than they did law enforcers. But until recently, Willis had most certainly been the smallest detective anyone in this city had ever seen, with narrow bones and an alert cocker-spaniel look on his thin face, a sort of younger Fred Astaire look-alike carrying a .38 Detective's Special instead of a cane and kicking down doors instead of dancing up staircases. Willis knew judo the way he knew the Penal Code, and he could lay a thief on his back faster than any six men using fists. He wondered now if he should toss one of the masked men over his shoulder, just to liven up the action a bit. He decided instead to tell what had happened back there at the garage.

"I pulled my gun," he said, and to demonstrate, pulled the .38 from its shoulder holster and fanned the air with it. "These two heroes here immediately yell, 'Don't shoot!' You want to know why? Because their *own* guns aren't loaded! Can you imagine that? They go in for a stickup, and they're carrying empty guns!"

"That ain't such a good story," the previously interested drunk said.

"So go ask for your money back," Willis said. "Sit down, punks," he said to the masked men.

"We're handcuffed together. How can we sit?" one of them said.

"On two chairs," Willis said, "like Siamese twins. And take off those stupid masks."

"Don't," one of them said to the other.

"Why not?" the other one said.

"We don't have to," the first one said. "We know our constitutional rights," he said to Willis.

"I'll give you *rights*," Willis said. "I could've got *shot*, you realize that?"

"How?" Meyer said. "You just told us the guns—"

"I mean *if* they'd been loaded," he said, and just then Genero came up the hall from the men's room. He said, "Who turned off my radio?" looked around for the pregnant hooker, the only one of his prisoners who wasn't in the detention cage, spotted her sitting on the edge of Hawes's desk, walked swiftly toward her, and was saying, "Okay, sister, let's . . ." when suddenly she began screaming at him. The scream scared Genero half out of his wits. He ducked and covered his head as if he'd suddenly been caught in a mortar attack. The scream scared all the drunks in the cage, too. In defense, *they* all began screaming as well, as if they'd just seen mice coming out of the walls and bats flying across the room to eat them.

The woman's strenuous effort, her penetrating, persistent, high-pitched angry scream—aside from probably breaking every window within an eight-mile radius—also broke something else. As the detectives and the drunks and the two masked men watched in male astonishment, they saw a huge splash of water cascade from between the pregnant hooker's legs. The drunks thought she had wet her pants. Willis and Hawes, both bachelors, thought so, too. Carella and Meyer, who were experienced married men, knew that the woman had broken water and that she might go into labor at any moment. Genero, his hands over his head, thought he had done something to provoke the lady to pee on the floor, and he was sure he would get sent to his room without dinner.

"*Madre de Dios!*" the woman said, shocked, and clutched her belly.

"Get an ambulance!" Meyer yelled to Hawes.

Hawes picked up the phone receiver and jiggled the hook.

"My baby's comin'," the woman said, very softly, almost reverently, and then very quietly lay down on the floor near Meyer's desk.

"Dave," Hawes said into the phone, "we need a meat wagon, *fast!* We got a pregnant lady up here about to give birth!"

"You know how to do this?" Meyer asked Carella.

"No. Do you?"

"Help me," the woman said with quiet dignity.

"For Christ's sake, *help* her!" Hawes said, hanging up the phone.

"*Me?*" Willis said.

"Somebody!" Hawes said.

The woman moaned. Pain shot from her contracting belly into her face.

"Get some hot water or something," Carella said.

"Where?" Willis said.

"The Clerical Office," Carella said. "Steal some of Miscolo's hot water."

"Help me," the woman said again, and Meyer knelt beside her just as the phone on Carella's desk rang. He picked up the receiver.

"Eighty-Seventh Squad, Carella," he said.

"Just a second," the voice on the other end said. "Ralph, will you please pick up that other *phone*, please!"

In the detention cage, the drunks were suddenly very still. They pressed against the mesh. They watched as Meyer leaned over the pregnant woman. They tried to hear his whispered words. The woman screamed again, but this time they did not echo her scream with their own screams. This was not a scream of anger. This was something quite different. They listened to the scream in awe and were hushed by it.

"Sorry," the voice on the phone said, "they're ringing it off the hook today. This is Levine, Midtown East. We had a shooting around midnight, D.O.A., girl named—"

"Listen," Carella said, "can you call back a little later? We've got a sort of emergency up here."

"This is a *homicide*," Levine said, as if that single word would clear all the decks for action, cause whoever heard it to drop whatever else he was doing and heed the call to arms. Levine was right.

"Shoot," Carella said.

"Girl's name was Sally Anderson," Levine said. "That mean anything to you?"

"Nothing," Carella said, and looked across the room. Willis had come back from the Clerical Office not only with Miscolo's boiling water, but with Miscolo himself. Miscolo was now kneeling on the other side of the woman on the floor. Carella realized all at once that Miscolo and Meyer were going to try delivering the baby.

"Reason I'm calling," Levine said, "it looks like this may be related to something you're working."

Carella moved his desk pad into place and picked up a pencil. He could not take his eyes off what was happening across the room.

"I got a call from Ballistics ten minutes ago," Levine said. "Guy named Dorfsman, smart guy, very alert. On the slugs they dug out of the girl's chest and head. You working a case involving a thirty-eight-caliber Smith and Wesson?"

"Yes?" Carella said.

"A homicide this would be. The case you're working. You sent some slugs to Dorfsman, right?"

"Yes?" Carella said. He was still writing. He was still looking across the room.

"They match the ones that iced the girl."

"You're sure about that?"

"Right down the line. Dorfsman doesn't make mistakes. The same gun was used in both killings."

"Uh-huh," Carella said.

Across the room, Miscolo said, "Bear down now."

"Hard," Meyer said.

"However you want to," Miscolo said.

"So what I want to know is who takes this one?" Levine asked.

"You're sure it's the same gun?"

"Positive. Dorfsman put the bullets under the microscope a dozen times. No mistake. The same thirty-eight-caliber Smith and Wesson."

"Midtown East is a long way from home," Carella said.

"I know it is. And I'm not trying to dump anything on you, believe me. I just don't know what the regs say in a case like this."

"If they're related, I would guess—"

"Oh, they're related, all right. But is it yours or mine, that's the question. I mean, you caught the original squeal."

"I'll have to check with the lieutenant," Carella said, "when he comes in."

"I already checked with mine. He thinks I ought to turn it over to you. This has nothing to do with how busy we are down here, Carella. One more stiff ain't gonna kill us. It's that you probably already done a lot of legwork . . ."

"I have," Carella said.

"And I don't know what you come up with so far, if anything . . ."

"Not much," Carella said. "The victim here was a small-time gram dealer."

"Well, this girl's a dancer, the victim here."

"Was she doing drugs?"

"I don't have anything yet, Carella. That's why I'm calling you. If I'm gonna start, I'll start. If it's your case, I'll back off."

"That's the way," Meyer said. "Very good."

"We can see the head," Miscolo said. "Now you can push a little harder."

"That's the way," Meyer said again.

"I'll check with the lieutenant and get back to you," Carella said. "Meanwhile, can you send me the paper on this?"

"Will do. I don't have to tell you—"

"The first twenty-four hours are the most important," Carella said by rote.

"So if I'm gonna move, it's got to be today."

"I've got it," Carella said. "I'll call you back."

"Push!" Miscolo said.

"Push!" Meyer said.

"Oh, my God!" the woman said.

"Here it comes, here it *comes!*" Meyer said.

"Oh, my God, my God, my *God!*" the woman said exultantly.

"That's *some* little buster!" Miscolo said.

Meyer lifted the blood-smeared infant and slapped its buttocks. A triumphant cry pierced the stillness of the squadroom.

"Is it a boy or a girl?" one of the drunks whispered.

THREE

CARELLA did not call Levine back until ten minutes past eleven, because that was how long it took to straighten out the protocol regarding the two corpses. By that time, the squadroom had quieted down considerably. The no-longer-pregnant hooker and her operatic new daughter had been taken by ambulance to the hospital, and the four drunks had been booked for Public Intoxication and led out of the station house to the waiting van by a triumphant Detective Genero, who perhaps did not realize that Public Intoxication was a mere violation as opposed to a misdemeanor or a felony and was punishable only by a sentence not to exceed fifteen days. There was not a man or woman in that squadroom on that bright February morning who did not realize that Genero was wasting the city's time and therefore money by dragging those drunks downtown, where they would undoubtedly be turned loose at once by a judge who knew that every available inch of cell space was needed for more serious offenders than a quartet of happy imbibers. Blithely, Genero went his way. The men—and the one woman who arrived at the squadroom at 11:00 a.m. that Saturday, just as Genero was leading his procession of prisoners out—shook their heads in unison and moved on to the more serious matters at hand.

The woman was a Detective/Second on loan from Headquarters Division's Special Forces Unit. Her name was Eileen Burke, and she worked out of the Eight-Seven only occasionally, usually on cases requiring a female decoy. Which meant that whenever Eileen worked up here, she walked the streets alone as bait for a mad rapist or any other kind of degenerate person out there. Eileen had red hair and green eyes; Eileen had long legs, sleek and clean, full-calved and tapering to slender ankles; Eileen had very good breasts and flaring hips; and Eileen was five feet nine inches tall, all of which added up to someone who could not be missed on a city street if someone else had rape on his mind. But Eileen had once worked a *mugging* case up here, too, with Hal Willis as her backup, and she'd coincidentally worked another case with Willis as her partner in a sleeping bag in the park, both of them pretending to be passionate lovers in a complicated stakeout that included Detectives Meyer and Kling dressed as nuns and sitting on a nearby bench.

Eileen could not later remember the *purpose* of the elaborate stakeout. She remembered only that Willis kept putting his hand on her behind while she tried to watch a third bench, on which there was a lunch pail that was supposed to contain fifty thousand dollars but instead contained fifty thousand scraps of newspaper. Willis—in his role as ardent lover—kissed her a lot while they huddled together in the sleeping bag on that bitterly cold day. The necking came to an abrupt halt when a young man picked up the lunch-pail bait and began walking away toward the bench upon which the fake blind man Genero was sitting, whereupon Genero leaped to his feet, ripped off his dark glasses, unbuttoned the third button of his coat the way he had seen detectives do on television, reached in for his revolver, and shot himself in the leg. In the sleeping bag, Willis managed to slide the walkie-talkie up between Eileen's breasts and began yelling to Hawes, who was parked in an unmarked car on Grover Avenue, that their man was heading his way—it was always fun working out of the Eight-Seven, Eileen thought now. She also thought it was a shame she only got to see Willis every once in a while. Idly, she wondered if Willis was married. Idly, she wondered why she had begun thinking of marriage so *often* these past few days. Was it because no one had sent her a valentine this year?

The squadroom was relatively quiet with Genero and all of his prisoners (the delivered hooker had escaped his grasp—for the time being, anyway) gone their separate ways. Cotton Hawes, at his desk, was taking a complaint from a fat black man who insisted that his wife threw hot grits all over him every time he got home late because she thought he was out larking around with another woman. Those were his words: larking around. Hawes found them somewhat poetic. Hal Willis had already gone down to book the two juves and was leading them into the alley running through the station house and adjacent to the detention cells on the street level, where Genero's drunks were already in the van that would take them downtown. The juves still refused to take off the ski masks. One of the drunks in the van asked them if they were going to a party. As Willis delivered them to the uniformed cop, who slammed the locked door of the van behind them, Eileen Burke perched herself on the edge of Willis's desk upstairs, and crossed her splendid legs, and then looked at her watch, and then lit a cigarette.

"Hello, Eileen," Hawes said to her as he led the fat black grits victim past her and out of the squadroom, presumably to confront the grits-tossing wife in the sanctity of their own peaceful home. Eileen watched Hawes as he disappeared down the corridor. He had red hair, much like her own. She wondered idly if the progeny of two redheaded people would *also* be redheads. She wondered idly if Hawes was married. She began jiggling one foot.

Some three feet away from where she smoked her cigarette and impatiently jiggled her foot, Meyer was on the telephone with his wife, telling her he'd delivered a baby right here in the squadroom with a little—but *only* a little—help from Alf Miscolo, who was at the moment down the hall in the Clerical Office, brewing another pot of coffee now that his hot water was no longer urgently needed in maternity cases. On another telephone, at his own desk, Carella finally made contact with Levine at Midtown East and began apologizing to him for having taken so long to get back.

It had taken him all this while to get back because a police department is like a small army, and a homicide is like a big battle in a continuing war. In big armies, even small battles get serious consideration. In a small army like a police department, a big battle like homicide commands a great deal of attention and participation from a great many people all up and down the line. In the city for which these men worked, the precinct detective assigned to any homicide was the one who'd caught the original squeal, generally assisted by any member of the detective team who'd been catching with him at the time. The moment a squadroom detective said, "I've got it," or "I'm rolling," or some such other colorful jargon to that effect, the case was officially his, and he was expected to stick with it until he solved it or cleared it (which was not the same thing as solving it) or simply threw up his hands in despair on it. But since homicide was such a big deal—a major offensive, so to speak—there were *other* people in the department who were terribly interested in the activity down there at the squadroom level. In this city, once a squadroom detective caught a bona fide or "good" homicide, he had to inform:

1. The Police Commissioner
2. The Chief of Detectives
3. The District Commander of the Detective Division
4. Homicide East or Homicide West, depending upon where the body was found
5. The Squad and Precinct Commanding Officers of the precinct in which the body was found

6. The Medical Examiner
7. The District Attorney
8. The Telegraph, Telephone and Teletype Bureau at Headquarters
9. The Police Laboratory
10. The Police Photo Unit

Not all of these people had to be consulted on protocol that Saturday morning. But the situation was knotty enough to cause Lieutenant Byrnes, in command of the 87th Squad, to wrinkle his brow and phone Captain Frick, in command of the entire 87th Precinct, who in turn hemmed and hawed a bit and then cleverly said, "Well, Pete, this would seem to be a matter of 'member of the force,' wouldn't it?" which Byrnes took to mean "member of the force handling the case," which is exactly what he'd called Frick about in the *first* place. Frick advised Byrnes to go to superior rank within the division on this, which necessitated a call to the Chief of Detectives, something Byrnes would have preferred avoiding lest his superior officer think he was not up on current regs. The Chief of Detectives did a little telephonic head scratching and told Byrnes he had not had one like this in a great many years and, since the police department changed its rules and regulations as often as it changed its metaphoric underwear, he would have to check on what *current* procedure might be, after which he would get back to Byrnes. Byrnes, eager to remind his superior officer that the men of the Eight-Seven were conscientious law enforcers, casually mentioned that there were *two* homicides involved here and *two* detectives in separate parts of the city waiting to get moving on the second and freshest of the killings (which wasn't quite true; neither Levine *nor* Carella were particularly hot to trot), so he would appreciate it if the Chief could get back to him as soon as possible on this. The Chief did not get back until close to 11:00 a.m., after he'd had a conversation with the Chief of Operations, whose office was two stories above the Chief's own in the Headquarters Building. The Chief told Byrnes that in the opinion of the Chief of Operations, the *former* homicide took priority over the *latter*; the member of the force handling the case should be the squadroom detective who'd caught the *initial* squeal, whenever that had been. Byrnes didn't know when it had been, either; he simply said, "Yes, whenever. Thank you, Chief," and hung up and summoned Carella to his office and said, "It's ours," meaning not that it was actually *theirs* (although in a greater sense it was) but that it was *his*—Carella's. When Carella reported all this to Levine, Levine said, "Good luck," managing to convey an enormous sense of relief in those two simple words.

Hal Willis came back into the squadroom some five minutes later, just as a windblown and frostbitten patrolman from Midtown East was delivering the packet promised by Levine when he'd first spoken to Carella earlier this morning. Willis spotted Eileen sitting on the edge of his desk, smiled, and virtually tap-danced over to her. Grinning, he said, "Hey, they sent *you*, huh?"

"Here's that stuff from Levine," Carella said to Meyer.

"You were hoping for Raquel Welch maybe?" Eileen said.

"Who's complaining?" Willis said.

"Who raped who *this* time?" Eileen asked.

"Don't talk dirty in my squadroom," Meyer said, and winked at Carella.

"Looks very thin," Carella said, hefting the yellow manila envelope he had just signed for.

"That it?" the patrolman asked, rubbing his hands together.

"That's it," Carella said.

"Anyplace I can get a cup of coffee here?" the patrolman asked.

"There's a machine downstairs in the swing room," Carella said.

"I got no change," the patrolman said.

"Oh, the old Got-No-Change Ploy," Meyer said.

"Huh?" the patrolman said.

"Try the Clerical Office down the hall," Carella said.

"Is your insurance paid up?" Meyer said.

"Huh?" the patrolman said, and shrugged and went down the hall.

"Where do you want to discuss this?" Willis asked Eileen.

"Oh, the old Your-Place-Or-Mine Ploy," Meyer said. He was feeling terrific! He had just delivered a baby! There was nothing like collaborating in an act of creation to make a man feel marvelous! "Is this the Laundromat case?" he asked Willis.

"It's the Laundromat case," Willis said.

"A rapist in a *Laundromat?*" Eileen asked, and stubbed out her cigarette.

"No, a guy who's been holding up Laundromats late at night. We figured we'd plant you in the one he's gonna hit next—"

"How do you know which one he'll hit next?" Eileen asked.

"Well, we're guessing," Willis said. "But there's sort of a pattern."

"Oh, the old Modus-Operandi Ploy," Meyer said, and actually burst out laughing. Carella looked at him. Meyer shrugged and stopped laughing.

"Dress you up like a lady with dirty laundry," Willis said.

"Sounds good to me," Eileen said. "You're the backup, huh?"

"I'm the backup."

"Where will *you* be?"

"In a sleeping bag outside," Willis said, and grinned.

"Sure," she said, and grinned back.

"Remember?" he said.

"Memory like a judge," she said.

"We'll leave you two to work out your strategy," Meyer said. "Come on, Steve, let's use the interrogation room."

"When do we start?" Eileen asked, and lit another cigarette.

"Tonight?" Willis said.

In the interrogation room down the hall, Meyer and Carella studied the single sheet of paper that had been in the envelope Levine sent them:

(DO NOT FOLD OR ROLL THIS REPORT)		
CRIME CLASSIFICATION Homicide	**POLICE DEPARTMENT** ——— **SUPPLEMENTARY COMPLAINT REPORT**	**DETECTIVE SQUAD** Midtown East **PRECINCT** Midtown East
HERETOFORE THIS CASE WAS CLASSIFIED AS FOLLOWS Homicide	(See Activity Report #379-61-0230)	**COMPLAINT NUMBER** 375-61-0241 **DATE OF THIS REPORT** Feb. 13
NAME OF COMPLAINANT Dominick Bonaccio re	**ADDRESS OF COMPLAINANT** 637 North Campbell	**DATE OF FIRST REPORT** same

victim SALLY ANDERSON

Complainant Dominick Bonaccio discovered victim lying on her
back in the snow at 12:30 AM on his way home from work. Recognized her from the coat she was wearing. Went up to his apartment, called 911, went down stairs again to wait for responding
police officers. (P. O. Frank O'Neal, P.O. Peter Nelson, Midtown
East, Charlie Car.) Victim D.O.A. on arrival. Officer O'Neal
radioed dispatcher, requesting detectives on scene. (See Activity report #375-61-0230) Homicide detectives (Monoghan and Monroe) cruising area, responded to call, arrived at scene before
M.E. Detectives Henry Levine and Ralph Coombes.
   Victim identified as SALLY ANDERSON, white female, age 25.
Hair blond. Eyes blue. Pending exact autopsy measurements,
height appears five feet eight inches, weight approximately one
twenty-five. Assistant M.E. David Lowenby pronounced victim dead
at scene, apparent cause of death gunshot wounds. Pending
autopsy report, wounds appear to be three: one in left side of
chest, two in face. No spent shell casings recovered at scene.
Contents girl's handbag: lipstick, eyebrow pencil, two sticks
chewing gum, address book, Kleenex tissues, wallet with three
photographs, twenty-three dollars U.S. currency, Actors Equity
I.D. card. Canvass of tenants 637 North Campbell no eye witnesses, but statements victim was a dancer employed in a musical called "Fatback," Wales Theater, 1134 North Adderley.
   Body sent to Haley Hospital Morgue. Personal effects in possession Midtown East for transfer to Laboratory. Ballistics section informed BOLO for any bullets recovered from body during
autopsy, early report requested.

Henry Levine

Detective (1st/Gr) Henry Levine
Shield #27842 (Midtown East)

"He types neat," Meyer said.

"Not much here, though," Carella said.

"This must've been before he got that call from Dorfsman, huh?"

"Got fast action with his BOLO," Carella said.

"Let's see what we've got on the *other* one," Meyer said.

In the Clerical Office, Alf Miscolo was brewing the city's worst coffee. Its strong aroma assailed their nostrils the moment they stepped into the room.

"Halloween has come and gone," Meyer said.

"What's that supposed to mean?" Miscolo said.

"You can stop throwing newts and frogs in your coffeepot."

"Ha-ha," Miscolo said. "You don't like it, don't drink it." He sniffed the air. "This is a new Colombian blend," he said, and rolled his eyes appreciatively.

"Your coffee smells just like Meyer's cigars," Carella said.

"I give him all my old butts," Meyer said, and then realized his *cigars* were being attacked. "What do you mean?" he said. "What's the matter with my cigars?"

"Did you come in here to waste my time, or what?" Miscolo said.

"We need the file on Paco Lopez," Carella said.

"That was only a few days ago, wasn't it?"

"The homicide on Culver," Carella said, nodding. "Tuesday night."

"It ain't filed yet," Miscolo said.

"So where is it?"

"Here on my desk someplace," Miscolo said, and gestured toward the wilderness of unfiled reports covering its top.

"Can you dig it out?" Carella said.

Miscolo did not answer. He sat in the swivel chair behind the desk and began sorting out the reports. "My wife gave me that coffee for Valentine's Day," he said, sulking.

"She must love you a lot," Meyer said.

"What'd *your* wife give *you?*"

"Valentine's Day isn't till tomorrow."

"Maybe she'll give you some terrific cigars," Carella said. "Like the ones you're already smoking."

"Here's a *Gofredo* Lopez. Is that who you're looking for?"

"Paco," Carella said.

"There's nothing wrong with my cigars," Meyer said.

"You know how many Lopezes we got up here in the Eight-Seven?" Miscolo said. "Lopez up here is just like Smith or Jones in the *real* world."

"Only one Lopez got shot last Tuesday," Carella said.

"I sometimes wish *all* of them would," Miscolo said.

"Give them a sip of your coffee instead," Meyer said. "Do 'em in as sure as a sawed-off shotgun."

"Ha-ha," Miscolo said. "Paco, where the hell's Paco?"

"When are you going to get around to filing all this stuff?" Meyer said.

"When I get around to it," Miscolo said. "If all our upstanding citizens out there would stop shooting each other, and robbing each other, and stabbing each other—"

"You'd be out of a job," Carella said.

"Shove the job," Miscolo said. "I've had the job up to here. Three more years, I'll be out of it. Three more years, I'll be living in Miami."

"No crime at all down there in Miami," Meyer said.

"Nothing that'll bother *me*," Miscolo said. "I'll be out on my boat fishing."

"Don't forget to take your coffeepot with you," Meyer said.

"Here it is," Miscolo said. "Paco Lopez. Bring it back when you're finished with it."

"So you can file it next Friday," Meyer said.

"Ha-ha," Miscolo said.

In the late-morning stillness of the squadroom, they looked over the sheaf of papers on Paco Lopez. The shooting had taken place last Tuesday night, a bit more than seventy-three hours before Sally Anderson was killed with the same gun half a city away. The girl's body had been found at 12:30 a.m. on the morning of the thirteenth; Paco Lopez had been killed at 11:00 p.m. on the night of the ninth. The dead girl had been twenty-five years old, a white female, gainfully employed. Lopez had been nineteen, a Hispanic male, with one previous arrest for possession of narcotics with intent to sell; he had gotten off with a suspended sentence because he'd been only fifteen at the time. When they'd gone through his pockets on Tuesday night, they'd found six grams of cocaine and a rubber-banded roll of hundred-dollar bills totaling eleven hundred dollars. Sally Anderson's wallet had contained twenty-three dollars. There seemed very little connection between the two victims. But the same gun had been used in both slayings.

The supplementary reports on Lopez confirmed that he'd continued dealing drugs after his initial bust; his street name was El Snorto. No such word existed in the Spanish language, but the Hispanic residents in the 87th Precinct were not without their own wry sense of humor. The people Carella and Meyer had interrogated and interviewed all seemed to agree that Paco Lopez was a mean son of a bitch who'd deserved killing. Many of them suggested alternate means of death slower and more painful than the two .38-caliber bullets that had been fired into his chest at close range. One of his previous girlfriends unbuttoned her blouse for the detectives and showed them the cigarette burns Lopez had left as souvenirs on both her breasts. Even Lopez's mother seemed to agree (although she'd crossed herself when she admitted this) that the world would be much better off without the likes of her son around.

A roundup of known gram dealers had brought up the

information that Lopez was truly a small-time operator, something slightly higher than a mule in the hierarchy of cocaine "redistribution"—as one of the dealers euphemistically called it. Lopez had enjoyed a small following of users whom he'd supplied on a modest basis, but if he pulled down ten, twelve bills a week, that was a lot. Listening to this, Meyer and Carella, who each and separately pulled down only twenty bills a *month*, wondered if perhaps they were not in the wrong profession. All of these more successful dealers agreed that Lopez hadn't even been *worth* killing. He was a threat to nobody, operating as he was on the fringes of gram-dealer society. They all figured some angry cokie had iced him. Maybe Lopez got fancy, started cutting his stuff too fine in an attempt to get more mileage out of the dust, and maybe an irate user had put the blocks to him. As simple as that. But how did a cocaine murder tie in with Sally Anderson?

"You know what I wish?" Carella said.

"What?"

"I wish we hadn't inherited this one."

But they had.

THE superintendent of Sally Anderson's building on North Campbell Street was not happy to see them. He had been awakened at close to one in the morning and interrogated by two other detectives, and he had not been able to fall asleep again till almost two-thirty, and then he'd had to get up at six to put out the garbage cans before the Sanitation Department trucks arrived, and then he'd had to shovel the sidewalk in front of the building clear of snow, and now it was ten minutes to twelve, and he was hungry, and he wanted his lunch, and he didn't want to be talking to two *more* detectives when he hadn't even seen what happened and hardly knew the girl from a hole in the wall.

"All I know is she lives in the building," he said. "Her name's Sally Anderson. She lives in apartment three-A." He kept using the present tense when referring to her, as though her death had never happened and, even if it had, was of small consequence to him—which was the truth.

"Did she live here alone?" Carella asked.

"Far as I know."

"What does that mean?"

"These girls today, who knows *who* they live with? A guy, *two* guys, another girl, a cat, a dog, a goldfish—who knows, and who cares?"

"But as far as you know," Meyer said patiently, "she was living here alone."

"As far as I know," the super said. He was a gaunt and graying man who had lived in this city all his life. There were burglaries day and night in this building and in all the other buildings he'd ever worked in over the years. He was no stranger to violence and had little patience with the minor details of it.

"Mind if we take a look at the apartment?" Carella asked.

"Makes no matter to me," the super said, and led them upstairs and unlocked the door for them.

The apartment was small and furnished eclectically, modern pieces and antiques rubbing elbows side by side, throw pillows on the black leather sofa and the carpeted floor surrounding it, framed three-sheets from various shows, including the current hit *Fatback*, hanging on all the walls. There were several framed professional photographs of the girl in ballet tights, in various ballet positions, hanging on the wall outside the bathroom. There was a poster for the Sadler's Wells Ballet. There was a bottle of white wine on the kitchen counter. They found her appointment calendar near the telephone in her bedroom, on a night table alongside a king-sized bed covered with a patchwork quilt.

"Did you call the lab?" Meyer asked.

"They're through here," Carella said, nodding, and picked up the appointment calendar. It was one of those large, spiral-bound

books that, when opened, showed each separate day at a glance. A
large, orange-colored, plastic paper clip allowed the calendar to fall
open easily to the twelfth of February. Meyer took out his notebook and began listing her daily appointments since the beginning
of the month. He had come through Thursday, February 4, when
the doorbell rang. Both detectives looked at each other. Carella
went to the door, half expecting the super would be standing out
there in the hall, asking for a search warrant or something.

The girl outside the door looked at Carella and said, "Oh."

She looked at the numeral on the door as if somehow she'd
made a mistake, and then she frowned. She was a tall, lissome
Oriental girl, perhaps five nine or five ten, with midnight-black
hair and slanted eyes the color of loam. She was wearing a black
ski parka over blue jeans tucked into knee-high black boots. A
yellow watch cap was tilted saucily over one brow. A long yellow-
and-black muffler hung loose over the front of the parka.

"Do I know you?" she asked.

"I don't think so," Carella said.

"Where's Sally?" she asked, and peered past him into the apartment. Meyer had come out of the bedroom and stood in the living room now, within her frame of vision. Both men were still
wearing overcoats. She glanced briefly at Meyer and then looked
back at Carella again.

"What *is* this?" she said. "What's going on here?"

She backed away a pace and then quickly glanced over her
shoulder toward the elevator. Carella knew just what she was
thinking. Two strangers in overcoats, no sign of her girlfriend
Sally—she was interrupting a burglary in progress. Before she
could panic, he said, "We're policemen."

"Oh, *yeah?*" she said skeptically, and glanced again toward the
elevator.

A native, Carella thought, and almost smiled.

He took a small leather case from his pocket and opened it to show his shield and his I.D. card. "Detective Carella," he said, "Eighty-Seventh Squad. This is my partner, Detective Meyer."

The girl bent to look at the shield. She bent from the waist, her legs and her back stiff. A dancer, he thought. She straightened up again and looked him dead in the eye.

"What's the matter?" she said. "Where's Sally?"

"Can you tell us who *you* are, please?" Carella asked.

"Tina Wong. Where's Sally?"

Carella hesitated.

"What are you doing here, Miss Wong?" he said.

"Where's Sally?" she said again, and moved past him into the apartment. She was obviously familiar with the place; she went first into the kitchen and then the bedroom and then came back into the living room, where the two detectives were waiting. "Where is she?" she said.

"Was she expecting you, Miss Wong?" Carella asked.

The girl did not answer him. Her eyes were beginning to reflect the knowledge that something was wrong. They darted nervously in her narrow face, moving from one detective to the other. Carella did not want to tell her, not yet, that Sally Anderson was dead. The story had not made the morning's papers, but it was certain to be in the afternoon editions, on the newsstands by now. If she already *knew* Sally was dead, Carella wanted the information to come from her.

"Was she expecting you?" he said again.

The girl looked at her watch. "I'm five minutes early," she said. "Would you mind telling me what's going on here? Was she robbed or something?"

A native for sure, he thought. In this city, burglary was always confused with robbery—except by the police. The police only had trouble distinguishing one *degree* of burglary from another.

"What were your plans?" Carella asked.

"Plans?"

"With Miss Anderson."

"Lunch and then the theater," Tina said. "It's a matinee day, half-hour is one-thirty." She planted her feet firmly, put her hands on her hips, and said again, "Where is she?"

"Dead," Carella said, and watched her eyes.

Only suspicion showed there. Not shock, not sudden grief, only suspicion. She hesitated a moment and then said, "You're putting me on."

"I wish I were."

"What do you mean *dead?*" Tina said. "I saw her only last night. *Dead?*"

"Her body was found at twelve-thirty a.m.," Carella said.

Something came into the eyes now. Belief. And then belated shock. And then something like fear.

"Who did it?" she asked.

"We don't know yet."

"How? Where?"

"Outside the building here," Carella said. "She was shot."

"Shot?"

And suddenly she burst into tears. The detectives watched her. She fumbled in her shoulder bag for a tissue, wiped her eyes, began crying again, blew her nose, and continued crying. They watched her silently. They both felt huge and awkward in the presence of her tears.

"I'm sorry," she said, and blew her nose again, and looked for an ashtray into which she could drop the crumpled tissue. She took another tissue from her bag and dabbed at her eyes again. "I'm sorry," she mumbled.

"How well did you know her?" Meyer asked gently.

"We're very good . . ." She stopped, correcting herself, realizing she was talking about Sally Anderson as though she were still alive. "We were very good friends," she said softly.

"How long had you known her?"

"Since *Fatback*."

"Are you a dancer, too, Miss Wong?"

She nodded.

"And you'd known her since the show opened?"

"Since we went into rehearsal. Even longer ago than that, in fact. From when we were auditioning. We met at the first audition."

"When was that, Miss Wong?" Meyer asked.

"Last June."

"And you've been good friends since."

"She was my *best* friend." She shook her head. "I can't *believe* this."

"You say you saw her only last night . . ."

"Yes."

"Was there a performance last night?"

"Yes."

"What time did the curtain come down?"

"About a quarter to eleven. We ran a little long last night. Joey—he's our comic, I don't know if you're familiar with the show . . ."

"No," Carella said.

"No," Meyer said.

The girl looked surprised. She shrugged, dismissing their ignorance, and then said, "Joey Hart. He was bringing down the house in the second act, so he milked it for all it was worth. We ran fifteen minutes over."

"The curtain usually comes down at ten-thirty, is that it?" Meyer asked.

"Give or take, either way. It varies. It depends on the house."

"And is that the last time you saw Sally Anderson alive?"

"In the dressing room later," Tina said.

"Who else was in the dressing room?"

"All the gypsies. The girls, anyway."

"Gypsies?"

"The dancers in the chorus."

"How many of them?"

"There are sixteen of us altogether. Boys and girls. Eight of us were in the girls' dressing room. Five blondes, two blacks, and a token Chink—*me.*" She paused. "Jamie digs blondes."

"Jamie?"

"Our choreographer. Jamie Atkins."

"So you were in the dressing room . . ."

"All eight of us. Taking off our makeup, getting out of our costumes . . . like that."

"What time did you leave the dressing room, Miss Wong?"

"I got out as fast as I could." She paused. "I had a date."

"Who was in the dressing room when you left?" Meyer asked.

"Just Sally and Molly."

"Molly?"

"Maguire." She paused. "She changed her name. It used to be Molly Materasso, which isn't too terrific for the stage, am I right?" Carella guessed it was not too terrific for the stage. "In fact, it means 'mattress.' " Carella knew it meant mattress. "In fact, that was her *maiden* name. She's married now, and her *real* name is Molly Boyd, but she still uses Molly Maguire on the stage. It's a good name. Because of the Molly Maguires, you know." Carella looked at her blankly. "It was a secret society in Ireland. In the 1840s," she said. Carella was still looking at her blankly. "And later in Pennsylvania," she said. "Anyway, you hear the name, you think you know her from someplace. The name gets her lots of jobs because directors and producers think, 'Hey, Molly *Maguire,* sure, *I* know *her.*' Actually, she's a pretty lousy dancer."

"But she was there alone in the dressing room with Sally when you left," Meyer said.

"Yes."

"What time was that?"

"About five after eleven."

"What were they talking about, do you know?"

"It was *Molly* who was doing all the talking."

"About what?"

"Geoffrey. Her husband. That's why I got out of there as fast as I could. Actually, I wasn't supposed to meet my date till midnight."

"I don't understand," Meyer said.

"Well, Molly keeps bitching about her husband, and it gets to be a drag. I wish she'd either shut up or else divorce him."

"Uh-huh," Meyer said.

"And that's the last time you saw her, right?" Carella said.

"Yeah, right. I *still* can't believe this. I mean . . . *God!* We had a cup of *coffee* together just before half-hour last night."

"What'd you talk about then, Miss Wong?"

"Girl talk," Tina said, and shrugged.

"Men?" Carella said.

"Of course men," Tina said, and shrugged again.

"Was she living with anybody?" Meyer asked.

"Not in that sense."

"What sense is that?"

"Most of *her* clothes were here, most of *his* were there."

"Whose clothes?" Carella asked.

"Timmy's."

"Is he a boyfriend or something?" Meyer asked.

"Or something," Tina said.

"Timmy what?" Carella asked.

"Moore."

"Is the Timmy for Timothy?"

"I think so."

"Timothy Moore," Meyer said, writing the name into his notebook. "Do you know where he lives?"

"Downtown, just outside the Quarter. He's a med student at Ramsey U. His apartment is near the school someplace."

"You wouldn't know the address, would you?"

"I'm sorry," Tina said.

"When you say 'or something . . .'" Carella said.

"Well, they were sort of on-again off-again."

"But they *were* romantically involved?"

"Do you mean were they sleeping together?"

"Yes, that's what I mean."

"Yes, they were sleeping together," Tina said. "Isn't everybody?"

"I suppose," Carella said. "Did she ever mention a man named Paco Lopez?"

"No. Who's Paco Lopez? Is he in show business?"

Carella hesitated a moment and then said, "Was Sally doing drugs?"

"I don't think so."

"Never mentioned drugs to you?"

"Are you talking about a little pot every now and then, or what?"

"I'm talking about the hard stuff. Heroin," he said, and paused. "Cocaine," he said, and watched her closely.

"Sally smoked pot," Tina said. "Who doesn't? But as for anything else, I don't think so."

"You're sure of that?"

"I couldn't swear to it in a court of law, if that's what you mean. But usually, you can get a pretty good idea of who's doing what when you're working in a show, and I don't think Sally was doing any kind of hard drugs."

"Are you suggesting that *some* members of the cast . . ."

"Oh, sure."

"Uh-huh," Carella said.

"Not heroin," Tina said. "Nobody's *that* stupid anymore. But some coke here and there, now and then, sure."

"But not Sally."

"Not to my knowledge." Tina paused. "Not *me*, either, if that's your next question."

"That wasn't my next question," Carella said, and smiled. "Did Sally ever mention any threatening letters or telephone calls?"

"Never."

"Did she owe anybody money? To your knowledge?"

"Not that I know of."

"Anything seem to be troubling her?"

"No. Well, yes."

"What?"

"Nothing serious."

"Well, what?"

"She wanted to take singing lessons again, but she didn't know how she could find the time. She had dance every day, you know, and she was seeing a shrink three times a week."

"And that's it? That's all that was troubling her?"

"That's all she ever mentioned to me."

"Would you know her shrink's name?"

"I'm sorry, no."

"How'd she get along with the rest of the cast?"

"Fine."

"How about management?"

"Who do you mean? Allan?"

"Who's Allan?"

"Our producer, Allan Carter. I mean, who do you mean by management? The company manager? The general manager?"

"Any or all of them. How'd she get along with the people who were *running* the show?"

"Fine, I guess," Tina said, and shrugged. "Once a show opens, you rarely *see* any of those people anymore. Well, in our case, because we're such a big hit, Freddie comes around to check it out once or twice a week, make sure we aren't coasting. But for the most part—"

"Freddie?"

"Our director. Freddie Carlisle."

"How do you spell that?" Meyer asked, beginning to write again.

"With an *i* and an *s*," Tina said. "C-a-r-l-i-s-l-e."

"And you said your producer's—"

"Allan Carter. Two *l*'s and an *a*."

"Who's your company manager?"

"Danny Epstein."

"And your general manager?"

"Lew Eberhart."

"Anybody else we should know about?" Carella asked.

Tina shrugged. "The stage managers? We've got three of them." She shrugged again. "I mean, there are thirty-eight people in the cast alone, and God knows how many musicians and electricians and carpenters and property men and—"

"Any of them Hispanic?"

"In the crew, do you mean? I guess so. I don't know too many of them. Except to pass them by in my underwear."

She smiled suddenly and radiantly and then seemed to remember what they were talking about here. The smile dropped from her face.

"How about the cast? Any Hispanics in the cast?" Carella asked.

"Two of the gypsies," Tina said.

"Could we have their names, please?" Meyer said.

"Tony Asensio and Mike Roldan. Roldan doesn't *sound* like a Spanish name, but it is. Actually, it's *Miguel* Roldan."

"Was Sally particularly friendly with either of them?"

"The gypsies in a show get to know each other pretty well," Tina said.

"How well did she know these two men?" Carella asked.

"Same as the rest of us," Tina said, and shrugged.

"Did she ever date either of them?"

"They're both faggots," Tina said. "In fact, they're living

together." As though talk of the show had suddenly reminded her of the afternoon performance, she looked swiftly at her watch. "Oh, my God," she said, "I've got to get out of here. I'll be late!" And suddenly a look of self-chastisement crossed her face, and it appeared as if she would burst into tears again. "The show must go on, huh?" she said bitterly, shaking her head. "*I'm* worrying about the goddamn *show*, and Sally's *dead*."

FOUR

FROM where the two patrolmen sat in the patrol car parked at the curb, it seemed evident that the priest was winning the fight. They had no desire to get out of the car and break up the fight, not with it being so cold out there, and especially since the priest seemed to be winning. Besides, they were sort of enjoying the way the priest was mopping up the street with his little spic opponent.

Up here in the Eight-Seven, you sometimes couldn't tell the spics (*Hispanics*, you were supposed to say in your reports) from the whites because some of them had high Spanish blood in them and looked the same as your ordinary citizen. For all the patrolmen knew, the *priest* was a spic, too, but he had a very white complexion, and he was bigger than most of the cockroach-kickers up here. The two patrolmen sat in the heated comfort of the car and guessed aloud that he was maybe six three, six four, something like that, maybe weighing in at two hundred and forty pounds or thereabouts. They couldn't figure which church he belonged to. None of the neighborhood churches had priests who dressed the way this one was dressed, but maybe he was visiting from someplace in California—they dressed that way in California, didn't they, at those missions they had out there in the Napa Valley? The priest was wearing a brown woolen robe, and his head was shaved like a monk's head, its bald crown glistening above the tonsure that encircled it like a wreath. One of the patrolmen in the car asked the other one what you called that brown thing the priest was wearing, that thing like a dress, you know? The other patrolman told him it was called a *hassock*, stupid, and the first patrolman said, "Oh yeah, right." They were both rookies who had been working out of the Eight-Seven for only the past two weeks, otherwise they'd have known that the priest wasn't a priest at all, even though he was known in the precinct as Brother Anthony.

Clearly, Brother Anthony was in fact beating the man to a pulp. The man was a little Puerto Rican pool shark who'd made the enormous mistake of trying to hustle him. Brother Anthony had dragged the little punk out of the pool hall and first had picked him up and hurled him against the brick wall of the tenement next door, just to stun him, you know, and then had swung a pool cue at his kneecaps, hoping to break them but breaking only the pool cue instead, and was now battering him senseless with his hamlike fists as the two patrolmen watched from the snug comfort of the patrol car. Brother Anthony weighed a lot, but he had lifted weights in prison, and there wasn't an ounce of fat on his body. He sometimes asked people to hit him as hard as they could in the belly, and laughed with pleasure whenever anyone told him how hard and strong he was. All year round, even in the hot summer months, he wore the brown woolen cassock. During the summer months, he wore nothing at all under it. He would lift the hem of the cassock and show his sandals to the neighborhood hookers. "See?" he would say. "That's all I got on under this thing." The hookers would oooh and ahhh and try to lift the cassock higher, making believe they didn't think he was really naked under it. Brother Anthony was very graceful for such a big man; he would laugh and dance away from them, dance away.

In the winter, he wore army combat boots instead of the sandals. He was using those boots now to stomp the little Puerto Rican pool hustler into the icy sidewalk. In the patrol car, the two cops debated whether they should get out and break this thing up before the little spic got his brains squashed all over the sidewalk. They were spared having to make any decision because their radio erupted with a 1010, and they radioed back that they were rolling on it. They pulled away from the curb just as Brother Anthony leaned over the prostrate and unconscious hustler to take his wallet from his pocket. Only ten dollars of the money in that wallet had been hustled from Brother Anthony, but he figured he might as well take *all* of it because of all the trouble the little punk had put him to. He was cleaning out the wallet when Emma came around the corner.

Emma was known in the neighborhood as the Fat Lady, and most of the people in the precinct tried to steer very clear of her because she was known to possess a short temper and a straight-edge razor. She carried the razor in her shoulder bag, hanging from the left shoulder, so that she could reach in there with her right hand, and whip open the razor in a flash, and lop off any dude's ear or slash his face or his hands or sometimes go for the money, open the man's windpipe and his jugular with one and the same stroke. Nobody liked to mess with the Fat Lady, which was perhaps why the crowd began to disperse the moment she came around the corner. On the other hand, the crowd might have dispersed anyway, now that the action had ended; nobody liked to stand around doing nothing on a cold day, especially in *this* neighborhood, where somehow it always seemed colder than anyplace else in the city. This neighborhood could have been Moscow. The park bordering this neighborhood could have been Gorky Park. Maybe it was. Or vice versa.

"Hello, bro," the Fat Lady said.

"Hello, Emma," he said, looking up from where he was

crouched over the unconscious hustler. He had stomped the man real good. A thin trickle of blood was beginning to congeal on the ice beneath the stupid punk's head. His face looked very blue. Brother Anthony tossed the empty wallet over his shoulder, stood up to his full height, and tucked the five hundred-odd dollars into the pouchlike pocket at the front of the cassock. He began walking, and Emma fell into step beside him.

Emma was perhaps thirty-two or thirty-three years old, in any event a good six or seven years older than Brother Anthony. Her full name was Emma Forbes, which had been her name when she was still married to a black man named Jimmy Forbes, since deceased, the unfortunate victim of a shoot-out in a bank he'd been trying to hold up. The man who'd shot and killed Emma's husband was a bank guard who'd been sixty-three years old at the time, a retired patrolman out of the 28th Precinct downtown. He'd never lived to be sixty-*four*, because Emma sought him out a month after her husband's funeral and slit his throat from ear to ear one fine April night when the forsythias were just starting to bud. Emma did not like people who deprived her or her loved ones of anything they wanted or needed. Emma was fond of saying, "The opera ain't over till the fat lady sings," an expression she used to justify her frequent vengeful attacks. It was uncertain whether the expression had preceded the nickname or vice versa. When someone was five feet six inches tall and weighed a hundred and seventy pounds, it was reasonable to expect—especially in *this* neighborhood, where street names were as common as legal names—that sooner or later someone would begin calling her the Fat Lady, even without having heard her operatic reference.

Brother Anthony was one of the very few people who knew that the name on her mailbox was Emma Forbes and that she had been born Emma Goldberg, not to be confused with the anarchist Emma Goldman, who'd been around long before Emma

Goldberg was even born. Brother Anthony was also one of the very few people who called her Emma, the rest preferring to call her either Lady (not daring to use the adjective in her presence) or nothing at all, lest she suddenly take offense at an inflection and whip out that razor of hers. Brother Anthony was the only person in the precinct, and perhaps the entire world, who thought Emma Goldberg Forbes a.k.a. the Fat Lady was exceptionally beautiful and extraordinarily sexy besides.

"Listen, there's no accounting for taste," a former acquaintance once said to Brother Anthony immediately after he'd mentioned how beautiful and sexy he thought Emma was. The man's thoughtless comment was uttered a moment before Brother Anthony plucked him off his stool and hurled him through the plate-glass mirror behind the bar at which they'd been sitting. Brother Anthony did not like people who belittled the way he felt about Emma. Brother Anthony saw her quite differently than most people saw her. Most people saw a dumpy little bleached blonde in a black cloth coat and black cotton stockings and blue track shoes and a black shoulder bag in which there was a straightedge razor with a bone handle. Brother Anthony—despite empirical knowledge to the contrary—saw a natural blonde with curly ringlets that framed a Madonna-like face and beautiful blue eyes; Brother Anthony saw breasts like watermelons and a behind like a brewer's horse; Brother Anthony saw thick white thighs and acres and acres of billowy flesh; Brother Anthony saw a shy, retiring, timid, vulnerable darling dumpling caught in the whirlwind of a hostile society, someone to cuddle and cherish and console.

Just walking beside her, Brother Anthony had an erection, but perhaps that was due to the supreme satisfaction of having beaten that pool hustler to within an inch of his life; it was sometimes difficult to separate and categorize emotions, especially when it was so cold outside. He took Emma's elbow and led her onto Mason Avenue toward a bar in the middle of a particularly sordid stretch of real estate that ran north and south for a total of three blocks. There was a time when the Street (as the three-block stretch was familiarly defined) was called the Hussy Hole by the Irish immigrants and later Foxy Way by the blacks. With the Puerto Rican influx, the street had changed its language—but not its major source of income. The Puerto Ricans referred to it as La Vía de Putas. The cops used to call it Whore Street before the word *hooker* became fashionable. They now referred to it as Hooker Heaven. In any language, you paid your money, and you took your choice.

Not too long a time ago, the madams who ran the sex emporiums called themselves Mama-this or Mama-that. In those days, Mama Teresa's was the best-known joint on the street. Mama Carmen's was the filthiest. Mama Luz's had been raided most often by the cops because of the somewhat exotic things that went on behind its crumbling brick façade. Those days were gone forever. The brothel, as such, was a thing of the past, a quaint memory. Nowadays, the hookers operated out of the massage parlors and bars that lined the street, and turned their tricks in the hot-bed hotels that blinked their eyeless neon to the night. The bar Brother Anthony chose was a hooker hangout named Sandy's, but at two in the afternoon most of the neighborhood working girls were still sleeping off Friday night's meaningless exercise. Only a black girl wearing a blond wig was sitting at the bar.

"Hello, Brother Anthony," she said. "Hello, Lady."

"*Dominus vobiscum,*" Brother Anthony said, cleaving the air with the edge of his right hand in a downward stroke, and then passing the hand horizontally across the first invisible stroke to form the sign of the cross. He had no idea what the Latin words meant. He knew only that they added to the image he had consciously created for himself. "All is image," he liked to tell Emma, the words rolling mellifluously off his tongue, his voice deep and resonant, "all is illusion."

"What'll it be?" the bartender asked.

"A little red wine, please," Brother Anthony said. "Emma?"

"Gin on the rocks, a twist," Emma said.

"See what the other lady will have," Brother Anthony said, indicating the black-and-blond hooker. He was feeling flush. His encounter with the ambitious pool hustler had netted him a five-hundred-dollar profit. He asked the bartender for some change, went to the juke box, and selected an assortment of rock-and-roll tunes. He loved rock-and-roll. He especially loved rock-and-roll groups that dressed up on stage so you couldn't recognize them later on the street. The black-and-blond hooker was telling the bartender she wanted another scotch and soda. As Brother Anthony went back to his stool at the other end of the bar, she said, "Thanks, Brother Anthony."

The bartender, who was also the Sandy who owned the place, wasn't too happy to see Brother Anthony in here. He did not like having to replace plate-glass mirrors every time Brother Anthony took it in his head to get insulted by something somebody said. Luckily, the only other person in here today, besides Brother Anthony and his fat broad, was the peroxided nigger at the end of the bar, and Brother Anthony had just bought *her* a drink, so maybe there'd be no trouble this afternoon. Sandy hoped so. This was Saturday. There'd be plenty of trouble here tonight, whether Sandy wanted it or not.

In this neighborhood, and especially on this street, Saturday night was never the loneliest night of the week, no matter *what* the song said. In this neighborhood, and especially on this street, nobody had to go lonely on a Saturday night, not if he had yesterday's paycheck in his pocket. Along about ten tonight, there'd be more hookers cruising this bar than there'd be rats rummaging in the empty lot next door, black hookers and white ones, blondes and brunettes and redheads, even some with pink hair or lavender hair, males and females and some who were AC/DC.

Two by two they came, it took all kinds to make a world, into the ark they came, your garden-variety scaly-legged twenty-dollar-a-blowjob beasts or your slinky racehorses who thought they should be working downtown at a C-note an hour, it took all kinds to make a pleasant family neighborhood bar. Two by two they came and were welcomed by Sandy, who recognized that all those men drinking at the bar were here to sample the flesh and not the spirits and who was anyway getting a piece of the action from each of the nocturnal ladies who were allowed to cruise here, his recompense (or so he told them) for having to pay off the cops on the beat and also their sergeant, who dropped in every now and again. Actually, Sandy was ahead of the game, except when the weekend trouble assumed larger proportions than it normally did. He dreaded weekends, even though it was the weekends that made it possible for the bar to remain open on weekdays.

"This is on the house," he said to Brother Anthony, hoping the bribe would keep him away from here tonight and then suddenly panicking when he realized Brother Anthony might *like* the hospitality and might decide to return for more of it later.

"I pay for my own drinks," Brother Anthony said, and fetched the roll of bills from the pouchlike pocket running across the front of his cassock, and peeled off one of the pool hustler's tens, and put it on the bar.

"Even so . . ." Sandy started, but Brother Anthony silently made the sign of the cross on the air, and Sandy figured who was he to argue with a messenger of God? He picked up the ten-spot, rang up the sale, and then put Brother Anthony's change on the bar in front of him. At the end of the bar, the black hooker in the frizzy blond wig lifted her glass and said, "Cheers, Brother Anthony."

"*Dominus vobiscum,*" Brother Anthony said, lifting his own glass.

Emma put her fleshy hand on his knee.

"Did you hear anything else?" she whispered.

"No," he said, shaking his head. "Did you?"

"Only that he had eleven bills in his wallet when he caught it."

"Eleven bills," Brother Anthony whispered.

"And also, it was a thirty-eight. The gun."

"Who told you that?"

"I heard two cops talking in the diner."

"A thirty-eight," Brother Anthony said. "Eleven bills."

"That's the kind of bread I'm talking about," Emma said. "That's *cocaine* bread, my dear."

Brother Anthony let his eyes slide sidelong down the bar, just to make sure neither the bartender nor the black hooker were tuning in. The bartender was leaning over the bar, in deep and whispered conversation with the hooker. His fingertips roamed the yoke front of her dress, brushing the cleft her cushiony breasts formed. Brother Anthony smiled.

"The death of that little *schwanz* has left a gap," Emma said.

"Indeed," Brother Anthony said.

"There are customers adrift in the night," Emma said.

"Indeed," Brother Anthony said again.

"It would be nice if we could *fill* that gap," Emma said. "Inherit the trade, so to speak. Find out who the man was servicing, become their *new* candyman and candylady."

"There's people who might not like that," Brother Anthony said.

"I don't agree with you. I don't think the little pisher was killed for his trade. No, my dear, I definitely disagree with you."

"Then why?"

"Was he killed? My educated guess?"

"Please," Brother Anthony said.

"Because he was a stupid little man who probably got stingy with one of his customers. That's my guess, bro. But, ah, my dear, when *we* begin selling the nose dust, it'll be a different story. We will be sugar-sweet to everybody; we will be Mr. and Mrs. Nice."

"How do we get the stuff to sell?" Brother Anthony asked.

"First things first," Emma said. "*First* we get the customers, *then* we get the candy."

"How many customers do you think he had?" Brother Anthony asked.

"Hundreds," Emma said. "Maybe thousands. We are going to get rich, my dear. We are going to thank God every day of the week that somebody killed Paco Lopez."

"*Dominus vobiscum,*" Brother Anthony said, and made the sign of the cross.

TIMOTHY Moore came into the squadroom not ten minutes after a package of Sally Anderson's effects was delivered by a patrolman from Midtown East. The accompanying note from Detective Levine mentioned that he had talked with the dead girl's boyfriend and they ought to expect a visit from him. So here he was *now*, standing just outside the slatted rail divider and introducing himself to Genero, who immediately said, "That ain't my case."

"In here, sir," Meyer said, signaling to Moore, who looked up, nodded, found the release catch on the inside of the gate, and let himself into the squadroom. He was a tall, angular young man with wheat-colored hair and dark brown eyes. The trench coat he was wearing seemed too lightweight for this kind of weather, but perhaps the long striped muffler around his neck and the rubber boots on his feet were some sort of compensation. His eyes were quite solemn behind the aviator eyeglasses he wore. He took Meyer's offered hand and said, "Detective Carella?"

"I'm Detective Meyer. *This* is Detective Carella."

"How do you do?" Carella said, rising from behind his desk and extending his hand. Moore was just a trifle taller than he was; their eyes met at almost the same level.

"Detective Levine at Midtown East . . ."

"Yes, sir."

"Told me the case had been turned over to you."

"That's right," Carella said.

"I went up there the minute I learned about Sally."

"When was that, sir?"

"This morning. I heard about it this morning."

"Sit down, won't you? Would you like some coffee?"

"No, thank you. I went up there at about ten o'clock, it must've been, right after I heard the news on the radio."

"Where was this, Mr. Moore?"

"In my apartment."

"And where's that?"

"On Chelsea Place. Downtown, near the university. Ramsey."

"We understand you're a medical student there," Carella said.

"Yes." He seemed puzzled as to how they already knew this, but he let it pass, shrugging it aside. "I went back up there a little while ago—"

"Up there?"

"Midtown East. And Mr. Levine told me the case had been turned over to you. So I thought I'd check with you, just to see if there was anything I could do to help."

"We appreciate that," Carella said.

"How long had you known Miss Anderson?" Meyer asked.

"Since last July. I met her shortly after my father died."

"How'd you happen to meet her?"

"At a party I crashed. She . . . The minute I saw her . . ." He looked down at his hands. The fingers were long and slender, the nails as clean as a surgeon's. "She was . . . very beautiful. I . . . was attracted to her from the first minute I saw her."

"So you began seeing her . . ."

"Yes . . ."

"Last July."

"Yes. She'd just gotten the part in *Fatback*."

"But you weren't living together or anything," Meyer said. "Or *were* you?"

"Not officially. That is, we didn't share the same apartment," Moore said. "But we saw each other virtually every night. I keep thinking . . ." He shook his head. The detectives waited. "I keep thinking if only I'd been with her *last* night . . ." He shook his head again. "I usually picked her up after the show. Last night . . ." Again he shook his head. The detectives waited. He said nothing further.

"Last night . . ." Carella prompted.

"It's stupid the way things work sometimes, isn't it?" Moore said. "My grades were slipping. Too much partying. Okay. I made a New Year's resolution to spend at least *one* weekend night studying. Either Friday, Saturday, or Sunday. This week it was Friday."

"You're saying—"

"I'm saying . . . Look, I don't know *who* did this to her, but chances are it was just some lunatic who ran across her on the street, am I right? Saw her on the street and killed her, am I right? A chance victim."

"Maybe," Carella said.

"So what I'm saying is if this had been *last* week, I'd have been there to pick her *up* on Friday night. Because last week I stayed home on *Sunday* to study. I remember there was a party she wanted me to go to on Sunday, and I told her no, I had to study. Or the week *before* that, it would've been a Saturday. What I'm saying is why did it have to be a *Friday* this week, why couldn't I have been *waiting* for her last night when she came out of that theater?"

"Mr. Moore," Meyer said, "in the event this *wasn't* a crazy—"

"It had to be," Moore said.

"Yes, well," Meyer said, and glanced at Carella, looking for some sort of expression on his face that would indicate whether or not it would be wise to mention Paco Lopez. Carella's face said nothing, which was as good as telling Meyer to cool it. "But we have to explore every possibility," Meyer said, "which is why the questions we're about to ask may sound irrelevant, but we have to ask them anyway."

"I understand," Moore said.

"As the person closest to Miss Anderson—"

"Well, her mother is alive, you know," Moore said.

"Does she live here in the city?"

"No, she lives in San Francisco."

"Did Miss Anderson have any brothers or sisters?"

"No."

"Then essentially—"

"Yes, I suppose you could say I was closest . . . to her."

"I'm assuming you confided things to each other."

"Yes."

"Did she ever mention any threatening letters or telephone calls?"

"No."

"Anyone following her?"

"No."

"Or lurking about the building?"

"No."

"Did she owe money to anyone?"

"No."

"Did anyone owe *her* money?"

"I don't know."

"Was she involved with drugs?"

"No."

"Or any other illegal activity?"

"No."

"Had she recently received any gifts from strangers?" Carella asked.

"I don't know what you mean."

"At the theater," Carella said. "Flowers . . . or candy? From unknown admirers?"

"She never mentioned anything like that."

"Did she ever have any trouble at the stage door?"

"What kind of trouble?"

"Someone waiting for her, trying to talk to her or touch her . . ."

"You don't mean autograph hounds?"

"Well, anyone who might have got overly aggressive."

"No."

"Or who was rejected by her . . ."

"No."

"Nothing you saw or that she later mentioned to you."

"Nothing."

"Mr. Moore," Carella said, "we've gone through Miss Anderson's appointment calendar and had a schedule typed up for every day this month. We've just now received her address book from Midtown East, and we'll be cross-checking that against the names on the calendar. But you might save us some time if you could identify—"

"I'll be happy to," Moore said.

Carella opened the top drawer of his desk and took out several photocopies of the sheet Miscolo had typed from their handwritten notes. He handed one of the copies to Moore and another to Meyer.

Monday, February 1

10:00 a.m.	Dance
12:00 Noon	Lunch, Herbie, Genelli's
4:00 p.m.	Kaplan
6:00 p.m.	Groceries
7:30 p.m.	Theater

"Kaplan's her shrink," Moore said. "She saw him at four o'clock every Monday, Thursday, and Friday."

"Would you know his first name?"

"Maurice, I think."

"Know where his office is?"

"Yes, on Jefferson. I picked her up there once."

"Who's this Herbie she had lunch with?"

"Herb Gotlieb, her agent."

"Know where *his* office is?"

"Midtown someplace. Near the theater."

Tuesday, February 2

10:00 a.m.	Dance
2:00 p.m.	Audition, Théâtre des Étoiles
4:30 p.m.	Call Mother M
7:30 p.m.	Theater

"That's when she was *due* at the theater," Moore said. "The curtain goes up at eight each night, two o'clock for the matinees. Half-hour is one-thirty for the matinees, seven-thirty for the evening performances. That means the company gets to the theater a half hour before curtain."

"What's this audition at two o'clock?" Carella asked. "Do they audition for other parts when they're already working in a hit?"

"Oh, yes, all the time," Moore said.

"We've got her clocked for two calls a week to 'Mother M,' " Meyer said. "Would that be her mother in San Francisco?"

"No," Moore said. "That's *my* mother. In Miami."

"She called *your* mother twice a week?"

"Every week. Sally didn't get along too well with her own mother. She left home at an early age, went to London to study ballet. Things were never the same afterward."

"So your mother was . . . sort of a substitute, huh?"

"A surrogate, if you will."

"Mother M. Does that stand for . . ."

"Mother Moore, yes."

"That's what she called her, huh?"

"Yes. We used to joke about it. Made my mother sound like a nun or something." He paused. "Has anyone contacted *Mrs.* Anderson? I'm sure she'd want to know. I guess."

"Would you know her first name?" Carella asked.

"Yes, it's Phyllis. Her number's probably in Sally's book. You *did* say Mr. Levine had sent you—"

"Yes, we have it here with some of her other stuff. The stuff the lab's finished with."

"What's the lab looking for?" Moore asked.

"Who knows *what* they look for?" Carella said, and smiled. He knew damn well what they looked for. They looked for anything that might shed a little light on either the killer or the victim. The killer because he was still loose out there, and the longer he stayed loose the harder it would be to get him. And the victim because very often the more you knew about what a person had *been*, the easier it became to learn why anyone would want that person to *cease* being.

"But surely," Moore said, "nothing in Sally's personal effects could possibly tell you anything about the lunatic who attacked her."

Again, neither of the detectives mentioned that the same "lunatic" had attacked and killed a young cocaine dealer named Paco Lopez three nights before he'd killed Sally. Instead, both of them looked at the schedules in their hands. Taking his cue, Moore also looked at his schedule.

Wednesday, February 3

10:00 a.m.　　Dance

12:00 Noon　　Antoine's

1:30 p.m.	Theater
5:00 p.m.	Herbie, Sands Bar
7:30 p.m.	Theater

"Two performances every Wednesday and Saturday," Moore said.

"Who's Antoine?" Carella asked.

"Her hairdresser," Moore said. "He's on South Arundel, six blocks from her apartment."

"There's Herbie again," Meyer said.

"Yes, she saw him often," Moore said. "Well, an agent is very important to an actress's career, you know."

The listings for the remaining nine days between Wednesday, February 3, and Friday, February 12—the last full day before she was murdered—followed much the same pattern. Dance class on Monday through Friday at ten in the morning. Kaplan at 4:00 p.m. three times a week. Calls to Moore's mother in Miami twice a week. Meetings with her agent Herbie at *least* twice a week, and sometimes more often. The page for Sunday, February 7, listed only the word "Del" without a time before it and then the words "8:00 p.m. Party. Lonnie's."

"She's one of the black dancers in the show," Moore said. "Lonnie Cooper. That's the party Sally wanted me to go to last week."

"And who's Del?" Carella asked.

"Del?"

"Right there on the sheet," Carella said. "Del. No time, no place. Just Del."

"Del? Oh," Moore said. "Of course."

"Who is he? Or she?"

"Neither," Moore said, and smiled. "That stands for delicatessen."

"Delicatessen?" Meyer said.

"Cohen's Deli," Moore said. "On the Stem and North Rogers. Sally went up there every Sunday. To pick up bagels and lox, cream cheese, the works."

"And she put that on her calendar, huh?"

"Well, yes, she put *everything* on her calendar."

"Went up there every Sunday."

"Yes."

"What time?"

"It varied."

"Uh-huh," Carella said, and looked at the sheet again.

On Thursday, February 11, Sally had gone to her hairdresser again and then later in the day to a meeting with a man named Samuel Lang at Twentieth Century-Fox. On the day before she was killed, she had taken her cat to the vet's at one in the afternoon. The listed calendar appointments naturally spilled over into the weeks beyond her death; even in this city, no one ever expected a gun exploding out of the night. She had, for example, meticulously noted "Dance" for every February weekday at 10:00 a.m. and had similarly noted her appointments with Kaplan, her twice-weekly calls to Moore's mother, and the times she was due at the theater. For Monday, February 15, she had noted that the cat had to be picked up at 3:00 p.m.

"Mr. Moore," Carella said, "I hope you won't mind if we ask some questions—"

"Anything," Moore said.

"Of a more personal nature," Carella said.

"Go ahead."

"Well . . . would you know whether or not there was any other man in her life? Besides you. Someone who might have been jealous of the relationship she shared with you? Someone she might have known *before* she met you?"

"Not that I know of."

"Or another woman?"

"No, of course not."

"No one who might have resented—"

"No one."

"How about her agent, Herb Gotlieb? How old a man is he?"

"Why?"

"I was just wondering," Carella said.

"Wondering what?"

"Well, she *did* see him a lot—"

"He was her agent; of *course* she saw him a lot."

"I'm not suggesting—"

"Yes, you *are*, as a matter of fact," Moore said. "First you ask me whether there was another man—or even another *woman*, for God's sake—in Sally's life, and then you zero in on Herb Gotlieb, who has to be at *least* fifty-five years old! How can you *possibly* believe someone like Herb could have—"

"I don't believe anything yet," Carella said. "I'm simply exploring the possibilities."

And one of the possibilities, it belatedly occurred to him, was that Mr. Timothy Moore himself was a possible suspect in at least the murder of Sally Anderson. Carella had learned a long time ago that some 30 percent of all reported homicides were generated by family situations and 20 percent were eventually identified as stemming from lovers' quarrels. By his own admission, Timothy Moore had been Sally Anderson's lover, and never mind that he had voluntarily walked into the squadroom—*two* squadrooms, in fact, by the most recent count.

"As a matter of fact," Moore said, "the only thing that interests Herb is money. Sally could have danced for him naked and he wouldn't have noticed unless she was *also* tossing gold doubloons in the air."

Carella decided to run with it.

"But she wouldn't have done that, right?" he said.

"Done *what*?"

"Danced naked for Herb Gotlieb. Or for anyone else."

"Is that a question?"

"It's a question."

"The answer is no."

"You're sure of that?"

"I'm absolutely positive."

"No other men or women in her life?"

"None."

"She told you that?"

"She didn't *have* to tell me. I *knew*."

"How about you?"

"What about me?"

"Any other women in your life?"

"No."

"Or men?"

"No."

"Then this was pretty serious between you, is that right?"

"It was serious enough."

"How serious is serious enough?"

"I don't get this," Moore said.

"What don't you get?"

"I came up here to offer—"

"Yes, and we're grateful for that."

"You don't *seem* too grateful," Moore said. "What are you going to ask *next*? Where I was last night when Sally was getting killed?"

"I wasn't going to ask that, Mr. Moore," Carella said. "You already told us you were home studying."

"*Were* you home?" Meyer asked.

"You weren't going to ask, huh? I was home."

"All night long?"

"Here we go," Moore said, and rolled his eyes.

"You were her boyfriend," Meyer said flatly.

"Which means I killed her, right?" Moore said.

"You seem to be asking the questions and giving the answers both," Meyer said. "*Were* you home all night?"

"All night."

"Anyone with you?"

"Not exactly."

"What does that mean, not exactly? Either someone is with you or you're alone. Were you alone?"

"I was alone. But I called a friend of mine at least half a dozen times."

"What about?"

"The study material. Questions back and forth."

"Is he a med student, too? This friend you called?"

"Yes."

"What's his name?"

"Karl Loeb."

"Where does he live?"

"In the Quarter."

"Do you know his address?"

"No. But I'm sure he's in the phone book."

"What time did you call him?"

"Off and on, all night long."

"Did you call him at midnight?"

"I don't remember."

"Did he call *you* at any time last night?"

"Several times."

"When's the last time you spoke to him?"

"Just before I went to sleep. I called Sally first. I tried her number—"

"Had you called *her* before that?"

"On and off, yes."

"Last night, we're talking about."

"Yes, last night. I called her on and off."

"Were you worried when you didn't get her?"

"No."

"How come? When's the last time you tried her?"

"About three in the morning. Just before I called Karl for the last time."

"And you got no answer?"

"No answer."

"And you weren't worried? Three in the morning, and she doesn't answer the phone—"

"You're talking about theater people," Moore said. "Night people. Three o'clock is still early for them. Anyway, she knew I was studying. I figured she must've made other plans."

"Did she tell you *what* plans?"

"No, she didn't."

"When did you call her again?"

"I didn't. I heard about . . . When I woke up, I turned on the radio and I . . . I . . . heard . . . I heard . . ."

He suddenly buried his face in his hands and began weeping. The detectives watched him. Carella was thinking they'd been too harsh with him. Meyer was thinking the same thing. But why'd he come up here? Carella wondered. Meyer wondered the same thing. And why had a medical student expressed ignorance of what sort of evidence might be turned up by an examination of Sally's personal effects? Weren't medical schools teaching prospective doctors about bloodstains anymore? Or traces of semen? Or fingernail scrapings? Or human hair? Or any of the other little physical leftovers that could later lead to positive identification? Moore kept weeping into his hands.

"Are you all right?" Carella asked.

Moore nodded. He fumbled in his back pocket for a handkerchief, tossing the tails of the trench coat aside. There was a stethoscope in the right-hand pocket of his jacket. He found the handkerchief, blew his nose, dried his eyes.

"I loved her," he said.

The detectives said nothing.

"And she loved me," he said.

Still they said nothing.

"I know what you're trained to look for. I know all about it. But I had nothing to do with her murder. I came up here because I wanted to *help*, period. You might do better to go looking for the son of a bitch who *did* it, instead of—"

"I'm sorry, Mr. Moore," Carella said.

"I'll bet you are," Moore said. He put the handkerchief back in his pocket. He looked up at the wall clock. He stood up and began buttoning the trench coat. "I've got to go," he said. "You'll find my number in Sally's book. You can reach me at night there. During the day, I'm at Ramsey."

"We appreciate your help," Meyer said.

"Sure," Moore said, and turned and walked out of the squadroom.

Both men looked at each other.

"What do you think?" Carella asked.

"The idea or the execution?"

"Well, I know I blew it, but the idea."

"Good one."

"I really *was* looking for a third party at first—"

"I know that. But the other way around, right?"

"Right. Some guy—"

"Or some lady—"

"Right, who was annoyed because Sally Anderson was seeing Moore—"

"Right."

"And who decided to put the blocks to her."

"A possibility," Meyer said.

"But then Moore blew sky-high—"

"Right, I could see the wheels clicking inside your head, Steve."

"Right, when I reversed field, right?"

"Right. You were thinking, 'Hey, maybe *Moore* is the jealous party, maybe *he's* the one who killed her.' "

"Well, yeah. But I blew it."

"Maybe not. Maybe now he'll run a bit scared. Two things we've got to find out, Steve."

"Right. The exact times he was on the phone talking to this guy Loeb."

"Right, the other med student."

"Right. And where he was on Tuesday night, when Lopez was getting his."

"You decided not to go with Lopez, huh?"

"I wanted to see if Moore would *volunteer* an alibi for Tuesday."

"Listen, you know something?" Meyer said. "Who *says* the same gun means the same killer?"

"Huh?" Carella said.

"*I* use a gun to kill somebody on Tuesday night. I throw the gun away. Somebody picks it up, and it finds its way onto the street. *You* come along and buy the gun to use on Friday night. No connection at all between the two murders, do you get it?"

"I get it," Carella said, "and you're making life difficult."

"Only because I can't see any connection at all between Paco Lopez and Sally Anderson."

"Monday's a holiday, isn't it?" Carella asked abruptly.

"Huh?"

"Monday."

"What about it?"

"It's Washington's Birthday, isn't it?"

"No, that's the twenty-second."

"But we're celebrating it on the fifteenth. We're calling it 'Presidents' Day.' "

"What's that got to do with Moore?"

"Nothing. I'm thinking about the cat."

"What cat?"

"Sally's cat. She was supposed to pick it up on Monday. Will the vet be open on Monday?"

"I guess if she put it in her book—"

"She listed a pickup for three o'clock."

"Then I guess he'll be open."

"So who'll pick up the cat?" Carella asked.

"Not me," Meyer said at once.

"Maybe Sarah would like a cat," Carella said.

"Sarah doesn't like cats," Meyer said. His wife did not like *any* animals. His wife thought animals were *animals*.

"Maybe the girl's mother will take the cat," Carella said very seriously.

"The girl's mother is in San Francisco," Meyer said, and looked at him.

"So who'll take the goddamn cat?" Carella said. He had once taken home a Seeing Eye dog he'd inherited on the job. Fanny, the Carella housekeeper, had not liked the dog. At *all*. The dog no longer resided at the big old house in Riverhead. Meyer was still looking at him.

"I just hate to think of that cat sitting there *waiting*," Carella said, and the telephone rang. He snatched the receiver from the cradle.

"Eighty-Seventh Squad, Carella," he said.

"This is Allan Carter," the voice on the other end said.

"Ah, Mr. Carter, good," Carella said, "I've been trying to reach you. Thanks for returning my call."

"Is this about Sally Anderson?" Carter asked.

"Yes, sir."

"I know nothing whatever about her death."

"We'd like to talk to you anyway, sir," Carella said. "As her employer—"

"I've never heard it described *that* way before," Carter said.

"Sir?"

"I've never heard a *producer* described as an *employer*," Carter said, raising his voice as though Carella hadn't quite heard him the first time around. "In any event, I was in Philadelphia last night. Her death came as a total surprise to me."

"Yes, sir, I'm sure it did," Carella said. He paused. "We'd *still* like to talk to you, Mr. Carter."

"We're talking now," Carter said.

"In *person*, Mr. Carter."

There was a silence on the line. Carella leaped into it.

"Can you see us at three?" he asked. "We won't take up much of your time."

"I have an appointment at three," Carter said.

"When *will* you be free, sir?"

"This is Saturday," Carter said. "I just got back from Philly. I'm calling you from home. Tomorrow's Sunday, and Monday's a holiday. Can we meet sometime Tuesday? Or Wednesday? I won't be going back to Philly till late Wednesday."

"No, sir," Carella said, "I'm afraid we can't."

"Why not?" Carter said.

"Because a twenty-five-year-old girl's been murdered," Carella said, "and we'd like to talk to you *today*, sir—if that's all right with you."

Carter said nothing for several seconds.

Then he said, "Four o'clock," and gave Carella the address and hung up abruptly.

FIVE

ALLAN Carter lived in a high-rise apartment building snugly nestled into a row of luxury hotels overlooking Grover Park West. Because the streets had not yet been plowed entirely clear of snow, it took the detectives almost a half hour to drive the fifty-odd blocks from the station house to Carter's building. Actually, if the forecast for more snow tomorrow was accurate, the sanitmen were laboring somewhat like Hercules in the Augean stables. The day was gloomy and bitterly cold. The snow had hardened and was difficult to move. As the detectives approached Carter's building, a uniformed doorman was trying to break away the ice that had formed in front of the doorway after the sidewalk had been shoveled. He worked with a long-handled ice chipper that would have made a good weapon, Carella thought. Meyer was thinking the same thing.

Another uniformed man was sitting behind a desk in the lobby. Carella and Meyer identified themselves, and the man picked up a phone, said, "Mr. Carella and Mr. Meyer to see you, sir," and then cradled the receiver and said, "You can go right up. It's apartment thirty-seven."

The uniformed elevator man said, "They say it's gonna snow again tomorrow."

Meyer looked at Carella.

They got off on the third floor, walked a long carpeted hallway to Carter's apartment, pressed the bell button set in the doorjamb, heard chimes sounding inside, and then a voice calling, "Come in. It's open!"

Carella opened the door and almost tripped over a piece of brown leather luggage in the entrance hall. He stepped around the bag, motioned for Meyer to be careful, and then moved from the foyer into a vast living room with wall-to-wall windows overlooking the park. The naked branches of the trees beyond were laden with snow. The sky behind them was gray and roiling. Allan Carter was sitting on a long sofa upholstered in a pale green springtime fabric. He had a telephone to his ear. He was wearing a dark brown business suit over a lemon-colored shirt. Gold cufflinks showed at his sleeves. A chocolate-brown tie hung loose over his massive chest. The top button of his shirt was unfastened. Listening to whoever was on the other end of the phone connection, he gestured for the detectives to come in.

"Yes, I understand that," he said into the phone. "But, Dave . . . uh-huh, uh-huh." He listened impatiently, sighing, pulling a face, tugging simultaneously at a lock of the thick white hair that crowned his head. The white hair was premature, Carella guessed; Carter seemed to be a man in his early forties. His eyes were a piercing blue, reflecting wan, fading winter light from the window wall. He looked suntanned. Carella wondered if the weather was better in Philadelphia than it was here. He suddenly thought of all the Philadelphia jokes he knew. He had never been to Philadelphia.

"Well, what did *Annie* get?" Carter said into the phone. He listened and then said, "That's exactly my point, Dave. This is a bigger hit than *Annie* ever was. Well, that's just too damn bad.

Things are tough all over. You tell Orion the price is firm, and if they can't meet it, tell them to pass, they're just wasting our time here. I recognize I'm talking deal-breaker, Dave. I'm not a babe in the woods. Tell them."

He hung up abruptly.

"Forgive me," he said, rising and coming to where the detectives were standing, his hand extended. "I'm Allan Carter. Can I get either one of you a drink?"

"No, thanks," Carella said.

"Thanks," Meyer said, shaking his head.

"So," Carter said. "Hell of a thing, huh?"

"Yes, sir," Carella said.

"Any idea yet who did it?"

"No, sir."

"Some lunatic," Carter said, shaking his head and walking toward the bar. He lifted a decanter. "Sure?" he said. "No?" He shrugged, poured two fingers of whiskey into a low glass, added a single ice cube to it, said, "Cheers," drank the entire contents of the glass in a single swallow, and poured more whiskey into it. "Philadelphia," he said, shaking his head as if simple *mention* of that city explained his need for alcoholic reinforcement.

"When did you learn about her death, Mr. Carter?" Carella asked.

"When I got off the train. I picked up a paper at the station."

"What were you doing in Philadelphia?"

"Trying out a new play there."

"Another musical?" Meyer asked.

"No, a straight play. Big headache," Carter said. "It's a thriller . . . Have you seen *Deathtrap?*"

"No," Meyer said.

"No," Carella said.

"It's sort of like *Deathtrap*. Except it's lousy. I don't know how I ever got talked into doing it. First time I've ever done a straight play." He shrugged. "Probably go right down the drain when it gets here. *If* it ever gets here."

"So you read about Miss Anderson in the papers," Carella prompted.

"Yes," Carter said.

"What'd you think?"

"What *could* I think? This city," he said, and shook his head.

"How well did you know her?" Carella asked.

"Hardly at all. Just another one of the dancers, you know? We've got sixteen of them in the show. Have you seen the show?"

"No," Meyer said.

"No," Carella said.

"I'll get you some house seats," Carter said. "It's a good show. Biggest hit this town has seen in a long time."

"Who hired her, Mr. Carter?"

"What? Oh, the girl. It was a joint decision."

"Whose?"

"Mine and Jamie's and—"

"Jamie?"

"Our choreographer, Jamie Atkins. But . . . are you asking who was actually *there* when the dancers were cast?"

"Yes."

"Well, as I said—this would be the final selection, you understand—*I* was there, and Freddie Carlisle, our director, and Jamie, and his assistant, and our musical director, and an Equity rep, I guess, and . . . let me see . . . two of the stage managers were there, and our press agent, I think, and, of course, a piano player. And . . . well, sure, the composer and the lyricist and the book writer."

"The book writer?"

"The librettist. I think that was about it. This was a long time ago. We went into rehearsal last August, you know. We must've been doing our final casting in July sometime."

"Quite a few people," Carella said.

"Oh, yes, decision by committee," Carter said, and smiled. "But when you figure a musical can cost anywhere between two and three million bucks—well, you've got to be cautious."

"So all these people got together and . . . well, what *did* they do?" Carella asked. "Vote?"

"Not really. It's more a sort of general agreement on a finalist, with the choreographer having the last word, of course. He's the one who's going to have to work with any given dancer, you know."

"How many dancers *didn't* get a part?"

"Thousands. Counting the cattle calls and the Equity calls . . . sure. We must've seen every unemployed dancer in the city."

"Miss Anderson must've been a good dancer," Meyer said.

"I'm sure she was. She was, after all, hired for the part."

"How'd she get along with the rest of the cast?"

"You'd have to ask either Freddie or Jamie about that."

"Your director and choreographer."

"Yes. But I'm sure there was no friction . . . aside from the usual tension generated by a show in rehearsal. What I'm saying . . . Let me try to explain this."

"Please," Carella said.

"The company of any show, particularly a musical, has to perform as a tightly knit unit. I'm sure if there was any friction between Miss Anderson and anyone else in the cast, Jamie would've had a good long talk with her. When two million five is at stake, there's no room for fooling around with artistic temperament."

"Is that how much *Fatback* cost?"

"Give or take."

"How long was the show in rehearsal, Mr. Carter?"

"Six weeks. Not counting previews. We did two weeks of previews before we felt we were ready for the critics."

"Were you present at all those rehearsals?"

"Not all of them. After Freddie had mounted a good part of the show, yes. Usually, you try to give your creative people a free hand in the beginning. Once the run-throughs start, a producer—well, *this* producer, anyway—tries to be present at all the rehearsals."

"Then you would have noticed if there was any friction between Miss Anderson and any other member of the cast."

"I detected no such friction. Gentlemen, I wish I could help you, believe me. But I hardly knew the girl. I'll confess something to you. When I read about her in the paper, I had difficulty recalling just which one of the dancers she was."

"I see," Carella said.

"Little redheaded thing, wasn't she?" Carter said.

"We didn't see the body, sir," Carella said.

"What?" Carter said.

"We weren't there at the scene, sir," Carella said.

"The body was found in another precinct," Meyer said at once.

"Sir," Carella said, "it would help us if we could get a list of names, addresses, and telephone numbers for everyone in the cast and crew, anyone who might have had even the slightest contact with Miss Anderson."

"You don't plan to visit them *all*, do you?" Carter said.

"Well . . . yes," Carella said.

Carter smiled. "Maybe I ought to give you some idea of what that would involve," he said. "*Fatback* is a very large show. We've got six principals, four featured players, sixteen dancers plus twelve *other* people in the chorus, eighteen stagehands, twenty-six musicians, three stage managers, three property men, fourteen wardrobe people, including the dressers, three electricians, two carpenters, one soundman, three lighting-board-and-follow-spot men, one makeup woman, and two standby dancers—what we call 'swing' dancers."

Carella looked at Meyer.

"That comes to a hundred and fourteen people," Carter said.

"I see," Carella said. He paused. Then he said, "But *does* such a list exist? Of all these people?"

"Well, yes, *several* lists, in fact. Our general manager has one, and our company manager, and the production secretary . . . In fact, I'm sure there's a list at the theater, too. Near the stage door phone. That might be your best bet. If you could stop by the theater—"

"Yes, sir, we'll do that."

"As a matter of fact, why don't you kill two birds with one stone?" Carter said.

"Sir?" Carella said.

"I mean, as long as you'll be at the theater."

The detectives looked at him, puzzled.

"I've guaranteed a pair for a friend of mine, but there was a message on my machine that he won't be coming into the city tonight because of the weather." Carter looked at their blank faces. "I'm talking about the show," he said. "Do you think you might like to see it? There's a pair of house seats guaranteed at the box office."

"Oh," Carella said.

"Oh," Meyer said.

"What do you think?" Carter asked.

"Well, thank you," Meyer said, "but my wife and I are meeting some friends for dinner tonight."

"How about you?"

"Well . . ." Carella said.

"You'll enjoy it, believe me."

"Well . . ."

He was hesitating because he didn't know what "house seats" were and he didn't know what "guaranteed" meant, but it sounded to him as if these might be free tickets, and he sure as hell wasn't about to accept a gift from a man who claimed to believe a five-foot-eight blond murder victim was a "little redheaded thing." Carella had learned early on in the game that if you wanted to survive as a cop, you either took nothing at all or you took everything that wasn't nailed down. Accept a cup of coffee on the arm from the guy who ran the local diner? Fine. Then also take a bribe from the friendly neighborhood fence who was running a tag sale on stolen goods every Sunday morning. A slightly dishonest cop was the same thing as a slightly pregnant woman.

"How much do these tickets cost?" he asked.

"Forget it," Carter said, and waved the question aside, and Carella knew the man had figured he was seeking the grease; he was, after all, a *cop* in this fair city, wasn't he? And cops *copped*, anytime and anyplace they could.

"Are house seats free tickets?" Carella asked.

"No, no, we *do* have investors, you know, we can't go giving away seats to a hit," Carter said. "But these are taken care of, don't worry about them."

"Who's taking care of them?" Carella asked.

"I personally guaranteed them," Carter said.

"I don't know what that means," Carella said. "Guaranteed."

"I personally agreed to pay for them. Even if they weren't claimed."

"Claimed?"

"By law, house seats have to be claimed forty-eight hours before any performance. By guaranteeing them, I was—in effect—claiming them."

"But they haven't been paid for yet."

"No, they haven't."

"Then I'll pay for them myself, sir," Carella said.

"Well, really—"

"I'd like to see the show, sir, but I'd like to pay for the tickets myself."

"Fine, whatever you say. They're being held at the box office in my friend's name: Robert Harrington. You can claim them anytime before the curtain goes up."

"Thank you," Carella said.

"I'll call the stage door, meanwhile, tell them you'll be stopping by for that list."

"Thank you."

"I *still* don't understand what house seats are," Meyer said.

"Choice seats set aside for each performance," Carter said. "For the producer, director, choreographer, stars—"

"Set aside?"

"Reserved," Carter said, nodding. "By contract. So many seats for each performance. The higher you are in the pecking order, the more seats you're entitled to buy. If you don't claim them, of course, they go right back on sale in the box office, on a first-come, first-served basis."

"Live and learn," Meyer said, and smiled.

"Yes," Carter said, and glanced at his watch.

"Anything else?" Carella asked Meyer.

"Nothing I can think of," Meyer said.

"Then thank you, sir," Carella said. "And thanks for making those seats available to me."

"My pleasure," Carter said.

The detectives were silent in the elevator down to the street. The elevator operator, who had already informed them earlier that it was going to snow tomorrow, seemed to have nothing more to say. The sky was even more threatening when they stepped outside again. Darkness was coming on. It would be a moonless night.

"I just want to make sure I heard her right," Meyer said.

"Tina Wong, do you mean?"

"Yeah. She *did* say 'Five blondes, two blacks, and a token Chink,' didn't she?"

"That's what she said."

"So how could Carter think Sally Anderson was a *redhead?*"

"Maybe one of the understudies is a redhead."

"Maybe *I'm* a redhead, too," Meyer said. "Didn't Carter say that once they started run-throughs, he was at every rehearsal?"

"That's what he said."

"So he *knows* that damn show. How could he *possibly* think there was a redhead up there?"

"Maybe he's color-blind."

"You *did* catch it, didn't you?"

"Oh, I caught it, all right."

"I was wondering why you didn't jump on it."

"I wanted to see how far he'd go with it."

"He didn't go *anywhere* with it. He let it lay there like a lox."

"Maybe he was just trying it for size."

"Backing up what he said about not knowing her from a hole in the wall. Just another one of the girls, another face in the crowd."

"Which may be true, Meyer. There are thirty-eight people in the cast. You can't expect a man to remember—"

"What's thirty-eight people, a *nation?*" Meyer said. "We've got close to two *hundred* cops in the precinct, and I know each and every one of them. By sight, at least."

"You're a trained observer," Carella said, smiling.

"How long does it take to get from Philadelphia by train?" Meyer asked.

"About an hour and a half."

"Easy to get here and back again," Meyer said. "Time enough to do anything that had to be done here. If a person had anything to do here."

"Yes," Carella said.

"Jamie digs blondes, remember?" Meyer said. "Isn't that what she told us? The choreographer digs blondes. So how come everybody in the world knows this but Carter? He was there when the whole *mishpocha* was picking the dancers. Decision by committee, remember? So how come, all of a sudden, he has trouble remembering what color her *hair* is? A little redheaded thing, he calls her. All of a sudden, his choreographer—who likes them blond—ends up with a *redhead* in his chorus line. Steve, that stinks. I'm telling you it stinks. Do *you* buy it?"

"No," Carella said.

BUYING the tickets came as something of a shock.

Carella had not seen a hit show in a long time, and he did not know what current prices were. When the woman in the box office shoved the little white envelope across the counter to him, he glanced at the yellow tickets peeking out, *thought* he saw the price on one of them, figured he must be wrong, and then had verbal confirmation when the woman said, "That'll be eighty dollars, please." Carella blinked. Eighty divided by two came to forty dollars a seat! "Will that be charge or cash?" the woman asked.

Carella did not carry a credit card; he did not know any cops who carried credit cards. He panicked for a moment. Did he *have* eighty dollars in cash in his wallet? As it turned out, he was carrying ninety-two dollars, which meant he would have to call home and ask Teddy to bring some cash with her tonight. He parted with the money reluctantly. This had better be *some* show, he thought, and walked to the pay phone in the lobby. Fanny, the Carella housekeeper, answered on the fourth ring.

"Carella residence," she said.

"Fanny, hi, it's me," he said. "Can you give Teddy a message? First tell her I've got tickets to a show called *Fatback*, and I thought we'd have dinner down here tonight before the show. Ask her to meet me at six-thirty, at a place called O'Malley's. She knows it—we've been there before. Next, tell her to bring a lot of cash; I'm running low."

"That's *three* messages," Fanny said. "How *much* cash?"

"Enough to cover dinner."

"I planned to make pork chops," Fanny said.

"I'm sorry," he said. "This came up all of a sudden."

"Mm," Fanny said.

He visualized her standing by the phone in the living room. Fanny Knowles was "fiftyish," as she put it in her faint Irish brogue, and she had blue hair, and she wore a pince-nez, and she weighed about 150 pounds, and she'd ruled the Carella household with an iron fist from the day she'd arrived there as a temporary gift from Teddy's father—ten years ago. Fanny was a registered nurse, and she'd originally been hired to stay with the Carellas for only a month, just long enough to give Teddy a hand till she was able to cope alone with the infant twins. It was Fanny who suggested that she ought to stay on a while longer, at a salary they could afford, telling them she never again wanted to stick another thermometer into a dying old man. She was still there. Her silence on the phone was ominous.

"Fanny, I'm really sorry," he said. "This is *sort* of business."

"What do I do with a dozen pork chops?" she said.

"Make a cassoulet," he said.

"What in hell is a cassoulet?" she asked.

"Look it up," he said. "Will you give her my message?"

"When she gets home," Fanny said, "which should be any minute now. She'll have to run a footrace to meet you downtown at six-thirty."

"Well, tell her, okay?"

"I'll tell her," Fanny said, and hung up.

He put the receiver back on the hook, went out of the theater, found the alley leading to the stage door, went to the door, and knocked on it.

An old man opened the door and peered out at him.

"Box office is up front," he said.

Carella showed him his shield and I.D. card. "I'm supposed to pick up a list," he said.

"What list?"

"Of everyone in the company."

"Oh, yeah, Mr. Carter phoned me about it. Come on in. I got one on the clipboard here, but I can't let you have it. It's the only one I got." The old man paused. "You can copy it down, if you like."

Carella went to the list hanging on the wall near the telephone and looked at it. Four typewritten pages. He glanced at his watch.

"Okay if I take it out and have it xeroxed?" he asked.

"No way," the old man said. "Only one I got."

"I was hoping—"

"How're we supposed to get in touch with anybody, case he don't show up for half-hour? How we supposed to know to put in a swing dancer case somebody's sick or something? That list has to stay right *there*, right where it is." The old man paused. "You want my advice?"

Carella sighed, sat on the high stool near the wall telephone, and began copying the list into his notebook.

THE Laundromat was on the corner of Culver and Tenth, a neighborhood enclave that for many years had been exclusively Irish but that nowadays was a rich melting-pot mixture of Irish, black, and Puerto Rican. The melting pot here, as elsewhere in this city, never seemed to come to a precise boil, but that didn't bother any of the residents; they all knew it was nonsense, anyway. Even though they all shopped the same supermarkets and clothing stores, even though they all bought gasoline at the same gas stations and rode the same subways, even though they washed their clothes at the same Laundromats and ate hamburgers side by side in the same greasy spoons, they all knew that when it came to socializing, it was the Irish with the Irish and the blacks with the blacks and the Puerto Ricans with the Puerto Ricans and never mind that brotherhood-of-man stuff.

Eileen Burke, what with her peaches-and-cream complexion and her red hair and green eyes, could have passed for any daughter of Hibernian descent in the neighborhood—which, of course, was exactly what they were hoping for. It would not do to have the Dirty Panties Bandit, as the boys of the Eight-Seven had wittily taken to calling him, pop into the Laundromat with his .357 Magnum in his fist, spot Eileen for a policewoman, and put a hole the size of a bowling ball in her ample chest. No, no. Eileen Burke did not want to become a dead heroine. Eileen Burke wanted to become the first lady Chief of Detectives in this city, but not over her own dead body. For the job tonight, she was dressed rather more sedately than she would have been if she'd been on the street trying to flush a rapist. Her red hair was pulled to the back of her head, held there with a rubber band and covered with a dun-colored scarf knotted under her chin and hiding the pair of gold loop earrings she considered her good-luck charms. She was wearing a cloth coat that matched the scarf, and knee-length brown socks and brown rubber boots, and she was sitting on a yellow plastic chair in the very cold Laundromat, watching her dirty laundry (or rather the dirty laundry supplied by the Eight-Seven) turn over and over in one of the washing machines while the neon sign in the window of the place flashed LAUNDROMAT first in orange and then LAVANDERÍA in green. In the open handbag on her lap, the butt of a .38 Detective's Special beckoned from behind a wad of Kleenex tissues.

The manager of the place did not know Eileen was a cop. The manager of the place was the night man, who came on at four and worked through till midnight, at which time he locked up the place and went home. Every morning, the owner of the Laundromat would come around to unlock the machines, pour all the coins into a big gray sack, and take them to the bank. That was the owner's job: emptying the machines of coins. The owner had thirty-seven Laundromats all over the city, and he lived in a very good section of Majesta. He did not empty the machines at closing time because he thought that might be dangerous, which in fact it would have been. He preferred that his thirty-seven night men all over the city simply lock the doors, turn on the burglar alarms, and go home. That was part of their job, the night men. The rest of their job was to make change for the ladies who brought in their dirty clothes, and to call for service if any of the machines broke down, and also to make sure nobody stole any of the cheap plastic furniture in the various Laundromats, although the owner didn't care much about that, since he'd got a break on the stuff from his brother-in-law. Every now and then it occurred to the owner that his thirty-seven night men each had keys to the thirty-seven separate burglar alarms in the thirty-seven different locations, and if they decided to go into cahoots with one of the crazies in this city, they could open the stores and break open the machines—but so what? Easy come, easy go. Besides, he liked to think all of his night men were pure and innocent.

Detective Hal Willis knew for damn sure that the night man at the Laundromat on Tenth and Culver was as pure and as innocent as the driven snow so far as the true identity of Eileen Burke was concerned. The night man did not know she was a cop, nor did he know that Willis himself, angle-parked in an unmarked green Toronado in front of the bar next door to the Laundromat, was *also* a cop. In fact, the night man did not have the faintest inkling that the Eight-Seven had chosen his nice little establishment for a stakeout on the assumption that the Dirty Panties Bandit would hit it next. The assumption seemed a good educated guess. The man had been working his way straight down Culver Avenue for the past three weeks, hitting Laundromats on alternate sides of the avenue, inexorably moving farther and farther downtown. The place he'd hit three nights ago had been on the south side of the avenue. The Laundromat they were staking out tonight was eight blocks farther downtown, on the north side of the avenue.

The Dirty Panties Bandit was no small-time thief, oh no. In the two months during which he'd operated unchecked along Culver Avenue, first in the bordering precinct farther uptown and then moving lower into the Eight-Seven's territory, he had netted—or so the police had estimated from what the victimized women had told them—six hundred dollars in cash, twelve gold wedding bands, four gold lockets, a gold engagement ring with a one-carat diamond, and a total of twenty-two pairs of panties. These panties had not been lifted from the victims' laundry baskets. Instead, the Dirty Panties Bandit—and hence his name—had asked all those hapless Laundromat ladies to please remove their panties for him, which they had all readily agreed to do since they were looking into the rather large barrel of a .357 Magnum. No one had been raped—yet. No one had been harmed—yet. And whereas there was something darkly humorous, after all, about an armed robber taking home his victims' panties, there was nothing at all humorous about the potential of a .357 Magnum. Sitting in the parked car outside the bar, Willis was very much aware of the caliber of the gun the Laundromat robber carried. Sitting inside the Laundromat, flanked by a Puerto Rican woman on her left and a black woman on her right, Eileen Burke was even more aware of the devastating power of that gun.

She looked up at the wall clock.

It was only ten-fifteen, and the place wouldn't be closing till midnight.

A LITTLE slip of paper in the program informed the audience that someone named Allison Greer would be replacing Sally Anderson that night, but none of the dancers in the show had character names, and they all looked very much alike with the exception of the two black girls (who in fact looked very much like each other) and Tina Wong, who looked like no one in the cast but herself. The blondes were indistinguishable one from the other. They were tall and leggy and, Carella thought, somewhat busty for dancers. They all had radiant smiles. They all were dressed in costumes that made them look even more alike, cut high on their thighs and hanging in tatters on their flashing legs, the sort of little nothing any young and ignorant southern girl might wear in the middle of a swamp, which was where *Fatback* was supposed to be taking place and which was what the dancers in the cast were supposed to be. Given such a premise, given a curtain rising on what looked like a primeval bog, with mist floating in over it and giant trees dripping moss onto slime-covered rocks, Carella had expected the worst. He turned to his right to look at Teddy. She was looking back at him. This was going to be yet another example of this city's critics praising yet another lousy show to the skies and thereby turning straw into gold—for the *investors*, at any rate.

Teddy Carella was a deaf-mute.

She often had difficulty at the theater. She could not hear what any of the performers were saying, of course, and usually she and Carella would be sitting too far back to read lips. Over the years, they had worked out a system whereby his hands—held chest high so as not to disturb anyone sitting behind them—flashed dialogue to her while she shifted her eyes back and forth from the stage to his rapidly moving fingers. Musicals, as a general rule, were somewhat easier for her. A singer usually faced the audience squarely when belting out a song, and his lip movements were more exaggerated than when he was simply speaking. Ballet was her favorite form of entertainment, and tonight she was delighted when—not ten seconds after the curtain had risen on that ominous bog—the entire stage seemed to fill with leaping, prancing, gyrating, twirling, frantically energetic dancers who virtually swung from the treetops and turned that steamy swamp into the sassiest, sexiest, most dazzling opening number Teddy had ever seen in her life. Spellbound, she sat beside Carella for what must have been ten full minutes of exposition through dance, squeezing his hand, her dark eyes flashing as she watched the story silently unfold. Carella sat there grinning. When the opening number ended, the house burst into tumultuous applause. He readied his hands for the translation he felt would be necessary as the act progressed, but he found that Teddy was impatiently nodding his moving fingers aside, understanding most of what was happening, able to read directly from the performers' lips because the seats were sixth row center.

She asked him some questions during intermission. She was wearing a black, wool-knit dress with a simple cameo just above her breasts, black leather boots, a gold bracelet on her wrist. She had pulled her long black hair to the back of her head and fastened it there with a gold barrette. Except for eye liner, shadow, and lipstick, there was no makeup on her face. She needed none; she was the most beautiful woman he'd ever known in his life. He watched her hands, watched the accompanying expressions that crossed her face. She wanted to know if she'd been right in assuming that the trapper and the girl moonshiner had had an affair years ago and that this was the first time they'd seen each other since? No? Then what was all that hugging and kissing about? Carella explained, responding with his voice so that she could read his lips, accompanying his voice with hand signals (and always there were the fascinated observers in the crowd, nudging each other—Hey, take a look, Charlie, see the grown man talking to the dummy?), and she watched his lips and watched his hands and then signed *Well, they seem awfully lovey-dovey for cousins,* and he explained that they were only *second* cousins, and she signed *Does that make incest legal?*

Now, forty-five minutes into the second act, Carella looked at his watch because he sensed the evening was coming to an end and he simply did not want it to. He was having too good a time.

EILEEN Burke was having a splendid time watching her laundry go round and round. The night man thought she was a little crazy, but then again, everybody in this town was a little crazy. She had put the same batch of laundry through the machine five times already. Each time, she sat watching the laundry spinning in the machine. The night man didn't notice that she alternately watched the front door of the place or looked through the plate-glass window each time a car pulled in. The neon fixture splashed orange and green on the floor of the Laundromat: LAVANDERÍA . . . LAUNDROMAT . . . LAVANDERÍA . . . LAUNDROMAT. The laundry in the machines went round and round.

A woman with a baby strapped to her back was at one of the machines, putting in another load. Eileen guessed she was no older than nineteen or twenty, a slender attractive blue-eyed blonde who directed a nonstop flow of soft chatter over her shoulder to her near-dozing infant. Another woman was sitting on the yellow plastic chair next to Eileen's, reading a magazine. She was a stout black woman, in her late thirties or early forties, Eileen guessed, wearing a bulky knit sweater over blue jeans and galoshes. Every now and then, she flipped a page of the magazine, looked up at the washing machines, and then flipped another page. A third woman came into the store, looked around frantically for a moment, seemed relieved to discover there were plenty of free machines, dashed out of the store, and returned a moment later with what appeared to be the week's laundry for an entire Russian regiment. She asked the manager to change a five-dollar bill for her. He changed it from a coin dispenser attached to his belt, thumbing and clicking out the coins like a streetcar conductor. Eileen watched as he walked to a safe bolted to the floor and dropped the bill into a slot on its top, just as though he were making a night deposit at a bank. A sign on the wall advised any prospective holdup man: MANAGER DOES NOT HAVE COMBINATION TO SAFE. MANAGER CANNOT CHANGE BILLS LARGER THAN FIVE DOLLARS. Idly, Eileen wondered what the manager did when he ran out of coins. Did he run into the bar next door to ask the bartender for change? Did the bartender next door have a little coin dispenser attached to *his* belt? Idly, Eileen wondered why she wondered such things. And then she wondered if she'd ever meet a man who wondered the same things she wondered. That was when the Dirty Panties Bandit came into the store.

Eileen recognized him at once from the police-artist composites Willis had shown her back at the squadroom. He was a short slender white man wearing a navy pea coat and watch cap over dark brown, wide-wale corduroy trousers and tan suede desert boots. He had darting brown eyes and a very thin nose with a narrow mustache under it. There was a scar in his right eyebrow. The bell over the door tinkled as he came into the store. As he reached behind him with his left hand to close the door, Eileen's hand went into the bag on her lap. She was closing her fingers around the butt of the .38 when the man's right hand came out of his coat pocket. The Magnum would have looked enormous in any event. But because the man was so small and so thin, it looked like an artillery piece. The man's hand was shaking. The gun in it flailed the room.

Eileen looked at the Magnum, looked at the man's eyes, and felt the butt of her own pistol under her closing fingers. If she pulled the gun now, she had maybe a thirty/seventy chance of bringing him down before he sprayed the room with bullets that could tear a man's head off his body. In addition to herself and the robber, there were five other people in the store, three of them women, one of them an infant. Her hand froze motionless around the butt of the gun.

"All right, all right," the man said in a thin, almost girlish voice, "nobody moves, nobody gets hurt." His eyes darted. His hand was still shaking. Suddenly, he giggled. The giggle scared Eileen more than the gun in his hand did. The giggle was high and nervous and just enough off center to send a shiver racing up her spine. Her hand on the butt of the .38 suddenly began sweating.

"All I want is your money, all your money," the man said. "And your—"

"I don't have the combination to the safe," the manager said.

"Who asked *you* for anything?" the man said, turning to him. "You just shut up, you hear me?"

"Yes, sir," the manager said.

"You hear me?"

"Yes, sir."

"I'm talking to the ladies here, not you, you hear me?"

"Yes, sir."

"So shut up."

"Yes, sir."

"You!" the man said, and turned to the woman with the baby strapped to her back, jerking the gun at her, moving erratically, almost dancing across the floor of the Laundromat, turning this way and that as though playing to an audience from a stage. Each time he turned, the woman with the baby on her back turned with him, so that she was always facing him, her body forming a barricade between him and the baby. She doesn't know, Eileen thought, that a slug from that gun can go clear through her *and* the baby *and* the wall behind them, too.

"Your money!" the man said. "Hurry up! Your rings, too, give me your rings!"

"Just don't shoot," the woman said.

"Shut up! Give me your panties!"

"What?"

"Your panties, take off your panties. Give them to me!"

The woman stared at him.

"Are you deaf?" he said, and danced toward her and jabbed the gun at her. The woman already had a wad of dollar bills clutched in one fist and her wedding ring and engagement ring in the other, and she stood there uncertainly, knowing she had heard him say he wanted her panties, but not knowing whether he wanted her to give him the money and the jewelry *first* or—

"Hurry up!" he said. "Take them off! Hurry up!"

The woman quickly handed him the bills and the rings and then reached up under her skirt and lowered her panties over her thighs and down to her ankles. She stepped out of them, picked them up, handed them to him, and quickly backed away from him as he stuffed them into his pocket.

"All of you!" he said, his voice higher now. "I want all of you to take off your panties! Give me your money! Give me all your money! And your rings! And your panties, take them off, hurry up!"

The black woman sitting on the chair alongside Eileen kept staring at the man as though he had popped out of a bottle, following his every move around the room, her eyes wide, disbelieving his demands, disbelieving the gun in his hand, disbelieving his very existence. She just kept staring at him and shaking her head in disbelief.

"You!" he said, dancing over to her. "Give me that necklace! Hurry up!"

"Ain't but costume jewelry," the woman said calmly.

"Give me your money!"

"Ain't got but a dollar an' a quarter in change," the woman said.

"Give it to me!" he said, and held out his left hand.

The woman rummaged in her handbag. She took out a change purse. Ignoring the man, ignoring the gun not a foot from her nose, she unsnapped the purse and reached into it and took out coin after coin, transferring the coins from her right hand to the palm of her left hand, three quarters and five dimes, and then closing her fist on the coins and bringing her fist to his open palm and opening the fist and letting the coins fall (disdainfully, it seemed to Eileen) onto his palm.

"Now your panties," he said.

"Nossir."

"Take off your panties," he said.

"Won't do no such thing," the woman said.

"What?"

"Won't do no such thing. Ain't just a matter of reachin' up under m'skirt way that lady with the baby did, nossir. I'd have to take off fust m'galoshes and then m'jeans, an' there ain't no way I plan to stan' here naked in front of two men I never seen in my life, nossir."

The man waved the gun.

"Do what I tell you," he said.

"Nossir," the woman said.

Eileen tensed.

She wondered if she should make her move now, a bad situation could only get worse, she'd been taught that at the academy and it was a rule she'd lived by and survived by all the years she'd been on the force, but a rule she'd somehow neglected tonight when this silly little son of a bitch walked through the door and pulled the cannon from his pocket, a bad situation can only get worse, make your move now, do it now, go for the money, go for broke, but now, *now!* And she wondered, too, if he would bother turning to fire at *her* once she pulled the gun from her handbag or would he instead fire at the black woman who was willing to risk getting shot and maybe killed rather than take off her jeans and then her panties in a room containing a trembling night man and an armed robber who maybe was or maybe wasn't bonkers, make your move, stop thinking, stop wondering—but what if the baby gets shot?

It occurred to her that maybe the black woman would actually succeed in staring down the little man with the penchant for panties, get him to turn away in defeat, run for the door, out into the cold and into the waiting arms of Detective Hal Willis—which reminds me, where the hell *are* you, Willis? It would not hurt to have my backup come in *behind* this guy right now, it would not hurt to have his attention diverted from me to you, two guns against one, the good guys against the bad guys, where the hell *are* you? The little man was trembling violently now, the struggle inside him so intense that it seemed he would rattle himself to pieces, crumble into a pile of broken pink chalk around a huge weapon—he's a closet rapist, she thought suddenly, the man's a closet rapist!

The thought was blinding in its clarity. She knew now, or felt she knew, why he was running around town holding up Laundromats. He was holding up Laundromats because there were *women* in Laundromats and he wanted to see those women taking off their panties. The holdups had nothing at all to do with money or jewelry. The man was after *panties!* The rings and the bracelets and the cash were all his cover, his beard, his smoke screen, the man wanted ladies' panties, the man wanted the aroma of women on his loot, the man probably had a garageful of panties wherever he lived, the man was a closet rapist and she knew how to deal with rapists, she had certainly dealt with enough rapists in her lifetime, but that was her alone in a park, that was when the only life at stake had been her own, make your move, she thought, make it *now!*

"You!" she said sharply.

The man turned toward her. The gun turned at the same time.

"Take mine," she said.

"What?" he said.

"Leave her alone. Take *my* panties."

"What?"

"Reach under my skirt," she whispered. "Rip off my panties."

She thought for a terrifying moment that she'd made a costly mistake. His face contorted in what appeared to be rage, and the gun began shaking even more violently in his fist. Oh, God, she thought, I've forced him out of the closet, I've forced him to see himself for what he is, that gun is his cock as sure as I'm sitting here, and he's going to jerk it off into my face in the next ten seconds! And then a strange thing happened to his face, a strange smile replaced the anger, a strange secret smile touched the corners of his mouth, a secret communication flashed in his eyes, his eyes to her eyes, *their* secret, a secret to share, he lowered the gun, he moved toward her.

"Police!" she shouted, and the .38 came up out of the bag in the same instant that she came up off the plastic chair, and she rammed the muzzle of the gun into the hollow of his throat and said so quietly that only he could hear it, "Don't even *think* it, or I'll shoot you dead!" And she would remember later and remember always the way the shouted word "Police!" had shattered the secret in his eyes, their shared secret, and she would always wonder if the way she'd disarmed him hadn't been particularly cruel and unjust.

She clamped the handcuffs onto his wrists and then stooped to pick up the Magnum from where he'd dropped it on the Laundromat floor.

SIX

CARELLA could not fall asleep.

He kept thinking that too many people were involved. He kept thinking that even if the lieutenant was willing to put another man on the case, even *then* it would take them at least a week to question all those people in the show, that was if the lieutenant agreed to give him another man. *Fat* chance he'd agree to that. Well, maybe he would. The death of Paco Lopez had gone by without a ripple; there weren't many people who cared about a two-bit dealer biting the dust—"Good riddance to bad rubbish," as Carella's mother used to say when he was but a mere lad coming along in this city he loved. He often wondered where his mother had picked up the expressions that had been her favorites. "Ike and Mike, they look alike," she would often say of him and his father. Or, whenever Carella managed to knock over a glass of milk at the dinner table, "Very good, Eddie." Or, regarding his aunt Clara, whom Carella had positively adored, "She dresses like Astor's pet horse." Or (speaking of horses), whenever anyone became insulted about something, Carella's mother would describe it with the words "He got on his high horse." Were Ike and Mike comic strip characters? Who in the world was Eddie? Good riddance to bad rubbish—was there such a thing as *good* rubbish?

Paco Lopez had been bad rubbish for sure, and no one had mourned his passing. But the Anderson girl's death had made headlines in the city's afternoon newspaper, and the muckraking journalists on that yellow sheet were beginning to clamor for a speedy arrest of the "maniac responsible." So maybe the lieutenant *would* give Carella the additional man he planned to request; maybe Pete himself was getting some pressure from upstairs.

The newspapers did not yet know, nor did Carella plan to tell them, that a man named Paco Lopez, whose death had gone unnoticed, had been killed with the same gun. There was nothing the journalists would have liked better than a possible romantic link (a possibility that had crossed Carella's mind) between a young blond dancer and a Puerto Rican dope dealer. A story like that would make even the *television* newscasters jump for joy. There were, after all, two Puerto Rican dancers in the show. Well, not necessarily Puerto Rican. Carella had asked only if there were any *Hispanics* in the show, and Tina Wong had told him there were two, so they could be anything: Puerto Rican, Cuban, Dominican, Colombian—you name it, this city had it. Both of them faggots. Carella wondered if either of them was doing nose candy. Carella wondered if either of them had known Paco Lopez. That was the damn trouble. A hundred and fourteen people involved with that show, one or more of whom may have been the connection between Sally Anderson and Paco Lopez, if there *was* any connection at all besides the .38-caliber gun that had killed them both.

Please don't let it be a crazy, he thought.

Please let it be a nice sensible murderer who killed both those people for a very good reason.

He kept staring up at the ceiling.

There were just too many people involved, he thought.

WILLIS was trying to explain why he hadn't happened to notice the Dirty Panties Bandit when he entered the Laundromat. They had sent down for pizza, and now they sat in the relative 1:00 a.m. silence of the squadroom, eating Papa Joe's really pretty good combination anchovies and pepperoni and drinking Miscolo's really pretty lousy Colombian coffee. Detective Bert Kling was sitting with them, but he wasn't eating or saying very much.

Eileen remembered him as a man with a huge appetite, and she wondered now if he was on a diet. He looked thinner than she recalled—well, that had been several years back—and he also looked somewhat drawn and pale and, well, unkempt. His straight blond hair was growing raggedly over his shirt collar and his ears, and the collar itself looked a bit frayed, and his suit looked unpressed, and there were stains on the tie he was wearing. Eileen figured he was maybe coming in off a stakeout someplace. Maybe he was *supposed* to look like somebody who was going to seed. And maybe those dark shadows under his eyes were all part of the role he was playing out there on the street, in which case he should get not only a commendation but an Academy Award besides.

Willis was very apologetic.

"I'll tell you the truth," he said, "I figured we didn't have a chance of our man showing. Because on the other jobs, he usually hit between ten and ten-thirty, and it was almost eleven when this guy came running out of the bar—"

"Wait a minute," Eileen said. "*What* guy?"

"Came running out of the bar next door," Willis said. "Bert, don't you want some of this?"

"Thanks," Kling said, and shook his head.

"Yelling, 'Police, police,' " Willis said.

"When was this?" Eileen asked.

"I told you, a little before eleven," Willis said. "Even so, if I thought we had a chance of our man showing, I'd have said screw it, let some other cop handle whatever it is in the bar there. But I mean it, Eileen, I figured we'd had it for tonight."

"So you went in the bar?"

"No. Well, yes. But not right away, no. I got out of the car, and I asked the guy what the trouble was, and he asked me did I see a cop anywhere because there was somebody with a knife in the bar, and I told him I was a cop, and he said I ought to go in there and take the knife away before somebody got cut."

"So naturally you went right in," Eileen said, and winked at Kling. Kling did not wink back. Kling lifted his coffee cup and sipped at it. He seemed not to be listening to what Willis was saying. He seemed almost comatose. Eileen wondered what was wrong with him.

"No, I still gave it a bit of thought," Willis said. "I would have rushed in *immediately*, of course—"

"Of course," Eileen said.

"To disarm that guy . . . who, by the way, turned out to be a girl . . . but I was worried about you being all alone there in the Laundromat in case Mr. Bloomers *did* decide to show up."

"Mr. Bloomers!" Eileen said, and burst out laughing. She was still feeling very high after the bust, and she wished that Kling wouldn't sit there like a zombie but would instead join in the general postmortem celebration.

"So I looked through the window," Willis said.

"Of the bar?"

"No, the Laundromat. And saw that everything was still cool. You were sitting there next to a lady reading a magazine, and this other lady was carrying about seven tons of laundry into the store, so I figured you'd be safe for another minute or two while I went in there and settled the thing with the knife, *especially* since I didn't think our man was going to show anyway. So I went in the bar, and there's this very nicely dressed middle-class–looking lady wearing eyeglasses and her hair swept up on her head and a dispatch case sitting on the bar as if she's a lawyer or an accountant who stopped in for a pink lady on the way home, and she's got an eight-foot-long switchblade in her right hand, and she's swinging it in front of her like this, back and forth, slicing the air with it, you know, and I'm surprised first of all that it's a lady and next that it's a switchblade she's holding, which is not exactly a lady's weapon. Also, I do not wish to get cut," Willis said.

"Naturally," Eileen said.

"Naturally," Willis said. "In fact, I'm beginning to think I'd better go check on you again, make sure the panties nut hasn't shown up after all. But just then the guy who came out in the street yelling, 'Police, police,' now says to the crazy lady with the stiletto, 'I warned you, Grace, this man is a policeman.' Which means I now have to uphold law and order, which is the last thing on earth I wish to do."

"What'd you do?" Eileen asked.

She was really interested now. She had never come up against a woman wielding a dangerous weapon, her line of specialty being men, of sorts. Usually she leveled her gun at a would-be rapist's privates, figuring she'd threaten him where he lived. Tonight, she had rammed the gun into the hollow of the man's throat. The barrel of the gun had left a bruise there, she had seen the bruise when she was putting the cuffs on him. But how do you begin taking a knife away from an angry *woman?* You couldn't threaten to shoot her in the balls, could you?

"I walked over to her and I said, 'Grace, that's a mighty fine knife you've got there. I wonder if you'd mind giving it to me.' "

"That was a mistake," Eileen said. "She might've given it to you, all right. She might've *really* given it to you."

"But she didn't," Willis said. "Instead, she turned to the guy who'd run out of the bar—"

"The 'Police, police' guy?"

"Yeah, and she said, 'Harry,' or whatever the hell his name was, 'Harry, how can you keep cheating on me this way?' and then she burst into tears and handed the knife to the *bartender* instead of to *me*, and Harry took her in his arms—"

"Excuse me, huh?" Kling said, and got up from behind the desk and walked out of the squadroom.

"Oh, God," Willis said.

"Huh?" Eileen said.

"I forgot," Willis said. "He probably thinks I told that story on purpose. I'd better go talk to him. Excuse me, okay? I'm sorry, Eileen, excuse me."

"Sure," she said, puzzled, and watched while Willis went through the gate in the slatted rail divider and down the corridor after Kling. There were some things she would never in a million years understand about the guys who worked up here. Never. She picked up another slice of pizza. It was cold. And she hadn't even got a chance to tell anyone about how absolutely brilliant and courageous and deadly forceful she'd been in that Laundromat.

AND whenever he couldn't sleep, Carella found himself thinking about Kling. Found himself wondering what Kling was doing at that moment. And to keep his mind off Kling, he started thinking about the case again, whichever case it happened to be; there was always some case or other he was working, some case or other that was driving him slowly crazy. And when he couldn't find an opening in the case, when he'd poked and pried and shaken the damn thing trying to find that one seam in the fabric that he could tear open with his hands—let some light in, climb in there inside the case, find out what the hell was making the case tick—when the case refused to yield, he began thinking about Kling again, wondering about Kling, hoping that Kling would not decide to eat his own gun one night.

It was a possibility.

It was more than a remote possibility.

Carella had been a Detective/Second for several years already before he'd met Kling—well, *really* met him; before that, he'd known him as a patrolman, but only to say hello to. When Kling got promoted into the squadroom (youngest man on the team back then), Carella took an immediate liking to him and recognized at once that his boyish good looks and quiet manner could be a tremendous asset to anyone partnered with him. Nor was he thinking only of your garden-variety Mutt-and-Jeff situations, where any cop in the world would be happy to play the heavy to Kling's apple-cheeked softie. It went beyond that. It involved something like a basic decency that civilians could sense, a decency that encouraged them to open up in his presence where they might not have to another cop.

It was easy to allow this precinct to burn you out. When you dealt with it day and night, it could get to you. All the ideals you'd come in with, the lofty notions about maintaining law and order, preserving society, all of it seemed to fade deeper and deeper into an innocent past as you came to grips with what it was *really* all about, when you realized it was a *war* you were fighting out there, the good guys versus the bad guys, and in a war you got tired, man, in a war you burned out.

So, yes, the police work had left its mark on Kling, too; only a man like Andy Parker could remain unfazed by police work, and the way *he* remained unfazed was by abdicating it. Parker was the worst cop in the precinct, perhaps the worst one in the entire city. Parker's credo was a simple one: you can't drown if you don't go in the water. Maybe Parker had once been young and idealistic. If so, Carella hadn't known him then. All he saw now was a man who never went in the water. The police work had touched Kling the way it had touched them all, but it wasn't the police work that made Carella worry he would eat his gun one night, it was the women, the way Kling kept having such bad luck with women. Carella had been with him that first time, in the bookshop on Culver Avenue, when Kling had knelt beside a dead girl wearing what appeared to be a red blouse, and had winced when he'd seen the two enormous bullet holes in the girl's side, the blood pouring steadily from those wounds, staining her white blouse a bright red. Kling had reached down to lift from the dead girl's face a book that had fallen from one of the shelves and lay tented over it, her broken string of pearls scattered on the floor like tiny luminescent islands in the sticky coagulation of her blood, his hand reaching out to lift the book, to reveal the girl's face, and then he'd whispered, "Oh, my Jesus Christ!" and something in his voice caused Carella to run toward the back of the shop at once. And then he heard Kling's cry, a single sharp anguished cry that pierced the dust-filled, cordite-stinking air of the shop.

"Claire!"

He was holding the dead girl in his arms when Carella reached him. His hands and his face were covered with Claire Townsend's blood, his fiancée's blood, and he kissed her lifeless eyes and her nose and her throat, and he kept murmuring over and over again, "Claire, Claire," and Carella would remember that name and the sound of Kling's voice as long as he lived.

And he would remember, too, the kind of cop Kling became— or almost became—after her murder. He thought they'd lose him then. He thought Kling would go the way of the Andy Parkers of the world, if indeed he remained a cop at all. Lieutenant Byrnes had wanted to transfer him out of the Eight-Seven. Byrnes was normally a patient and understanding man, who could appreciate the reasons for Kling's behavior, but this in no way made Kling any nicer to have around the office. The way Byrnes figured it, psychology was certainly an important factor in police work because it helped you to recognize there were no longer any villains in the world; there were only disturbed people. It was a very nice tool to possess, psychology was, until a cheap thief kicked you in the groin one night. It then became somewhat difficult to imagine the thief as a put-upon soul who'd had a shabby childhood. In much the same way, though Byrnes completely understood the trauma that had been responsible for Kling's behavior (God, how many *years* ago was this? Carella wondered), he nonetheless was finding it more and more difficult to accept Kling as anything but a cop who was going to hell with himself.

He had not gone to hell with himself.

Not that time nor the time afterward, either, when the girl he'd begun dating and eventually living with decided to dump him once and for all on a Christmas Eve, which was not a particularly good time to finally and irrevocably end a relationship, especially if later that night you were forced to shoot somebody dead, which was just what happened with Kling on that Christmas Eve, the man lunging across the room toward him, Kling squeezing the trigger once, and then again, aiming for the man's trunk, both slugs catching him in the chest, one of them going directly through his heart and the other piercing his left lung. Kling had lowered the gun. He remained sitting on the floor in the corner of the room, and watched the man's blood oozing into the sawdust, and wiped the sweat from his lip, and blinked and then began crying.

Long ago, Carella thought. All of it long ago.

Meeting Augusta Blair—or so all the guys in the squadroom had thought at the time—was perhaps the best thing that ever could have happened to Kling. He'd been investigating a burglary—victim came home from a ski trip to find the apartment a shambles—and there she was, auburn-haired and green-eyed, the most beautiful woman he'd ever seen in his life. Augusta Blair. Whose face and figure only adorned every fashion magazine in America. How could a Detective/Second earning only $24,600 a year even *hope* to ask a famous fashion model for a date? Nine months later, he told Carella he was thinking of marrying her.

"Yeah?" Carella said, surprised.

"Yeah," Kling said, and nodded.

They were in an unmarked police car, heading for the next state. It was bitterly cold outside. The windows, except for the windshield, were entirely covered with rime. Carella busied himself with the heater.

"What do you think?" Kling asked.

"Well, I don't know. Do you think she'll say yes?"

"Oh, yeah, I think she'll say yes."

"Well then, ask her."

"Well," Kling said, and fell silent.

They had come through the tollbooth. Behind them, Isola thrust its jagged peaks and minarets into a leaden sky. Ahead, the terrain consisted of rolling, smoke-colored hills through which the road snaked its lazy way. As it turned out, Kling's doubts had largely to do with whether or not the relationship he then enjoyed with Augusta would somehow *change* once they were married. He finally got around to asking Carella why he himself had got married. Carella thought it over for a long while. Then he said, "Because I couldn't bear the thought of any other man ever touching Teddy."

And in the long run, that was what had ended the marriage between Kling and Augusta, wasn't it? Another man touching her? Not so long ago, that. No. Only last August. This was now February, and Kling had found his wife in bed with another man only last August and had almost killed that man, but had hurled his gun away before he'd fired it. The divorce had been simple and clean. Augusta needed no alimony and wanted none from him; she had always earned more than three times what he did, anyway. They had split their possessions equally down the middle. It was Kling who'd moved out of the apartment they'd once shared. It was Kling who'd found a new apartment downtown, almost at the opposite end of the city, almost as though he wanted to put as much geographical distance between them as was humanly possible. It was Kling who'd carted all his possessions downtown with him, his clothes, his share of the records and books—and his guns. He owned two guns. They were both .38-caliber Police Specials. He preferred carrying the one with the burn mark on the walnut stock, and kept the other one only as a spare. It was the guns that bothered Carella.

He had never seen Kling this despondent, not even after the senseless murder of Claire Townsend in that bookshop. He had talked Byrnes into offering Kling two weeks' vacation immediately after the divorce was final, even though Kling wasn't up for another vacation till the summertime. Kling had refused the offer. He had invited Kling to several dinner parties at the Riverhead house. Kling had turned down the invitations. He had tried to work out his schedule so that he and Kling were partnered more often than any other two men on the squad, so that he could talk to Kling, help him through *this* bad time the way he had helped him through all the *other* bad times. But Kling had learned of the maneuver and had asked that he be put on "floater" status, filling in for whoever was off sick or in court or on vacation or whatever. Carella now believed that Kling was deliberately trying to avoid him, and only because he was a painful reminder of what had happened; he had, after all, been the first person to whom Kling had confided his suspicions.

Tomorrow was Valentine's Day—well, *today*, actually; the bedside clock read one-thirty in the morning. Holidays, even minor-league ones, were a bad time for anyone who'd lost a partner through death or divorce. Carella felt there was a fifty-fifty chance the lieutenant would give him the extra man he and Meyer desperately needed. So, all right, if the lieutenant *did* say okay, then why not zero in on Kling, tell the lieutenant Kling was the only man who could properly help them track down all those hundred and fourteen names on the company list, and then question a third of those people and eliminate the ones who couldn't possibly have killed either Sally Anderson *or* Paco Lopez—damn it, where was the connection? He fell asleep thinking that even if the lieutenant *did* assign Kling as a triple, the job would take them forever. He did not know that at that very moment the case was about to take a turn that would bring Kling into it, anyway, and would furthermore obviate the urgent need for questioning all those hundred and fourteen people.

THE man was wearing under his overcoat a plaid jacket, gray flannel slacks, and a vest. He was also wearing a .32-caliber pistol in a holster on the left-hand side of his body. The overcoat button closest to his waist was unbuttoned so that he could reach in for a clean, right-handed draw if ever the need arose. He had never had to use the pistol since he'd got the carry permit for it, six years ago.

He should not have worked so late tonight.

When he'd closed his shop downtown and then rolled down the metal grille and fastened the padlock in place, bolting the protective grille to the sidewalk, there had not been another soul anywhere on the street. He had walked quickly and nervously to the all-night garage where he normally parked his car, grateful for the gun at his waist. In the empty hours of the morning, the midtown area of this city turned into something resembling a moonscape. He had driven steadily uptown, stopping at each red light, nervously anticipating a sudden attack from any of the denizens who were abroad. When finally he entered the Grover Park transverse road, he felt a bit more secure; he would only have to stop at two traffic lights inside the park itself (if, in fact, they were red when he approached them) and a possible third one when he came out of the park farther uptown on Grover Avenue.

He caught the first of the lights and waited impatiently for it to change. The next one was green. The one at the end of the exit ramp was also green; he made his right turn onto Grover Avenue, drove uptown for several blocks, past the police station with its green globes flanking the front doorstep, the numerals 87 on each globe, and continued driving for another three blocks uptown before he made a left turn and headed north for Silvermine Road. He parked the car in the garage under his building, the way he always did, locking it and then heading for the elevator at the far end of the garage. It occurred to him, each and every time he parked the car under the building, that the security guard at the front door upstairs wasn't of very much use down here. But the distance from his assigned parking space to the red door of the elevator was perhaps fifty feet, if that, and rarely did he get home later than 7:00 p.m., when there were a great many other tenants coming and going.

There was no one else in the garage at a quarter to two in the morning.

The pillars supporting the roof stood like bulky sentinels spaced some ten feet apart from each other, four of them marking off the distance between him and the elevator. The garage was brightly lighted. His heels clicked on the cement floor as he moved toward the elevator. His footfalls echoed. He was passing the third pillar when a man with a gun in his hand stepped out from behind it, directly into his path.

He reached immediately into his coat for his own gun.

His hand closed on the stock.

He was starting to pull the gun free of its holster when the man standing in his path fired. The man fired directly into his face. He felt only the fierce sharp pain of the first bullet. His body was already jerking backward with the force of the impact when the second bullet entered his head. He did not feel this bullet. He did not feel anything anymore. His hand was still inside his coat, the fingers wrapped around the butt of the pistol, when he collapsed to the cold cement floor of the garage.

It was beginning to snow again. Lightly. Fat fluffy flakes drifting down lazily from the sky. Arthur Brown was driving. Bert Kling sat beside him on the front seat of the five-year-old unmarked sedan. Eileen Burke was sitting in the back. She had still been in the squadroom when the homicide squeal came in, and she'd asked Kling if he'd mind dropping her off at the subway on his way to the scene. Kling had merely grunted. Kling was a charmer, Eileen thought.

Brown was a huge man who looked even more enormous in his bulky overcoat. The coat was gray and it had a fake black fur collar. He was wearing black leather gloves that matched the black collar. Brown was supposed to be what people nowadays called a "black" man, but Brown knew that his complexion did not match the color of either the black collar or the black gloves. Whenever he looked at himself in the mirror, he saw someone with a chocolate-colored skin looking back at him, but he did not think of himself as a "chocolate" man. Neither did he think of himself as a Negro anymore; somehow, if a black man thought of himself as a Negro, he was thinking obsequiously. *Negro* had become a derogatory term, God alone knew when or how. Brown's father used to call himself "a person of color," which Brown thought was a very hoity-toity expression even when it was still okay for black men to call themselves Negroes. (Brown noticed that *Ebony* magazine capitalized the word *Black*, and he often wondered why.) He guessed he still thought of himself as colored, and he sincerely hoped there was nothing wrong with that. Nowadays, a nigger didn't know *what* he was supposed to think.

Brown was the kind of black man white men crossed the street to avoid. If you were white, and you saw Brown approaching on the same side of the street, you automatically assumed he was going to mug you or cut you with a razor or do something else terrible to you. That was partially due to the fact that Brown was six feet four inches tall and weighed two hundred and twenty pounds. It was also partially (*mostly*) due to the fact that Brown was black, or colored, or whatever you chose to call him, but he certainly was not white. A white man approaching Brown might not have crossed the street if Brown had also been a white man; unfortunately, Brown never had the opportunity to conduct such an experiment. The fact remained that when Brown was casually walking down the street minding his own business, white people crossed over to the other side. Sometimes even white *cops* crossed over to the other side. Nobody wanted trouble with someone who looked the way Brown looked. Even *black* people sometimes crossed the street when Brown approached, but only because he looked so bad-ass.

Brown knew he was, in fact, very handsome.

Whenever Brown looked in the mirror, he saw a very handsome chocolate-colored man looking back at him out of soulful brown eyes. Brown liked himself a lot. Brown was very comfortable with himself. Brown was glad he was a cop because he knew that the *real* reason white people crossed the street when they saw him was because they thought all black people were thieves or murderers. He frequently regretted the day he was promoted into the Detective Division, because then he could no longer wear his identifying blue uniform, the contradiction to his identifying brown skin. Brown especially liked to bust people of his own race. He especially liked it when some black dude said, "Come on, brother, give me a break." That man was no more Brown's brother than Brown was brother to a hippopotamus. In Brown's world, there were the good guys and the bad guys, white or black, it made no difference. Brown was one of the good guys. All those guys breaking the law out there were the bad guys. Tonight, one of the bad guys had left somebody dead and bleeding on the floor of a garage under a building on fancy Silvermine Road, and Kling had caught the squeal, and Brown was his partner, and they were two good guys riding out into the gently falling snow, with another good guy (who happened to be a girl) sitting on the back seat—which reminded him; he had to drop her off at the subway station.

"The one on Culver and Fourth, okay?" he asked her.

"That'll be fine, Artie," Eileen said.

Kling was hunkered down inside his coat, looking out at the falling snow. The car heater rattled and clunked, something wrong with the fan. The car was the worst one the squad owned. Brown wondered how come whenever it was his turn to check out a car, he got *this* one. Worst car in the entire *city*, maybe. Ripe tomato accelerator, rattled like a two-dollar whore, something wrong with the exhaust, the damn car always smelled of carbon monoxide, they were probably *poisoning* themselves on the way to the homicide.

"Willis says you nabbed the guy who was running around pulling down bloomers, huh?" Brown said.

"Yeah," Eileen said, grinning.

"Good thing, too," Brown said. "This kind of weather, lady *needs* her underdrawers." He began laughing. Eileen laughed, too. Kling sat staring through the windshield.

"Will you be all right on the subway, this hour of the night?" Brown asked.

"Yeah, I'll be fine," Eileen said.

He pulled the car into the curb.

"You sure now?"

"Positive. G'night, Artie," she said, and opened the door. "G'night, Bert."

"Good night," Brown said. "Take care."

Kling said nothing. Eileen shrugged and closed the door behind her. Brown watched as she went down the steps into the subway. He pulled the car away from the curb the moment her head disappeared from sight.

"What was that address again?" he asked Kling.

"One-one-one-four Silvermine," Kling said.

"That near the Oval?"

"Few blocks west."

There were two patrol cars parked at the curb when Brown pulled in. Their dome lights were flashing blue and red into the falling snow. Kling and Brown got out of the car, had a brief conversation with the patrolman who'd been left at the sidewalk to keep an eye on both cars (the theft of police cars not being unheard of in this city), and then walked down the ramp into the underground garage. The place was lighted with sodium lamps. The three patrolmen from the cars upstairs were standing around a man lying on the cement floor some eight feet from the elevator. The elevator door was red. The man's blood flowed from his open skull toward the matching red elevator door.

"Detective Brown," Brown said. "My partner, Detective Kling."

"Right," one of the patrolmen said, and nodded.

"Who was the first car on the scene?"

"We were," another patrolman said. "Boy Car."

"Anybody down here when you arrived?"

"Nobody."

"Nobody?" Kling said. "Who called it in? Who found the body?"

"Don't know, sir," the patrolman said. "Dispatcher radioed us a Ten-Ten—investigate shots fired. We didn't even know where we were supposed to look, they just gave us the address. So we asked the guy in the lobby, the security guard there, did he call nine-one-one to report a man with a gun, and he said no, he didn't. So we looked around the building and also the backyard, and we were about to call it back as a Ten-Ninety, when Benny here, he says, 'Let's check out the garage under the building.' By that time, Charlie Car was here—"

"We'd been checking out an alarm on Ainsley," one of the other patrolmen said.

"So the three of us come down here together," the first patrolman said.

"And there he is," the third patrolman said, nodding toward the body on the floor.

"Has Homicide been informed?" Kling asked.

"I guess so," the first patrolman said.

"What do you mean, you *guess* so?"

"I gave it to the desk sergeant as a D.O.A. It ain't my responsibility to inform Homicide."

"Who's talkin' about Homicide behind our backs?" a voice from the top of the ramp said.

"Speak of the devil," Brown said.

It was rare that Homicide detectives—or any detectives, for that matter—worked as triples, but the three men who came down the ramp now, advancing as steadily as Sherman tanks, were known throughout the city as the Holy Trinity, and it was rumored that they never did *anything* except as a trio. Their names were Hardigan, Hanrahan, and Mandelbaum. It occurred to Brown that he had never learned their first names. It further occurred to him that he had never learned the first name of *any* Homicide detective. Did Homicide detectives *have* first names? The three detectives were all wearing black. Homicide detectives in this city favored black. There was a rumor afoot that the stylistic trend had been started years back by a very famous Homicide dick. Brown's surmise was a much simpler one: Homicide cops dealt exclusively with corpses; they were only wearing the colors of mourning. It occurred to him that Genero had begun wearing a lot of black lately; was Genero hoping for a transfer to Homicide? It further occurred to him that nobody in the squadroom ever called Genero by his first name, which was Richard. It was always, "Come here, Genero" or—more likely— "Go away, Genero." Occasionally, he was called Genero the Asshole, the way an ancient king might have been dubbed affectionately Amos the Simple or Herman the Rat. If Homicide cops had no first names, and if Genero had a first name no one ever used, then perhaps Genero might one day enjoy a successful career with the Homicide Division. Brown devoutly hoped so.

"This here the victim here?" Hardigan asked.

"No, this here is a paper doily here," Brown said.

"I forgot I was dealing with the Eight-Seven," Hardigan said.

"Comedians," Hanrahan said.

"*Morons*," Mandelbaum said. "Two o'clock in the *morning*."

"We get you out of your little beddie?" Brown asked.

"Shove it up your ass," Mandelbaum said pleasantly.

"In spades," Hardigan said, and Brown wondered if he was making a racist remark.

"Who *is* he?" Hanrahan asked.

"We haven't tossed him yet," Kling said.

"So do it," Hanrahan said.

"Not until the M.E.'s finished with him."

"Who says?"

"New regs—only a year old already."

"Hell with the regs, we'll freeze out here waiting for the M.E. here. This is Saturday night, you know how many people are getting themselves killed out there tonight?"

"How many?" Kling said.

"Toss him. Do what I tell you. This is Homicide here," Hanrahan said.

"Put it in writing," Kling said. "That I should toss him before the M.E. pronounces him dead."

"You can *see* he's dead, can't you? What do you need? The

man's got no face left, why do you need an M.E. to tell you he's
dead?" Hardigan said, backing his partner.

"Then *you* toss him," Brown said, backing *his* partner.

"Okay, we'll wait for the M.E., okay?" Hanrahan said.

"We'll freeze down here waiting for the M.E., okay?" Mandelbaum said.

"Will that make you guys happy?" Hardigan said.

Neither Brown nor Kling answered.

The M.E. did not arrive until almost 3:00 a.m. By that time the
Mobile Crime Unit was on the scene doing everything they *could*
do without touching the body itself. The boys from the Photo
Unit were taking their pictures, and the Crime Scene signs
were up, and Brown and Kling were making their drawings, and
everybody was freezing to death but nobody had yet come to pronounce the stiff (very *literally* stiff) dead. The M.E. made a grand
entrance, striding down the ramp like a stand-up burlesque comic
ready to pitch popcorn and prizes.

"Sorry to be late, gentlemen," he said, and Hardigan farted.

The M.E. bent over the corpse. He unbuttoned the corpse's
overcoat. The first thing all of them saw was the corpse's hand
clutched around the butt of a pistol in a holster.

"Well, well," Hanrahan said.

With some difficulty, the M.E. unbuttoned the man's plaid
jacket. He was about to slide his stethoscope under the man's vest
and then under his shirt and onto his chest, the better to determine that the bullets pumped into his face had caused his heart to
cease functioning, when he noticed—as did the five detectives and
the three patrolmen and the photographer and the two lab tech-
nicians—that the man's vest had perhaps a dozen pockets sewn
into it.

"Last time I saw that was on a pickpocket," Mandelbaum said.
"Had all these pockets on his vest, used to drop stolen goods in
them."

The man was not a pickpocket.

Not unless he'd been very fortunate that day.

As soon as the M.E. was finished with him (and he *was* indeed dead), they went through all those little pockets sewn into his vest. And in each one of those little pockets, they found little plastic packets. And in each one of those little plastic packets, they found diamonds of various sizes and shapes.

"The guy's a walking jewelry store," Hardigan said.

"Only he ain't walking no more," Hanrahan said.

"*Look* at all that ice, willya?" Mandelbaum said.

SEVEN

THEY had promised only snow, but by morning the snow had changed to sleet and then to freezing rain, and the streets were dangerously slick. Carella almost slipped on his way to the subway, catching his balance a moment before he flew into the air. His mother had told him two atrocity stories when he was a child, and both of them had remained with him into his adult years. The first had to do with his Uncle Charlie, whom he'd never met, who had accidentally blinded himself in one eye with the point of a scissors while trying to trim his eyebrows. Carella occasionally had his eyebrows trimmed in a barber shop, but never did he attempt that dangerous task himself. His mother had also told him how his Uncle Salvatore had slipped on the ice outside his haberdashery in Calm's Point and landed on his back, which was why he was confined to a wheelchair. Whenever Carella spotted a patch of ice on a sidewalk or a road, he walked or drove over it very, very carefully.

Carella *had* known (and incidentally had loved) his Uncle Salvatore, and whenever his uncle asked him why he didn't wear a hat, Carella felt a bit guilty. "You should wear a hat," his uncle said. "If you don't wear a hat, forty percent of your body heat escapes from your head, and you feel cold all over." Carella did not like hats. He told his uncle he did not like hats. His uncle tapped his temple with his forefinger. "*Pazzo*," he said, which meant "crazy" in Italian. It was Carella's uncle who'd told him the only haberdashery joke he'd ever heard in his life. "A man walks into a haberdashery," his uncle said. "The haberdasherer comes over to him and says, 'Yes, sir, do you have anything in mind?' The man says, 'I have *pussy* in mind, but let me see a hat.' " Carella was sixteen years old when his uncle told him that story. They were in his uncle's haberdashery, which he was still running from a wheelchair. He died three years later.

It took Carella two hours to get to work that morning. He spent the time on the subway trying to figure out what he would buy Teddy for Valentine's Day—which was today, a Sunday, when most of the city's shops would be closed. He had expected to pick up something yesterday, but that was before he'd inherited the Sally Anderson homicide. Teddy had told him at breakfast this morning, a secretive smile on her mouth, her hands flashing, that she would be getting him *his* gift sometime this afternoon and would present it to him tonight when he got home from work. He told her there was no rush; despite the makeshift Presidents' Day holiday tomorrow, many of the stores would be open, and besides, the roads would be cleared and sanded by then. Teddy told him she'd already made the appointment. An appointment for *what?* he wondered.

Meyer Meyer was wearing his Valentine's Day present.

His Valentine's Day present was a woolen watch cap that would have caused Carella's Uncle Salvatore to beam with pride. Meyer's wife, Sarah, had knitted the watch cap herself. It was a white cap with a border of linked red hearts. Meyer was marching around the squadroom with the hat pulled down over his ears, showing it off.

"You can hardly tell you're bald with that hat," Tack Fujiwara said, and noticed Carella coming through the gate in the railing. "Hello, cousin," he said.

"Oh-hi-oh," Carella said.

"What do you mean '*hardly*'?" Meyer said. "Do I look bald?" he asked Carella.

"You look hairy," Carella said. "Where'd you get that hat?"

"Sarah made it. For Valentine's Day."

"Very nice," Carella said. "Is the Loot in?"

"Ten minutes ago," Fujiwara said. "What'd *you* get for Valentine's Day?"

"A murder," Carella said.

"Shake hands with Kling," Fujiwara said, but Carella was already knocking on the lieutenant's door, and he didn't catch the words.

"Come!" Byrnes shouted.

Carella opened the door. The lieutenant was sitting behind his desk studying the open lid of a box of candy. "Hello, Steve," he said. "This chart tells you what each piece of candy in the box is. Would you like a piece of candy?"

"Thanks, Pete, no," Carella said.

Byrnes kept studying the chart, running his finger over it. He was a compact man with a head of thinning iron gray hair, flinty blue eyes, and a craggy nose that had been broken with a lead pipe when he was still a patrolman in Majesta, but that had miraculously knitted itself together without any trace of the injury save a faintly visible scar across the bridge. No one ever noticed the scar except when Byrnes touched it, as he sometimes did during a particularly knotty skull session in his office. He was touching it now as he studied the varied selection promised by the chart on the inside lid of the candy box.

"My Valentine's present," he said, fingering the scar on his nose, studying the list of goodies to be sampled.

"I'll be getting mine tonight," Carella said, feeling somehow defensive.

"So have some candy now," Byrnes said, and plucked a square-shaped piece of chocolate from the box. "The square ones are always caramels," he said. "I don't need a chart to tell me this is a caramel." He bit into it. "See?" he said, smiling and chewing. "Good, too. Have one," he said, and shoved the box across his desk.

"Pete, we've got a hundred and fourteen people to track down," Carella said. "That's how many people are in the *Fatback* company, and that's how many people Meyer and I have got to question if we're going to get any kind of a lead on this dead dancer."

"What's her connection with this Lopez character?" Byrnes asked, chewing.

"We don't know yet."

"Dope?" Byrnes asked.

"Not that we know. The lab's checking."

"Was he her boyfriend or something?"

"No, her boyfriend is a med student at Ramsey."

"Where was *he* when the girl was cashing it in?"

"Home studying."

"Who says?"

"He says."

"Check it."

"We will. Meanwhile, Pete—"

"Let me guess," Byrnes said. "You sure you don't want one of these?" he said, and took another chocolate from the box.

"Thanks," Carella said, and shook his head.

"Meanwhile," Byrnes said, "I'm trying to guess what you want from me."

"Triple us," Carella said.

"Who'd you have in mind?"

"Bert Kling."

"Bert's got headaches of his own just now."

"What do you mean?"

"He caught a homicide last night."

"Well, that takes care of that," Carella said. "Who *can* you spare?"

"Who said I can spare anybody?"

"Pete, this girl is all over the newspapers."

"So what?"

"She'll be making news as long as that show runs . . . and that'll be forever."

"So what?"

"So how long do you think it'll be before the Chief of Detectives picks up the telephone and gives you a little jingle? 'Hello, Pete, about this dancer? In that big hit musical? Any leads yet, Pete? Lots of reporters calling here, Pete. What are your boys doing up there, Pete, besides sitting on their duffs while people go around shooting other people?' "

Byrnes looked at him.

"Never mind the Chief of Detectives," he said. "The Chief of Detectives doesn't have to come to work up *here* every day, the Chief of Detectives has a nice big corner office in the *Headquarters* Building downtown. And if the Chief of Detectives thinks we're moving too slowly on this one, then maybe we ought to remind him it wasn't even *ours* to begin with, the girl was shot and killed in Midtown *East*, if the Chief of Detectives would like to know, and not up here in the Eight-Seven. What we have as our very own up *here* is the murder of a crumby little gram dealer, if that would interest the Chief of Detectives, though I doubt he could care less. Now if you want to make your request to me on the basis of something *sensible*, Steve, like how talking to a hundred and fourteen people—are there *really* that many people attached to that show?"

"A hundred and fourteen, yes."

"If you want to come to me and tell me it'll take you and Meyer a week, ten days, two weeks, *however* long to question all hundred and fourteen of those people while a murderer is running around out there with a gun in his hand, if you want to present your case sensibly and logically and not threaten me with what the Chief of *Detectives* is going to think . . ."

"Okay, Pete, how's this?" Carella said, smiling. "It's going to take Meyer and me at least ten days to question all those people while a murderer is running around out there with a gun in his hand. We can cut the working time to maybe five days, unless we hit pay dirt before then, so all I'm asking for is *one* other man on the case, triple us up, Pete, and turn us loose out there. Okay? Who can you spare?"

"Nobody," Byrnes said.

SHE tried to remember how long ago it had been. Years and years, that was certain. And would he think her frivolous now? Would he accept what she had done (what she was *about* to do, actually, since she hadn't yet done it, and could still change her mind about it) as the gift she intended it to be, or would he consider it the self-indulgent whim of a woman who was no longer the young girl he'd married years and years ago? Well, who *is?* Teddy thought. Even Jane Fonda is no longer the young girl she was years and years ago. But does Jane Fonda worry about such things? Probably, Teddy thought.

The section of the city through which she walked was thronged with people, but Teddy could not hear the drifting snatches of their conversations as they moved past her and around her. Their exhaled breaths pluming on the brittle air were, to her, only empty cartoon balloons floating past in a silent rush. She walked in an oddly hushed world, dangerous to her in that her ears could provide no timely warnings, curiously exquisite in that whatever she saw was unaccompanied by any sound that might have marred its beauty. The sight (and aroma) of a bluish-gray cloud of carbon monoxide, billowing onto the silvery air from an automobile exhaust pipe, assumed dreamlike proportions when it was not coupled with the harsh mechanical sound of an automobile engine. The uniformed cop on the corner, waving his arms this way and that, artfully dodging as he directed the cross-purposed stream of lumbering traffic, became an acrobat, a ballet dancer, a skilled mime the moment one did not have to hear his bellowed, "*Move* it, let's keep it *moving!*" And yet—

She had never heard her husband's voice.

She had never heard her children's laughter.

She had never heard the pleasant wintry jingle of automobile skid chains on an icy street, the big-city cacophony of jackhammers and automobile horns, street vendors and hawkers, babies crying. As she passed a souvenir shop whose window brimmed with inexpensive jade, ivory (illegal to import), fans, dolls with Oriental eyes (like her husband's), she did not hear drifting from a small window on the side wall of the shop the sound of a stringed instrument plucking a sad and delicate Chinese melody, the notes hovering on the air like ice crystals—she simply did not hear.

The tattoo parlor was vaguely anonymous, hidden as it was on a narrow Chinatown side street. The last time she'd been here, the place had been flanked by a bar and a Laundromat. Today, the bar was an offtrack betting parlor and the Laundromat was a fortune-telling shop run by someone named Sister Lucy. Progress. As she passed Sister Lucy's emporium, Teddy looked over the curtain in the front window and saw a Gypsy woman sitting before a large phrenology poster hanging on the wall. Except for the poster and the woman, the shop was empty. The woman looked very lonely and a trifle cold, huddled in her shawl, looking straight ahead of her at the entrance door. For a moment, Teddy was tempted to walk into the empty store and have her fortune told. What was the joke? Her husband was very good at remembering jokes. What was it? Why couldn't women remember jokes? Was that a sexist attitude? What the hell was the *joke?* Something about a Gypsy band buying a chain of empty stores?

The name on the plate glass window of the tattoo parlor was Charlie Chen. Beneath the name were the words Exotic Oriental Tattoo. She hesitated a moment, and then opened the door. There must have been a bell over the door, and it probably tinkled, signaling Mr. Chen from the back of his shop. She had not heard the bell, and at first she did not recognize the old Chinese man who came toward her. The last time she'd seen him, he had been a round fat man with a small mustache on his upper lip. He had laughed a lot, and each time he laughed, his fat little body quivered. He had thick fingers, she remembered, and there had been an oval jade ring on the forefinger of his left hand.

"Yes, lady?" he said.

It was Chen, of course. The mustache was gone, and so was the jade ring, and so were the acres of flesh, but it was surely Chen, wizened and wrinkled and shrunken, looking at her now out of puzzled brown eyes, trying to place her. She thought, *I've* changed, too, he doesn't recognize me, and suddenly felt foolish about what she was here to do. Maybe it was too late for things like garter belts and panties, ribbed stockings and high-heeled, patent leather pumps, merry widows and lacy teddies, too late for Teddy, too late for silly, sexy playfulness. Was it? Oh my God, *was* it?

She had asked Fanny to call yesterday, first to find out if the shop would be open today and next to make an appointment for her. Fanny had left the name Teddy Carella. Had Chen forgotten her name as well? He was still staring at her.

"You Missa Carella?" he said.

She nodded.

"I know you?" he said, his head cocked, studying her.

She nodded again.

"You know me?"

She nodded.

"Charlie Chen," he said, and laughed, but nothing about him shook, his laughter was an empty wind blowing through a frail old body. "Everybody call me Charlie *Chan*," he explained. "Big detective Charlie Chan. But me Chen, *Chen*. You know Charlie Chan, detective?"

The same words he had spoken all those years ago.

Oddly, she felt like weeping.

"Big detective," Chen said. "Got stupid sons." He laughed again. "Me got stupid sons, too, but me no detec—" And suddenly he stopped, and his eyes opened wide, and he said, "Detective wife, you detective *wife!* I make butterfly for you! Black lacy butterfly!"

She nodded again, grinning now.

"You no can talk, right? You read my lips, right?"

She nodded.

"Good, everything hunky-dory. How you been, lady? You still so pretty, most beautiful lady ever come my shop. You still got butterfly on shoulder?"

She nodded.

"Best butterfly I ever make. Nice small butterfly. I want do *big* one, remember? You say no, small one. I make tiny delicate black butterfly, very good for lady. Very sexy in strapless gown. You husband think was sexy?"

Teddy nodded. She started to say something with her hands, caught herself—as she so often had to—and then pointed to a pencil and a sheet of paper on Chen's counter.

"You wanna talk, right?" Chen said, smiling, and handed her the pencil and paper.

She took both and wrote, *How have you been, Mr. Chen?*

"Ah, well, not so good," Chen said.

She looked at him expectantly, quizzically.

"Old Charlie Chen gotta Big C, huh?" he said.

She did not understand him for a moment.

"Cancer," he said, and saw the immediate shocked look on her face and said, "No, no, lady, don't worry, old Charlie be hunky-dory, yessir." He kept watching her face. She did not want to cry. She owed the old man the dignity of not having to watch her cry for him. She opened her hands. She tilted her head. She raised her eyebrows ever so slightly. She saw on his face and in his eyes that he knew she was telling him how sorry she was. "Thank you, lady," he said, and impulsively took both her hands between his own and, smiling, said, "So, why you come here see Charlie Chen? You write down what you like, yes?"

She picked up the pencil and began writing again.

"Ah," he said, watching. "Ah. Very smart idea. Very smart. Okay, fine."

He watched the moving pencil.

"Very good," he said. "Come, we go in back. Charlie Chen so happy you come see him. My sons all married now, I tell you? My oldest son a doctor Los Angeles. A *head* doctor!" he said, and burst out laughing. "A shrink! You believe it? My oldest *son!* My other two sons . . . come in back, lady . . . my other two sons . . ."

FROM where Captain Sam Grossman stood at the windows looking down at High Street, he could see out over almost all of the downtown section of the city. The new Headquarters Building was a structure made almost entirely of glass (or so it appeared from the outside), and Grossman sometimes wondered if anyone down there in the street was watching him as he went about his daily commonplace chores—like trying to get through to the Eight-Seven on the telephone, which was both commonplace *and* irritating. Actually, Grossman rarely thought of his work in the lab as being anything but important and exciting and very far from commonplace, but he would not have admitted that to anyone in the world, with the possible exception of his wife. The number was still busy. He momentarily pressed one of the receiver rest buttons, got a fresh dial tone, and dialed the number again. He got another busy signal. Sighing, Grossman cradled the receiver and looked at his watch. I shouldn't even *be* here today, he thought. This is Sunday.

He was here today because someone thought it might be amusing to restage the Valentine's Day Massacre right here in *this* city instead of in Chicago, where it had originally taken place in 1929. What had happened back then, if Grossman's memory of history served, was that some nice fellows from Al Capone's gang forced seven unarmed but equally nice fellows from the Bugs Moran gang to line up against a garage wall and then shot them down with machine guns. Oh boy, that was some massacre. It was also a pretty good joke since the guys from the Capone gang were all dressed as policemen. There were some wags in Chicago at the time who maintained that the hoods were only *behaving* like policemen, too, but that was mere conjecture. Nonetheless, at nine o'clock this morning—which by Grossman's watch was almost three hours ago—several uniformed "policemen" had broken into a garage housing not bootleggers but instead narcotics traffickers, and had asked them to line up against the wall, and had shot them down in cold blood. One of the surprise shooters had spray-painted the outline of a big red heart on the wall. The killers hadn't even bothered to take with them the estimated four kilos of heroin the traffickers had been processing when they'd broken in; perhaps they felt the red heart on the wall, and the red blood all over the floor, complemented the pristine white of the uncut heroin on the table. Either way, there were seven dead men on the Lower Platform, as the area closest to the city's Old Quarter was called, and those men had bullets in them, and those bullets had been recovered from their respective cadavers and sent to the laboratory together with the empty spray can and a slew of fingerprints lifted from hither and yon, not to mention some paint scrapings taken from the lamp-post opposite the garage, presumably left there when the getaway car backed into it, leaving as well a deposit of taillight glass splinters on the pavement, all in all a nice batch of material for the lab to ponder on a nice Sunday morning.

Grossman dialed the number again.

Would miracles never? It was actually ringing!

"Eighty-Seventh Squad, Genero," a harried-sounding voice said.

"Detective Carella, please," Grossman said.

"Can he call you back?" Genero said. "We're very busy up here just now."

"I've been trying to get through for the past ten minutes," Grossman said.

"Yeah, that's 'cause the lines've been busy," Genero said. "All hell is busting loose up here. Give me your name and I'll ask him to call back."

"No, give him my name and tell him I'm on the line *waiting*," Grossman said, annoyed.

"Well, what *is* your name, mister?" Genero said, somewhat snottily.

"Captain Grossman," Grossman said. "What's *your* name?"

"He'll be right with you, sir," Genero said, forgetting to tell Grossman his name. Grossman heard the receiver clattering onto a hard surface. There was a great deal of yelling and hollering in the background, but that was usual for the Eight-Seven, even on a Sunday.

"Detective Carella," Carella said. "Can I help you, sir?"

"Steve, this is Sam Grossman."

"*Sam?* He told me it was a Captain *Holtzer*."

"No, it's a Captain Grossman. What's going on up there? It sounds like World War Three."

"We have a delegation of angry citizens," Carella said.

"Angry about what?"

"A person shitting in the hallways."

"Don't send me samples," Grossman said at once.

"*You* may think it's comical," Carella said, lowering his voice, "and frankly, so do I. But the tenants of 5411 Ainsley do not find it amusing at all. They are here en masse, demanding police action."

"What do they want you to *do*, Steve?"

"Apprehend the Mad Shitter," Carella said, and Grossman burst out laughing. Carella started laughing, too. In the background, over Carella's laughter, Grossman could hear someone yelling in Spanish. He thought he detected the word *mierda*.

"Steve," he said, "I hate to take you away from matters of great moment—"

"Matters of great *movement*, you mean," Carella said, and both men burst out laughing again; there was nothing a grown cop liked better than a scatalogical joke unless it was a joke about a cop on the take. Both cops laughed for what must have been a full two minutes while behind them everyone was shouting like the Bay of Pigs. At last, the laughter subsided. So did all the Spanish voices in the background.

"Where'd they all *go*, all of a sudden?" Grossman asked.

"*Home!*" Carella said, and burst out laughing again. "Genero told them he'd arrange a *lineup* for them! Can you picture eight cops and a possible perp throwing moons at twenty-six concerned Hispanic tenants?"

Grossman began laughing so hard he thought he would wet his pants. Another two minutes went by before either of the men could speak. It was not always like this when Carella and Grossman got on the phone together, but both men were grateful for those times when it was. Usually, Grossman presented a much soberer demeanor to the detectives with whom he worked. Tall and blue-eyed, rather somber-looking in his unrimmed spectacles, he resembled a New England farmer more than he did a scientist, and his clipped manner of speaking did little to belie the notion. Standing face to face with Sam Grossman in the sterile orderliness of his laboratory, you had the feeling that if you asked him directions to the next town, he'd say you couldn't get there from here. But every so often, perhaps because he liked Carella so much, Grossman seemed to forget momentarily that his job was often inextricably linked with violent death.

"About this girl's handbag," he said, and Carella knew he was getting down to business.

"The Anderson girl?" he said.

"Sally Anderson, right," Grossman said. "I'll send you the full report later, right down to what brand of cigarettes she smoked. But for now . . . this was flagged for possible cocaine, wasn't it?"

"Because the other victim was a—"

"That's what the card says, anyway."

"Did you find anything that *might* be cocaine?"

"A residue on the bottom of the bag. Not enough to run as many tests as I'd have liked."

"How many *did* you run?"

"Four. Which in the process of elimination—you should pardon the expression—isn't a hell of a lot. But I knew what you were looking for, so I deliberately chose my color tests for the most dramatic reactions. For example, cocaine shows colorless on both the Mercke and the Marquis, so I avoided those. Instead, I went with nitrosylsulfuric acid for my first color test. I got a pale yellow reaction, with no change when ammonia was added, and with a change to colorless when water was added. That's a cocaine reaction. For the second color test—am I boring you?"

"No, no, go on," Carella said. He considered himself a scientific nitwit and was in fact fascinated whenever Grossman began spewing formulas and such.

"For the second color test, I used tetrabitromathane, which again—if we're looking for cocaine—would give us a more dramatic reaction than some of the other tests. Sure enough, we initially got yellow with an orange cast to it, turning eventually to full yellow. Cocaine," Grossman said.

"Cocaine," Carella repeated.

"And when I ran my tests for precipitation and crystallization, I got virtually the same results. With platinum chloride as my reagent and normal acetic acid as my solvent, I got an immediate cocaine reaction—thousands of aggregate crystalline blade forms, arranged in bizarre fashion, moderate birefringence, predominantly—"

"You're losing me, Sam," Carella said.

"No matter. It was typically cocaine. When I used gold chloride with the acid, I got ruler-edged crystals forming from amorphous . . . again, no matter. It, too, was typically cocaine."

"So . . . are you saying the substance you found at the bottom of her bag *is* cocaine?"

"I'm saying there's a very strong *likelihood* it's cocaine. I can't say positively, Steve, without having run a great many more tests, but I simply ran out of available substance before I could. If it makes you any happier . . . you *are* looking for a drug connection here, I assume."

"I am."

"Well, we found shreds of marijuana, as well as marijuana seeds at the bottom of the bag. Ladies' handbags are wonderful receptacles for all *kinds* of crap."

"Okay, thanks, Sam."

"Would it help further to know that the girl chewed sugarless gum?"

"Not in the slightest."

"In that case, I won't mention that she chewed sugarless gum. Good luck, Steve, I have bullets here from seven people who were shot by cops today."

"What?" Carella said, but Grossman had hung up.

Smiling, Grossman stood with his hand on the cradled receiver for a moment and then looked up when he heard the door opening. He was surprised to see Bert Kling coming into the room, not because Kling never visited the lab, but only because Grossman had not ten seconds earlier been talking to *another* cop from the Eight-Seven. Considering the laws of probability, Grossman would have guessed . . . well, no matter.

"Come in, Bert," he said. "How's it going?"

He knew how it was going. Everyone in the department knew how it was going. Bert Kling had found his wife in bed with another man last August, *that's* how it was going. He knew that Kling and his wife were now divorced. He knew that Carella was concerned about him because Carella had expressed that concern to Grossman, who had suggested that he talk to one of the department psychologists, who in turn had advised Carella to try to get Kling to come in personally, which Carella had not been able to convince Kling to do. Grossman liked Kling. There were not many cops in the Eight-Seven he disliked, as a matter of fact—well, yes, Parker, he guessed. Parker very definitely. Parker was mean-spirited and lazy and altogether a person to dislike passionately. Grossman liked Kling, and he hated seeing him *looking* this way, like a man who'd just been released from the state penitentiary at Castleview and was still wearing the ill-fitting civilian threads the state gave him gratis with his parole papers and his minimum-wage check. Like a man who needed a shave, even though the blond stubble on Kling's cheeks and jaws was less noticeable than it might have been on a man with a heavier beard. Like a man carrying an enormous weight on his shoulders.

Like a man whose eyes appeared a trifle too moist, a bit too precariously poised on the edge of tears. Grossman looked into those eyes as the men shook hands. Was Carella's concern a legitimate one? *Did* Kling look like a man who might one day decide to chew on the barrel of his gun?

"So," Grossman said, smiling, "what brings you down here?"

"Some bullets," Kling said.

"*More* bullets? We had the Valentine's Day Massacre all over again this morning," Grossman said. "Seven guys killed in a garage down on the Lower Platform. Guys who did it were dressed like cops. I have to admit it took style, but I don't like the extra work it's given us on a weekend. What bullets?"

"We caught a homicide last night on Silvermine Road," Kling said. "Man named Marvin Edelman, gunshot victim. I asked the morgue to send whatever they recover over to you. I thought I might mention it."

"You came all the way down here to tell me some *bullets* are on the way?" Grossman said.

"No, no, I was in the area, anyway."

Grossman knew that the Criminal Court Building was right next door, and at first he figured Kling might be down here on court business. There was only one court open on Sunday, though, and that strictly for the arraignment of anyone arrested the day before. And then Grossman remembered that the Psychological Counseling Unit had recently moved into new quarters on the third floor of the building. Had Carella finally convinced Kling to see someone about his obvious depression?

"So what *did* bring you down here on a Sunday?" Grossman asked in what he hoped was a casual way.

"I had a lady in yesterday, her husband . . . Well, it's a long story," Kling said.

"Let me hear it," Grossman said.

"No, you've got bullets to worry about," Kling said. "Anyway, keep an eye out for whatever comes from the morgue, will you? The guy's name is Edelman."

"A *landsman*," Grossman said, smiling, but Kling did not return the smile.

"See you," Kling said, and walked out of the lab and into the marble corridor outside. The story he'd been about to tell was about this woman who'd come to see him yesterday because her husband's former girlfriend had accosted him on the street and slashed his arm from the shoulder to the wrist with a bread knife she'd pulled from her handbag. In describing the former girl-friend, the woman used the words "black as that telephone there" and then went on to describe her further as an extremely thin woman whose name was Annie—she didn't know Annie *what*, and neither did her husband. Her husband, according to the woman's story, was a Dutch seaman who came into this city's port every other month or so and who, until they'd met and married, used to spend his wages on various prostitutes either uptown on La Vía de Putas or else downtown on the stretch of hooker-packed turf known as Slit City. The wife had been witness to the knifing and had heard the girl Annie say, "I'm goan juke you good," and it was perhaps the use of the word *juke* that rang a bell for Kling.

A working cop doesn't always know *how* he remembers the myriad little details of the numberless criminal transgressions that cross his desk and his path every day of the week. To remember them is enough. The fact that the knife wielder had been black had not been enough to trigger recall. Neither had the name Annie, or the knowledge that the girl was extremely thin and a working prostitute. But the first time Kling had ever heard the word *juke* in his life was on Mason Avenue, when an anorectic black whore who'd slashed a customer's face later claimed, "I di'n juke that dumb trick." Cotton Hawes, who had answered the squeal with him, informed Kling that he himself had first heard the expression in New Orleans, and that it meant, of course, "to stab." The hooker's name had been Annie Holmes. The moment the victim's wife repeated what Annie had said as she carved up her former playmate's arm, Kling snapped his fingers.

He was down here today—even though it was his day off—because: (a) he lived only six blocks away, in a small apartment in the shadow of the Calm's Point Bridge, and (b) he could not question Marvin Edelman's widow until tomorrow because she was on her way home from the Caribbean after receiving a call from her daughter informing her that Edelman had been shot and killed last night, and (c) there was not much more he could do on the homicide until Grossman's people came up with some information on the gun used in the slaying, and (d) he knew the Identification Section was open seven days a week (although the Mayor had been threatening cutbacks), and he hoped he might be able to pick up a picture of Annie Holmes, which he could then show to the man she'd stabbed and his wife, who'd witnessed the stabbing, hoping for a positive I.D. that would be good enough for an arrest.

That was why he was here.

He had not told Grossman why he was here, even though he'd started to, because somehow the triangle of Dutch Seaman–Present Wife–Former Bedmate recalled vividly and blindingly the scene in the bedroom of the apartment Kling had shared with Augusta as man and wife, the triangular scene in that room, Augusta naked in their bed, absurdly clutching the sheet to her breasts, hiding her shame, protecting her nakedness from the prying eyes of her own husband, her green eyes wide, her hair tousled, a fine sheen of perspiration on the marvelous cheekbones that were her fortune, her lip trembling the way the gun in Kling's hand was trembling. And the man with Augusta, the *third* side of the triangle, was in his undershorts and reaching for his trousers folded over a bedside chair, the man was short and wiry, he looked like *Genero*, for Christ's sake, with curly black hair and brown eyes wide in terror, but he was not Genero, he was Augusta's lover, and as he turned from the chair where his trousers were draped, he said only, "Don't shoot," and Kling leveled the gun at him.

I *should* have shot him, he thought now. If I'd shot him, I wouldn't still be living with the shame. I wouldn't have to stop telling a story about a Dutch seaman and his hooker girlfriend for fear that even a decent man like Sam Grossman will remember, will think, Ah yes, Kling and his cheating wife, Ah yes, Kling did *nothing*, Ah yes, Kling did not *kill* the man who was—

"Hey, hi!" the voice said.

He was approaching the elevators, his head bent, his eyes on the marble floor. He did not recognize the voice, nor did he even realize at first that it was he who was being addressed. But he looked up because someone had stepped into his path. The someone was Eileen Burke.

She was wearing a simple brown suit with a green blouse that was sort of ruffly at the throat, the green the color of her eyes, her long red hair swept efficiently back from her face, standing tall in high-heeled brown pumps a shade darker than the suit. She was carrying a shoulder bag, and he could see into the bag to where the barrel of a revolver seemed planted in a bed of crumpled Kleenexes. The picture on her plastic I.D. card, clipped to the lapel of her suit, showed a younger Eileen Burke, her red hair done in the frizzies. She was smiling—in the picture and in person.

"What are you doing down *here?*" she asked. "Nobody comes here on a Sunday."

"I need a picture from the I.S.," he said. She seemed waiting for him to say more. "How about you?" he added.

"I work here. Special Forces is here. Right on this floor, in fact. Come on in for a cup of coffee," she said, and her smile widened.

"No, thanks, I'm sort of in a hurry," Kling said, even though he was in no hurry at all.

"Okay," Eileen said, and shrugged. "Actually, I'm glad I ran into you. I was going to call later in the day, anyway."

"Oh?" Kling said.

"I think I lost an earring up there. Either there or in the Laundromat with the panty perpetrator. If it *was* the Laundromat, good-bye, Charlie. But if it was the squadroom or maybe the car—when you were dropping me off last night, you know . . ."

"Yeah," Kling said.

"It was just a simple gold hoop earring, about the size of a quarter. Nothing ostentatious when you're doing dirty laundry, right?"

"Which ear was it?" he asked.

"The right," she said. "Huh? What difference does it make? I mean, it *was* the right ear, but earrings are interchangeable, so—"

"Yeah, that's right," Kling said. He was looking at her right ear, or at the space beyond her right ear, or wherever. He was certainly not looking at her face, certainly not allowing his eyes to meet her eyes. What the hell is *wrong* with him? she wondered.

"Well, take a look up there, okay?" she said. "If you find it, give me a call. I'm with Special Forces—well, you know that—but I'm in and out all the time, so just leave a message. That is, if you happen to find the earring." She hesitated, and then said, "The *right* one, that is. If you find the *left* one, it's the *wrong* one." She smiled. He did not return the smile. "Well, see you around the pool hall," she said, and spread her hand in a farewell fan, and turned on her heel, and walked away from him.

Kling pressed the button for the elevator.

TINA Wong had been jogging in the snow, and she was surprised to find the detectives waiting in the lobby of her building when she came out of the park. She was wearing a gray sweat suit and a woolen hat that was less colorful than the one Meyer had received as a present. Her track shoes were wet, as were the legs of the sweat suit pants. She said, "Oh," and then inexplicably looked over her shoulder, as though her car were illegally parked at the curb or something.

"Sorry to bother you, Miss Wong," Meyer said. He was not wearing his Valentine's Day gift. Instead, he had on a blue snap-brim fedora that he felt made him look more stylish if a trifle more bald than the watch cap did.

"Just a few questions we'd like to ask," Carella said. They had been standing in the lobby for close to forty minutes, after having been advised by Tina's doorman that Miss Wong was "out for her run."

"Sure," Tina said, and gestured toward an array of furniture clustered around an imitation fireplace. The lobby was very hot. Tina's face was flushed red from the cold outside and the energetic jogging she had done. She yanked off the woolen hat and shook out her hair. All three sat in chairs around the fake fireplace. At the switchboard across the room, the doorman looked bored as he read the headline on the morning paper. There was a mechanical hum in the room; the detectives could not locate its source. The lobby had the feel and smell of slightly damp clothes in a cloistered alcove. Outside the glass entrance doors, the wind blew fiercely, its rising and falling keen counterpointing the steady hum.

"Miss Wong," Carella said, "when we spoke to you yesterday, do you remember our asking whether or not Sally was doing anything like cocaine?"

"Uh-huh," Tina said.

"And you remember you told us—"

"I said that to my knowledge she wasn't."

"Does that mean you never *saw* her using cocaine?"

"Never."

"Does that also mean she never mentioned it to you?"

"Never."

"*Would* she have mentioned something like that?"

"We were close friends. There's nothing so terrible about snorting a few lines every now and then. I suppose if she'd been using it, she might have mentioned it."

"But she didn't."

"No, she didn't."

"Miss Wong, according to Timothy Moore, there was a party Sally Anderson went to last Sunday night. Someone named Lonnie. One of the black dancers in the show."

"Yes?" Tina said.

"Were you at that party?"

"Yes, I was."

"But Mr. Moore wasn't."

"No, he wasn't. He had to study. He made this New Year's Eve resolution—"

"Yes, he told us. At any time that night, did you notice Miss Anderson sniffing coke?"

"No, I didn't."

"How about anyone else?"

"I don't know what you mean."

"Were there any other cast members there?"

"Oh, sure."

"Do you remember when we talked yesterday, you mentioned that some people in the cast *were* doing coke."

"Yes, I may have said that."

"Well, you said that some of them were doing a little coke, here and there, now and then."

"I suppose that's what I said."

"Were any of them doing coke last Sunday night? That you may have noticed?"

"I'm not sure I ought to answer that," Tina said.

"Why not?" Meyer said.

"Anyway, why do you think *Sally* was into cocaine?"

"*Was* she?" Carella asked at once.

"I told you, not to my knowledge. But all these questions you're asking . . . what *difference* does it make if she was or she wasn't? She's dead, she was shot to death. What does *cocaine* have to do with anything?"

"Miss Wong, we have good reason to believe she was a user."

"How? What reason?"

"We tested a residue of powder from her handbag."

"And it was cocaine?"

"We're reasonably certain it was."

"What does that mean? Was it or wasn't it?"

"The tests weren't exhaustive, but from what—"

"Then it could have been *anything*, right? Face powder or—"

"No, it wasn't face powder, Miss Wong."

"Why are you so anxious to prove she was doing coke?"

"We're not. We simply want to know who *else* was."

"How am *I* supposed to know who else was?"

"When we talked to you yesterday—"

"Yesterday, I didn't know this would turn into a third degree."

"This isn't a third degree, Miss Wong. When we talked to you yesterday, you said—and I think I'm quoting you exactly—'Usually, you can get a pretty good idea of who's doing what when you're working in a show.' Isn't that what you said?"

"I don't remember my exact words."

"But that's what you meant, isn't it?"

"I suppose so."

"Okay. If you have a pretty good idea of who's doing what, we'd like you to share it with us."

"What for? So I can get decent people in trouble for no reason at all?"

"*Which* decent people?" Carella asked.

"I don't know anybody who was involved with drugs, okay?"

"That's not what you said yesterday."

"It's what I'm saying today." She looked at them steadily and then added, "I think I'd better call my lawyer."

"We're not looking for a drug bust here," Meyer said.

"I don't know what you're looking for, but you're not going to get it from me."

"Your best friend was murdered," Carella said softly.

She looked at him.

"We're trying to find the person who did it," Carella said.

"Nobody in the show did it."

"How do you know that?"

"I *don't* know it. I just know . . ." She fell silent. She folded her arms across her chest. She lifted her chin stubbornly. Carella looked at Meyer. Meyer nodded almost imperceptibly.

"Miss Wong," Carella said, "on the basis of what you told us yesterday, we have good cause to believe you know who, if anyone, in the cast was using cocaine. This is a murder we're investigating. We can subpoena you before a grand jury, who'll ask you the same questions we've been asking you—"

"No, you can't," she said.

"Yes, we can," Carella said, "and we *will* if you continue refusing to—"

"What is this, Russia?" Tina asked.

"This is the United States," Carella said. "You've got *your* rights, but we've also got *ours*. If you refuse to answer a grand jury, you'll be held in contempt of court. Take your choice."

"I can't believe this," she said.

"Believe it. If you know who's doing coke—"

"I hate strong-arm macho shit," Tina said.

Neither of the detectives said anything.

"*Mafia* tactics," Tina said.

Still, they said nothing.

"As if it has anything at *all* to do with who killed her," Tina said.

"Let's go, Meyer," Carella said, and stood up.

"Just a minute," Tina said.

He did not sit down again.

"There were maybe half a dozen people snorting at that party."

"Anyone in the cast?"

"Yes."

"Who?"

"Sally, of course."

"Who else?"

"Mike."

"Mike who?"

"Roldan. Miguel Roldan."

"Thank you," Carella said.

"If you cause him any trouble—"

"We're not looking to cause him trouble," Meyer said. "How well did Sally Anderson know your producer?"

The question took her totally by surprise. Her eyes opened wide. She hesitated a moment before answering. "Allan?" she said.

"Allan Carter," Carella said, nodding.

"Why?"

"Did Sally ever mention him in anything but a professional way?"

"I don't know what that means."

"I think you know what it means, Miss Wong."

"Are you asking if she was *involved* in some way with him? Don't be ridiculous."

"Why do you think that's ridiculous, Miss Wong?"

"Because . . . well, she had a boyfriend. You *know* that, I told you that yesterday."

"Why would that exclude an involvement with Mr. Carter?"

"I just know there was nothing going on between them."

"How do you know that?"

"There are some things you just *know*."

"Did you ever see them together?"

"Of course."

"Outside of the theater, I mean."

"Occasionally."

"When's the *last* time you saw them together?"

"Last Sunday night."

"Under what circumstances?"

"He was at Lonnie's party."

"Is that usual? For the producer of a show to attend a party given by one of the dancers?"

"You're not going to stop till you get *everybody* in trouble, are you?"

"Who are we getting in trouble now?" Meyer asked.

"Allan was with *me*," Tina said, "okay? *I* asked him to the party."

The detectives looked at each other, puzzled.

"He's *married*, okay?" Tina said.

AT THIS point, they only wanted to talk to two people connected with the show.

The first was Miguel Roldan, who, coincidentally, was both Hispanic and a cocaine user. Sally Anderson had been a cocaine user, and Paco Lopez had been Hispanic. They wanted to ask Roldan where he got his stuff and whether Sally got it from the same place and whether that place happened to be Paco Lopez's little candy stand. The second was Allan Carter, married producer of *Fatback*, who—according to Tina Wong—had been enjoying a little backstage romance with the Chinese dancer ever since September, when they'd discovered each other at the show's opening-night party. They wanted to ask Carter why he had thought Sally Anderson was "a little redheaded thing." Had Carter been involved in an *extra* extramarital fling with the blond dancer as well? If not, why had he gone to such lengths to indicate he'd scarcely known her? They had not asked Tina anything at all about Carter's seeming confusion. If there *had* existed any sort of relationship between him and the dead girl, it was entirely possible that Tina knew nothing about it, in which case they did not want her to alert him. They knew intuitively that he'd been lying when he denied remembering Sally Anderson. Now they wanted to find out *why* he'd been lying.

They did not find out that late Sunday afternoon.

The doorman at Carter's building on Grover Park West told the detectives that both he and Mrs. Carter had left at close to 4:00 p.m. He did not know where they'd gone or when they'd be back. He suggested that perhaps Mr. Carter had gone down to Philadelphia again, but that didn't seem to tie in with the fact that a chauffeured limousine had picked up the couple; Mr. Carter usually took the train to Philadelphia, and besides, he always went down alone. The Philadelphia possibility seemed unlikely to Carella as well. Carter had mentioned on the phone yesterday that he would not be going back to Philadelphia until late Wednesday. The detectives drove uptown and crosstown to the brownstone Miguel Roldan shared with Tony Asensio, the other Hispanic dancer in the show. No one was home there, either, and there was no doorman to offer suggestions or possibilities.

Carella said good night to Meyer at ten minutes past six and only then remembered he had not yet bought Teddy a present. He shopped the Stem until he found an open lingerie shop, only to discover that it featured panties of the open-crotch variety and some that could be eaten like candy, decided this was not quite what he had in mind, thank you, and then shopped fruitlessly for another hour before settling on a heart-shaped box of chocolates in an open drugstore. He felt he was letting Teddy down.

Her eyes and her face showed no disappointment when he presented the gift to her. He explained that it was only a temporary solution and that he'd shop for her *real* present once the pressure of the case let up a little. He had no idea when that might be, but he promised himself that he would buy her something absolutely mind-boggling tomorrow, come hell or high water. He did not yet know that the case had already taken a peculiar turn or that he would learn about it tomorrow, when once again it would postpone his grandiose plans.

At the dinner table, ten-year-old April complained that she had received only one Valentine's card, and that one from a doofus. She pronounced the word with a grimace her mother might have used more suitably, managing to look very much like Teddy in that moment—the dark eyes and darker hair, the beautiful mouth twisted in an expression of total distaste. Her ten-year-old brother, Mark, who resembled Carella more than he did either his mother or his twin sister, offered the opinion that anyone who would send a card to April *had* to be a doofus, at which point April seized her half-finished pork chop by its rib and threatened to use it on him like a hatchet. Carella calmed them down. Fanny came in from the kitchen and casually mentioned that these were the same pork chops she'd taken out of the freezer the night before and she hoped they tasted okay and wouldn't give the whole family trichinosis. Mark wanted to know what trichinosis was. Fanny told him it was related to a cassoulet and winked at Carella.

They put the children to bed at nine.

They watched television for a while, and then they went into the bedroom. Teddy was in the bathroom for what seemed an inordinately long time. Carella guessed she was angry. When she came into the bedroom again, she was wearing a robe over her nightgown. Normally, she wasn't quite so modest in their own bedroom. He began to think more and more that his gift of chocolates without even a selection chart under the lid had truly irritated her. So deep was his own guilt ("Italians and Jews," Meyer was fond of saying, "are the guiltiest people on the face of the earth") that he did not remember until she pulled back the covers in the dark and got into bed beside him that *she* hadn't given *him* anything at *all*.

He snapped on the bedside lamp.

"Honey," he said, "I'm really sorry. I know I should have done it earlier. It was stupid of me to leave it for the last minute. I promise you tomorrow I'll—"

She put her fingers to his lips, silencing him.

She sat up.

She lowered the strap of her nightgown.

In the glow of the lamplight, he saw her shoulder. Where previously there had been only a single black butterfly tattoo, put there so long ago he could hardly remember when, he now saw *two* butterflies, the new one slightly larger than the other, its wings a bright yellow laced with black. The new butterfly seemed to hover over the original, as though kissing it with its outstretched wings.

His eyes suddenly flooded with tears.

He pulled her to him and kissed her fiercely and felt his tears mingling with hers as surely as did the butterflies on her shoulder.

EIGHT

FOR some people, it was still St. Valentine's Day.

Many people do not believe a day ends at midnight. It is still the same day until they go to sleep. When they wake up in the morning, it is the next day. Two people who thought it was still St. Valentine's Day were Brother Anthony and the Fat Lady. Even though it was 1:00 a.m. on the morning of February 15, they thought of it as still being a day for lovers, especially since they had learned the name of Paco Lopez's girlfriend. Actually, they had learned her name when it *was* still St. Valentine's Day, which they considered a good omen. But it was not until 1:00 a.m. that Brother Anthony knocked on the door of Judite Quadrado's apartment.

In this neighborhood, a knock on the door at 1:00 a.m. meant only trouble. It meant either the police coming around to ask about a crime that had been committed in the building, or it meant a friend or neighbor coming to tell you that a loved one had either hurt someone or *been* hurt by someone. Either way, it meant bad news. The people in this neighborhood knew that a knock on the door at 1:00 a.m. did not mean a burglar or an armed robber. Thieves did not knock on doors unless it was going to be a shove-in, and in this neighborhood most thieves knew that doors were double-locked and often reinforced as well with a Fox lock, the steel bar hooked into the door and wedged into a floor plate. Brother Anthony knew that someone awakened at one in the morning would be frightened; that was why he and Emma had waited until that time, even though they'd had their information at 10:00 p.m.

From behind the door, Judite said, "Who is it?"

"Friends," Brother Anthony said.

"Friends? Who? What friends?"

"Please open the door," he said.

"Go away," Judite said.

"It's important that we speak to you," Emma said.

"Who are you?"

"Open the door just a little," Emma said, "and you'll see for yourself."

They heard lock tumblers falling. One lock, then another. The door opened just a crack, held by a night chain. In the wedge of the open door, they saw a woman's pale face. A kitchen light burned behind her.

"*Dominus vobiscum,*" Brother Anthony said.

"We have money for you," Emma said.

"Money?"

"From Paco."

"Paco?"

"He said to make sure we gave it to you if anything happened to him."

"Paco?" Judite said again. She had not seen Paco for at least two months before he was killed. It was Paco who had scarred her breasts, the rotten bastard. Who was this priest in the hallway? Who was this fat woman claiming they had money for her? Money from Paco? Impossible.

"Go away," she said again.

Emma took a sheaf of bills from her pocketbook, the money remaining from what Brother Anthony had taken from the pool hustler. In the dim hallway light, she saw Judite's eyes widen.

"For you," Emma said. "Open the door."

"If it's for me, hand it to me," Judite said. "I don't need to open the door."

"Never mind," Brother Anthony said, and put his hand on Emma's arm. "She doesn't want the money."

"How much money is it?" Judite asked.

"Four hundred dollars," Emma said.

"And Paco said he wanted *me* to have it?"

"For what he did to you," Emma said, lowering her voice and her eyes.

"Just a minute," Judite said.

The door closed. They heard nothing. Brother Anthony shrugged. Emma returned the shrug. Had their information been wrong? The man who'd told them about Judite was her cousin. He said she'd been living with Paco Lopez before he was killed. He said Paco had burned her breasts with cigarettes. Which was one of the reasons Brother Anthony had suggested they call on her at one in the morning. It was Brother Anthony's opinion that no woman allowed herself to be treated brutally unless she was a very frightened woman. One o'clock in the morning should make her even more frightened. But where was she? Where had she gone? They waited. They heard the night chain being removed. The door opened wide. Judite Quadrado stood in the open doorway with a pistol in her fist.

"Come in," she said, and gestured with the pistol.

Brother Anthony had not expected the pistol. He looked at Emma. Emma said, "*No hay necesidad de la pistola,*" which Brother Anthony did not understand. Until that moment, in fact, he hadn't known Emma could speak Spanish.

"*Hasta que yo sepa quien es usted,*" Judite said, and again gestured with the gun.

"All right," Emma answered in English. "But *only* until you know who we are. I don't like doing favors for a woman with a gun in her hand."

They went into the apartment. Judite closed and locked the door behind them. They were in a small kitchen. A refrigerator, sink, and stove were on one wall, below a small window that opened onto an areaway. The window was closed and rimed with ice. A table covered with white oilcloth was against the right-angled wall. Two wooden chairs were at the table.

Brother Anthony did not like the look on Judite's face. She did not look like a frightened woman. She looked like a woman very much in command of the situation. He was thinking they'd made a mistake coming up here. He was thinking they'd lose what was left of the money he'd taken from the pool hustler. He was thinking maybe the ideas he and Emma hatched weren't always so hot. Judite was perhaps five feet six inches tall, a slender, dark-haired, brown-eyed girl with a nose just a trifle too large for her narrow face. She was wearing a dark blue robe; Brother Anthony figured that was why she'd left them waiting in the hall so long. So she could go put on the robe. And get the gun from wherever she kept it. He did not like the look of the gun. It was steady in her hand. She had used a gun before; he sensed that intuitively. She would not hesitate to use it now. The situation looked extremely bad.

"So," she said. "Who are you?"

"I'm Brother Anthony," he said.

"Emma Forbes," Emma said.

"How did you know Paco?"

"A shame what happened to him," Emma said.

"How did you know him?" Judite said again.

"We were friends for a long time," Brother Anthony said. It

kept bothering him that she held the gun so steady in her hand. The gun didn't look like any of the Saturday-night specials he had seen in the neighborhood. This one was at *least* a .38. This one could put a very nice hole in his cassock.

"If you're his friends, how come *I* don't know you?" Judite said.

"We've been away," Emma said.

"Then how did you get the money if you've been away?"

"Paco left it for us. At the apartment."

"What apartment?"

"Where we live."

"He left it for *me?*"

"He left it for you," Emma said. "With a note."

"Where's the note?"

"Where's the note, Bro?" Emma said.

"At the apartment," Brother Anthony said, assuming an attitude of annoyance. "I didn't know we'd need a *note*. I didn't know you needed a *note* when you came to deliver four hundred dollars to—"

"Give it to me then," Judite said, and extended her left hand.

"Put away the gun," Emma said.

"No. First give me the money."

"Give her the money," Brother Anthony said. "It's hers. Paco wanted her to have it."

Their eyes met. Judite did not notice the glance that passed between them. Emma went to the table and spread the bills in a fan on the oilcloth. Judite turned to pick up the bills, and Brother Anthony stepped into her at the same moment, smashing his bunched fist into her nose. Her nose had not looked particularly lovely beforehand, but now it began spouting blood. Brother Anthony had read somewhere that hitting a person in the nose was very painful and also highly effective. The nose bled easily, and blood frightened people. The blood pouring from Judite's nose caused her to forget all about the pistol in her hand. Brother

Anthony seized her wrist, twisted her arm behind her back, and yanked the pistol away from her.

"Okay," he said.

Judite was holding her hand to her nose. Blood poured from her nose onto her fingers. Emma took a dish towel from where it was lying on the counter and tossed it to her.

"Wipe yourself," she said.

Judite was whimpering.

"And stop crying. Nobody's going to hurt you."

Judite didn't exactly believe this. She had *already* been hurt. She had made a mistake, opening the door at one in the morning, even *with* the gun. Now the gun was in the priest's hand, and the fat woman was picking up the money on the table and stuffing it back into her shoulder bag.

"Wh . . . what do you want?" Judite said. She was holding the towel to her nose now. The towel was turning red. Her nose hurt; she suspected the priest had broken it.

"Sit down," Brother Anthony said. He was smiling, now that the situation was in his own capable hands.

"Sit down," Emma repeated.

Judite sat at the table.

"Get me some ice," she said. "You broke my nose."

"Get her some ice," Brother Anthony said.

Emma went to the refrigerator. She took out an ice tray and cracked it open into the sink. Judite handed her the bloodstained towel, and Emma wrapped it around a handful of cubes.

"You broke my nose," Judite said again, and accepted the towel and pressed the ice pack to her nose. On the street outside, she could hear the rise and fall of an ambulance siren. She wondered if she would need an ambulance.

"Who were his customers?" Brother Anthony asked.

"What?" She didn't know who he meant at first. And then it occurred to her that he was talking about Paco.

"His *customers*," Emma said. "Who was he *selling* to?"

"Paco, do you mean?"

"You know who we mean," Brother Anthony said. He tucked the gun into the pouchlike pocket at the front of his robe and gestured to the fat woman. The fat woman reached into her bag again. For a dizzying moment, Judite thought they were going to let her go. The priest had put the gun away, and now the fat woman was reaching into her bag again. They were going to give her the money, after all. They were going to let her go. But when the fat woman's hand came out of the bag, there was something long and narrow in it. The fat woman's thumb moved, and a straight razor snapped open out of its case, catching tiny dancing pinpricks of light. Judite was more afraid of the razor than she had been of the gun. She had never in her life been shot, but she'd been cut many, many times, once even by Paco. She bore the scar on her shoulder. It was a less hideous scar than the ones he had burned onto her breasts.

"Who were his customers?" Brother Anthony asked again.

"I hardly even knew him," Judite said.

"You were living with him," Emma said.

"That doesn't mean I knew him," Judite said, which, in a way, was an awesome truth.

She did not want to tell them who Paco's customers had been because *his* customers were now *her* customers, or at least *would* be as soon as she got her act together. She had reconstructed from memory a list of an even dozen users, enough to keep her living in a style she thought would be luxurious. Enough to have caused her to buy a gun before she embarked on her enterprise; there were too many bastards like Paco in the world. But the gun was now in the priest's pocket, and the fat woman was turning the razor slowly in her hand, so that its edge caught glints of light. Judite thought, and this in itself was an awesome truth, that life had a peculiar way of repeating itself. Remembering what Paco had done to her breasts, she pulled the robe instinctively closed over her nightgown, using her free left hand. Brother Anthony caught the motion.

"Who were his customers?" Emma said.

"I don't know. *What* customers?"

"For the nose candy," Emma said, and moved closer to her with the razor.

"I don't know what that means, nose candy," Judite said.

"What you *sniff*, my dear," Emma said, and brought the razor close to her face. "Through your *nose*, my dear. Through the nose you won't *have* in a minute if you don't tell us who they were."

"No, not her face," Brother Anthony said, almost in a whisper. "Not her face."

He smiled at Judite. For another dizzying moment, Judite thought he was the one who would let her go. The woman seemed menacing, but surely the priest—

"Take off the robe," he said.

"What for?" she asked, and clutched the robe closed tighter across her chest.

"Take it off," Brother Anthony said.

She hesitated. She pulled the towel away from her nose. The flow of blood seemed to be tapering. She put the towel back again. Even the pain seemed to be ebbing now. Perhaps this would not be so bad, after all. Perhaps, if she just went along with them, played along with them—surely the fat woman wasn't *serious* about cutting off her nose? Were the names of Paco's customers really that important to them? Would they risk so much for so little? Anyway, they were *her* customers now, damn it! She would give them whatever else they wanted, but not the names that were her ticket to what she imagined as freedom. She did not know what kind of freedom. Just freedom. She would never give them the names.

"Why do you want me to take off the robe?" she asked. "What is it you want from me?"

"The customers," Emma said.

"Do you want to see my body?" she asked. "Is that it?"

"The customers," Emma said.

"You want me to blow you?" she asked Brother Anthony.

"Take off the robe," Brother Anthony said.

"Because if you want me to—"

"The robe," he said.

She looked at him. She tried to read his eyes. Paco had told her she gave better head than most of the hookers he knew. If she could reach the priest—

"Can I stand up?" she asked.

"Stand up," Emma said, and retreated several steps. The open razor was still in her hand.

Judite put down the towel. Her nose had stopped bleeding entirely. She took off the robe and draped it over the back of the chair. She was wearing only a pale blue baby-doll nightgown. The nightgown ended just an inch below her crotch. She was not wearing the panties that had come with the nightgown when she'd bought it. The nightgown and panties had cost her twenty-six dollars. Money she could easily get back from her new cocaine trade. She saw where the priest's eyes went.

"So what do you say?" she asked, arching one eyebrow and trying a smile.

"I say take off the nightgown," Brother Anthony said.

"It's cold in here," Judite said, hugging herself. "The heat goes off at ten." She was being seductive and bantering, she thought. She had captured the priest's eye—they were all supposed to be celibate, some joke—and now she thought she'd make it a bit more interesting and spicy, tease him along a little, make a big production out of taking off the nightgown. The fat woman would go along with whatever the priest decided; Judite knew women, and that's the way it was.

"Just take it off," Brother Anthony said.

"What for?" Judite said, the same light tone in her voice. "You can *see* what you're getting, can't you? I'm practically naked here, you can practically see right through this thing, so why do I have to take it off?"

"Take off the fucking nightgown!" Emma said, and all at once Judite thought she'd made a big error in judgment. The fat woman was moving closer to her again, the razor flashing.

"All right, don't . . . just don't get . . . I'll take it off, okay? Just . . . take it easy, okay? But, really, I don't know what you're talking about, Paco's customers. I swear to God I don't know what you mean by—"

"You know what we're talking about," Brother Anthony said.

She pulled the gown up over her waist, lifted it over her breasts and shoulders, and, without turning, placed it on the seat of the wooden chair. Gooseflesh erupted immediately on her arms and across her chest and shoulders. She stood naked and trembling in the center of the kitchen, her bare feet on the cold linoleum, the ice-rimed window behind her. She was quite well formed, Brother Anthony thought. Her shoulders were narrow and delicately turned, and there was a gently rounded swell to her belly and a ripe flare to her hips. Her breasts, too, were large and firm, quite beautiful except for the angry brown burn scars on their sloping tops. Very well formed, he thought. Not as opulent a woman as Emma, but very well formed indeed. He noticed that there was a small knife scar on her left shoulder. She was a woman who'd been abused before, perhaps regularly, a very frightened woman.

"Cut her," he said.

The thrust of the razor came so swiftly that for a moment Judite didn't even realize she'd been cut. The slash drew a thin line of blood across her belly, not as frightening as the blood pouring from her nose had been, really just a narrow line of blood oozing from the flesh, nothing so terribly scary. Even the searing aftermath of the razor slash was less painful than the blow to her nose had been. She looked down at her belly in amazement. But somehow, she was less frightened now than she'd been a moment earlier. If this was what it would be like, if this was the *worst* they would do to her—

"We don't want to hurt you," the priest said, and she knew this meant they *did* want to hurt her, would in *fact* hurt her more than they already had if she did not give them the names they wanted. Her mind worked quickly, frantically searching for a way to protect her own interests, give them the names of the customers, why not, but withhold the name of the ounce dealer—you could always find new customers if you knew where to get the stuff. Hiding her secret, hiding her fear as well, she calmly gave them all the names they wanted, all of the twelve she had memorized, writing them down at their request, scribbling the names and addresses on a sheet of paper, trying to conceal the shaking of her fist as she wrote. And then, after she had given them all the names and had even clarified the spelling of some of them, after she thought it was all over, thought they had what they wanted from her now and would leave her alone with her broken nose and the bleeding slash across her belly, she was surprised to hear the priest ask, "Where did he get the stuff?" and she hesitated before answering, and realized all at once that her hesitation had been another mistake, her hesitation had informed them that she knew the source of Paco's supply, knew the name of his ounce dealer and wanted it from her now.

"I don't know where," she said.

Her teeth were beginning to chatter. She kept looking at the razor in the fat woman's hand.

"Cut off her nipple," the priest said, and her hands went instinctively to her scarred breasts as the fat woman approached with the razor again, and suddenly she was more frightened than she'd ever been in her life, and she heard herself telling them the name, heard herself giving away her secret and her freedom, saying the name over and over again, babbling the name, and thought that would truly be the end of it, and was astonished to see the razor flashing out again, shocked beyond belief when she saw blood spurting from the tip of her right breast and knew, *Oh dear Jesus*, that they were going to hurt her anyway, *Oh sweet Mary*, maybe kill her, *Oh sweet mother of God*, the razor glinting and slashing again and again and again until at last she fainted.

IN THE station house, the squadroom looked exactly the same every day of the week, weekends and holidays included. But on Monday mornings, everyone *knew* it was Monday, the feel was just different. Like it or not, it was the start of another week. Sameness or not, it was somehow different.

Carella was at his desk at 7:30 a.m., fifteen minutes before he was scheduled to relieve the graveyard shift. The men on the night watch were wrapping it up, winding down over coffee and crullers from an all-night greasy spoon on Crichton, talking softly about the events that had transpired in the empty hours of the night. The shift had been a relatively quiet one. They kidded Carella about coming in fifteen minutes early. Was he bucking for Detective/First? Carella was bucking for a conversation with Karl Loeb, the med-student friend Timothy Moore claimed to have telephoned several times on the night Sally Anderson was shot to death.

There were three columns of Loebs in the Isola telephone directory, but only two of the listings were for men named *Karl* Loeb, and only one of those listed an address on Perry Street, three blocks from Ramsey University. Moore had told Carella that he could be reached at the school during the daytime. Carella didn't know whether or not Ramsey would be observing a cockamamie holiday like Presidents' Day, but he didn't want to take any chances. Besides, if the school *was* closed today, Loeb might decide to go out for a picnic or something. He wanted to catch him at home, before he left one way or the other. He dialed the number.

"Hello?" a woman said.

"Hello. May I speak to Karl Loeb, please?" Carella said.

"Who's this, please?" the woman asked.

"Detective Carella of the Eighty-Seventh Squad."

"What do you mean?" the woman said.

"Police department," Carella said.

"Is this a joke?" she said.

"No joke."

"Well . . . just a sec, okay?"

She put down the phone. He heard her calling to someone, presumably Loeb. When Loeb came onto the line, he sounded puzzled.

"Hello?" he said.

"Mr. Loeb?"

"Yes?"

"This is Detective Carella, Eighty-Seventh Squad."

"Yes?"

"If you have a few minutes, I'd like to ask you some questions."

"What about?" Loeb said.

"Do you know a man named Timothy Moore?"

"Yes?"

"Were you at home Friday night, Mr. Loeb?"

"Yes?"

"Did Mr. Moore call you at any time on Friday night? I'm talking now about Friday, February twelfth, this past Friday."

"Well . . . can you tell me what this is about, please?"

"Is this an inconvenient time for you, Mr. Loeb?"

"Well, I was shaving," Loeb said.

"Shall I call you back?"

"No, but . . . I *would* like to know what this is about."

"Did you speak to Mr. Moore at any time this past Friday night?"

"Yes, I did."

"Do you remember what you discussed?"

"The exam. We have a big exam coming up. In Pathology. Excuse me, Mr. Coppola, but—"

"Carella," Carella said.

"Carella, excuse me. Can you tell me what this is about, please? I'm not really in the habit of getting mysterious phone calls from the police. In fact, how do I even *know* you're a policeman?"

"Would you like to call me back here at the precinct?" Carella said. "The number here—"

"Well, no, I don't think that's necessary. But, really—"

"I'm sorry, Mr. Loeb, but I'd rather *not* tell you what it's about just yet."

"Is Timmy in some kind of trouble?"

"No, sir."

"Then what . . . I just don't understand."

"Mr. Loeb, I'd appreciate your help. Do you remember *when* Mr. Moore called you?"

"He called me several times."

"How *many* times, would you estimate?"

"Five or six? I really couldn't say. We were swapping information back and forth."

"Did you call *him* at any time?"

"Yes, two or three times."

"So between the two of you—"

"Maybe four times," Loeb said. "I really couldn't say. We were sort of studying together on the phone."

"So you exchanged calls nine or ten times, is that right?"

"Roughly. Maybe a dozen times. I don't remember."

"Throughout the night?"

"Well, not *all* night."

"When was the first call?"

"Around ten o'clock, I guess."

"Did you call Mr. Moore, or did—"

"He called me."

"At ten o'clock."

"Around ten. I'm not sure of the exact time."

"And the next call?"

"I called him back about a half hour later."

"To swap information."

"To ask him a question, actually."

"And the next one?"

"I really couldn't say with any accuracy. We were on the phone together constantly that night."

"When you made *your* three or four calls . . . was Mr. Moore at home?"

"Yes, of course."

"You called him at his home number?"

"Yes."

"When was the *last* time you spoke to him?"

"It must've been about two in the morning, I guess."

"Did you call him? Or did he—"

"I called him."

"And you got him at home?"

"Yes. Mr. Carella, I *would* like to—"

"Mr. Loeb, did you exchange any phone calls between eleven o'clock and midnight this past Friday night?"

"With Timmy, do you mean?"

"Yes, with Mr. Moore."

"Between eleven and midnight?"

"Yes, sir."

"I believe so, yes."

"Did he call you, or did you call him?"

"He called me."

"Can you remember the exact times?"

"Well, no, not the *exact* times."

"But you're certain those calls came between eleven and midnight."

"Yes, I am."

"How *many* calls during that hour?"

"Two, I believe."

"And Mr. Moore made both those calls?"

"Yes."

"Can you try to remember the precise times of—"

"I really couldn't say with any accuracy."

"Approximately, then."

"I guess he called at . . . it must've been a little past eleven, the first call. The news was just going off. It must've been about five past eleven, I guess."

"The news?"

"On the radio. I was studying with the radio on. So was Timmy. I like to study with background music, do you know? I find it soothing. But the news was on when he called."

"And you say *he* was listening to the radio, too?"

"Yes, sir."

"How do you know that?"

"I could hear it. In fact, he said something about turning it down."

"I'm sorry, turning it—"

"His radio. He said something like . . . I really don't remember exactly . . . 'Let me turn this down a minute, Karl,' something like that."

"And then he turned down the radio?"

"Yes, sir."

"The volume on the radio?"

"Yes, sir."

"And you had your conversation."

"Yes, sir."

"How long did you talk to him during that call? This was at five after eleven, you say?"

"Yes, sir, approximately. We talked for five or ten minutes, I guess. In fact, when he called *back*, there were still some things he didn't understand about—"

"When was that, Mr. Loeb? The next call, I mean."

"A half hour later? I can't say exactly."

"Sometime around eleven-thirty-five?"

"Approximately."

"Was his radio still on?"

"What?"

"His radio. Could you still hear it in the background?"

"Yes, sir, I could."

"What did you talk about *that* time?"

"The same thing we'd talked about at eleven. Well, five *after* eleven, actually. The test is on diseases of the bone marrow. We went over the material on leukemia. How specific do you want me to get?"

"Went over the same material again, is that it?"

"Well, leukemia isn't quite as simple as it may sound, Mr. Carella."

"I'm sure it isn't," Carella said, feeling reprimanded. "And you say the last time you spoke to him was at two in the morning or thereabouts?"

"Yes, sir."

"Did you speak to him at any time between eleven-thirty-five and two a.m.?"

"I believe so, yes."

"Who called who?"

"We called each other."

"At what time?"

"I don't remember exactly. I know the phone was busy at one point, but—"

"When you called him?"

"Yes, sir."

"What time would that have been?"

"I really couldn't say with any accuracy."

"Before midnight? After midnight?"

"I'm not sure."

"But you *did* speak again after that eleven-thirty-five call?"

"Yes, sir. Several times."

"Calling back and forth."

"Yes, sir."

"To discuss the exam again."

"Yes, the material that would be on the exam."

"Was his radio still on?"

"I think so."

"You could hear the radio?"

"Yes, sir. I could hear music."

"The same sort of music you'd heard earlier?"

"Yes, sir. He was listening to classical music. I heard it in the background each time he called."

"And the last time you spoke was at two in the morning."

"Yes, sir."

"When *you* called him."

"Yes, sir."

"At home."

"Yes, sir."

"Thank you very much, Mr. Loeb, I really appreciate—"

"Well, what *is* this all about, Mr. Carella? I really—"

"Routine," Carella said, and hung up.

BLUE Monday.

The threatening blue glare of ice. The brilliant robin's-egg blue of a sky that stretched from horizon to horizon over the city's towers and peaks, the kind of sky that always came as a surprise in January and February even though—like the snow and the wind and the freezing rain—it was not an unusual occurrence in this city. The darker blue of smoke pouring from the tall stacks of the factories across the river Dix in Calm's Point. The almost-black blue of the uniforms on the cops who stood outside the tenement on Ainsley Avenue and looked down at the mutilated woman on the icebound sidewalk.

The woman was naked.

A trail of blood led from where she lay on the sidewalk to the front door of the tenement behind her and into the tenement hallway, bloody palm prints on the inner vestibule door, blood on the stairs and banisters leading to the upper stories.

The woman was still bleeding profusely.

The woman's breasts had been brutally slashed.

There was a giant bleeding cross on the woman's belly.

The woman had no nose.

"Jesus!" one of the patrolmen said.

"Help me," the woman moaned, and blood bubbled from her mouth.

THE woman who answered the door to Allan Carter's apartment was perhaps thirty-five years old, Carella guessed, wearing a brocaded housecoat at ten in the morning, her long black hair sleekly combed and hanging straight on either side of a delicate oval face, her brown eyes slanted enough to give her the same faintly Oriental appearance that caused the cops of the Eight-Seven to kid Carella about being Fujiwara's cousin. She could have been an older Tina Wong; it always amazed Carella that when a man began cheating on his wife, he often chose a woman who looked somewhat *like* her.

"Mr. Carella?" she said.

"Yes, ma'am."

"Come in, please, my husband's expecting you." She extended her hand. "I'm Melanie Carter."

"How do you do?" Carella said, and took her hand. It felt extremely warm to the touch, perhaps because his own hand was so icy cold after walking gloveless (*and* hatless, yes, I *know*, Uncle Sal) from where he'd parked the police sedan.

Carter came out of what Carella assumed to be a bedroom. He was wearing a Japanese-style kimono over dark blue pajamas. Carella idly wondered if the kimono had been a gift from Tina Wong. He let the thought pass.

"Sorry to bother you so early in the morning," he said.

"No, no, not at all," Carter said, and took his hand. "Some coffee? Melanie?" he said. "Could we get some coffee?"

"Yes, certainly," Melanie said, and went out into the kitchen.

"No partner today?" Carter asked.

"There are only two of us," Carella said, "and we have a lot of people to see."

"I'll bet," Carter said. "So. What can I do for you?"

"I was hoping we could talk privately," Carella said.

"Privately?"

"Yes, sir. Just the two of us," he said, and nodded toward the kitchen.

"My wife can hear anything we have to say," Carter said.

"I'm not sure of that, sir," Carella said, and their eyes met and held. Carter said nothing. Melanie came out of the kitchen carrying a silver tray on which there was a silver coffeepot, a silver sugar bowl and creamer, and two cups and saucers. She set the tray down on the coffee table before them, said, "I forgot spoons," and went out into the kitchen again. Neither of the men said a word. When she came back, she said, "There we are," and put two spoons onto the tray. "Would you like anything else, Mr. Carella? Some toast?"

"No, thank you, ma'am," Carella said.

"Melanie," Carter said, and hesitated. "I'm sure this will bore you to tears. If you have anything you need to do . . ."

"Of course, dear," Melanie said. "If you'll forgive me, Mr. Carella." She nodded briefly, smiled, and went out into the bedroom, closing the door behind her. Carter rose suddenly and went to the bank of stereo equipment set into a bookcase on the far wall. He knows what we're going to talk about, Carella thought. He wants a sound cover. The door between the rooms isn't enough for him. Carter turned on the radio. Music flooded the room. Something classical. Carella could not place it.

"That's a little loud, isn't it?" he said.

"You said you wanted to talk privately."

"Yes, but I don't want to *shout* privately."

"I'll lower it," Carter said.

He went to the radio again. Carella remembered that there had been classical music in the background when Loeb had spoken to Moore on the telephone Friday night. There was only one classical music station in this entire cultured city. Apparently it had more listeners than it realized.

Carter came back to where Carella was sitting on the sofa upholstered in the pale green springtime fabric and took the chair opposite him. The chair was upholstered in a lemon-colored fabric. Outside the windows at the far end of the room, the sky was intensely blue, but the wind howled fiercely.

"This is about Tina, huh?" Carter said at once.

CARELLA admired him for getting directly to what he surmised was the point, but actually he wasn't here to talk about Tina Wong. Tina Wong was only his form of official blackmail. Coercion, it might have been called in the Penal Code. Carella was not above a little coercion every now and again.

"Sort of," he answered.

"So you know," Carter said. "So what? Actually, my wife *could* have heard this."

"Oh?" Carella said.

"She isn't exactly a nun," Carter said.

"Oh?" Carella said again.

"She finds ways to busy herself while I'm occupied elsewhere, believe me. Anyway, what does Tina have to do with Sally Anderson?"

"Well, gee," Carella said, "that's just what *I'd* like to know."

"That was very nicely delivered," Carter said, unsmiling. "The next time I have a part for a shit-kicking bumpkin, I'll call you. What are you after, Mr. Carella?"

"I want to know why you thought Sally Anderson was a redhead."

"Isn't she?" Carter said.

"Very nicely delivered," Carella said. "The next time *I* have a role for a smart-ass liar, I'll call *you*."

"Touché," Carter said.

"I didn't come here to fence," Carella said.

"Why *did* you come here? So far, I've been very patient with you. I'm not without legal resources, you know. I have a lawyer on retainer, and I'm sure he'd like nothing better than to—"

"Go ahead, call him," Carella said.

Carter sighed. "Let's cut the crap, okay?" he said.

"Fine," Carella said.

"Why did I think Sally was a redhead? That was your question, wasn't it?"

"That was my question."

"Is it a crime to believe a redhead was a redhead?"

"It's not even a crime to think a *blonde* was one."

"Then what's the problem?"

"Mr. Carter, you *know* she was a blonde."

"What makes you think so?"

"Well, for one thing, your choreographer favors blondes, and every white girl in the show *is* a blonde. It was a nice show, by the way. Thanks for making those tickets available to me."

"You're welcome," Carter said, and nodded sourly.

"For another thing, you were present at the final selection of all the dancers—"

"Who told you that?"

"You did. And you *had* to know there were no redheads in the show, especially since you attended all the run-throughs after the show was put together . . . which you *also* told me."

"So?"

"So I think you were lying when you told me you thought she was a redhead. And when someone is lying, I begin wondering why."

"I *still* think she was a redhead."

"No, you don't. Her picture's been in the papers for the past three days. She's clearly shown as a blonde, and she's described as such. Even if you thought she was a redhead on the day after she was murdered, you certainly don't think so now."

"I haven't seen the papers," Carter said.

"How about television? They showed her picture on television, too. In full color. Come on, Mr. Carter. I told you I wasn't here to fence."

"Let me hear what *you* think, Mr. Carella."

"I think you knew her better than you're willing to admit. For all I know, you were playing around with *her* as *well* as Tina Wong."

"I wasn't."

"Then why'd you lie to me?"

"I didn't. I thought she was a redhead."

Carella sighed.

"I did," Carter said.

"I'll tell you something, Mr. Carter. Shit-kicking bumpkin that

I am, I nonetheless believe that if a man *continues* lying even after he's been *caught* in a lie, then he's *really* got something to hide. I don't know what that something might be. I know that a girl was shot to death last Friday night, and you're lying about having known her better than you *did* know her. Now what would *you* think, Mr. Carter, big-shot producer that you are?"

"I would think you're way off base."

"Were you at a party on the Sunday before the murder? A party given by a dancer named Lonnie Cooper? One of the black girls in the cast?"

"I was."

"Was Sally Anderson there?"

"I don't remember."

"She was there, Mr. Carter. Are you telling me you didn't recognize her *then*, either? There are only *eight* female dancers in your show. How could you *not* know Sally Anderson if you ran into her?"

"*If* she was there—"

"*If* she was there—and she *was*—she sure as hell wasn't wearing a red wig!" Carella said, and stood up abruptly. "Mr. Carter, I hate to sound like a clichéd detective in a B-movie, but I wouldn't advise you to go to Philadelphia this Wednesday. I'd suggest, instead, that you stay right here in this city, where we can reach you if we want to ask you any other questions. Thanks for your time, Mr. Carter."

He was starting for the door when Carter said, "Sit down."

He turned to look at him.

"Please," Carter said.

Carella sat.

"Okay, I knew she was a blonde," Carter said.

"Okay," Carella said.

"I was simply afraid to say I'd known her, that's all."

"Why?"

"Because she was murdered. I didn't want to get involved, not in any way possible."

"In what way *could* you have got involved? You didn't kill her, did you?"

"Of course not!"

"Were you having an affair with her?"

"No."

"Then what were you afraid of?"

"I didn't want people poking around. I didn't want anyone to find out about Tina and me."

"But we *have* found out, haven't we? And besides, Mr. Carter, your wife isn't exactly a nun, remember? So what difference would it have made?"

"People behave strangely when murder is involved," Carter said, and shrugged.

"Is that a line from the play you're rehearsing in Philadelphia?"

"It's a lame excuse, I know—"

"No, it happens to be true," Carella said. "But usually, the only people who behave strangely are the ones with something to hide. I *still* think you have something to hide."

"Nothing, believe me," Carter said.

"*Did* you, in fact, see Sally at that party last Sunday night?"

"I did."

"Did you talk to her?"

"I did."

"What about?"

"I don't remember. The show, I suppose. When people are involved in a show—"

"Anything besides the show?"

"No."

"Were you present when Sally and some other people began snorting cocaine?"

"I was not."

"Then how do you know they were doing it?"

"What I'm saying is I didn't *see* anyone doing anything of the sort. Not while I was there."

"What time did you leave the party, Mr. Carter?"

"At about midnight."

"With Tina Wong?"

"Yes, with Tina."

"Where'd you go from there?"

"To Tina's place."

"How long did you stay there?"

"All night long."

"Tina saw Sally Anderson snorting. Together with a group of other people, including Mike Roldan, who's *also* in your show. If *Tina* saw them, how come *you* didn't see them?"

"Tina and I are *not* Siamese twins. We are *not* joined at the hip."

"Meaning what?"

"Lonnie has one of these big old rent-controlled apartments on the park. There were sixty or seventy people there that night. It's entirely possible that Tina was in one part of the apartment while I was in another."

"Yes, that's entirely possible," Carella said. "And I guess Tina would be willing to swear you weren't with her when she witnessed Sally Anderson using cocaine."

"I don't know *what* Tina would be willing to swear."

"Do *you* use cocaine, Mr. Carter?"

"I certainly do not!"

"Do you know who was supplying Sally?"

"I do not."

"Do you know a man named Paco Lopez?"

"No."

"Where were you last Friday night between eleven and twelve midnight?"

"I told you. In Philadelphia."

"Where were you on Tuesday night at about the same time?"

"Philadelphia."

"I suppose there are any number of people—"

"Any number."

"What are you trying to hide, Mr. Carter?"

"Nothing," Carter said.

AT ST. Jude's Hospital—familiarly called St. Juke's by the cops, because of the many knifing victims carted there day and night—Judite Quadrado kept calling for a priest. At least that's what they thought she wanted. They thought she knew she was dying and wanted a priest to administer the rites of extreme unction. Actually, she was trying to tell them that a priest had come into her apartment together with a fat woman and that the two of them had done this terrible thing to her.

Judite was in the intensive care unit, with tubes coming out of her nose and her mouth and tubes running from her arms to a galaxy of machines that beeped and glowed with electronic oranges and blues all around her bed. It was difficult to talk around the tube in her mouth. When she tried to say "Brother Anthony," which was the name the priest had given her, it came out as a scrambled "Branny," and when she tried to say "Emma Forbes," which had been the fat woman's name, it came out only as what sounded like a cross between a mumble and a hum. She went back to saying "priest," which came out as "preese," but which at least they seemed to understand.

The priest came into the unit at seven minutes past eleven that Monday morning.

He was a little too late.

Judite Quadrado had died six minutes earlier.

IF THERE is one thing criminals and cops alike share—aside from the symbiotic relationship that makes each of their jobs possible—it is the sense of smell that tells them when someone is frightened. The moment they catch that whiff, cops and criminals alike turn into savage beasts of prey, ready to tear out the throat and devour the entrails. Miguel Roldan and Antonio Asensio were scared witless, and Meyer smelled their fear the instant Roldan, unsolicited, told him that he and Asensio had been living together as man and wife for the past three years. Meyer didn't care *what* their persuasion was. The offered information told him only that the two men were frightened. He knew they weren't afraid they'd be busted as homosexuals—not in *this* city. So what *were* they afraid of? Until that moment, he had been calling them, respectively and respectfully, Mr. Roldan and Mr. Asensio. He now switched to "Mike" and "Tony," an old cop trick designed to place any suspect at a disadvantage, a ploy somewhat similar to the one nurses used in hospitals. "Hello, Jimmy, how are we feeling this morning?" they would say to the chairman of the board of a vast conglomerate, immediately letting him know who was boss around here and who was privileged to take your rectal temperature. It worked even better with policemen and anyone who came into their purlieu. Calling a man Johnny instead of Mr. Fuller was the same thing as calling him Boy. It put him in his place at once and instantly made him feel (a) inferior, (b) defensive, and (c) oddly dependent.

"Mike," Meyer said, "why do you think I'm here?"

They were sitting in the living room of the brownstone Roldan and Asensio shared. The room was pleasantly furnished with antiques Meyer wished he could have afforded. A fire was going on the hearth. The fire crackled and spit into the room.

"You're here about Sally, of course," Roldan said.

"Is that what *you* think, Tony?"

"Yes, of course," Asensio said.

Meyer wasted no time.

"You know she was using cocaine, don't you?" he said.

"Well . . . no," Roldan said. "How would we know that?"

"Well, come on, Mike," Meyer said, and smiled knowingly. "You were at a party with her a week ago Sunday, and she was doing cocaine, so you *must* know she was a user, right?"

Roldan looked at Asensio.

"You were using it that night, too, weren't you, Mike?"

"Well . . ."

"I know you were," Meyer said.

"Well . . ."

"How about you, Tony? You snort a few lines last Sunday night?"

Asensio looked at Roldan.

"Who were you and Sally getting your stuff from?" Meyer asked.

"Listen," Roldan said.

"I'm listening."

"We had nothing to do with her murder."

"Didn't you?" Meyer said.

"We didn't," Asensio said, shaking his head and then looking at Roldan. Meyer wondered which of them was the wife and which was the husband. They both seemed very demure. He tried to reconcile this with the fact that the homosexual murders in the precinct were among the most vicious and brutal the cops investigated.

"Do you know who *might* have killed her?" he asked.

"No, we don't," Roldan said.

"We don't," Asensio agreed.

"So who do you get your stuff from?" Meyer asked again.

"Why is that important?" Roldan asked.

"That's assuming we're users," Asensio said quickly.

"Yes," Roldan said. "*If* we're users . . ."

"You are," Meyer said, and again smiled knowingly.

"Well, *if* we are, what does it matter *who* we were getting it from?"

"*Were?*" Meyer asked at once.

"*Are,*" Roldan said, correcting himself.

"Assuming we're users, that is," Asensio said.

"Did something happen to your dealer?" Meyer asked.

"No, no," Roldan said.

"That's assuming we even *needed* a dealer," Asensio said.

"*Needed?*" Meyer said.

"*Need,* I mean," Asensio said, and looked at Roldan.

"Well, Tony," Meyer said, "Mike . . . assuming you *are* users, and assuming you *do* have a dealer, or *did* have a dealer, who *is* the dealer? Or *was* the dealer, as the case may be."

"Cocaine isn't habit-forming," Roldan said.

"A sniff every now and then never hurt anybody," Asensio said.

"Ah, I know," Meyer said. "It's a shame it's against the law, but what can you do? Who are you getting it from?"

The two men looked at each other.

"Something *did* happen to your dealer, huh?" Meyer said.

Neither of them answered.

"Were you getting it from Sally Anderson?" Meyer asked, taking a wild stab in the dark and surprised when both men nodded simultaneously. "From *Sally?*" he said. The men nodded again. "*Sally* was dealing cocaine?"

"Well, not what you'd call *dealing,*" Roldan said. "Would you call it *dealing,* Tony?"

"No, I wouldn't call it *dealing,*" Asensio said. "Besides, the coke had nothing to do with her murder."

"How do you know?" Meyer said.

"Well, it wasn't that big a deal."

"How big a deal was it?"

"I mean, she wasn't making any *money* from it, if that's what you think," Roldan said.

"What *was* she doing?" Meyer asked.

"Just bringing in a few grams a week, that's all."

"How many grams?"

"Oh, I don't know. How many grams, Tony?"

"Oh, I don't know," Asensio said.

"By bringing it in—"

"To the theater. For whichever of the kids needed it."

"Well, I wouldn't say *needed* it," Roldan said. "Cocaine isn't habit-forming, you know."

"Whoever *wanted* it, I should have said," Asensio agreed, nodding.

"How many people *wanted* it?" Meyer asked.

"Well . . . Tony and I," Roldan said. "And some of the other kids."

"How many other kids?"

"Not many," Asensio said. "Six or seven? Would you say six or seven, Mike?"

"I'd say six or seven," Roldan said. "Not including Sally herself."

"So what are we talking about here?" Meyer said. "A dozen grams a week, something like that?"

"Something like that. Maybe two dozen."

"Two dozen grams," Meyer said, nodding. "What was she charging?"

"The going street price. I mean, Sally wasn't *making* anything on the deal, believe me. She just picked up *our* stuff when she was getting her *own*. She may have even got a discount for a bulk purchase, who knows?"

"I think, in fact," Roldan said to Asensio, "that we were getting it cheaper than the going street price."

"Maybe so," Asensio said.

"How much were you paying?" Meyer said.

"Eighty-five dollars a gram."

Meyer nodded. A gram of cocaine was the approximate equivalent of one twenty-eighth of an ounce. The going street price ranged from a hundred to a hundred and a quarter a gram, depending on the purity of the cocaine.

"Who was *she* getting it from?" he asked.

"I don't know," Roldan said.

"I don't know," Asensio said.

"Who's Paco Lopez?" Meyer asked.

"Who is he?" Roldan said.

Asensio shrugged.

"Are we supposed to know him?" Roldan said.

"You don't know him, huh?"

"Never heard of him."

"How about you, Tony?"

"Never heard of him," Asensio said.

"Is he a dancer?" Roldan asked.

"Is he gay?" Asensio asked.

"He's dead," Meyer said.

REBECCA Edelman was a woman in her late forties, splendidly tanned and monumentally grief-stricken. The detectives had called her early this morning, eager to talk to her after her flight back from Antigua the night before, but they had been advised by a daughter-in-law that Marvin Edelman's funeral would be taking place at eleven that morning, in keeping with the Jewish tradition of burying a person within twenty-four hours after his death. As it was, the funeral and burial had been delayed, anyway, by the mandatory autopsy required in any cases of traumatic death.

Neither Kling nor Brown had ever witnessed a family sitting shiva before. The windows in the Edelman living room faced the river Harb. The sky beyond was still intensely blue, the light less golden than it might have been in that it was partially reflected from the icebound water below. There was a knife-edged clarity to the atmosphere that afternoon; Brown could make out in the sharpest detail the high rises that perched atop the cliffs on the shore opposite, in the next state. Farther uptown, he could see the graceful curves of the Hamilton Bridge, its lacy outlines etched against the brilliant blue of the sky. In the living room, the family and friends of Marvin Edelman sat on wooden boxes and talked to each other in hushed voices.

She led them into a small room she obviously used as a sewing room, a machine in one corner, a basket of brightly colored fabrics sitting left of the treadle. She sat in the chair before the machine. They sat on a small sofa facing her. Her brown eyes were moist in her tanned face. She kept wringing her hands as she spoke. The sun had not been kind to her. Her face was wrinkled, her hands were wrinkled, her lips looked parched without lipstick. She directed her entire conversation to Kling, even though Brown asked most of the questions. Brown was used to this; sometimes even the *blacks* turned to the white cop, as though he himself were invisible.

"I told him he should come with me," Mrs. Edelman said. "I told him he could use the vacation, he should be good to himself, am I right? But no, he said he had too much work to do just now, planning for his trip to Europe next month. He told me he'd take a vacation when he got back, in April sometime. Who needs a vacation in April? In April, we have flowers, even here in the city. So he wouldn't come. Now he'll *never* have another vacation, never," she said, and turned her head away because tears were beginning to form in her eyes again.

"What sort of work did he do, ma'am?" Brown asked. "Was he in the jewelry business?"

"Not what you would call a regular jeweler," Mrs. Edelman said, and took a paper tissue from her bag and dabbed at her eyes with it.

"Because he was wearing this vest—" Brown started.

"Yes," Mrs. Edelman said. "He bought and sold gems. That's what he did for a living."

"Diamonds?"

"Not only diamonds. He dealt in all kinds of precious gems. Emeralds, rubies, sapphires—diamonds, of course. Precious gems. But he neglected the most precious thing of all. His life. If he'd come with me . . ." She shook her head. "A stubborn man," she said. "God forgive me, but he was a stubborn man."

"Was there any *special* reason he wanted to stay here in the city?" Brown asked. "Instead of going with you to Antigua." He pronounced the word "An-tee-gwa."

"It's a hard g," Mrs. Edelman said.

"What?"

"It's the British pronunciation they use. An-*tee*-ga."

"Oh," Brown said. He looked at Kling. Kling said nothing. "But in any event," Brown said, "*was* there?"

"Only the usual. Nothing he couldn't have left for a week. So look what happens," she said, and again dabbed at her eyes.

"By the usual—" Brown said.

"His usual business. Buying and selling, selling and buying." She was still directing all of her conversation to Kling. Brown cleared his throat, to remind her *he* was here, too. It had no effect.

Perhaps prompted by her steady gaze, Kling said, "Did he go very often to Europe?"

"Well, when he had to. That's the diamond center of the world, you know. Amsterdam. For emeralds, he went to South America. He could run all over the world for his business, am I right?" she said. "But when it comes to flying only four, five hours away, for a week in the sun, this he can't do. He has to stay here instead. So someone can shoot him."

"Do you have any idea who might have—"

"No," Mrs. Edelman said.

"No enemies you can think of?" Brown said.

"None."

"Any employees he might have—"

"He worked alone, my husband. That's why he could never take any time off. All he wanted to do was make money. He told me he wouldn't be happy till he was a multimillionaire."

"Did the possibility exist in his business?" Brown said. "Making millions of dollars, I mean?"

"Who knows? I suppose. We lived comfortably. He was always a good earner, my husband."

"But when you're talking about millions of dollars—"

"Yes, it was possible to make such money," Mrs. Edelman said. "He had a very sharp eye for quality gems. He turned a very good profit on almost anything he bought. He knew what he was buying, and he drove very hard bargains. Such a dope," she said. "If only he'd come with me, like I wanted him to."

Her eyes were misting with tears again. She dabbed at them with her crumpled tissue and then reached into her bag for a fresh one.

"Mrs. Edelman," Kling said, "where was your husband's place of business, can you tell us?"

"Downtown. On North Greenfield, just off Hall Avenue. What they call the Diamond Mart, the street there."

"And he worked alone there, you said?"

"All alone."

"In a street-level shop?"

"No, on the second floor."

"Was he ever held up, Mrs. Edelman?"

She looked at him in surprise.

"Yes," she said. "How did you know that?"

"Well, being a diamond merchant . . ."

"Yes, last year," she said.

"When last year?" Brown asked.

"August, I think it was. The end of July, the beginning of August, sometime in there."

"Was the perpetrator apprehended?" Brown asked.

"What?" Mrs. Edelman said.

"Did they catch the man who did it?"

"Yes."

"They *did?*"

"Yes, two days later. He tried to pawn the gems in a shop three doors down from my husband's, can you believe it?"

"Would you remember the man's name?"

"No, I wouldn't. He was a black man," she said, and—for the first time during their visit—turned to look at Brown, but only fleetingly. Immediately, she turned her attention back to Kling again.

"Can you be more exact about that date?" Kling asked. He had taken out his pad and was beginning to write.

"Why? Do you think it was the same person? They told me nothing was stolen. He had diamonds in his vest. Nobody touched them. So how could it be anybody who wanted to rob him?"

"Well, we don't know, really," Kling said, "but we'd like to follow up on that robbery if you can give us a few more details."

"All I know is he was working late one night, and this black man came in with a gun and took everything from the worktable. He didn't bother with the safe. He just told my husband to dump everything from the worktable into this little sack he had. The *good* stuff was in the safe, my husband was tickled to dea—"

She cut herself short before she could finish the word. The tears began again. She busied herself with searching for another tissue in her bag. The detectives waited.

"You say it was sometime toward the end of July, the beginning of August," Kling said at last.

"Yes."

"The last week in July, would that have been? The first week in August?"

"I can't say for sure. I think so."

"We can track it from the address," Brown said to Kling. "It'll be on the computer."

"*Could* we have the address, please?" Kling said.

"Six-twenty-one North Greenfield," Mrs. Edelman said. "Room two-oh-seven."

"Was the man convicted, would you know?" Brown asked.

"I think so. I don't remember. My husband had to go to court to identify him, but I don't know whether he was sent to jail or not."

"We can check with Corrections," Brown said to Kling. "Mrs. Edelman, had you spoken to your husband at any time since you left for Antigua?" This time, he pronounced it correctly.

"No. Do you mean, did we *call* each other? No. Antigua's not around the corner, you know."

"*Before* you left, did he mention anything that might have been disturbing him? Threatening telephone calls or letters, quarrels with customers, anything like that? Was anything at *all* troubling him, that you know of?"

"Yes," Mrs. Edelman said.

"What?" Brown asked.

"How he could make his millions of dollars," Mrs. Edelman said to Kling.

THIS time, the call came from Dorfsman himself.

It came at twenty minutes past four that Monday, the day after Valentine's Day, but Dorfsman apparently was still enjoying the influence of the brief lovers' holiday. The first thing he said to Carella was, "Roses are red, violets are blue, wait'll you hear what *I've* got for *you!*"

Carella thought Dorfsman had lost his marbles; it happened

often enough in the police department, but he had never heard of it happening to anyone in Ballistics.

"What *have* you got for me?" he asked warily.

"Another one," Dorfsman said.

"Another what?"

"Another corpse."

Carella waited. Dorfsman sounded as if he was enjoying himself immensely. Carella did not want to spoil his fun. A corpse on the day of the observance of Washington's Birthday, even if it was a week *before* Washington's Birthday, was certainly amusing.

"I haven't even called Kling yet," Dorfsman said. "You're the first one I'm calling."

"Kling?" Carella said.

"Kling," Dorfsman said. "Don't you guys ever *talk* to each other up there? Kling caught the squeal Saturday night. Sunday morning, actually. Two o'clock Sunday morning."

"What are you talking about?" Carella asked.

"A homicide on Silvermine Oval. Guy named Marvin Edelman, two slugs pumped into his head." Dorfsman still sounded as if he was smiling. "I'm calling you first, Steve," he said.

"So I gather. How come?"

"Same gun as the other two," Dorfsman said cheerfully.

It was beginning to look like they had a crazy on their hands.

NINE

CRAZIES make police work difficult.

When you've got a crazy on your hands, you might just as well throw away the manual and work the case by the seat of your pants, because that's the way the crazy is working *his* case. There were a lot of crazies in this city, but thankfully most of them were content to walk up and down Hall Avenue carrying signs about doomsday or else muttering to themselves about the Mayor and the weather. The crazies in this city seemed to think the Mayor was responsible for the weather. Maybe he was.

Detective Lieutenant Peter Byrnes seemed to think his squad was responsible for the lack of communication on what now appeared to be *three* linked murders. Byrnes, when apprised of what Dorfsman had said on the telephone, agreed emphatically with him: Didn't the guys up here ever *talk* to each other?

"You get a murder last Tuesday night and another one on Saturday night, Sunday morning, when*ever* it was," Byrnes said. "The first one is on Culver Avenue, and the next one is on Silvermine Road, just a few blocks *away!* Both of them are *gunshot* murders, but does it ever occur to you masterminds to do an in-house *cross*-check? I'm not even *mentioning* the little girl who got killed downtown on *Friday* night, I wouldn't *dream* of mentioning a *third* gunshot murder to sleuths of such remarkable perception," Byrnes said, gathering steam, "but does anyone up here even *glance* at the activity reports, which is why we *keep* activity reports in the *first* place, so that every cop in this precinct, uniformed *or* plainclothes, will know what the hell is going *on* up here!"

In the squadroom outside, Miscolo and a handful of uniformed patrolmen were milling about apprehensively, listening to Byrnes's angry voice from behind the frosted glass door to his office and knowing that someone in there was getting chewed out mightily. Actually, there were *four* someones in there, but none of the squadroom eavesdroppers knew that because the detectives had been called at home early that Tuesday morning and asked to report at the crack of dawn (well, 7:30 a.m.) and the uniformed force hadn't begun trickling in until 7:45 a.m., when roll call took place every morning in the muster room downstairs. The four plainclothes someones were, in alphabetical order, Detectives Brown, Carella, Kling, and Meyer. They were all looking at their shoes.

Byrnes's rage was comprised of one part pressure from "rank" downtown and one part sheer indignation over the stupidity of men he had hoped, after all these years, could do their jobs with at least a modicum of routine efficiency. Secretly, he suspected Kling was more at fault than any of the others because of the clamlike posture he had developed after his divorce. But he did not want to single out Kling as the sole perpetrator here, because that would only serve to embarrass him and perhaps cause disharmony among four detectives who now seemed fated to work together on solving three separate murders. So Byrnes ranted and raved about simple procedures, which—if only followed to the letter—would dispel confusion, eliminate duplication, and ("A consummation devoutly to be wished," he actually said) maybe solve a *case* every now and then around here.

"All right," he said at last, "that's that."

"Pete—" Carella started.

"I said all right, that's the end of it," Byrnes said. "Have a piece of candy," he said, shoving the half-depleted box across the desk toward his surprised detectives. "Tell me what you've got."

"Not much," Carella said.

"Is this a crazy we're dealing with here?"

"Maybe," Brown said.

"Have you got a line on that thirty-eight yet?"

"No, Pete, we've been—"

"Round up your street gun dealers, find out who was shopping for a gun that fits the description."

"Yes, Pete," Carella said.

"How does Lopez tie in with these other two?"

"We don't know yet."

"Were either of them doing drugs?"

"The girl was. We don't know about Edelman yet."

"Was Lopez supplying her?"

"We don't know yet. We *do* know she was bringing coke in for some of the other people in the show."

"This last one was a diamond merchant, huh?"

"Precious gems," Kling said.

"Did he know either Lopez or the girl?"

"We don't know yet," Kling said. "But he was held up sometime last summer, and that may be something to go on. We'll be running it through the computer this morning."

"Don't go squeezing them," Byrnes said to Meyer, who was reaching for a chocolate in the box. "Take all you want, but *eat* the ones you touch, and don't go squishing up the whole box."

Meyer, who had in fact been about to squeeze one of the chocolates, gave Byrnes an offended look.

"What's with her boyfriend?" Byrnes said. "The girl's boyfriend."

"He was on the phone most of last Friday night," Carella said. "The night the girl was killed."

"On the phone? Who with?"

"Another student. The boyfriend's a med student at Ramsey."

"What's his name again?"

"Timothy Moore."

"And his friend's name?"

"Karl Loeb."

"You checked with him?"

"Loeb? Yes. They were gabbing till almost two in the morning."

"Who called who?" Byrnes asked.

"Back and forth."

"What else?"

"The producer of the show, man named Allan Carter, is playing house with one of the dancers."

"So what?" Byrnes asked.

"He's married," Meyer said.

"So what?" Byrnes asked again.

"We think he's lying to us," Meyer said.

"About his little tootsie?" Byrnes said, using one of the quaint, archaic terms that sometimes crept into his vocabulary, for which the younger men on the squad almost always forgave him.

"No, he was straight on about that," Carella said. "But he claims to have known the dead girl only casually, and it doesn't smell right."

"Why would he lie about that?" Byrnes asked.

"We don't know yet," Carella said.

"You think they were doing a two-on-one?" Byrnes asked, using one of the more voguish terms that sometimes crept into his vocabulary.

"We don't know yet," Meyer said.

"What the hell *do* you know?" Byrnes asked heatedly, and then gained control of himself once again. "Have some candy, for Christ's sake!" he said. "I'll get fat as a horse here."

"Pete," Carella said, "this is a complicated one."

"Don't tell *me* it's a complicated one. Don't I know a complicated one when I see a complicated one?"

"Maybe it *is* a crazy," Brown suggested.

"That's the easy way out," Byrnes said, "blaming it on a crazy. You want to know something? In *my* book, *anybody* who kills anybody is a crazy."

The detectives had no quarrel with him there.

"Okay," Byrnes said, "start vacuuming the street. Or, better yet, call some of our snitches, see if they can come up with a line on that goddamn gun. Bert, Artie, run your computer check on that holdup . . . Have you been to that guy's shop yet? Edelman's?"

"Not yet," Brown said.

"Go there, go through everything in the place. You come across even a *speck* of white dust, shoot it over to the lab for a cocaine test."

"We're not sure cocaine is the connection," Meyer said.

"No? Then what *is*? The girl was doing coke and supplying half the cast with it."

"Not that many, Pete."

"How*ever* goddamn many! I don't care if she was the *star* of that show, which I gather she wasn't. On my block, she was delivering dope, and that made her a *mule*. We *know* Lopez was in the business of selling cocaine—he had six grams and eleven hundred bucks in his pocket when he was killed. So find out some more about little Miss Goody Two Shoes. Where'd she get the stuff she was spreading around the cast? Was she turning a profit or just doing a favor? And put the blocks to this producer, whatever the hell his name is, Carter. If he was sleeping with both that other dancer *and* the dead girl, I want to know about it. That's it. Call Danny Gimp, call Fats Donner, call any snitch who's in town instead of in Florida, where *I* should be. I want this case moved off the *dime*, have you got that? The next time the Chief calls me, I want to tell him something *positive*."

"Yes, Pete," Carella said.

"Don't 'Yes, Pete' me. Just *do* it."

"Yes, Pete."

"And another thing. I'm not buying this as a crazy until you guys can convince me there was absolutely *no* connection between the three victims."

Byrnes paused.

"Find that connection," he said.

THEY arranged to meet on a bench in Grover Park, not too far from the skating rink and the statue of General Ronald King, who had once stormed a precious hill during the Spanish-American War, thereby shortening the tenure of the foreign tyrants who (according to William Randolph Hearst and Joseph Pulitzer) were oppressing the honest Cuban cane cutters and fishermen. A bygone Mayor had commissioned the statue of the general, not because of his indisputable gallantry, but only because King (like the Mayor himself) was reputed to have been a card mavin whose specialty had been poker and whose favorite game within the genre had been something called "Shove," which was also the Mayor's favorite. For his patience in standing out there in bronze in all sorts of weather, the general had been further honored by the city's Hispanic (though not Cuban) population, who scrawled their names in spray paint across his bold chest and who occasionally pissed on his horse's legs.

School had been canceled today because of hazardous road conditions. As Carella waited for Danny Gimp on the bench near the statue of the general, he could hear the voices of young boys playing ice hockey on the outdoor rink. He was frozen to the marrow. He was not normally a philosophical man, but as he sat huddled inside his heaviest coat—*and* his jacket beneath that, *and* a sweater beneath that, *and* a flannel shirt beneath that, *and* woolen underwear beneath that—he thought that winter was a lot like police work. Winter wore you down. The snow, and the sleet, and the freezing rain, and the ice just kept coming at you till you were ready to throw up your hands in surrender. But you hung in there somehow until the spring thaw came and everything seemed all right again—till *next* winter.

Where the hell was Danny?

He saw him limping slowly up the path, turning his head this way and that to check the snow-covered terrain, just like an undercover agent out in the cold, which—to tell the truth—Danny sometimes fancied himself to be. He was wearing a red-and-blue plaid mackinaw and a red watch cap pulled down around his ears and blue woolen gloves and green corduroy trousers tucked into the tops of black galoshes, a somewhat garish costume for someone trying to appear inconspicuous. He walked directly past the bench on which Carella sat freezing (there were times when he carried this spy stuff a *bit* too far), walked almost to the statue of the general, peered around cautiously, and then came back to the bench, sat beside Carella, took a newspaper from the side pocket of his mackinaw, opened it to hide his face, and said, "Hello, Steve. Cold, huh?"

Carella took off his glove and offered his hand to Danny. Danny lowered the newspaper, took off his glove, and reached out for Carella's hand. They shook hands briefly and put on their gloves again. There were not too many detectives who shook hands with informers. Most cops and their informers were business associates of a sort, but they did not shake hands. Not many cops held snitches in very high regard. A snitch was usually someone who "owed" something to the cops. The cops were willing to look the other way in return for information. Some of the snitches who provided information were among the city's worst citizens. But if politics made strange bedfellows, criminal investigation made even stranger ones. Hal Willis's favorite snitch was a man named Fats Donner, whose penchant for twelve-year-old girls made him universally despised. But he was a good and valuable informer. Of all the snitches Carella worked with, he liked Danny Gimp best. And he would never forget that once upon a time, more years ago than he cared to remember, Danny had come to see him in the hospital when he was recovering from a bullet wound. That was why he always shook hands with Danny Gimp. He would shake hands with Danny Gimp even if the Commissioner were watching.

"How's the leg?" he asked.

"It hurts when it's cold," Danny said.

"Just once," Carella said, "I would like to meet someplace that isn't Siberia."

"I have to be careful," Danny said.

"You can be careful *inside.*"

"Inside there are ears," Danny said.

"Well, let's make this fast, okay?"

"It's your nickel," Danny said, inappropriately in that they were not on the telephone, and anyway a nickel telephone call had gone the way of the buggy whip.

"I'm looking for a thirty-eight Smith and Wesson that was used in three murders," Carella said.

"When was this?" Danny asked.

"The first one was a week ago today, the ninth. The second one was last Friday night, the twelfth. The last one was on Saturday night, the thirteenth."

"All of them up here?"

"Two of them."

"Which two?"

"A coke dealer named Paco Lopez—ever hear of him?"

"I think so."

"And a diamond merchant named Marvin Edelman."

"Doing business up here?"

"No, downtown. He lived on Silvermine Road."

"Fancy," Danny said.

"Who's the *third* party?"

"A girl named Sally Anderson. Dancer in a musical downtown."

"So where's the connection?" Danny asked.

"That's what we're trying to find out."

"Mmm," Danny said. "Lopez, huh?"

"Paco," Carella said.

"Paco Lopez," Danny said.

"Ring a bell?"

"Did he burn some chick's tits a while back?"

"That's the guy."

"Yeah," Danny said.

"Do you know him?"

"I seen him around. This was months ago. He must've been living with the chick, they were together all the time. So he bought it, huh? That's no great loss, Steve. He was bad news all around."

"How so?"

"Mean," Danny said. "I don't like people who are mean, do you? Did you talk to the chick yet?"

"The day after Lopez got killed."

"And?"

"Nothing. She told us what he'd done to her . . ."

"Something, huh?" Danny said, and shook his head.

"But they'd stopped living together two months ago. She didn't know anything."

"Nobody *ever* knows anything when it comes to cops in this neighborhood. Maybe *she's* the one who done it. For marking her that way."

"I doubt it, Danny, but be my guest. Frankly, I'm more interested in knowing whether a thirty-eight changed hands sometime during this past week."

"Lots of thirty-eights in this city, Steve."

"I know that."

"Changing hands all the time." He was silent for a moment. "The first one was last Tuesday, huh? What time?"

"Eleven o'clock."

"P.m.?"

"P.m."

"Where?"

"On Culver Avenue."

"Inside or out?"

"On the street."

"Not too many people out doing mischief in this weather," Danny said. "The cold keeps them home. Murderers and thieves like their comfort," he said philosophically. "Nobody seen the killer, huh?"

"Would I be here freezing my ass off if we had a witness?" Carella said.

"*I'm* freezing, too, don't forget," Danny said, somewhat offended. "Well, let me see what I hear. How urgent is this?"

"Urgent," Carella said.

" 'Cause there's a bet I want to place before I get to work."

"Anything good?" Carella asked.

"Only if he wins," Danny said, and shrugged.

BROTHER Anthony and Emma were smoking dope and drinking wine and going over the list of names and addresses Judite Quadrado had given them two days ago. A kerosene heater was going in one corner of the room, but the radiators were only lukewarm, and the windows were nonetheless rimed with ice. Brother Anthony and Emma were sitting very close to the kerosene heater, even though both of them insisted that cold weather never bothered them. They were both in their underwear.

They had smoked a little pot an hour ago, before making love in the king-sized bed in Brother Anthony's bedroom. Afterward, they had each and separately pulled on their underwear and walked out into the living room to open a bottle of wine and to light two more joints before sitting down again with the list of potential customers. Brother Anthony was wearing striped boxer shorts. Emma was wearing black bikini panties. Brother Anthony thought she looked radiantly lovely after sex.

"So what it looks like to me," Emma said, "is that he had a dozen people he was servicing."

"That's not so many," Brother Anthony said. "I was hoping for something bigger, Em, I'll tell you the truth. Twelve rotten names sounds like very small potatoes for all the trouble we went to." He looked at the list again. "Especially in such small quantities. Look at the quantities, Em."

"Do you know the joke?" she asked him, grinning.

"No. What joke?" He loved it when she told jokes. He also loved it when she went down on him. Looking at her huge breasts, he was beginning to feel the faintest stirrings of renewed desire, and he began thinking that maybe he would let her tell her joke and then they would forget all about Lopez's small-time list and go make love again. That sounded like a very good thing to do on a cold day like today.

"This lady is staying at a Miami Beach hotel, you know?" Emma said, still grinning.

"I wish *I* was staying at a Miami Beach hotel," Brother Anthony said.

"You want to hear this joke or not?"

"Tell it," he said.

"So she eats a couple of meals in the dining room, and then she goes to the front desk and starts complaining to the manager."

"What about?" Brother Anthony said.

"Will you let me tell it, please?"

"Tell it, tell it."

"She tells the manager the food in the dining room is absolute poison. The *eggs* are poison, the *beef* is poison, the *potatoes* are poison, the *salads* are poison, the *coffee* is poison, everything is poison, poison, poison, she says. And you know what *else?*"

"What else?" Brother Anthony asked.

"The *portions* are so small!" Emma said, and burst out laughing.

"I don't get it," Brother Anthony said.

"The lady is complaining the food is *poison* . . ."

"Yeah?"

"But she's *also* complaining the portions are too small."

"So what?"

"If it's *poison*, why does she want bigger portions?"

"Maybe she's crazy," Brother Anthony said.

"No, she's not crazy," Emma said. "She's complaining about the food, but she's *also* telling the manager the portions—"

"I understand," Brother Anthony said, "but I still don't get it. Why don't we go in the other room again?"

"You're not ready yet," Emma said, glancing at his lap.

"You can make me ready."

"I know I can. But I like it better when you're ready *before* I make you ready."

"Sweet mouth," Brother Anthony said, lowering his voice.

"Mmm," Emma said.

"So what do you say?"

"I say business before pleasure," Emma said.

"Anyway, what made you even *think* of that joke?" he asked.

"You said something about the small quantities."

"They *are* small," Brother Anthony said. "Look at them," he said, and handed the list to her. "Two or three grams a week, most of them. We ain't gonna get rich on two, three grams a week."

"We don't have to get rich all at once, Bro," Emma said. "We'll take things slow and easy at first, start with these people who used to be Lopez's customers, build from there."

"How?"

"Maybe the lady can put us onto some other customers."

"What lady? The one eating poison?"

"The one who was supplying Lopez. His ounce dealer."

"Why would she want to help us that way?"

"Why not? There has to be a chain of supply, Bro. An ounce dealer needs gram dealers, a gram dealer needs users. The lady puts us onto some users, we buy our goods from her, and everybody's happy."

"I think you're dreaming," Brother Anthony said.

"Would it hurt to ask?" Emma said.

"She'll tell us to get lost."

"Who knows? Anyway, first things first. First we have to let her know we've taken over from Lopez and would like to continue doing business with her. That's the first thing."

"That's the first thing, for sure."

"So what I think you should do," Emma said, "is get dressed and go pay this Sally Anderson a little visit."

"Later," Brother Anthony said, and took her in his arms.

"Mmm," Emma said, and cuddled closer to him and licked her lips.

EILEEN Burke called the squadroom while Kling was still on the phone with Communications Division. Brown asked her to wait and then put a note on Kling's desk, advising him that Detective Burke was on six. Kling nodded. For a moment, he didn't know who Detective Burke *was*.

"I've got the printout right here in my hand," the supervisor in the Dispatcher's Office said. "That was last July twenty-eighth, eight-oh-two p.m., six-twenty-one North Greenfield, room two-oh-seven. Adam Car responded at eight-twelve."

"What'd they find?"

"Radioed back with a Ten-Twenty. That's a Robbery Past."

Kling knew what a 10-20 was.

"Which precinct was that?"

"Midtown East," the supervisor said.

"Would you know who handled the case there?"

"That's not on the printout."

"Okay, thanks," Kling said, and pressed the lighted 6 button in the base of his phone. "Kling," he said.

"Bert, it's Eileen."

"I didn't get a chance to look for that earring," he said.

"Didn't turn up in the squadroom, huh?"

"Well, we've got a lost-and-found box, but there's nothing in it."

"How about the car?"

"I haven't checked the car yet," he said. "I haven't used that particular car since Saturday night."

"Well, if you *do* get a chance . . ."

"Sure," he said.

"It's just that . . . they're sort of my good-luck earrings."

Kling said nothing.

"I feel naked without them," she said.

He still said nothing.

"Can't go around wearing just *one* good-luck earring, can I?" she said.

"I guess not," he said.

"Cut my luck in half," she said.

"Yeah," he said.

"How's the weather up there?" she asked.

"Cold."

"Here, too," she said. "Well, let me know if you find it, okay?"

"I will."

"Thanks," she said, and hung up.

On the same slip of paper Brown had placed on his desk, Kling scrawled "E's earring" and then put the slip of paper in his jacket pocket. He flipped his precinct directory till he found the number for Midtown East, dialed it, told the desk sergeant there what he was looking for, and was put through to a detective named Garrido, who spoke with a Spanish accent and who remembered the case at once because he himself had been staked out in the back of the Greenfield Street pawnshop when the armed robber walked in trying to hock all the stuff he'd stolen from Edelman two days earlier and three doors south.

"The whole list," Garrido said, "ever'ting on it from soup to nuts. We had him cold."

"So what happened?" Kling asked.

"Guess who we got for the jutch?" Garrido asked.

"Who?" Kling asked.

"Harris."

Kling knew the Honorable Wilbur Harris. The Honorable Wilbur Harris was known in the trade as Walking Wilbur. His specialty was allowing criminals to march out of his courtroom.

"What happened?" Kling asked.

"The kid wass a junkie, first time he did anyting like this. He was almos' cryin' in the cour'room. So Harris less him off with a suspended sentence."

"Even though you caught him with the goods, huh?"

"*All* of it!" Garrido said. "Ever'ting on the list! Ah, wha's the sense?"

"What was the kid's name?"

"Andrew someting. You wann me to pull the file?"

"If it's not any trouble."

"Sure," Garrido said. "Juss a secon', okay?"

He was back five minutes later with a name and a last known address for the seventeen-year-old boy who had held up Marvin Edelman the summer before.

THE APARTMENT ALLAN CARTER had described as "one of those big old rent-controlled apartments on the park" was in fact on the park, and most certainly old, and possibly rent-controlled, but only a dwarf would have considered it "big." Lonnie Cooper, one of the two black dancers in *Fatback*, was almost as tall as the two detectives she admitted into her home that late Tuesday morning; together, the three of them caused the tiny place to assume the dimensions of a clothes closet. Compounding the felony, Miss Cooper had jammed the place chock-full of furniture, knickknacks, paintings, and pieces of sculpture so that there was hardly an uncovered patch of wall or floor surface; both Meyer and Carella felt they had wandered into the business office of a fence selling stolen goods.

"I like clutter," the dancer explained. "Most dancers don't, but I do. On stage, I can fly. When I'm home, I like to fold my wings."

She was even more beautiful than Carella remembered her on stage, a lissome woman with skin the color of cork, high cheekbones, a nose like Nefertiti's, a generous mouth, and a dazzling smile. She was wearing a man's red woolen shawl-collared sweater over a black leotard top and black tights. She was barefooted, but she was wearing striped leg warmers over the tights. She asked the detectives if they would like some coffee or anything, and when they declined, she asked them to make themselves comfortable. Carella and Meyer took seats beside each other on a sofa cluttered with throw pillows. Lonnie Cooper sat opposite them in an easy chair with antimacassars pinned to the back and the arms. A coffee table between them was covered with glass paperweights, miniature dolls, letter openers, campaign buttons, and a Trylon-and-Perisphere souvenir ashtray from New York City's 1939 World's Fair. Catching Carella's glance, she explained, "I collect things."

"Miss Cooper," he said, "I wonder if—"

"Lonnie," she said.

"Fine," he said. "Lonnie, I—"

"What's *your* first name?" she asked.

"Steve," he said.

"And yours?" she asked Meyer.

"Meyer," he said.

"I thought that was your last name."

"It is. It's also my first name."

"How terrific!" she said.

Meyer shrugged. He had never thought of his name as being particularly terrific, except once when a lady fiction writer used it as the title of a novel about a college professor. He had called Rollie Chabrier in the D.A.'s office, wanting to know if he could sue. Chabrier told him he should feel honored. Meyer guessed he'd felt a *little* bit honored. But it continued to bother him that somebody out there had used the name of a *real* person for a mere character in a work of fiction. A college professor, no less.

"Are you sure you don't want any coffee?" Lonnie asked.

"Positive, thanks," Carella said.

"We're about coffeed out," Meyer said. "This weather."

"Yeah, do you find yourself drinking a lot of coffee, too?" Lonnie said.

"Yes," Meyer said.

"Me, too," she said. "Gee."

There was something very girlish about her, Carella decided. She looked to be about twenty-six or twenty-seven, but her movements and her facial expressions and even her somewhat high-pitched voice were more like those of a seventeen-year-old. She curled up in the easy chair now and folded her legs under her, the way his daughter, April, might have.

"I guess you realize we're here about Sally Anderson," Carella said.

"Yes, of course," she said, and her face took on the studied, sober look of a child trying to cope with grown-up problems.

"Miss Cooper—"

"Lonnie," she said.

"Lonnie—"

"Yes, Steve?"

Carella cleared his throat. "Lonnie, we understand there was a party here a week ago last Sunday, that would've been the seventh of February. Do you recall such a party?"

"Yeah, wow," she said, "it was a *great* party!"

"Was Sally Anderson here?"

"Yeah, sure."

"And Tina Wong?"

"Yep."

"And Allan Carter?"

"Sure, lots of people," Lonnie said.

"How about Mike Roldan and Tony Asensio?" Meyer asked.

"You guys really do your homework, don't you?" Lonnie said.

Meyer had never thought of it as homework; he smiled weakly.

"They were here, too, Meyer," Lonnie said, and smiled back—dazzlingly.

"From what we've been able to determine," Carella said, "there was some cocaine floating around that night."

"Oh?" she said, and the smile dropped from her face.

"Was there?"

"Who told you that?"

"Several people."

"Who?"

"That's not important, Miss Cooper."

"It's important to *me*, Steve. And please call me Lonnie."

"We've had it from three different sources," Meyer said.

"Who?"

He looked at Carella. Carella nodded.

"Tina Wong, Mike Roldan, and Tony Asensio," Meyer said.

"Boy," Lonnie said, and shook her head.

"Is it true?" Carella said.

"Listen, who am I to contradict them?" Lonnie said, and shrugged and grimaced and then shifted her position in the chair. "But I thought this was about Sally."

"It is."

"I mean, is this going to turn into a *cocaine* thing?"

"It's *already* a cocaine thing," Meyer said. "We know Sally was doing coke that night, and we also know—"

"You're talking about last Sunday?"

"A week ago last Sunday, yes. You *do* remember that Sally was doing coke, don't you?"

"Well . . . yes. Now that you mention it."

"Plus some other people as well."

"Well, a few others."

"Okay. Where'd the stuff come from?"

"How would I know?"

"Miss Cooper—"

"Lonnie."

"Lonnie, we're not looking for a drug collar here. Sally Anderson was *murdered*, and we're trying to find out *why*. If cocaine had anything to do with her death—"

"I don't see how it could have."

"How do you know that?"

"Because she's the one who *brought* the coke."

"We know that. But where'd *she* get it, would you know?"

"Uptown someplace."

"Where uptown?"

"I have no idea."

"How far uptown? Are we talking about below the park or—"

"I really don't know."

"How often did she bring the stuff in?"

"Usually once a week. On Monday nights, before the show. We're dark on Sunday—"

"Dark?"

"No performances. So she usually got the stuff on Sundays, I guess, went uptown for it on Sundays, or else had it delivered, I really don't know. Anyway, she brought it to the theater on Monday nights."

"And distributed it among the cast."

"Those who wanted it, yes."

"How many of those were there?"

"Half a dozen? Seven? Something like that."

"How much money was involved here, would you say?"

"You don't think she was in this for the *money*, do you?"

"Why *was* she in it?"

"She was doing us a favor, that's all. I mean, why duplicate the effort? If you've got a good contact and he delivers good dust, why not make one *big* buy every week instead of six or seven *small* buys from dealers you maybe can't trust? It only makes sense."

"Uh-huh," Carella said.

"Well, doesn't it?"

"So what are we talking about here?" Meyer said. "For the six or seven grams, what'd she—"

"Well, sometimes more than that. But she only charged what she herself was paying for it, believe me. I know street prices, and that's all she was getting."

"Nothing for all the trouble of having to go uptown?"

"What trouble? She had to go anyway, didn't she? And besides, maybe the man was delivering it, who knows? You're really barking up the wrong tree if you think *that's* how Sally—"

She stopped suddenly.

"How Sally what?" Carella asked at once.

"How she . . . uh—"

Lonnie grimaced and shrugged as though utterly baffled as to how she might finish the sentence she had started.

"Yes?" Carella said. "How she *what?*"

"Earned her living," Lonnie said, and smiled.

"Well, we *know* how she earned her living, don't we?" Meyer said. "She was a dancer."

"Well, yes."

"Then why would we think she earned her living some *other* way?"

"Well, you've been talking about coke here and asking how much money was involved—"

"Yes, but you told us she wasn't making any profit on the coke."

"That's right."

"Was she earning extra cash someplace *else?*" Carella asked.

"I don't know anything about any extra cash."

"But there *was* extra cash someplace, wasn't there?"

"Gee, did *I* say that?" Lonnie said, and rolled her eyes.

"You seemed to indicate—"

"No, you misunderstood me, Steve."

"Where'd she get this extra cash?" Carella asked.

"What extra cash?" Lonnie said.

"Let's start all over again," Carella said. "What did you mean when you used the words 'how she earned her living'?"

"As a dancer," Lonnie said.

"That's not what I'm asking you."

"I don't know what you're asking me."

"I'm asking you where she earned additional income."

"Who said she did?"

"I thought that's what you implied."

"Anyway," Lonnie said, "sometimes a performer will do a nightclub gig or something. While she's still in a show that's running."

"Uh-huh," Carella said. "*Was* Sally doing nightclub gigs?"

"Well . . . no. Not that I know of."

"Then what *was* she doing?"

"I only said . . ." Lonnie shook her head.

"You said she was doing something that earned her a living. What was it?"

"It goes on all over town," Lonnie said.

"What does?"

"If Sally was lucky enough to get cut in on it, more power to her."

"Cut in on *what?*"

"It isn't even against the law, that I know of," Lonnie said. "Nobody gets hurt by it."

"What are we talking about?" Meyer asked. It sounded as if she'd been describing prostitution, but surely she knew *that* was against the law. And besides, who *said* nobody got hurt by it?

"Tell us what you mean," Carella said.

"I don't have anything else to tell you," she said, and folded her arms across her chest like a pouting six-year-old.

"We can subpoena you before a grand jury," Carella said, figuring if the ploy had worked at least a thousand times before, it might work yet another time.

"So subpoena me," Lonnie said.

WHEN Brown went out back to where the precinct's vehicles were parked, he was surprised first to see that it was the same rotten decrepit automobile they'd pulled last Saturday night, and next to see Kling on his hands and knees in the back seat.

"I told them I didn't want this car again," he said to Kling's back. "What are you doing?"

"Here it is," Kling said.

"Here's what?"

"Eileen's earring," he said, and held up a small gold circle.

Brown nodded. "You want to drive?" he asked. "I *hate* this car."

"Sure," Kling said.

He put the earring in his coat pocket, dusted off the knees of his trousers, and then climbed in behind the wheel. Brown got in beside him on the passenger side. "This door doesn't close right," he said, slamming and reslamming the door until it seemed at last to fit properly into the frame. He turned on the heater at once. The heater began rattling and clanging. "Terrific," he said. "Where we headed?"

"Diamondback," Kling said, and started the car.

"Terrific," Brown said.

A police department adage maintained that the best time and place to get killed in this city was at twelve midnight on a Saturday in the middle of August on the corner of Landis Avenue and Porter Street. Brown and Kling were happy that they reached that particular corner at twelve noon on a freezing day in February, but they weren't particularly delighted to be in Diamondback at all. Brown appreciated their destination even less than did Kling. Diamondback, in the 83rd Precinct, was almost exclusively black, and many of the residents here felt that a black cop was the worst kind of cop in the world. Even the honest citizens up here—and they far outnumbered the pimps, pushers, junkies, armed robbers, burglars, hookers, and assorted petty thieves—felt that if you had any kind of law trouble, it was better to go to Whitey than to one of your own brothers. A black cop was like a reformed hooker who'd gone tight and dry.

"What's this kid's name?" Brown asked.

"Andrew Fleet," Kling said.

"White or black?"

"Black," Kling said.

"Terrific," Brown said.

The last known address for Fleet was in a row of grimy tenements on St. Sebastian Avenue, which started at the eastern end of Grover Park and then ran diagonally northward and eastward for a total of thirteen blocks between Landis and Isola avenues, to become—inexplicably—*another* thoroughfare named Adams Street, presumably after the second president of the United States or per-

haps even the sixth. St. Sab's, as it was familiarly called by everyone in the neighborhood, looked particularly dismal that Tuesday
afternoon. You could always tell a neighborhood of poor people
in this city because the streets were always the last to be plowed
and sanded, and the garbage, especially in bad weather, was
allowed to pile up indefinitely, presumably as an inducement to
free enterprise among the rat population. It was not unusual in
Diamondback to see rats the size of alley cats striding boldly
across an avenue at high noon. It was ten minutes past twelve
when Kling pulled up alongside a snowbank outside Fleet's building. There was not a rat in sight, but all the garbage cans along
the street were overflowing, and the sidewalks were cluttered
with the loose debris of urban waste, much of it frozen into the
icy pavement. Up here, people didn't use plastic garbage bags.
Plastic garbage bags cost money.

Two old black men were standing around a fire in a sawed-off
gasoline drum, warming their hands as Brown and Kling
approached the front stoop of the building. The men knew
immediately that Brown and Kling were detectives. There's a
smell. Brown and Kling knew immediately that the men around
the gasoline drum knew immediately they were detectives.
There's a symbiosis. The two men didn't even look up at Brown
and Kling as they climbed the front steps. Brown and Kling didn't
look at the two men. The unspoken rule was that if you hadn't
done anything wrong, you had no bona fide business with each
other.

In the small vestibule, they checked the mailboxes. Only two of
them had nameplates.

"Have we got an apartment for him?" Brown asked.

"Three-B," Kling said.

The lock on the inner vestibule door was broken. Naturally.
The socket hanging from the ceiling just inside the door had no
lightbulb in it. Naturally. The hallway was dark, and the steps

leading upstairs were darker, and there was the aggressive aroma of tight cramped living, a presence as tangible as the brick walls of the building.

"Shoulda taken a flash from the car," Brown said.

"Yeah," Kling said.

They climbed the steps to the third floor.

They listened outside the door to Fleet's apartment.

Nothing.

They listened some more.

Still nothing.

Brown knocked.

"Johnny?" a voice said.

"Police," Brown said.

"Oh."

"Open it up," Brown said.

"Sure, just a second."

Brown looked at Kling. Both men shrugged. They heard footsteps inside, approaching the door. They heard someone fumbling with a night chain. They heard the tumblers of a lock falling. The door opened. A thin young black man wearing blue jeans and a tan V-necked sweater over a white undershirt stood in the doorframe, peering out into the hallway.

"Yeah?" he said.

"Andrew Fleet?" Brown said, and showed him his shield and I.D. card.

"Yeah?"

"*Are* you Andrew Fleet?"

"Yeah?"

"Few questions we'd like to ask you. Okay to come in?"

"Well, uh, sure," Fleet said, and glanced past them toward the stairwell.

"Or were you expecting somebody?" Kling asked at once.

"No, no, come on in."

He stepped aside to allow them entrance. They were standing in a small kitchen. A single ice-rimed window opened onto the brick wall of the tenement opposite. There were dirty dishes stacked in the sink. An empty wine bottle was on the small table. A clothesline was stretched across the room from one wall to the wall opposite. A single pair of Jockey shorts was draped over the line.

"It's a little chilly in here," Fleet said. "The heat's slow coming up today. We already called the Ombudsman's Office."

"Who's *we?*" Brown asked.

"A guy on the tenants' committee."

Through an open door off the kitchen, they could see an unmade bed. The floor around the bed was heaped with dirty clothes. On the wall over the bed, there was a framed picture of Jesus Christ with his hand hovering in blessing over his exposed and bleeding heart.

"You live here alone?" Brown asked.

"Yes, sir," Fleet said.

"Just these two rooms?"

"Yes, sir."

He was suddenly all "sirs"; the formality was not lost on the two detectives. A glance passed between them. They were both wondering what he was afraid of.

"Okay to ask you a few questions?" Brown said.

"Sure. But . . . uh . . . you know, like you said, I *was* kind of expecting someone."

"Who?" Kling said. "Johnny?"

"Well, yeah, actually."

"Who's Johnny?"

"A friend."

"You still doing heroin?" Brown asked.

"No, no. Who told you that?"

"Your record, for one thing," Kling said.

"I ain't *got* a record. I never done time in my life."

"Nobody said you did time."

"You were arrested last July," Brown said. "Charged with Rob One."

"Yeah, but—"

"You walked, we know."

"Well, it was a suspended sentence."

"Because you were a poor, put-upon junkie, right?" Brown said.

"Well, I was hooked pretty bad back then, that's true."

"But no more, huh?"

"No. Hey, no. You gotta be crazy to fool around with that shit."

"Uh-huh," Brown said. "So who's this friend Johnny?"

"Just a friend."

"Not a dealer by any chance?"

"No, no. Hey, come on, man."

"Where were you last Saturday night, Andrew?" Kling asked.

"Last Saturday night?"

"Actually Sunday morning. Two o'clock on the morning of the fourteenth."

"Yeah," Fleet said.

"Yeah what?"

"I'm trying to remember. Why? What happened last Saturday night?"

"You tell us," Brown said.

"Saturday night," Fleet said.

"Or Sunday morning, take your choice."

"Two o'clock in the morning," Fleet said.

"You've got it," Kling said.

"I was here, I think."

"Anybody with you?"

"Is this an Article Two-Twenty?" Fleet asked, using the penal law number for the section defining drug abuses.

"Anybody with you?" Kling repeated.

"Who remembers? That was . . . what was it? Three days ago? Four days ago?"

"Try to remember, Andrew," Brown said.

"I'm trying."

"Do you remember the name of the man you held up?"

"Yeah."

"What was his name?"

"Edelbaum."

"Try again."

"That was his name."

"Ever see him since the holdup?"

"Yeah, at the trial."

"And you think his name is Edelbaum, huh?"

"That *is* his name."

"Do you know where he lives?"

"No. Where does he live?"

"No idea where he lives, huh?"

"How would I know where he lives?"

"Do you remember where his shop is?"

"Sure. On North Greenfield."

"But you don't remember where he lives, huh?"

"I *never* knew where, so how can I *remember* where?"

"But if you wanted to find *out* where, you'd look it up in the phone book, right?" Brown said.

"Well, sure, but why would I want to do that?"

"Where were you on February the fourteenth at two in the morning?" Kling asked.

"I told you. Right here."

"Anybody with you?"

"If this is an Article—"

"Anybody with you, Andrew?"

"We were shooting a little dope, okay?" Fleet said. "Is that what you want to know? Fine, you got it, man. We were shooting dope, I'm still a junkie, okay? Big deal. Go through the place if you want to, you won't find anything but a little pot. Not enough for a bust, that's for sure. Go ahead, take a look."

"Who's *we?*" Brown asked.

"What?"

"The person who was with you on Saturday night."

"It was Johnny, okay? What are we gonna *do* here, get the whole *world* in trouble?"

"Johnny who?" Kling asked.

A knock sounded on the door. Fleet looked at the two cops.

"Answer it," Brown said.

"Listen—"

"Answer it."

Fleet sighed and went to the door. He turned the knob on the lock and opened the door.

"Hi," he said.

The black girl standing in the hallway couldn't have been more than sixteen years old. She was wearing a red ski parka over blue jeans and high-heeled boots. She was not unattractive, but the lipstick on her mouth was a shade too garish, and her cheeks were heavily rouged, and her eyes were made up with shadow and liner that seemed far too nocturnal for twenty minutes past noon.

"Come in, miss," Brown said.

"What's the beef?" she asked, recognizing them immediately as cops.

"No beef," Kling said. "Want to tell us who you are?"

"Andy?" she said, turning her eyes to where Fleet was standing.

"I don't know what they want," Fleet said, and shrugged.

"You got a warrant?" the girl asked.

"We don't need a warrant. This is a field investigation, and your friend here invited us in," Brown said. "Why? What've you got to hide?"

"Is this an Article Two-Twenty?" she asked.

"You both seem pretty familiar with Article Two-Twenty," Brown said.

"Yeah, well, live and learn," the girl said, shrugging.

"What's your name?" Kling said.

She looked at Fleet again. Fleet nodded.

"Corrine," she said.

"Corrine what?"

"Johnson."

The dawn broke slowly. It illuminated first Brown's face and then Kling's.

"Johnny, is it?" Brown asked.

"Yeah, Johnny," the girl said.

"Is that what you call yourself?"

"If *your* name was Corrine, would *you* call yourself Corrine?"

"How old are you, Johnny?"

"Twenty-one," she said.

"Try again," Kling said.

"Eighteen, okay?"

"Is it sixteen?" Brown said. "Or even younger?"

"Old enough," Johnny said.

"For what?" Brown asked.

"For anything I've got to do."

"How long have you been on the street?" Kling asked.

"I don't know what you're talking about."

"You're a hooker, aren't you, Johnny?" Brown asked.

"Who says?"

Her eyes had turned to ice as opaque as that on the window. Her hands were in the pockets of the ski parka now. Both Kling and Brown were willing to bet her unseen fists were clenched.

"Where were you last Saturday night?" Kling asked.

"Johnny, they—"

"Shut up, Andrew!" Brown said. "Where were you, miss?"

"*When* did you say?"

"Johnny—"

"I told you to shut *up!*" Brown said.

"Last Saturday night. Two a.m.," Kling said.

"Here," the girl said.

"Doing what?"

"Shooting up."

"How come? Was it slow on the street?"

"The *snow*," Johnny said angrily. "Keeping all the johns in they own beds."

"What time did you get here?" Brown asked.

"I *live* here, man," she said.

"Thought you lived here alone, Andrew," Kling said.

"Yeah, well, I didn't want to get anybody else in trouble, you know, man?"

"So you were here all night, huh?" Brown said.

"I didn't say that," the girl answered. "I went out around . . . what was it, Andy?"

"Never mind Andy. *You* tell us."

"Ten o'clock, musta been. Usually that's when the action starts. Damn streets was empty as a hooker's heart."

"When did you get back?"

"Around midnight. We started partying around midnight, wasn't it, Andy?"

Fleet was about to answer, but Brown's stare silenced him.

"And you were here from midnight till two?" Kling asked.

"I was here from midnight till the next *morning*. I told you, man, I *live* here."

"Did Andrew leave the apartment at any time that night?"

"No, *sir*," Johnny said.

"No, *sir*," Fleet repeated, nodding emphatically.

"Where'd you go the next morning?"

"Out. See if I could score."

"What time?"

"Early. Around eleven o'clock, I guess it was."

"*Did* you score?"

"Snow's hinderin' the traffic," she said. She was not talking about automobile traffic. "You get your junk comin' up from Florida, minute they hit North Carolina, they're ass-deep in snow. I tell you two things it don't pay to be in this weather, man. One's a hooker, the other's a junkie."

Brown could think of a lot of other things it didn't pay to be in this weather.

"Bert?" he said.

Kling looked at the two kids.

Then he said, "Yeah, let's go."

They walked down to the street in silence. The two old men were still standing around the gasoline drum, trying to warm themselves. When Kling started the car, the heater began rattling and clanging.

"They look clean, don't you think?" Brown asked.

"Yeah," Kling said.

"Didn't even know the man's *name*," Brown said.

They drove downtown in silence. As they were approaching the station house, Brown said, "It's a goddamn crying shame," and Kling knew he wasn't talking about the fact that they'd come up blank on the Edelman killing.

TEN

THE superintendent of Sally Anderson's building had been pestered by cops ever since her murder, and now there was a monk to contend with. The super was not a religious man, he did not give a damn about heaven *or* hell, and he did not feel like cooperating with a monk while he was sprinkling rock salt on the pavement outside the building, trying to melt the sheet of ice there.

"What's she got to do with you?" he asked Brother Anthony.

"She ordered a Bible," Brother Anthony said.

"A what?"

"A Bible. From the Order of Fraternal Pietists," he said, figuring that sounded very holy.

"So?"

"I am of that order," Brother Anthony said solemnly.

"So?"

"I would like to deliver her Bible. I've been upstairs to the apartment listed in her mailbox, and there's no answer. I was wondering if you could tell me—"

"You bet there's no answer," the super said.

"That's right," Brother Anthony said.

"Ain't *never* gonna be no answer up there," the super said. "Not from *her*, anyway."

"Oh?" Brother Anthony said. "Has Miss Anderson moved?"

"You mean you're not in touch?"

"In touch?"

"With God?"

"With God?"

"You mean God doesn't send down daily bulletins?"

"I'm not following you, sir," Brother Anthony said.

"Doesn't God have a list he sends down to you guys? Telling you who expired and where she was sent?" the super said, flinging rock salt onto the sidewalk with atheistic zeal. "Whether it was heaven or hell or in between?"

Brother Anthony looked at him.

"Sally Anderson is dead," the super said.

"I'm sorry to hear that," Brother Anthony said. *"Dominus vobiscum."*

"Et cum spiritu tuo," the super said; he had been raised as a Catholic.

"May God have mercy on her eternal soul," Brother Anthony said. "When did she die?"

"Last Friday night."

"What was the cause of her death?"

"Three bullet holes was what was the cause of her death."

Brother Anthony's eyes opened wide.

"Right here on the sidewalk," the super said.

"Do the police know who did it?" Brother Anthony asked.

"The police don't know how to blow their noses," the super said. "Don't you read the papers? It's been all over the papers."

"I wasn't aware," Brother Anthony said.

"Too busy with your Latin, I suppose," the super said, hurling rock salt. "Your kyrie eleisons."

"Yes," Brother Anthony said. He had never heard those words before. They sounded good. He decided to use them in the future. Toss in a few kyrie eleisons with his *Dominus vobiscums. Et cum spiritu tuo. That* was a good one, too. And then it occurred to him that this was a remarkable coincidence here, Paco Lopez buying a couple of slugs on *Tuesday* night, and his supplier taking three of them on *Friday* night.

Suddenly, this did not seem like such small potatoes anymore. All at once, the two murders seemed like the kind of action the big-time spic drug dealers in this city were into. He wondered if he wanted to get involved in such goings-on. He certainly did not want to wake up dead in the trunk of an automobile in the parking lot at Spindrift Airport. Still, he sensed he had stumbled onto something that might just possibly net him and Emma some *really* big bucks. Provided they played it right. Provided they did their sniffing around without getting their feet wet. At first, anyway. Plenty of time to move in once they knew what was going on.

"What did she do for a living?" he asked the super, figuring if this Anderson girl had been into something big with Lopez, then maybe one or more of her business associates were into the same thing. It was someplace to start. Such remarkable coincidences didn't fall into his lap every day of the week.

"She was a dancer," the super said.

A dancer, Brother Anthony thought, visualizing somebody teaching the tango up at Arthur Murray's. Once, a long time ago, when he was married to a lady who ran a luncheonette upstate, she had convinced him to go with her to a dance studio. Not Arthur Murray's. Not Fred Astaire's, either. Something called—he couldn't remember. To learn the cha-cha; she'd been crazy about the cha-cha. Brother Anthony got an erection the first time he was alone in the room with his instructor, a pretty little brunette wearing a slinky gown, looked more like a hooker than a person supposed to teach him the cha-cha. The girl told him he was very light on his feet, which he already knew. He had his hands spread on her satiny little ass when his wife walked in and decided maybe they should stop taking cha-cha lessons. Step Lively, that had been the name of the place. That was a long time ago, before his wife met with the untimely accident that had cost him a year in Castleview on a bum manslaughter rap. All water under the bridge, Brother Anthony thought, kyrie eleison.

"In that big musical downtown," the super said.

"What do you mean?" Brother Anthony asked.

"*Fatback*," the super said.

Brother Anthony still didn't know what he meant.

"The show," the super said. "Downtown."

"Where downtown?" Brother Anthony asked.

"I don't know the name of the theater. Buy yourself a newspaper. Maybe they got one printed in Latin."

"God bless you," Brother Anthony said.

THE phone on Kling's desk began ringing just as he and Brown were leaving the squadroom. He leaned over the slatted rail divider and picked up the receiver.

"Kling," he said.

"Bert, it's Eileen."

"Oh, hi," he said. "I was going to call you later today."

"Did you find it?"

"Just where you said it was. Back seat of the car."

"You know how many earrings I've lost in the back seats of cars?" Eileen said.

Kling said nothing.

"Years ago, of course," she said.

Kling still said nothing.

"When I was a teenager," she said.

The silence lengthened.

"Well," she said, "I'm glad you found it."

"What do you want me to do with it?" Kling asked.

"I don't suppose you'll be coming down this way for anything, will you?"

"Well . . ."

"Court? Or the lab? D.A.'s Office? Anything like that?"

"No, but . . ."

She waited.

"Actually, I live down near the bridge," Kling said.

"The Calm's Point Bridge?"

"Yes."

"Oh, well, good! Do you know A View From the Bridge?"

"What?"

"It's *under* the bridge, actually, right on the Dix. A little wine bar."

"Oh."

"It's just . . . I don't want to take you out of your way."

"Well . . ."

"Does five sound okay?" Eileen asked.

"I was just leaving the office. I don't know what time—"

"It's just at the end of Lamb Street, under the bridge, right on the river. You can't miss it. Five o'clock, okay? My treat. It'll be a reward, sort of."

"Well—"

"Or have you made other plans?" Eileen asked.

"No. No other plans."

"Five o'clock, then?"

"Okay," he said.

"Good," she said, and hung up.

Kling had a bewildered look on his face.

"What was that?" Brown asked.

"Eileen's earring," Kling said.

"What?" Brown said.

"Forget it," Kling said.

BY THREE O'CLOCK THAT afternoon, they had been through Edelman's small second-floor office a total of three times—four times, if you counted the extra half hour they'd spent going through his desk again. Brown wanted to call it quits. Kling pointed out that they hadn't yet looked inside the safe. Brown mentioned that the safe was locked. Kling put in a call to the Safe, Loft & Truck Squad. A detective there told him they'd try to get somebody up there within the half hour. Brown lighted a cigarette, and they began going over the office yet another time.

The office was the first in the hallway at the top of the stairs, which probably accounted for the fact that Andrew Fleet had chosen it for his stickup last July, a junkie robber being interested only in expediency and opportunity. A frosted-glass panel on the front door was lettered in gold leaf with the words EDELMAN BROS. and beneath that PRECIOUS GEMS. Mrs. Edelman had told them her husband worked alone, so both Brown and Kling figured the firm had been named when there *was* a brother-partner, and that either the brother was now dead or else no longer active in the business. They each made a note, in their separate pads, to call Mrs. Edelman and check on this.

Just inside the entrance doorway, there was a space some four feet wide, leading to a chest-high counter behind which was a grille fashioned of the same steel mesh as that on the squadroom's detention cage. A glass-paneled door covered with the same protective mesh was to the left of the counter. A button on the *other* side of the counter, when pressed, released the lock on the door to the inner office. But the mesh, somewhat like what you might find in a Cyclone fence around a school playground, could not have prevented an intruder from sticking a gun through any one of its diamond-shaped openings and demanding that the release button for the door be pressed. Presumably, this was what had happened on that night last July. Andrew Fleet had barged into the office, pointed his gun at Edelman, and ordered him to unlock the door. The steel mesh grille had been as helpful as a bathing suit in a blizzard.

The office side of the dividing counter resembled an apothecary chest, with dozens of little drawers set into it, each of them labeled with the names of the gems they presumably contained. No one had been in this office since the night of Edelman's murder, but the drawers were surprisingly empty, which led both Kling and Brown to assume that Edelman had locked his stuff in the safe before heading home that night. The men were both wearing cotton gloves as they went through the office. It was unlikely that the murderer had been here before heading uptown to ambush Edelman in the garage under his building, but the Crime Unit boys had not yet been through the place, and they weren't taking any chances. If they found a residue of anything that even remotely resembled cocaine, they would place a call downtown at once. They were working this by the book. You didn't summon the harried Crime Unit to a place that *wasn't* the scene of the crime unless you had damn good reason to suspect this other place was somehow *linked* to the crime. They had no reason to suspect that as yet.

The detective from Safe, Loft & Truck arrived forty minutes later, which wasn't bad considering the condition of the roads. He was wearing a sheepskin car coat, a cap with earflaps, fleece-lined gloves, heavy woolen trousers, a turtleneck shirt, and black rubbers. He was also carrying a black satchel. He put the satchel down on the floor, took off his gloves, rubbed his hands briskly together, said, "Some weather, huh?" and extended his right hand. "Turbo," he said, and shook hands first with Brown and then with Kling, who introduced themselves in turn.

Turbo reminded Brown of the pictures of Santa Claus in the illustrated version of "The Night Before Christmas," which he ritually read to his kid every Christmas Eve. Turbo didn't have a beard, but he was a roly-poly little man with bright red cheeks, no taller than Hal Willis, but at least a yard wider. He had retrieved his right hand and was again rubbing both hands briskly together. Brown figured he was going to try the combination, the way Jimmy Valentine might have.

"So where is it?" Turbo said.

"Right there in the corner," Kling said.

Turbo looked.

"I was hoping it'd be an old one," he said. "That box looks brand new."

He walked over to the safe.

"I coulda punched an old box in three seconds flat. This one's gonna take time."

He studied the safe.

"You know what I'm gonna find here, most likely?" he said. "A lead spindle shaft with the locknuts *away* from the shaft so I won't be able to pound it through the gut box and break the nuts that way."

Brown and Kling looked at each other. Turbo sounded as if he were speaking a foreign language.

"Well, let's see," Turbo said. "You think he may have left it on day combination, no such luck, huh?" He was reaching for the dial when his hand stopped. "The Crime Unit been in here?" he asked.

"No," Kling said.

"Is that why you're wearing the Mickey Mouse gloves?"

Both men looked at their hands. Neither of them had removed the cotton gloves when shaking hands with Turbo, a lack of etiquette he seemed not to have minded.

"What *is* this case, anyway?" he asked.

"Homicide," Kling said.

"And no Crime Unit?"

"He was killed uptown."

"So what's this, his place of business?"

"Right," Brown said.

"Whose authority do I have to open this thing?"

"It's our case," Kling said.

"So what does *that* mean?" Turbo asked.

"That's your authority," Brown said.

"Yeah? You go tell that to my lieutenant, that I busted open a safe on the authority of two flatfoots from the boonies," Turbo said, and went to the phone. Mindful of the fact that the Crime Unit hadn't yet been here, he opened his satchel, took out his *own* pair of white cotton gloves, and pulled them on. The three detectives now looked like waiters in a fancy restaurant. Brown expected one of them to start passing around the finger bowls. Turbo lifted the phone receiver, dialed a number, and waited.

"Yeah," he said, "Turbo here. Let me talk to the Loot." He waited again. "Mike," he said, "it's Dom. I'm here on North Greenfield. There's two guys from uptown want me to open a safe for them." He looked at Kling and Brown. "What's your names again?" he asked.

"Kling," Kling said.

"Brown," Brown said.

"Kling and Brown," Turbo said into the phone, and listened again. "What precinct?" he asked them.

"The Eight-Seven," Kling said.

"The Eight-Seven," Turbo said into the phone. "A homicide. No, this is the guy's place of business, the victim's. So what should I do? Uh-huh. Uh-huh. I just want my ass covered, you understand, Mike? 'Cause next thing you know, I'll be doing time on a Burglary Three rap." He listened. "*What* release form? Who's got a release form? Well, no, I *don't*. So what should it say? Uh-huh. Uh-huh. You want both of them to sign it, or what? Uh-huh. Uh-huh. And that'll do it, huh? Okay, Mike, you're the boss. I'll see you later," he said, and hung up. "I need a release from you guys," he said. "Authorizing me to open that thing. One signature'll do it, whoever caught the squeal. I'll give you the language."

He dictated the words to Kling, who wrote them down in his pad and then signed the page.

"Date it, please," Turbo said.

Kling dated it.

"And you'd better let me have your rank and shield number, too."

Kling scribbled his rank and shield number under his signature.

"I'm sorry to get so technical," Turbo said, pocketing the sheet of paper Kling tore from his pad, "but if there's anything of value in that safe, and it happens to disappear . . ."

"Right, you're just covering your ass," Brown said.

"Right," Turbo said, and shot him a glare. "So let's see if this guy left it on day comb." He went to the safe again. "Lots of guys who are in and out of a box all day long, they'll just give the dial a tiny little twist when they close it, you know? Then all they have to do is turn it back to the last number—saves a lot of time." He turned the dial slowly and yanked on the handle. "No such luck," he said. "Let's try the old five-ten."

The detectives looked at him.

"Lots of guys, they have trouble remembering numbers, so when they order a safe, they'll ask for the combination to be three numbers in a multiplication table. Like five, ten, fifteen. Or four, eight, twelve. Or six, twelve, eighteen, or whatever. Hardly ever the *nine* table. That's a bitch, the nine table. What's nine times three?" he asked Kling.

"Twenty-seven," Kling said.

"Yeah, well, that's the exception that proves the rule. So let's give it a shot."

As he began trying the multiplication-table combinations, he said, "Would you know this guy's birthday?"

"No," Brown said.

" 'Cause sometimes they use their birthdays, you know, anything to make it easy to remember. Like if he was born on October 15, 1926, the combination would be ten left, fifteen right, and then twenty-six left again. But you don't know his birthday, huh?"

"No," Brown said.

"Take a look at the phone there. What's the number on it?"

"What?" Brown said.

"The *phone*. The phone I just *used* there. On the guy's *desk*. What's the first six digits? Sometimes they'll use the first six digits of their phone number."

"You want me to write this down, or what?" Brown asked.

"Yeah, write it down. I'm still only up to the six table. I usually only take it to eleven, because after that the tables get too tricky. Who the hell even *knows* what fourteen times three is?" he said.

"Forty-two," Kling said, and Turbo gave him a sour look.

"Okay, give me that phone number," he said.

Brown handed him the slip of paper on which he'd written down the first six digits of the number. Turbo tried them.

"No such luck," he said. "Okay, let's bring up the heavy artillery." He opened his satchel and took from it a small sledgehammer and a punch. "Best burglars in this city are on the Safe, Loft & Truck Squad," he said proudly, and with one swift blow knocked off the combination dial. "Looks like a lead spindle," he said. "We'll find out in a minute." He began pounding on the exposed spindle. The spindle started mushrooming under the hammer blows. "Lead, sure as hell," he said. "This here is what you call a money box here. That means it's made of heavy steel layers, with a punch-resistant spindle, and sometimes a boltwork relock device, or even a copper sheet in the door so an acetylene torch on it don't mean nothing. If I'da known what this was gonna be, I'da brought nitro." He smiled suddenly. "I'm kidding. Your best burglars these days hardly *ever* use explosives. What I got to do here is I got to peel back the steel until I can get a big enough hole to force a jimmy in. Once I get to that lock, I can pry it loose and open the door. Make yourselves comfortable. This may take a while."

Kling looked up at the clock. It was ten minutes past four, and he had promised Eileen he'd meet her at five. He debated calling her, decided not to.

"Can we get a little light in here?" Turbo asked. "Or were you partners with this dead guy?"

Brown flicked on the wall switch.

Turbo got to work.

He opened the box in twenty minutes. He was obviously very pleased with himself, and so both Brown and Kling congratulated him effusively before getting down on their hands and knees to see what was inside there.

There were not very many gems in the safe. Several pouches of rubies, emeralds, and sapphires, and one small pouch of diamonds. But on a shelf at the rear of the safe, stacked neatly there, the detectives found $300,000 in hundred-dollar bills.

"We're in the wrong business," Turbo told them.

DETECTIVE Richard Genero had been very leery about answering the telephone ever since he'd inadvertently yelled at a captain from downtown two days ago. You never knew who was going to be on the other end. That was the mystery of the telephone. There were other mysteries in life as well, which was why his mother constantly advised him to "mind his own business," a warning that seemed absurd when directed to a policeman, whose business *was* minding other people's business. When the telephone on Carella's desk rang at four-thirty that Tuesday afternoon, Genero debated answering it. Carella was at the other end of the squadroom, putting on his coat, preparatory to leaving. Suppose this was that captain again? Carella and the captain seemed to be good friends. Carella had laughed a lot when he was talking to the captain on the telephone. Suppose the captain yelled at Genero again? The phone kept ringing.

"Will somebody please pick that *up?*" Carella shouted from across the room, where he was buttoning his coat.

Since Genero was the only other person in the room, he picked up the receiver, very gingerly, and held it a little distance from his ear, in case the captain started yelling again. "Hello?" he said, not wanting to give his name in case this was the captain again.

"Detective Carella, please," the voice on the other end said.

"Who's this, please?" Genero asked very carefully.

"Tell him it's Danny," the voice said.

"Yes, sir," Genero said, not knowing whether or not Danny was the same captain who'd called on Sunday or perhaps even *another* captain. "Steve!" he yelled. "It's Danny."

Carella came across the room to his desk. "Why does it always ring when I'm on my way out?" he said.

"That's the mystery of the telephone," Genero said, and smiled like an angel. Carella took the receiver from him. Genero went back to his own desk, where he was working on a crossword puzzle and having trouble with a three-letter word that meant feline.

"Hello, Danny," Carella said.

"Steve? I hope this ain't an inconvenient time."

"No, no. What've you got?"

Meyer came up the corridor from the men's room, zipping up his fly. He pushed his way through the gate in the slatted rail divider and went to the coatrack. The woolen hat his wife had knitted for him was in the right-hand pocket of his coat. He debated putting it on. Instead, he took his blue fedora from the rack, seated it on his bald head, shrugged into his coat, and walked to where Carella was on the phone.

"What do you mean, 'interesting'?" Carella said.

"Well, I thought I might be able to talk to this chick who

wouldn't give you the right time, you know the one I mean?" Danny said.

"The Quadrado girl, yes."

"Right. The one who used to live with Lopez. Give her a song and dance, tell her I was looking to buy some dope, whatever. Just to get her talking, you know what I mean?"

"So what was so interesting, Danny?"

"Well . . . you probably know this already, Steve, but maybe you don't."

"What is it, Danny?" Carella said, and looked at Meyer and shrugged. Meyer shrugged back.

"She was cut to ribbons Sunday night."

"What?"

"Yeah. She died at Saint Juke's yesterday morning, around eleven o'clock."

"Who told you this?"

"The lady who lives next door to her."

"Danny . . . are you *sure?*"

"I always check at the source, Steve. I called Saint Juke's the minute I left the building. She's dead, all right. They're still waiting for somebody to come claim the body. Has she got any relatives?"

"A cousin," Carella said blankly.

"Yeah," Danny said, and paused. "Steve . . . you still want me to look for a thirty-eight? I mean . . . the lady was *cut*, Steve."

"Yes, please keep looking, Danny," Carella said. "Thanks. Thanks a lot."

"See you," Danny said, and hung up. Carella held the receiver a moment before replacing it on the cradle.

"What?" Meyer said.

Carella took a deep breath. He shook his head. Still wearing his overcoat, he walked to the lieutenant's door and knocked on it.

"Come!" Byrnes shouted.

Carella took another deep breath.

THE ceiling of A View From the Bridge was adorned with wineglasses, the foot of each glass captured between narrow wooden slats, the stem and bowl hanging downward to create an overall impression of a vast, wall-to-wall chandelier glistening with reflected light from the fireplace on one wall of the room. The fireplace wall was made of brick, and the surrounding walls were wood-paneled except for the one facing the river, a wide expanse of glass through which Kling could see the water beyond and the tugboats moving slowly through the rapidly gathering dusk. It was 5:30 p.m. by the clock over the bar facing the entrance doorway. He had made it downtown as quickly as possible, leaving Brown to contact the lieutenant with the startling news that Edelman's safe had contained three hundred thousand smackeroos.

The wine bar at this hour was crowded with men and women who, presumably, worked in the myriad courthouses, municipal buildings, law offices, and brokerage firms that housed the judicial, economic, legal, and governmental power structure in this oldest part of the city. There was a pleasant conversational hum in the place, punctuated by relaxed laughter, a coziness encouraged by the blazing fire and the flickering glow of candles in ruby-red holders on each of the round tables. Kling had never been to England, but he suspected that a pub in London might have looked and sounded exactly like this at the end of a long working day. He recognized an assistant D.A. he knew, said hello to him, and then looked for Eileen.

She was sitting at a table by the window, staring out over the river. The candle in its ruby holder cast flickering highlights into her hair, red reflecting red. Her chin was resting on the cupped palm of her hand. She looked pensive and contained, and for a moment he debated intruding on whatever mood she was sharing with the dark waters of the river beyond. He took off his coat, hung it on a wall rack just inside the door, and then moved across the room to where she was sitting. She turned away from the river as he moved toward her, as though sensing his approach.

"Hi," he said. "I'm sorry I'm late. We ran into something."

"I just got here myself," she said.

He pulled out the chair opposite her.

"So," she said. "You found it."

"Right where you said it'd be." He reached into his jacket pocket. "Let me give it to you before it gets lost again," he said, and placed the shining circle of gold on the table between them. He noticed all at once that she was wearing the mate to it on her right ear. He watched as she lifted the earring from the table, reached up with her left hand to pull down the lobe of her left ear, and crossed her right hand over her body to fasten the earring. The gesture reminded him suddenly and painfully of the numberless times he had watched Augusta putting on or taking off earrings, the peculiarly female tilt of her head, her hair falling in an auburn cascade. Augusta had pierced ears; Eileen's earrings were clip-ons.

"So," she said, and smiled, and then suddenly looked at him with something like embarrassment on her face, as though she'd been caught in an intimate act when she thought she'd been unobserved. The smile faltered for an instant. She looked quickly across the room to where the waiter was taking an order at another table. "What do you prefer?" she asked. "White or red?"

"White'll be fine," he said. "But listen, *I* want to pay for this. There's no need—"

"Absolutely out of the question," she said. "After all the trouble I put you to?"

"It was no trouble at—"

"No way," she said, and signaled to the waiter.

Kling fell silent. She looked across at him, studying his face, a policewoman suddenly alerted to something odd.

"This really *does* bother you, doesn't it?" she said.

"No, no."

"My paying, I mean."

"Well . . . no," he said, but he meant yes. One of the things that had been *most* troubling about his marriage was the fact that Augusta's exorbitant salary had paid for most of the luxuries they'd enjoyed.

The waiter was standing by the table now, the wine list in his hand. Clued by the fact that she was the one who'd signaled him, and no longer surprised by women who did the ordering and picked up the tab, he extended the leather-covered folder to her. "Yes, miss?" he said.

"I believe the gentleman would like to do the ordering," Eileen said. Kling looked at her. "He'll want the check, too," she added.

"Whatever turns you on," the waiter said, and handed the list to Kling.

"I'm not so good at this," he said.

"Neither am I," she said.

"Were you thinking of a white or a red?" the waiter asked.

"A white," Kling said.

"A *dry* white?"

"Well . . . sure."

"May I suggest the Pouilly-Fumé, sir? It's a nice dry white with a somewhat smoky taste."

"Eileen?"

"Yes, that sounds fine," she said.

"Yes, the . . . uh . . . Pooey Foo May, please," Kling said, and handed the wine list back as if it had caught fire in his hands. "Sounds like a Chinese dish," he said to Eileen as the waiter walked off.

"Did you see the French movie . . . It's a classic," she said. "I forget the title. With Gerard Philippe and . . . Michelle Morgan, I think. She's an older woman, and he's a very young man, and he takes her to a fancy French restaurant—"

"No, I don't think so," Kling said.

"Anyway, he's trying to impress her, you know, and when the wine steward brings the wine he ordered and pours a little into his glass to taste it, he takes a little sip—she's watching him all the while, and the steward is watching him, too—and he rolls it around on his tongue and says, 'This wine tastes of cork.' The wine steward looks at him—they're all supposed to be such bastards, you know, French waiters—and he pours a little of the wine into his little silver tasting cup, whatever they call it, and *he* takes a sip and rolls it around in his mouth, and everybody in the place is watching them because they know they're lovers, and there's nothing in the world a Frenchman likes better than a lover. And finally the steward nods very solemnly and says, 'Monsieur is correct—this wine *does* taste of cork,' and he goes away to get a fresh bottle, and Gerard Philippe smiles, and Michelle Morgan smiles, and everybody in the entire place smiles."

Eileen was smiling now.

"It was a very lovely scene," she said.

"I don't much care for foreign movies," Kling said. "I mean, the ones with subtitles."

"This one had subtitles," Eileen said. "But it was beautiful."

"That scene *did* sound very good," Kling said.

"*Le Diable au Corps*, that was it."

Kling looked at her, puzzled.

"The title," she said. "It means 'Devil in the Flesh.' "

"That's a good title," Kling said.

"Yes," Eileen said.

"The Pouilly-Fumé," the waiter said, and pulled the cork. He wiped the lip of the bottle with his towel and then poured a little wine into Kling's glass. Kling looked at Eileen, lifted the glass, brought it to his lips, sipped at the wine, rolled the wine around in his mouth, raised his eyebrows, and said, "This wine tastes of cork."

Eileen burst out laughing.

"Cork?" the waiter said.

"I'm joking," Kling said. "It's really fine."

"Because, *really*, if it's—"

"No, no, it's fine, really."

Eileen was still laughing. The waiter frowned at her as he poured the wine into her glass and then filled Kling's. He was still frowning when he walked away from the table. They raised their glasses.

"Here's to golden days and purple nights," Eileen said, and clinked her glass against his.

"Cheers," he said.

"My uncle Matt always used to say that," Eileen said. "He drank like a fish." She brought the glass to her lips. "Be funny if it *really* tasted of cork, wouldn't it?" she said, and then sipped at the wine.

"*Does* it?" Kling asked.

"No, no, it's very good. Try it," she said. "For *real* this time."

He drank.

"Good?" she said.

"Yes," he said.

"Actually, it was Micheline Presle, I think," she said. "The heroine."

They sat silently for several moments. Out on the river, a tugboat hooted into the night.

"So," she said, "what are you working on?"

"That homicide we caught when you were up there Saturday night."

"How does it look?"

"Puzzling," Kling said.

"That's what makes them interesting," Eileen said.

"I suppose."

"*My* stuff is hardly ever puzzling. I'm always the bait for some lunatic out there, hoping he'll take the hook."

"I wouldn't want to be in your shoes," Kling said.

"It does get scary every now and then."

"I'll bet."

"So listen, who asked me to become a cop, right?"

"How'd you happen to get into it?"

"Uncle Matt. He of the golden days and purple nights, the big drinker. He was a cop. I loved him to death, so I figured *I'd* become a cop, too. He worked out of the old Hundred and Tenth in Riverhead. That is, till he caught it one night in a bar brawl. He wasn't even on duty. Just sitting there drinking his sour mash bourbon when some guy came in with a sawed-off shotgun and a red plaid kerchief over his face. Uncle Matt went for his service revolver, and the guy shot him dead." Eileen paused. "The guy got fifty-two dollars and thirty-six cents from the cash register. He also got away clean. I keep hoping I'll run into him one day. Sawed-off shotgun and red plaid kerchief. I'll blow him away without batting an eyelash."

She batted both eyelashes now.

"Tough talk on the lady, huh?" she said, and smiled. "So how about *you?*" she said. "How'd *you* get into it?"

"Seemed like the right thing to do at the time," he said, and shrugged.

"How about now? Does it *still* seem like the right thing?"

"I guess so." He shrugged again. "You get sort of . . . it wears you down, you know."

"Mm," she said.

"Everything out there," he said, and fell silent.

They sipped some more wine.

"What are *you* working on?" he asked.

"Thursday," she said. "I won't start till Thursday night."

"And what's that?"

"Some guy's been raping nurses outside Worth Memorial. On their way to the subway, when they're crossing that park outside the hospital. Do you know the park? In Chinatown?"

"Yes," Kling said, and nodded.

"Pretty big park for that part of the city. He hits the ones coming off the four-to-midnight, three of them in the past three months, always when there's no moon."

"I gather there'll be no moon this Thursday night."

"No moon at all," she said. "Don't you just *love* that song?"

"What song?"

" 'No Moon at All.' "

"I don't know it," Kling said. "I'm sorry."

"Well, this certainly isn't the 'We-Both-Like-the-Same-Things' scene, is it?"

"I don't know what scene that is," Kling said.

"In the movies. What's your favorite color? Yellow. Mine, too! What's your favorite flower? Geraniums. Mine, too! Gee, we both like the same things!" She laughed again.

"Well, at least we both like the *wine*," Kling said, and smiled, and poured her glass full again. "Will you be dressed like a nurse?" he asked.

"Oh, sure. Do you think that's sexy?"

"What?"

"Nurses. Their uniforms, I mean."

"I've never thought about it."

"Lots of men have things for nurses, you know. I guess it's because they figure they've seen it all, nurses. Guys lying around naked on operating tables and so forth. They figure nurses are experienced."

"Mm," Kling said.

"Somebody once told me—this man I used to date, he was an

editor at a paperback house—he told me if you put the word *nurse* in a title, you're guaranteed a million-copy sale."

"Is that true?"

"It's what he told me."

"I guess he would know."

"But nurses don't turn you on, huh?"

"I didn't say that."

"I'll have to show you what I look like," Eileen said. Her eyes met his. "In my nurse's outfit."

Kling said nothing.

"It must have something to do with white, too," Eileen said. "The fact that a nurse's uniform is white. Like a bride's gown, don't you think?"

"Maybe," Kling said.

"The conflicting image, do you know? The *experienced* virgin. Not that too many brides today are virgins," she said, and shrugged. "Nobody would even *expect* that today, would they? A man, I mean. That his bride's going to be a virgin?"

"I guess not," Kling said.

"You've never been married, have you?" she said.

"I've been married," he said.

"I didn't know that."

"Yes," he said.

"And?"

Kling hesitated.

"I was recently divorced," he said.

"I'm sorry," she said.

"Well," he said, and lifted his wineglass, avoiding her steady gaze. "How about you?" he said. He was looking out over the river now.

"Still hoping for Mr. Right," she said. "I keep having this fantasy . . . Well, I really shouldn't tell you this."

"No, go ahead," he said, turning back to her.

"Well . . . really, it's *silly*," she said, and he could swear that she was blushing, but perhaps it was only the red glow of the candle in its holder. "I keep fantasizing that one of those rapists out there will *succeed* one night, do you know? I won't be able to get my gun on him in time, he'll do whatever he *wants*, and—*surprise*—he'll turn out to be Prince *Charming!* I'll fall madly in love with him, and we'll live happily ever after. Whatever you do, don't tell that to Betty Friedan or Gloria Steinem. I'll get drummed out of the women's movement."

"The old rape fantasy," Kling said.

"Except that I happen to deal with *real* rape," Eileen said. "And I know it isn't fun and games."

"Mm," Kling said.

"So why should I fantasize about it? I mean, I've come within a *hairs*breadth so *many* times . . ."

"Maybe that's what accounts for the fantasy," Kling said. "The fantasy makes it seem less frightening. Your work. What you have to do. Maybe," he said, and shrugged.

"We've just had our 'I-Don't-Know-Why-I'm-Telling-You-All-This' scene, haven't we?"

"I suppose so," he said, and smiled.

"Somebody ought to write a book about all the different kinds of clichéd scenes," she said. "The one I like best, I think, is when the killer has a gun on the guy who's been chasing him, and he says something like, 'It's safe to tell you this now because in three seconds flat you'll be dead,' and then proceeds to brag about all the people he killed and how and why he killed them."

"I wish it was that easy," Kling said, still smiling.

"Or what I call the '*Uh*-oh!' scene. Where we see a wife in bed with her lover, and then we cut away to the husband putting his key in the door latch, and we're all supposed to go, '*Uh*-oh, here it comes!' Don't you just *love* that scene?"

The smile dropped from his face.

She looked into his eyes, trying to read them, knowing she'd somehow made a dreadful mistake and trying to understand what she'd said that had been so terribly wrong. Until that moment, they'd seemed—

"I'd better get the check," he said.

She knew better than to press it. If there was one thing she'd learned as a decoy, it was patience.

"Sure," she said. "I've got to run, too. Hey, thanks for bringing the earring back, really. I appreciate it."

"No problem," Kling said, but he wasn't looking at her. He was signaling to the waiter instead.

They sat in silence while they waited for the check. When they left the place, they shook hands politely on the sidewalk outside and walked off in opposite directions.

"I HATE scenes that are played offstage," Meyer said.

"So why didn't you come in there *with* me?" Carella said.

"It was bad enough listening to him yell from outside," Meyer said. "You want to tell me what it was all about?"

They were sitting side by side in the front seat of one of the precinct's newest sedans. Each time they checked out the car, Sergeant Murchison came out back to list any scratches or dents on it. That way he would know who was responsible for any *new* scratches or dents. The car was cozy and warm. The rear tires were snow tires with studs. Hawes and Willis, who had last used the car, said that it actually ran on *ice*. Carella and Meyer— heading downtown for Timothy Moore's apartment—were having no difficulties on the city's frozen tundra.

"So let me hear it," Meyer said.

"Very simple," Carella said. "Paco Lopez's girlfriend was stabbed Sunday night."

"What!"

"Died yesterday morning at Saint Jude's."

"Where'd this happen?" Meyer asked.

"That's just it. Charlie Car found her outside her building on Ainsley Avenue. It's all on the activity-report spindle, Meyer. A Ten-Twenty-four described as a cutting, victim taken to Saint Jude's."

"Who was catching Sunday night?"

"That's not the point. The blues didn't find her till Monday *morning*. The graveyard shift had already been relieved—this was the eight-to-four."

"That's when *we* were catching!" Meyer said.

"You're beginning to get the message."

"So why the hell didn't the blues call it in?"

"They did."

"Then why didn't *we* get it?"

"Officer's discretion," Carella said. "Charlie Car called for a meat wagon and then accompanied it to the hospital. The girl was still alive when they delivered her. That's the way it appears on the activity report they wrote up at the end of their tour."

"At four o'*clock*, you mean? What time did the girl *die?*"

"Around eleven."

"Is *that* on an activity report, too?"

"How could it be? I found out from Danny Gimp."

"Great! A snitch pulling together the pieces!"

"Exactly Pete's words."

"So what now?"

"Now we ask Timothy Moore about the 'extra' cash his girl-friend was making."

"I mean, what about the Quadrado girl?"

"She was *cut*, Meyer. Does that sound like the same M.O. to you?"

"Maybe the guy's running out of bullets."

"Maybe. Or maybe this was just another one of the hundred cuttings we get every day of the week. I want to talk to her cousin later, the kid who first put us onto her when we caught the Lopez murder. Maybe *he'll* know something."

"If this is related to cocaine . . ."

"It might be."

"Then it's starting to look like gang shit," Meyer said. "And gang shit, I can do without."

"Let's talk to Moore," Carella said.

WELL, they knew it was a big city. And in a big city, mistakes were bound to occur. Chances were that even if they'd known of Judite Quadrado's condition *before* she'd died, the girl might not have been able to tell them anything of value in cracking their case—or *cases* as the case happened to be. Knowing about her in time to have questioned her, and perhaps to have elicited a deathbed statement, might have proved a pointless exercise, anyway. Even in a big city, though, it was nice to know things.

Carella was very happy, for example, to have learned from Lieutenant Byrnes (between his readings of the Riot Act) that Brown and Kling had found $300,000 in hundred-dollar bills in the safe of Marvin Edelman, the last—or at least the most *recent;* they *hoped* he'd prove to be the last—of the murder victims killed with the same .38 Smith & Wesson revolver. The presence of such a large bundle might have been attributed, of course, to the very nature of the man's business: a precious-gems merchant did not normally accept subway tokens in exchange for his commodity. But why such an *awesome* amount of money had been kept in his office safe, instead of in a bank account or even a bank's safety-deposit box, was something that troubled the detectives. It might not have troubled them so much if Edelman's fellow victims hadn't been involved, in one way or another, with cocaine. When cocaine was on the scene, big bucks were mandatory. And the bucks in Edelman's safe were very big indeed.

In street parlance over the years, cocaine had been known

under various names: C, coke, snow, happy dust, sleigh ride, gold dust, Bernice, Corrine, girl, flake, star dust, blow, white lady, and—of course—nose candy. When combined with heroin, it was called a speedball, although the street jargon for this combination had recently changed to "Belushi cocktail." Whatever you chose to call it, cocaine was a headache. Up in the Eight-Seven, the heroin dealers had taken to giving their wares "brand" names. You bought your little glassine bag, and it came with a label pasted on it, and the label read Coolie High or Murder One or Rush or Jusey Whales or Quick Silver or Rope of Dope or Cousin Eddie or Bunny or Stay High or Crazy Eddie Shit or Good Pussy, hardly names that would ever be considered by General Foods. But since the people selling dope were criminals and since there truly *was* no honor among thieves, within hours after a reputable dealer's terrific stuff hit the street with a brand name like Devil, for example, or Prophecy or New Admissions, some slimy little pusher at the bottom of the ladder would be selling you a bag with the same brand name on it but with the heroin cut almost to nothing—a "beat bag," as it was known to addicts and dealers alike. But that was heroin.

Cocaine was something else.

The most recent federal report handed around the squadroom estimated that an approximate sixty metric tons of cocaine had been smuggled into the United States in the past year, at a wholesale value of fifty billion dollars.

Cocaine was fashionable.

That was the biggest problem with cocaine. You didn't *have* to be a raggedy-pantsed slum kid to snort a line. You could be running a big Hollywood studio, making multimillion-dollar decisions about the next movie you'd be foisting on an unsuspecting public, and that night you could sit around your Malibu beach house listening to the pounding of the surf and the pounding of your own head as you inhaled coke from the little gold spoon you wore on a slender gold chain under your custom-tailored silk shirt. In fact, if you wanted to start doing cocaine, it *helped* to be among the nation's biggest wage earners. Every working cop knew the mathematics of cocaine. Every working cop was also an expert on the metric system of weights and measures. To understand the economy, you had to know that an ounce of cocaine was the same thing as 28.3 grams, and a kilo was the equivalent of 35.2 ounces, or 2.2 pounds by avoirdupois measure. Your average Colombian coca farmer sold his leaves to a trafficker for about a dollar a pound—two bucks a kilo, give or take a penny. By the time this raw material was transformed into cocaine hydrochloride and then diluted again and again—"stepped on" or "whacked" or "hit"—and then sold in little packets about the size of the one you might find in a sugar bowl, a *gram* could cost you anywhere between a hundred and a hundred and twenty-five bucks, depending on the quality. The astronomical bucks to be realized in the cocaine trade were attributable to the extraordinary number of middlemen between the source and the consumer, and the ruthless dilution—all the way down the line—from a high of 90 to 98 percent pure in South America to a low of 12 percent pure on the city's streets.

Both Meyer and Carella had mixed feelings about a possible cocaine connection to the murders. On the one hand, they were eager to close out the Lopez/Anderson/Edelman (and possibly Quadrado) file. On the other hand, if the murders had anything to do with the South American gangsters who operated out of Majesta across the river, in a neighborhood dubbed Baby Bogotá by the police—well, they just weren't sure that was a can of peas they particularly cared to open. Organized crime wasn't their bag, and the Colombian underworld was perhaps something more than a pair of flatfoots from an undernourished precinct could cope with effectively. As they knocked on the door to Timothy Moore's second-floor apartment on Chelsea Place, they were hoping he *would* be able to tell them Sally Anderson was into some big-time drug dealing that was netting her the "extra" cash the black dancer Lonnie had hinted at—but they were *also* hoping the lead was a false one; better a bona fide crazy than a Colombian hit man.

There was music playing behind the door. Classical music. Lots of strings. Both of the detectives were musical ignoramuses; neither of them could identify it. The music was very loud. It flooded out past the wooden door and into the corridor. They knocked again.

"Hello!" a voice yelled.

"Police!" Carella yelled back.

"Okay, hold on!"

They held on. The music was all-pervasive, strings giving way to brasses and then to what Carella guessed was an oboe. Beneath the melodious din, he heard a lock being turned. The door opened. The music swelled more loudly into the hallway.

"Hey, hi," Timothy Moore said.

He was wearing a gray sweat shirt imprinted in purple with the name and seal of Ramsey University. He was also wearing brown corduroy trousers and frayed house slippers.

"Come on in," he said. "I just got home a few minutes ago."

Home appeared to be a three-room apartment: living room, bedroom, and kitchen. In this section of town, so close to the school, it was probably costing him something like six hundred dollars a month. The entrance door opened onto the small living room, furnished with a thrift-shop sofa, chairs, and lamp, and unpainted bookcases brimming with thick tomes Carella assumed were medical texts. A human skeleton hung on a rack in one corner of the room. On an end table near the battered sofa, a telephone rested alongside the portable radio that was blaring the symphony or concerto or sonata or whatever it was. The radio was one of those little Japanese jobs like Genero's, similar in every respect except one: Genero's was usually tuned to a rock station. Beyond the sofa, a door opened into a bedroom with an unmade bed. On the opposite wall, another door opened into the kitchen.

"Let me turn this down," Moore said, and went immediately to the radio. As he lowered the volume, Carella wondered why he simply didn't turn it *off.* He said nothing.

"There," Moore said.

The volume was still loud enough to make it annoying. Carella wondered if Moore was a little hard of hearing and then wondered if he wasn't overreacting. All Teddy had to learn was that he'd been annoyed by the listening habits of someone who might be a bit *deaf.*

"We didn't want to bother you at the school," he said over the sound coming from the radio. Clarinets now, he guessed. Or maybe flutes.

"I wonder if you could lower that a bit more," Meyer said, apparently unburdened by any guilt over hurting the feelings of the possibly handicapped.

"Oh, sorry," Moore said, and went immediately to the radio again. "I have it on all the time, I sometimes forget how loud it is."

"There've been studies," Meyer said.

"Studies?"

"About the rock-and-roll generation growing up deaf."

"Really?"

"Really," Meyer said. "From all the decibels."

"Well, I'm not deaf *yet,*" Moore said, and smiled. "Can I get you anything? Coffee? A drink?"

"Nothing, thanks," Carella said.

"Well, sit down, won't you? You said you tried me at the school—"

"No, we didn't want to *bother* you at the school."

"Well, thanks, I appreciate that. The way I'm falling behind these days, all I'd have needed was to be yanked out of class." He looked first at Carella and then at Meyer. "What is it? Is there some good news?"

"Well, no," Carella said. "That's not why we're here."

"Oh. I thought for a moment . . ."

"No, I'm sorry."

"Do you think . . . is there still a chance you may get him?"

"We're working on it," Carella said.

"Mr. Moore," Meyer said, "we had a long talk with a girl named Lonnie Cooper yesterday—she's one of the dancers in *Fatback*."

"Yes, I know her," Moore said.

"She told us all about the party that took place in her apartment a week ago Sunday—the party you missed."

"Yes?" Moore said, looking puzzled.

"She confirmed that there was cocaine at the party."

"Confirmed?"

"We had previously heard it from three separate sources."

"Yes?" Moore said. He still looked puzzled.

"Mr. Moore," Carella said, "the last time we spoke to you, we asked if Sally Anderson was involved with drugs. You told us—"

"Well, I really don't remember exactly what—"

"We asked you, specifically, 'Was she involved with drugs?' and you answered, specifically, no. We also asked if she was involved in any other illegal activity, and you answered no to that one, too."

"As far as I know, Sally was not involved in drugs or any other illegal activity, that's correct."

"You still maintain that?"

"I do."

"Mr. Moore, four different people so far have told us that Sally Anderson was sniffing coke at that party."

"Sally?" He was already shaking his head. "No, I'm sorry, I can't believe that."

"You knew nothing about her habit, huh?"

"Well, you know, of course, that cocaine isn't habit-forming. I'm speaking from a strictly physiological standpoint. There's absolutely no evidence of any dependence potential for methyl-ester of benzoylecgonine. None whatever."

"How about a *psychological* dependence?"

"Well, yes, but when you ask me whether or not Sally had a *habit*—"

"We asked whether you *knew* about her habit, Mr. Moore."

"I take exception to the word *habit*, that's all. But in any event, to answer your question, I do not believe Sally Anderson was using cocaine. Or any *other* drug, for that matter."

"How about marijuana?"

"Well, I don't consider that a drug."

"We found marijuana fibers and seeds in her handbag, Mr. Moore."

"That's entirely likely. But, as I just said, I do not consider marijuana a *drug*, per se."

"We also found a residue of cocaine."

"That surprises me."

"Even after what we told you about that party?"

"I don't know who told you Sally was sniffing cocaine—"

"Do you want their names?"

"Yes, please."

"Tina Wong, Tony Asensio, Mike Roldan, and Lonnie Cooper."

Moore sighed heavily and then shook his head. "I don't under-stand that," he said. "I have no reason to doubt you, but—"

"She never used cocaine in your presence, is that it?"

"Never."

"And this all comes as a total surprise to you."

"Yes, it does. In fact, I'm flabbergasted."

"Mr. Moore, in your relationship with Miss Anderson, did you ever see her on Sundays?"

"Sundays?" he said, and the telephone rang. "Excuse me," he said, and lifted the receiver. "Hello?" he said. "Oh, hi, Mom. How are you?" he said. He listened and then said, "No, nothing new. In fact, I have the two detectives with me right this minute. The ones working on the case. No, not yet." He listened again. "Still very cold," he said. "How is it down there? Well, Mom, sixty-eight isn't what I'd consider *cold.*" He listened, rolled his eyes toward the ceiling, and then said, "I'm really not sure. Right now, I'm in the middle of exams. Maybe during the spring break. I'll see. I know I haven't been down there in a while, Mom, but . . . well, August wasn't all that long ago, really. No, it *hasn't* been eight months, Mom. It's only been *six* months. *Less* than six months, in fact. Are you feeling okay? How's your arm? Oh? I'm sorry to hear that. You did, huh? Well, what did *he* say it was? Well, he's probably right. Mom, he's an orthopedist. He'd certainly know better than I what . . . Well, not yet, Mom. Well, thank you, but I'm not a doctor *yet.* Not for a *while* yet. An opinion from me wouldn't be worth much, Mom. Well . . . uh-huh . . . uh-huh . . . Well, if you want to think I saved that boy's life, fine. But that doesn't make me a doctor yet. And besides, anyone could have done what I did. The Heimlich maneuver. Heimlich. What difference does it make *how* you spell it, Mom?" He rolled his eyes again. "Mom, I *really* have to go now. I have these detectives . . . What? Yes, I'll tell them. I'm sure they're doing their best, anyway, but I'll tell them. Yes, Mom. I'll talk to you soon. Good-bye, Mom."

He put the phone back on the cradle, sighed in relief, turned to the detectives, and said unnecessarily, "My mother."

"Is she Jewish?" Meyer asked.

"Mother? No, no."

"She sounded Jewish," Meyer said, and shrugged. "Maybe *all* mothers are Jewish, who knows?"

"She gets lonely down there," Moore said. "Ever since my father died . . ."

"I'm sorry," Carella said.

"Well, it was a while ago. Last June, in fact. But they say it takes at least a year to get over either a death or a divorce, and she's still taking it pretty hard. Sally was a tonic for her, but now . . ." He shook his head. "It's just that she misses him so terribly much, you see. He was a wonderful man, my father. A doctor, you know. A surgeon, which is what I plan to be. Took care of us as if we were royalty. Even *after* he died. Made sure my mother wouldn't have to worry for the rest of her life, even left *me* enough money to see me through medical school and set up a practice afterward. A wonderful man." He shook his head again. "I'm sorry for the interruption," he said. "You were asking me . . ."

"What was that about the Heimlich maneuver?" Carella asked.

Moore smiled. "When I was down there last August, a kid began turning purple in a restaurant. Twelve-year-old Cuban kid, all dressed up for the big Sunday dinner with his family. I realized he was choking, and I jumped up and did the Heimlich on him. My mother thought I'd lost my mind, grabbing the kid from behind and—well, I'm sure you know the maneuver."

"Yes," Meyer said.

"Anyway, it helped him," Moore said modestly. "His parents were very grateful. You'd have thought I liberated Cuba single-handedly. And, of course, I've been a hero to my mother ever since."

"Her son the doctor," Meyer said.

"Yeah," Moore said. He was still smiling.

"So," Carella said.

"So, yeah, what were we talking about?"

"Sundays and Sally."

"Uh-huh."

"Did you ever see her on Sundays?"

"Occasionally. She was usually pretty busy on Sundays. Her day off, you know, no show that night."

"Busy doing what?"

"Oh, getting her errands done, mostly. Running here and there. We *saw* each other, of course, but only rarely. Did a little window-shopping together, went to the zoo every now and then, or the museum, like that. For the most part, Sally liked her privacy on Sundays. During the *day*time, anyway."

"Mr. Moore, did you ever go uptown with her? On the times you saw her, those Sundays you saw her, did you ever go uptown?"

"Well, sure. Uptown?"

"*All* the way uptown," Carella said. "Culver and Eighteenth."

"No," Moore said. "Never."

"Do you know where that is?"

"Sure."

"But you never went up there with Sally?"

"Why would I? That's one of the worst neighborhoods in the city."

"Did Sally ever go up there alone? On a Sunday?"

"She may have. Why? I don't under—"

"Because Lonnie Cooper told us that Sally went uptown every Sunday to pick up cocaine for herself and several other people in the show."

"Well, now we're back to cocaine again, aren't we? I've already told you that as far as I know, Sally wasn't involved with cocaine or any other drug."

"Except marijuana."

"Which I don't consider a drug," Moore said.

"But *definitely* not cocaine. Which you don't consider habit-forming."

"That's not *my* opinion, Mr. Carella. It happens to be . . . Look, what *is* this? Can you please tell me?"

"Did you know that Sally was supplying the cast with cocaine?"

"I did not."

"She kept this from you, did she?"

"I didn't think there were any secrets between us, but if she was engaged in . . . in this . . . illicit traffic or whatever you want to call it—"

"That's what we call it," Carella said.

"Then, yes, she kept it from me. I had no idea."

"How big a spender was she, Mr. Moore?"

"Pardon?"

"Did she ever seem to spend beyond her means?"

"Her means?"

"What she was earning as a dancer."

"Not that I noticed. She always dressed well, and I don't think she denied herself much . . . Mr. Carella, if you can tell me what you're *looking* for, perhaps—"

"Someone we talked to hinted at Sally earning extra cash. We're certain she was supplying cocaine in at least a limited way. We'd like to know if her activities in the drug market extended *beyond* that."

"I'm sorry. I wish I could help you with that, but I really didn't know until just now that she was in *any* way involved with drugs."

"Except marijuana," Carella said again.

"Well, yes."

"Can you think of any *other* way she might have been earning extra cash?"

"I'm sorry, no."

"She wasn't hooking, was she?" Meyer asked.

"Of course not!"

"You're sure about that?"

"Positive. We were very close. We spent virtually every *day* together. I'd certainly know—"

"But you *didn't* know about the coke."

"No, I didn't."

"Did she ever mention *any* kind of outside activity to you? Anything that might have been bringing in this extra cash?"

"I'm trying to remember," Moore said.

"Please," Carella said.

Moore was silent for what seemed like a very long time, thinking, his head bent. Then, suddenly, as if the idea had just occurred to him, he nodded and looked up at the detectives.

"Of course," he said. "I didn't realize what she was saying at the time, but of course, that has to be it."

"Has to be what?"

"How she was getting the extra cash you're talking about."

"How was she getting it?" Meyer said.

"What was she into?" Carella said.

"Ice," Moore said.

ELEVEN

THEY had not been able to reach Allan Carter the night before, and when they called his apartment early this morning, they learned that he had already left for his office. They considered the delay a stroke of good luck; it gave them time to do a little homework on the subject they planned to broach with the producer. The sky was clear, and the temperature was surprisingly mild on that Wednesday, February 17. This was bad news. If they knew this city, and they did, the springtime bonanza would be followed immediately by a howling blizzard; God gave with one hand and took away with the other. In the meantime, the snow and the ice were melting.

Carter's office was in a building a block north of the Stem, in Midtown East territory. The building was flanked by a Spanish restaurant on one side and a Jewish delicatessen on the other. A sign in the restaurant window read WE SPEAK ENGLISH HERE. A sign in the deli window read AQUI HABLA ESPAÑOL. Meyer wondered if the Spanish restaurant served blintzes. Carella wondered if the Jewish deli served tortillas. The building was an old one, with massive brass doors on the single elevator in the lobby.

A directory opposite the elevator told them that Carter Productions, Ltd., was in room 407. The elevator was self-service. They took it up to the fourth floor, searched for room 407, and found it in the middle of the corridor to the left of the elevator.

A girl with frizzied blond hair was sitting behind a desk immediately inside the entrance door. She was wearing a brown jump suit and she was chewing gum as she typed. She looked up from the machine, said, "Can I help you?" and picked up an eraser.

"We'd like to see Mr. Carter, please," Carella said.

"We're not auditioning till two o'clock," the girl said.

"We're not actors," Meyer said.

"Even so," the girl said, and erased a word on the sheet she'd typed and then blew at the paper.

"You should use that liquid stuff," Meyer said. "You use an eraser, it clogs the machine."

"The liquid stuff takes too long to dry," the girl said.

"We're from the police," Carella said, showing his shield. "Would you tell Mr. Carter that Detectives Meyer and Carella are here?"

"Why didn't you say so?" the girl said, and immediately picked up the phone. As she waited, she leaned over the desk to study the shield more carefully. "Mr. Carter," she said, "there's a Detective Meyer and Canella here to see you." She listened. "Yes, sir," she said. She put down the phone. "You can go right in," she said.

"It's Carella," Carella said.

"What did I say?" the girl asked.

"Canella."

The girl shrugged.

They opened the door to Carter's office. He was sitting behind a huge desk littered with what Carella assumed were scripts. Three walls of the office were covered with posters advertising his shows before *Fatback*, none of which Carella recognized. The fourth wall was a window wall streaming early-morning sunlight. Carter rose when they came into the room, indicated a sofa facing the desk, and said, "Sit down, won't you?" The detectives sat. Carella got straight to the point.

"Mr. Carter," he said, "what is ice?"

"Ice?"

"Yes, sir."

Carter smiled. "What water becomes when it freezes," he said. "Is this a riddle?"

"No riddle," Carella said. "You don't know what ice is, huh?"

"Oh," Carter said. "You mean *ice*."

"That's what I said."

"*Theater* ice, do you mean?"

"Theater ice," Carella said.

"Well, certainly, I know what ice is."

"So do we," Carella said. "Check us and see if we're right."

"I'm sorry, but what—"

"Bear with us, Mr. Carter," Carella said.

"I have an appointment at ten."

"That's fifteen minutes away," Meyer said, glancing up at the wall clock.

"We'll make it fast," Carella said. "First *we'll* talk, then *you'll* talk, okay?"

"Well, I really don't know what—"

"The way we understand this," Carella said, "ice is a common practice in the theater—"

"Not in *my* theater," Carter said.

"Be that as it may," Carella said, and went on as if he hadn't been interrupted. "A common practice that accounts for something like twenty million dollars a year in cash receipts unaccountable to either the tax man *or* a show's investors."

"That figure sounds high," Carter said.

"I'm talking citywide," Carella said.

"It still sounds high. Ice isn't practical unless a show is a tremendous hit."

"Like *Fatback*," Carella said.

"I hope you're not suggesting that anyone involved with *Fatback*—"

"Please listen, and tell me if I've got it right," Carella said.

"I'm sure you've got it right," Carter said. "You don't seem like the sort of man who'd come in unprepared."

"I simply want to make sure I understand it."

"Uh-huh," Carter said, and nodded skeptically.

"From what I can gather," Carella said, "a great many show business people have become rich on the proceeds of ice."

"There are stories to that effect, yes."

"And the way it works—please correct me if I'm wrong—is that someone in the box office puts aside a ticket, usually a *house* seat, Mr. Carter, and later sells it to a broker for a much higher price. Am I right so far?"

"That's my understanding of how ice works, yes," Carter said.

"The going price for a choice seat to *Fatback* is forty dollars," Carella said. "That was for sixth row center, the house seats you generously made available to me."

"Yeah," Carter said, and nodded sourly.

"How many house seats would you say are set aside for any performance of any given musical?" Carella asked.

"Are we talking about *Fatback* now?"

"Or *any* musical. Take *Fatback* as an example, if you want to."

"We've got about a hundred house seats set aside for each performance," Carter said.

"Who gets those house seats?"

"I get some of them as producer. The theater owner gets some. The creative people, the stars, some of the unusually big investors, and so on. I think we already discussed this once, didn't we?"

"I just want to get it straight," Carella said. "What happens to those seats if the people they're set aside for don't claim them?"

"They're put on sale in the box office."

"When?"

"In this city, it's forty-eight hours before any given performance."

"For sale to whom?"

"Anyone."

"Some guy who walks in off the street?"

"Well, not usually. These are choice seats, you realize."

"So who *does* get them?"

"They're usually sold to brokers."

"At the price printed on the ticket?"

"Yes, of course."

"No, *not* of course," Carella said. "That's where the ice comes in, isn't it?"

"If someone connected with a show is involved in ice, yes, that's where it would come in."

"In short, the man in charge of the box office—"

"That would be our company manager."

"Your company manager, or someone on his staff, would take these unclaimed house seats and sell them to a broker—or any number of brokers—at a price higher than the established price for the ticket."

"Yes, that would be the ice. The difference between the legitimate ticket price and whatever the iceman can get for it."

"Sometimes *twice* the ticket price, isn't it?"

"Well, I really wouldn't know. As I told you—"

"Eighty dollars for a forty-dollar ticket, wouldn't that be possible?"

"It would be possible, I suppose. For a tremendous hit."

"Like *Fatback.*"

"Yes, but no one—"

"And the broker would then take this ticket for which he's paid eighty dollars, and he'll sell it to a favored customer for something like a hundred and fifty dollars, isn't that so?"

"You're talking about scalping now. Scalping is against the law. A ticket broker can legally charge only two dollars more than the price on the ticket. That's his markup. Two dollars. By *law*."

"But there are brokers who break the law."

"That's *their* business, not mine."

"Incidentally," Carella said, "ice is *also* against the law."

"It may be against the law," Carter said, "but in my opinion, it doesn't really hurt anyone."

"It's just a victimless crime, huh?" Meyer said.

"In my opinion."

"Like prostitution," Meyer said.

"Well, prostitution is another matter," Carter said. "The girls themselves *are*, of course, victimized. But with ice . . ." He shrugged. "Let's assume someone in a show's box office *is* doing ice. He doesn't *steal* those house seats, you know. If the ticket costs forty dollars, he'll put forty dollars in the cash drawer before he sells that ticket to a broker."

"For twice the price," Carella said.

"That doesn't matter. The point is the show *got* the forty dollars it was *supposed* to get for the ticket. The *show* doesn't lose any money on that ticket. The *investors* don't lose any money."

"But the people running the ice operation *make* a lot of money."

"There's not that much involved," Carter said, and shrugged again. "I'll tell you the truth, on some shows I was involved with, I've had general managers come to me proposing ice, but I always turned them down cold—no pun intended," Carter said, and smiled. "Why risk a brush with the law when peanuts are involved?"

"Peanuts? You said there were a hundred house seats—"

"That's right."

"At a forty-dollar markup per seat, that comes to four thousand dollars a performance. How many performances are there a week, Mr. Carter?"

"Eight."

"Times four thousand is thirty-two thousand a week. That comes to something like . . . What does it come to, Meyer?"

"What?" Meyer said.

"In a year."

"Oh. Close to two million dollars a year. Something like a million six, a million seven."

"Is that peanuts, Mr. Carter?"

"Well, you know, the ice on a show is usually split up. Sometimes four or five ways."

"Let's say it's split five ways," Carella said. "That would still come to something like two, three hundred thousand dollars a person. That's a lot of money, Mr. Carter."

"It's not worth going to jail for," Carter said.

"Then why are you doing it?" Meyer asked.

"I beg your pardon?" Carter said.

"Why are you taking ice on *Fatback?*"

"Is that a flat-out accusation?" Carter said.

"That's what it is," Carella said.

"Then maybe I ought to call my lawyer."

"Maybe you ought to hear us out first," Carella said. "You always seem to be in a hurry to call your lawyer."

"If you're accusing me of—"

"Mr. Carter, isn't it true that Sally Anderson was a courier in your ice operation?"

"*What* ice operation?"

"We've been told Sally Anderson delivered house seats to various brokers, and collected cash for those seats, and then brought the cash back to your company manager. Isn't that true, Mr.

Carter? Wasn't Sally Anderson, in effect, a bag lady for your ice operation?"

"If someone in my theater is making money on ice—"

"Someone *is*, Mr. Carter."

"Not me."

"Let's take this a step further, shall we?" Carella said.

"No, let's call my lawyer," Carter said, and picked up the phone receiver.

"We have proof," Carella said.

He was lying; they had no proof at all. Lonnie Cooper had hinted that Sally had been earning extra cash someplace. Timothy Moore had told them she'd been running ice money for Carter. None of that was proof. But Carella's words stopped Carter dead in his tracks. He put the receiver back onto the cradle. He shook a cigarette free from the package on his desk and lighted it. He blew out a cloud of smoke.

"What proof?" he said.

"Let's go back a bit," Carella said.

"What proof?" Carter said again.

"Why'd you tell us you hardly knew Sally?" Carella asked.

"Here we go again," Carter said.

"Once more 'round the mulberry bush," Meyer said, and smiled.

"*We* think it's because she was involved in this ice operation with you," Carella said.

"I don't know anything about any ice operation."

"And maybe wanted a bigger piece of the pie—"

"Ridiculous!"

"Or maybe even threatened to blow the whistle—"

"I don't know what you're talking about," Carter said.

"We're talking about murder."

"Murder? For *what*? Because you think Sally was somehow involved with *ice*?"

"We *know* she was involved," Meyer said. "And not *somehow*. She was involved with *you*, Mr. Carter. She was your goddamn courier. She delivered tickets, and she picked up—"

"*Once!*" Carter shouted.

The room went silent.

The detectives looked at him.

"I had nothing to do with her murder," Carter said.

"We're listening," Meyer said.

"It was only once."

"When?"

"Last November."

"Why only once?"

"Tina was sick."

"Tina Wong?"

"Yes."

"What happened?"

"She couldn't make the rounds that day. She asked Sally to substitute for her."

"Without your knowledge?"

"She checked with me first. She was sick in bed with the flu, she had a fever. I told her it would be okay. Sally was her closest friend. I figured we could trust her."

"Is that why you denied knowing her?"

"Yes. I figured . . . well, if any of this came to light, you might think—"

"We might think exactly what we *are* thinking, Mr. Carter."

"No. You're mistaken. It was just that once. Sally *never* wanted anything more. Sally *never* threatened me with—"

"How much did she get for her services?" Meyer asked.

"Two hundred bucks. But that was the one and only time."

"How much do you give Tina? Is she your regular bag lady?"

"Yes. She gets the same."

"Two hundred for each pickup and delivery?"

"Yes."

"Twelve hundred a week?"

"Yes."

"And your end?"

"We're splitting it four ways."

"Who?"

"Me, my general manager, my company manager, and the box-office treasurer."

"Splitting thirty-two thousand a week?"

"More or less."

"So your end is something like four hundred grand a year," Meyer said.

"Tax free," Carella said.

"Weren't the show's profits enough for you?" Meyer asked.

"Nobody's getting hurt," Carter said.

"Except you and your pals," Carella said. "Get your coat."

"Why?" Carter said. "Are you wired?"

The detectives looked at each other.

"Let's hear the proof," Carter said.

"A man named Timothy Moore knows all about it," Carella said. "So does Lonnie Cooper, one of your dancers. Maybe Sally wasn't as trustworthy as you thought she was. Get your coat."

Carter stubbed out his cigarette and smiled thinly. "Let me put it this way," he said. "*If* there's ice—and I don't remember having this conversation today, do you?—and *if* Sally Anderson, once upon a time very long ago, really and truly delivered some tickets and picked up some cash, it seems to me you'd need more proof than . . . hearsay, do you call it? So let's say you run over to my box office straight from here. Do you know what you'll find? You'll find that all of our brokers, from this minute on, are getting only their legitimate allotments of tickets, and anything we sell them *beyond* their usual quotas will be at box-office prices. Our top ticket sells for forty dollars. If we send a house seat to a broker, that's what he'll pay for it. Forty dollars. Everything open and honest. Now tell me, gentlemen, are you going to try tracking down whatever cash has changed hands since the show opened? Impossible."

The detectives looked at each other.

"You can go to the attorney general with this," Carter said, still smiling, "but without proof you'd only look foolish."

Carella began buttoning his coat.

Meyer put on his hat.

"And, anyway . . ." Carter said.

The detectives were already heading for the door.

". . . a hot show *always* generates ice."

In the corridor outside, Meyer said, "Nothing ever hurts anybody, right? Snow isn't habit-forming, and ice is a time-honored scam. Marvelous."

"Lovely," Carella said, and pressed the button for the elevator.

"He knows we have no proof. He knows we can't do a damn thing. So he walks," Meyer said.

"Maybe he'll clean up his act, though."

"For how long?" Meyer asked.

Both men fell silent, listening to the elevator as it lumbered slowly up the shaft. Through a window at the far end of the corridor, they could see that the sunshine was waning, the day was turning gray again.

"What do you think about the other?" Carella asked.

"The dead girl?"

"Yes."

"I think he's clean, don't you?"

"I think so."

The elevator doors slid open.

"There ain't no justice in this world," Meyer said.

YEARS ago, when Brother Anthony was spending a little time at Castleview State Penitentiary on that manslaughter conviction, his cellmate was a burglar. Guy named Jack Greenspan. Big Jack Greenspan, they used to call him. Jewish guy. You hardly ever ran into any Jewish burglars. Big Jack taught him a lot of things, but Brother Anthony never figured any of them would help him on the outside.

Until today.

Today, all the things Big Jack had told him all those years ago seemed of immense value to Brother Anthony because what he planned to do was break into the Anderson girl's apartment. This was not a sudden whim. He had discussed it thoroughly with Emma yesterday, after he'd learned that the Anderson girl had been killed. The reason he had gone to see her in the first place was because Judite Quadrado had told them she was the source from which the sweet snow flowed. It was one thing to have a list of customers, but customers weren't worth beans without what to sell them. So he had gone there yesterday hoping to strike up a business relationship with the girl, only to discover she wouldn't be doing business as usual no more; someone had seen to that.

The reason he wanted to get into her apartment—well, there were two reasons, actually. The first reason was that maybe the girl had stashed away a whole pile of dope the cops hadn't found. He didn't think that was likely, but it was worth a shot. Cops were as careless as anybody else in the world, and maybe she'd stashed away a couple of kilos someplace, which would be like found money with a key going for something like sixty grand before it was stepped on. The second reason was that if the girl was an ounce dealer, which Judite Quadrado had said she was, then she was sure as hell getting those ounces from somebody *else*, unless she was in the habit of running down to South America every other weekend, which Brother Anthony doubted. The super of the building had told him she was a dancer in a hit show, right? Well, dancers couldn't go running off whenever they wanted to. No, the way he figured it, she was being supplied by somebody else.

So . . .

If she was getting her stuff from somebody else, then wouldn't there be something in the apartment that might tell him *where* she was getting it? If he could learn where she was getting it, why then he would just go to the man and tell him he'd bought out Sally, or some such bullshit, and would the man care to do business with him instead? Unless the man turned out to be the one who'd killed her, in which case Brother Anthony would make the sign of the cross, pick up his skirts, and disappear like an Arab in the night. One thing he didn't want was any heavy action from a guy who lived in Baby Bogotá.

He was carrying in the pouch at the front of his cassock two things that were essential to a successful break-in, again according to Big Jack, and assuming that the lock on the dead girl's door was a Mickey Mouse lock. If the lock looked like something Brother Anthony couldn't handle, he'd find some other way of getting in, like maybe climbing up the fire escape and smashing a window, although Big Jack said that was Amateur Night in Dixie, smashing windows, something only junkie burglars did. The two things Brother Anthony had in his pouch were a box of toothpicks and a strip of plastic he had torn from one of those milk bottles with a handle and a screw-top cap.

The toothpicks were his own portable burglar alarm.

The strip of plastic was to open the door.

The way Big Jack explained it, a credit card was the best way to loid a Mickey Mouse lock, but any thin strip of plastic or celluloid would do. That was where the expression *loid* had come from: before credit cards were even invented, the old-time burglars used to use strips of celluloid to work open a lock. Brother Anthony didn't *have* any credit cards, and he wasn't sure the plastic he'd torn from the milk bottle would work; still, Big Jack had said *any* strip of plastic, right?

He had checked out the lobby downstairs before entering the

building; no security, and the old fart superintendent was nowhere in sight. He had been up to the girl's apartment yesterday, when he'd knocked and got no answer, so he knew she was in apartment 3-A, but he checked the mailboxes in the lobby just to make sure, and then he took the steps up to the third floor and stepped out into an empty corridor, not a sound anywhere. Big Jack was right about apartment buildings being mostly empty during the daytime. If he played this right, according to Big Jack's rules, he should be inside the apartment in maybe a minute and a half.

It took him half an hour.

He kept sliding the plastic shim into the crack where the door met the jamb, working it, jiggling it, trying to find purchase on the bolt, turning it this way and that, beginning to sweat, removing it from the crack, inserting it again, worrying it, pushing at it, glancing over his shoulder down the hallway, coaxing it, whispering to it (Come on, baby, come on), positive some lady would come out of her apartment down the hall and start screaming at the top of her lungs, jerking the plastic shim, catching the bolt, losing the bolt, sweating more profusely now, the heavy cassock clinging to his body, his hands working feverishly, a full half *hour* before he finally felt the latch beginning to yield (Careful, don't *lose* it now!), felt it beginning to slide back as the plastic insinuated itself between the steel of the bolt and the wood of the jamb, twisting the shim slowly now, feeling the bolt give and then surrender entirely. He seized the knob and turned it, and the door was open.

He was drenched with sweat.

He stepped quickly into the apartment, closed the door immediately behind him, and leaned against it, breathing hard, listening, pouring sweat. When he had caught his breath, he fished in his pouch for the box of wooden toothpicks, opened the box, took a toothpick from it, and then carefully opened the door just a crack and peered out into the hallway, looking, listening again. Nothing.

He opened the door wider.

He wedged the toothpick into the keyway on the lock and then broke it off flush with the cylinder. He closed the door again and turned the thumb-bolt, locking it. The way Big Jack had explained it, if anybody came to the apartment with a key, they'd try to put the key in the lock, not knowing a toothpick was wedged there in the keyway, and they'd keep fumbling with the key, trying to get it in there, and the guy inside the apartment would hear all the clicking noise of metal against metal and would go out the window or whatever he'd chosen for his escape route. Your kitchen was a good escape route, Big Jack had told him. Some kitchens had service doors, and most kitchens had fire escapes. He didn't know why so many kitchens had fire escapes, they just did. Brother Anthony went into the kitchen now.

He leaned over the kitchen sink and looked through the window. No fire escape. He began roaming through the apartment, looking out over the windowsills for a fire escape. The only fire escape was outside the bedroom window. He turned the latch on the window, opened the window just a trifle so he could throw it *all* the way open in a second if anybody came in here, and then walked into the living room. This was a nice place—carpet on the floor, nice furniture. He wished Emma and him could live in a place like this. Posters on all the walls, nice black leather sofa with pillows. There were some framed pictures of a girl wearing tights and one of those little short frilly skirts ballet dancers wore. He figured she was the dead girl. Good-looking broad. Blond hair, nice figure, but a little on the thin side. He wondered where you could buy those little skirts ballet dancers wore. There were probably places in the city you could buy them. He'd like to buy one of them for Emma, have her run around the apartment naked except for the little skirt.

There was a poster for some ballet company hanging on the wall outside the bathroom. He figured he'd start with the bathroom first because Big Jack had told him lots of people stashed their valuables in the toilet tank, in the water inside the tank. He lowered the toilet seat and lifted the top of the toilet tank and put it down on the seat. He looked inside there. A lot of rusty water. He stuck his hand down into the water, felt around. Nothing. He pulled his hand back, wiped it on a towel hanging on a rod across from the toilet bowl, and then put the top of the tank back on again, trying to remember where else Big Jack said a person should look.

Well, let's try the bedroom, he thought. Big Jack had told him that a lot of bedroom dressers, the bottom drawer rested just on the frame of the dresser itself. There wasn't a shelf or anything under the bottom drawer. This meant there was a space of about two, three inches between the drawer and the floor of the room. What a lot of people did, they pulled out the drawer, and then put their valuables right on the floor itself before they put the drawer back in. An inexperienced burglar would go through the drawer, but he wouldn't think of pulling *out* the drawer to look on the floor.

Brother Anthony pulled out the bottom drawer. It was full of the girl's panties and brassieres. Little nylon bikinis in all colors. Tiny little brassieres—she must've had small tits. He tried to visualize her in just her panties. She was really too skinny, but some of those skinny ones, the closer the bone, the sweeter the meat. He picked up a pair of panties, the purple ones, and held them in his hands for several moments before throwing them back into the drawer. He was here to find two things: either a stash of cocaine or something that would tell him where the girl was getting her stuff.

He got down on his hands and knees and looked into the empty space where the drawer had been. He couldn't see a thing.

He stood up, turned on the lamp on the dresser, and got down on his hands and knees again. He still couldn't see anything. He reached into the dresser and began feeling around with both hands. There was nothing on the floor. He picked up the drawer from where he had left it on the floor, carried it to the bed—nice big bed with a patchwork quilt—and dumped the contents on the bed. Nothing but brassieres and panties; damn girl must've changed her underwear three times a day. He guessed maybe dancers did that. Worked up a sweat, changed their underwear a lot.

He took out all the other drawers in the dresser and dumped them on the bed, too. Nothing but clothes. Blouses and sweaters and tights and T-shirts, a whole pile of girl stuff. No cocaine. Not a scrap of paper with anything written on it. The cops had probably fine-combed the place, taken anything that looked interesting. They probably sold whatever dope they confiscated, the cops. Worse crooks than the *honest* crooks in this city. He put his hands on his hips and looked around. *Now* where? he wondered.

Big Jack had told him you could sometimes find heroin in a person's sugar bowl, that's if you got lucky enough to bust into some dealer's apartment. You found a stash of dope, it was better than finding cash or credit cards or even coin collections. He went back into the kitchen again, looked for the sugar bowl, found it on the bottom shelf of one of the cabinets, took off the lid, and discovered that the bowl was full of pink Sweet'N Low packets. So much for that, may God have mercy on your soul. He went through all the cereal boxes in the cabinet, figuring she might have hidden a plastic-wrapped kilo inside one of the boxes, dumping out cornflakes and wheat germ and whatever, but he couldn't find a thing. He went through the refrigerator. Nothing but an open container of yogurt and a lot of wilted vegetables. He went through every drawer in the living room and felt under every tabletop, figuring the stuff might be taped under one of them. Nothing. He went back into the bedroom and opened the door to the closet.

Girl had more clothes than a Hall Avenue department store. Even a fur coat. Raccoon, it looked like. Must have been making a bundle selling the snow, so where the hell *was* it? He began pulling dresses and coats from the hangers, patting down all the coat pockets, throwing everything on the floor behind him. Nothing. He opened all her shoe boxes. Sexy whore shoes, some of them, with high heels and ankle straps. He thought of her panties again. Nothing but shoes in any of the boxes. So where *was* it? He dug deeper into the closet.

He found a man's clothes hanging on the rod, pushed to the far corner of the closet. Well, sure, it figured. Little whore with her sexy panties and her high-heeled shoes, of *course* there had to be some guy putting it to her. Nice cardigan sweater, brown. Brother Anthony would have taken it with him except that it looked too small. Pair of checked slacks, wouldn't be caught dead in them even if they *did* fit him. A black silk robe with the monogram TM over the breast pocket. Little kinky sex, T. M.? You put on your black silk robe, she puts on her silk panties and her high-heeled hooker shoes, you sniff a little blow, and it's off to the races! Very nice, T. M. Nice clothes you got here, T. M. But not too *many* of them, so you couldn't have been *living* here with her, could you? Maybe you just dropped in every now and then; maybe you're some married stockbroker who was knocking off an uptown piece every Wednesday afternoon when the market closed. No more nookie, T. M. The lady's dead and gone.

Nice cashmere jacket, soft, tan. Another pair of pants. Green! Who would wear green pants except an Irishman on St. Patrick's Day? A down ski parka. Blue. A small one, though. Must've been the girl's, with one of those zipper collars that had a hood folded up inside it, in case you got cold on the ski lift at St. Moritz, my dear. He wouldn't strap a pair of skis to his feet if you paid him a million dollars! Yeah, here was the guy's parka, a black one, like the robe. Are you a skier, T. M.? Did you take your little sweetheart skiing every now and then? He patted down all the pockets in the cashmere jacket and then threw it on the floor behind him. He patted down the girl's ski parka, the blue one. Nothing. He was about to toss it on the floor with all the other clothes when he felt something strange about the collar.

He took it in both hands and twisted it.

Something felt a little stiff in there.

He twisted the collar again. There was a faint crackling sound. Something was zipped up inside that collar, something in addition to the hood. He carried the parka to the bed. He sat on the edge of the bed, the panties and brassieres scattered everywhere around him. He felt the collar again. Yes, there was definitely something in there. Quickly, he unzipped it.

At first, he was only disappointed.

What he was holding in his hands was an envelope folded lengthwise, once and then again, so that it formed a narrow oblong that had easily fitted inside the zipped-up collar of the parka. He unfolded the envelope once. He unfolded it again. The letter was addressed to Sally Anderson. He looked at the return address in the upper left-hand corner. The name there meant nothing to him, but the *place* triggered an instant reaction, and he suspected at once that whereas he hadn't found the coke itself, he *might* have found the primary *source* of the coke. He reached into the envelope and took out the handwritten letter. He began reading it. He could hear the ticking of his own watch. He realized he was holding his breath. Suddenly, he began giggling.

Now we *move*, he thought. Straight up into the big time, man, Cadillacs and Cuban cigars, champagne and caviar, man! Still giggling, he tucked the letter into his pouch, considered whether it was safe to go out the way he had come in, decided it was, and headed uptown to share the wealth with Emma.

ALONSO QUADRADO WAS NAKED when they walked in on him at four o'clock that afternoon. They considered this an advantage. A naked man feels uncomfortable talking to a person who is fully dressed. This was why burglars had an edge whenever they surprised some guy asleep in his bedroom, and he jumped out of bed naked and stood there with everything hanging out, facing an intruder who was wearing an overcoat and holding a gun in his hand. Alonso Quadrado was taking a shower in the locker room at the Y.M.C.A. on Landis Avenue when the two detectives walked in. The two detectives were both wearing overcoats. One of them was wearing a hat. Quadrado was wearing nothing but a thin layer of soapsuds.

"Hello, Alonso," Meyer said.

Quadrado got soap in his eyes. He said, "Damn it!" and began splashing water onto his face. He was an exceptionally thin man, with narrow bones and a pale olive complexion. The Pancho Villa mustache over his upper lip was almost bigger than he was.

"Few more questions we'd like to ask you," Carella said.

"You picked some time," Quadrado said. He rinsed himself off, turning this way and that under the needle spray. He turned off the shower, picked up a towel, and began drying himself. The detectives waited. Quadrado wrapped the towel around his waist and walked into the locker room. The detectives followed him.

"I just got done playing handball," he said. "You play handball?"

"I used to," Meyer said.

"Best game there is," Quadrado said, and sat on the bench, and opened the door to one of the lockers. "So what now?" he said.

"Do you know your cousin's dead?" Meyer asked.

"Yeah, I know it. The funeral's tomorrow. I ain't going. I hate funerals. You ever been to a Spanish funeral? All those old ladies throwing themselves on the coffin? Not for me, man."

"She was cut, do you know that?"

"Yeah."

"Any idea who did it?"

"No. If Lopez was still alive, I'da said it was him. But *he's* dead, too."

"Anybody else you can think of?"

"Look, you know what she was into. It coulda been anybody."

He was drying his feet. He reached into the locker, took out a pair of socks, and began putting them on. It was interesting the way people dressed themselves, Meyer thought. It was like the different ways people ate an ear of corn. No two people ate corn the same way, and no two people got dressed the same way. Why was Quadrado starting with his socks? *Black* socks, at that. Was he about to audition for a porn flick? Meyer wondered if he would put on his shoes next, before he put on his Jockey shorts or his pants. Another of life's little mysteries.

"What *was* she into?" Carella said.

"Well, not *exactly* into it, not yet. But *working* on it, let's say."

"And what was that?"

"The only thing she inherited from Lopez."

"Spell it out," Carella said.

Quadrado reached into the locker again. He took a pair of boxer shorts from where they were hanging on a hook and pulled them on. "Lopez's trade," he said, and reached into the locker for his pants.

"His dope trade?"

"Yeah, she had the list."

"What list?"

"Of his customers."

"How'd she get that?"

"She was living with him, wasn't she?"

"Is this a *real* list you're talking about? Names and addresses? Written down on a piece of paper?"

"No, no, what piece of paper? But she was living with him. She knew who his customers were. She told me she was gonna move on it, get the coke the same place *he* was getting it, make herself a little extra change, you know?"

"When did she tell you this?" Meyer asked.

"Right after he got shot," Quadrado said, and put on his shirt.

"Why didn't you mention this the last time we talked?"

"You didn't ask me."

"Did this sound like a *new* thing for her?" Carella asked.

"What do you mean?"

"Dealing."

"Oh. Yeah."

"She wasn't working with him *before* he got killed, was she? They weren't partners or anything?"

"No, no. Lopez? You think *he'd* share a good thing with a chick? No way."

"But he told her who his customers were."

"Well, he didn't say, 'This guy takes four grams, and this guy takes six grams,' nothing like that. I mean, he didn't hand her the list on a platter. But when a guy's livin' with somebody, they *talk*, you know what I mean? He'll say, 'I got to deliver a coupla three grams to Luis today,' something like that. They'll talk, you know?"

"Pillow talk," Meyer said.

"Yeah, pillow talk, right," Quadrado said. "That's a good way of putting it. Judite was a smart girl. When Lopez talked, she listened. Look, I'll tell you the truth. Judite didn't think this thing was gonna *last* very long, you know what I mean? After the guy hurt her . . . I mean, how much can a chick put up with? He was a crazy bastard to begin with, and he still had other women, never mind just Judite. So I guess she listened a lot. She had no way of knowing he was gonna get killed, of course, but I guess she figured it wouldn't hurt to—"

"How do you know that?"

"How do I know what?"

"That she didn't know he was going to get killed?"

"I'm just assuming. You guys mind if I smoke?"

"Go right ahead," Meyer said.

" 'Cause I like a little smoke after I finish playing," Quadrado said, and reached into the bag on the floor of the locker and pulled out a Sucrets tin. They knew what was in the tin even before he opened it. They were surprised, but not *too* surprised. Nowadays, people smoked grass even on the park bench across the street from the station house. They watched as Quadrado fired the joint. He sucked on it. He let out a stream of smoke.

"Care for a toke?" he asked, blithely extending the joint to Meyer.

"Thanks," Meyer said drily. "I'm on duty."

Carella smiled.

"Who were these other women?" he asked.

"Jesus, who could *count* them?" Quadrado said. "There's this one-legged hooker he was putting it to. You know Anita Diaz? She's gorgeous, but she's got only one leg. They call her *La Mujer Coja* in the neighborhood. She's the best lay in the world, you ever happen to run into her. Lopez was making it with her. And there was . . . You know the guy who owns the candy store on Mason and Tenth? His wife. Lopez was making it with her, too. This was all while he was living with Judite. Who knows why she put up with it for so long?" He sucked on the joint. "I figure she was scared of him, you know? Like, he was all the time threatening her, and finally he burned her with the cigarette, so that must've *really* scared her. So I guess she figured she'd just keep her mouth shut, let him run around with whoever he wanted to."

"How'd she plan to supply these people?"

"What do you mean?"

"Lopez's customers. Where'd she plan to get the stuff?"

"Same place Lopez got it."

"And where was that?"

"From the Anglo ounce dealer."

"What Anglo ounce dealer?"

"The one Lopez used to live with. The way Judite figured it, bygones are bygones, and business is business. If the chick was supplying Lopez, why couldn't she *also* supply Judite?"

"This was a woman, huh?"

"The blonde he used to live with, yeah."

Carella looked at Meyer.

"*What* blonde?" he said.

"I told you. The Anglo chick he used to live with."

"A *blonde?*" Meyer said.

"Yeah, a blonde," Lopez said. "What is it with you guys? You're hard of hearing?"

"When was this?" Meyer said.

"A year ago? Who remembers? Lopez had them coming and going like subway trains."

"What's her name, would you know?"

"No," Quadrado said, and took a last draw on the roach before dropping it on the floor. He was about to step on it when he realized he was still in his stocking feet. Meyer stepped on it for him. Quadrado sat, pulled on a pair of high-topped black sneakers, and began lacing them.

"Where'd they live?" Carella asked.

"On Ainsley. We still got a handful of Anglos living up here. The rent's cheap. They're mostly people trying to make it, you know? Like starving painters, or musicians, or these guys who make statues, you know?"

"Sculptors," Meyer said.

"Right, sculptors," Quadrado said. "That's a good way of putting it."

"Let me get this straight," Carella said. "You're saying that a year ago—"

"Around then."

"Lopez was living with a blond cocaine dealer—"

"No, not then."

"He *wasn't* living with her?"

"He *was* living with her, but she wasn't dealing coke. Not then."

"What *was* she doing?"

"Trying to make it. Same as anybody else."

"Trying to make it *how?*"

"I think she was a dancer or something."

Carella looked at Meyer again.

"I think she finally moved away because she got a part in a show," Quadrado said. "Last summer sometime. Moved back downtown, you know?"

"And surfaced again dealing coke," Carella said.

"Yeah."

"When?"

"The coke? Musta been last fall sometime. October, sometime."

"Began supplying Lopez with coke."

"Yeah."

"Who told you this?"

"Judite."

"Are you sure the girl wasn't coming up here to *buy* coke?"

"No, no. She was an ounce dealer, she was selling it. That's how come Judite figured she could pick up the trade now that Lopez was dead and gone. Same customers, same ounce dealer."

"How often did she come up here?"

"The blonde? Every week."

"You know that for a fact?"

"I know it because that's what Judite told me."

"And this started in October sometime?"

"Yeah, that's when Lopez went into business. Again, this is all according to Judite. I got no personal knowledge of it myself."

"When did she come up?"

"On Sundays, usually."

"To deliver the coke."

"And maybe a little something else besides."

"What do you mean?"

"Renew old times, you know? In the sack."

"With Lopez?"

"According to Judite. Who knows if it's true or not? You get a chick taking all kinds of shit from a guy, she begins to imagine things, you know? She starts finding panties that ain't hers under every pillow, you know what I mean? She starts smelling other women on her sheets. It gets to her. Listen, my cousin was a little nuts, I'll tell you the truth. You *have* to be a little nuts to take up with a guy like Lopez."

"But you don't know the girl's name, huh?"

"No."

"Do you know the name of the show she was in?"

"No."

"But you're *sure* she used to live with Lopez."

"Positive. Not at first. She had an apartment in this building where there's a couple other Anglos. But then she moved in with him. Yeah, I'm sure of that. I mean, *that* I seen with my own eyes."

"What did you see?"

"Him and her coming in and going out of the building together, all hours of the day and night. Look, it was common knowledge Lopez had himself a blond chick from downtown."

"What building was this?" Meyer asked.

"The building he was living in."

"When he got shot?"

"No, no. That's where he was living with *Judite.* That was on *Culver.* This was on *Ainsley.*"

"Do you know the address?"

"No. It's near the drugstore there. On the corner of Ainsley and Sixth, I think it is. The Tru-Way drugstore."

"Would you recognize the girl if you saw her again?"

"The blonde? Oh, sure. Nice-looking chick. What *she* saw in Lopez is *another* mystery, right?"

"Alonso, would you do us a favor?" Meyer said. "Would you come over to the station house with us? For just a minute?"

"Why? What'd *I* do?" Quadrado said.

"Nothing," Meyer said. "We want to show you some pictures."

TWELVE

ARTHUR Brown did not want to be doing what he was doing. Arthur Brown wanted to be watching television with his wife.

He did not want to be wading through all this stuff he and Kling had got, first from Marvin Edelman's widow and next from Marvin Edelman's safety-deposit box. If Arthur Brown had wanted to become an accountant, he would not have taken the patrolmen's test all those years ago. Accounting bored Brown. Even his *own* accounting bored him. He normally asked Caroline to balance the family checkbooks, something she did marvelously well.

It was twenty minutes past eleven.

The news would be over in ten minutes, and Johnny Carson would be coming on. Brown sometimes felt that the only two things uniting the people of the United States were Johnny Carson and the weather. Nothing short of a nuclear war could make everyone in the good old U.S. of A. feel more united than Johnny Carson and the weather. This winter, the weather was rotten all over the country. If you flew from here to Minneapolis, the weather would be the same. It gave you a feeling that here and Minneapolis were one and the same place. It united the people in adversity. If you flew from here to Cincinnati, the weather would be rotten there, too, and you'd step off the plane and immediately feel this enormous sense of brotherhood. Then, when you got to the hotel room and ordered your drink from room service, and unpacked your bag, and turned on your television set, why there would be old Johnny Carson at 11:30 p.m. sharp all over the country, and you knew that in Los Angeles they were watching Johnny Carson at the very same time, and in New York they were watching him, and in Kalamazoo, and Atlanta, and Washington, D.C., they were all watching Johnny Carson, and it made you feel like an essential part of the greatest people on earth, all of them sitting there with their fingers up their asses, watching Johnny Carson.

Brown figured that if Johnny Carson ran for the presidency, he would win hands down. What he wanted to do right now—well, ten minutes from now—was watch Johnny Carson. He did not want to be cross-checking the contents of Marvin Edelman's safety-deposit box against Marvin Edelman's bank statements and canceled checks for the past year or so. That was something for an accountant to be doing. What a *cop* should be doing was sitting on the sofa with his arm around Caroline while they watched Lola Falana, who was scheduled to be Johnny's guest tonight and whom Brown considered the most beautiful black woman in the world— next to Caroline, of course. He had never mentioned to Caroline how beautiful he thought Lola Falana was. After all these years on the force, he had learned that you never opened a door until you knew for certain what was behind it, and he wasn't quite sure what might be lurking behind Caroline's door these days. Brown had once mentioned that Diana Ross wasn't bad looking, and Caroline had thrown an ashtray at him. He had threatened to arrest her for attempted assault, and she had told him he could damn well glue the ashtray together *himself*. That had been a long time ago, and he hadn't tried opening that particular door since. He had the feeling he might find the same familiar tigress behind it.

He was very happy that Mrs. Edelman had found the duplicate key to her husband's safety-deposit box, because the discovery had saved him and Kling the trouble of going all the way downtown to apply for a court order to open the box, which application might or might not have been granted depending on which magistrate they'd have come up against that afternoon. Some of the judges downtown, you got the feeling they were on the side of the *bad* guys. You got a judge like Walking Wilbur Harris, you could go into his courtroom with a guy holding a machete in one bloody hand and a severed head in the other, and old Wilbur would cluck his tongue and say, "My, my, we've been a naughty boy today, haven't we? Prisoner released on his own recognizance." Or he'd set a ridiculous bail like ten thousand bucks for somebody who'd killed his mother, his father, his Labrador retriever, and all his pet goldfish. You got a judge like Walking Wilbur, it sometimes made you feel you were on the job for no reason at all in the world. You worked your tail off out there, you made your collar, and Wilbur let the man walk, sometimes clear to China, never to be heard from since. So what was the use? He was happy he hadn't had to go downtown today to beg for a court order to open that box.

He had not been happy when he'd seen the *size* of the safety-deposit box, and he had been even less happy when he and Kling discovered just how many papers were *inside* the damn thing. Those papers were scattered before him on the desk in the spare room now, together with Edelman's bank statements and canceled checks and a can of beer. From the other room—his daughter Connie's playroom during the day, his and Caroline's television room at night—he could hear the identifying theme song of the Johnny Carson show. He kept listening. He heard Ed McMahon announcing the list of guests (Lola Falana *was* one of them, sure as hell), and then he heard the familiar "Heeeeeere's Johnnnnnnnnnny!" and he sighed and took a long swallow of his beer and then started separating the various documents they'd taken from the safety deposit box.

It was going to be a long night.

WHEN the telephone rang, it startled Kling.

The phone was on an end table beside the bed, and the first ring slammed into the silence of the room like a pistol shot, causing him to sit bolt upright, his heart pounding. He grabbed for the receiver.

"Hello?" he said.

"Hi. This is Eileen," she said.

"Oh, hi," he said.

"You sound out of breath."

"No, I . . . It was very quiet in here. When the phone rang, it surprised me." His heart was still pounding.

"You weren't asleep, were you? I didn't—"

"No, no, I was just lying here."

"In bed?"

"Yes."

"I'm in bed, too," she said.

He said nothing.

"I wanted to apologize," she said.

"What for?"

"I didn't know about the divorce," she said.

"Well, that's okay."

"I wouldn't have said what I said if I'd known."

What she meant, he realized, was that she hadn't known about the *circumstances* of the divorce. She had found out since yesterday, it was common currency in the department, and now she was apologizing for having described what she'd called an "Uh-oh!" scene: the wife in bed with her lover, the husband coming up the steps, the very damn thing that had happened to Kling.

"That's okay," he said.

It was not okay.

"I've just made it worse, haven't I?" she said.

He was about to say, "No, don't be silly, thanks for calling," when he thought, unexpectedly, Yes, you *have* made it worse, and he said, "As a matter of fact, you have."

"I'm sorry. I only wanted—"

"What'd they tell you?" he asked.

"Who?"

"Come on," he said. "Whoever told you about it."

"Only that there'd been some kind of problem."

"Uh-huh. What kind of problem?"

"Just a problem."

"My wife was playing around, right?"

"Well, yes, that's what I was told."

"Fine," he said.

There was a long silence on the line.

"Well," she said, and sighed. "I just wanted to tell you I'm sorry if I upset you yesterday."

"You didn't upset me," he said.

"You sound upset."

"I *am* upset," he said.

"Bert . . ." she said, and hesitated. "Please don't be mad at *me*, okay? Please *don't!*" and he could swear that suddenly she was crying. The next thing he heard was a click on the line.

He looked at the phone receiver.

"*What?*" he said to the empty room.

THE trouble with Edelman's records was that they didn't seem to add up. Or maybe Brown was just adding them up wrong. Either way, the arithmetic didn't come out right. There seemed to be large sums of money unaccounted for. The constant factor in Brown's calculations was the $300,000 they'd found in Edelman's safe. To Brown, this indicated at least *one* cash transaction.

Possibly a *series* of cash transactions, fifty thou a throw, say, allowed to accumulate in his safe before—

Before *what?*

According to his bank statements and canceled checks, Edelman had not made any truly large deposits or withdrawals during the past year. His various outlays for business expenses were for trips to Amsterdam, Zürich, and other European cities—the airfares, the hotel rooms, the checks written to gem merchants in the Dutch city. But the purchases he'd made (and he was, after all, in the *business* of buying and selling precious gems) were relatively small ones: five thousand dollars here, ten thousand here, a comparatively big check for twenty thousand dollars written to one Dutch firm. The subsequent bank deposits here in America seemed to indicate that Edelman turned a good, if not spectacular, profit on each of his purchases abroad.

From what Brown could figure, Edelman did a business somewhere in the vicinity of $200,000 to $300,000 a year. His current tax return had not yet been prepared—this was still only February, and it was not due till April 15—but on the last return he'd filed, he'd indicated a gross income of $265,523.12 for the year, with a taxable income of $226,523.12 after allowable deductions and business expenses. A little calculation told Brown that Edelman had deducted about 15 percent from his gross. With Uncle Sam, he was playing it entirely safe: the tax due had been $100,710.56; a check written on April 14 last year indicated that Edelman had completely satisfied his obligation to the government—at least on the income he'd *reported.*

It was the $300,000 in cash that kept bothering Brown.

Doggedly, he turned to the documents they had taken from Edelman's safety-deposit box.

KLING looked at the telephone for a long time.

Had she been crying?

He hadn't wanted to make her *cry;* he hardly *knew* the girl. He went to the window and stared out at the cars moving steadily across the bridge, their headlights piercing the night. It was snowing again. Would it ever stop snowing? He had not wanted to make her cry. What the hell was *wrong* with him? *Augusta* is wrong with me, he thought, and went back to bed.

It might have been easier to forget her if only he didn't have to see her face everywhere he turned. Your average divorced couple, especially if there were no kids involved, you hardly ever ran into each other after the final decree. You started to forget. Sometimes you forgot even the *good* things you'd shared, which was bad but which was the nature of the beast called divorce. With Augusta, it was different. Augusta was a model. You couldn't pass a magazine rack without seeing her face on the cover of at least one magazine each and every month, sometimes two. You couldn't turn on television without seeing her in a hair commercial (she had such beautiful hair) or a toothpaste commercial, or just last week in a nail-polish commercial, Augusta's hands fanned out in front of her gorgeous face, the nails long and bright red, as if they'd been dipped in fresh blood, the smile on her face— ahh, Jesus, that wonderful smile. It got so he didn't want to turn on the TV set anymore, for fear Augusta would leap out of the tube at him, and he'd start remembering again and begin crying again.

He lay fully dressed on the bed in the small apartment he was renting near the bridge, his hands behind his head, his head turned so that he could see through the window, see the cars moving on the bridge to Calm's Point—the theater crowd, he guessed. The shows had all broken by now, and people were heading home. People going home together. He took a deep breath.

His gun was in a holster on the dresser across the room.

He thought about the gun a lot.

Whenever he wasn't thinking about Augusta, he was thinking about the gun.

He didn't know why he'd let Brown take all that stuff home with him. He'd have welcomed the opportunity to go through it himself, give him something to do tonight instead of thinking about either Augusta or the gun. He knew Brown hated paperwork; he'd have been happy to take the load off his hands. But Brown had tiptoed around him. They all tiptoed around him these days: No, Bert, that's fine, you just go out and have a good time, hear? I'll be through with this stuff by morning. We'll talk it over then, okay? It was as if somebody very close to him had died. They all knew somebody had died, and they were uncomfortable with him, the way people are always uncomfortable with mourners, never knowing where to hide their hands, never knowing what to say in condolence. He'd be doing them all a favor, not only himself. Take the gun and . . .

Come on, he thought.

He turned his head on the pillow and looked up at the ceiling.

He knew the ceiling by heart. He knew every peak and valley in the rough plaster, knew every smear of dirt, every cobweb. He didn't know some *people* the way he knew that ceiling. Sometimes, when he thought of Augusta, the ceiling blurred, he could not see his old friend the ceiling through his own tears. If he used the gun, he'd have to be careful of the angle. Wouldn't want to have the bullet take off the top of his skull and then put a hole in the ceiling besides, not his old friend the ceiling. He smiled. He figured somebody smiling wasn't somebody about to eat his own gun. Not yet, anyway.

Damn it, he really *hadn't* wanted to make her cry.

He sat up abruptly, reached for the Isola directory on the end table, and thumbed through it, not expecting to find a listing for her and not surprised when he didn't. Nowadays, with thieves getting out of prison ten minutes after you locked them up, not too many cops were eager to list their home numbers in the city's telephone books. He dialed Communications downtown, a number he knew by heart, and told the clerk who answered the phone that he wanted extension 12.

"Departmental Directory," a woman's voice said.

"Home number for a police officer," Kling said.

"Is *this* a police officer calling?"

"It is," Kling said.

"Your name, please?"

"Bertram A. Kling."

"Your rank and shield number, please?"

"Detective/Third, seven-four-five-seven-nine."

"And the party?"

"Eileen Burke."

There was a silence on the line.

"Is this a joke?" the woman said.

"A joke? What do you mean?"

"*She* called here ten minutes ago, wanting *your* number."

"We're working a case together," Kling said, and wondered why he'd lied.

"So did she *call* you?"

"She called me."

"So why didn't you ask *her* what her number was?"

"I forgot," Kling said.

"This isn't a *dating* service," the woman said.

"I told you, we're working a case together," Kling said.

"Sure," the woman said. "Hold on, let me run this through."

He waited. He knew she was making a computer check on him, verifying that he was a bona fide cop. He looked through the window. It was snowing more heavily now. Come *on*, he thought.

"Hello?" the woman said.

"I'm still here," Kling said.

"Our computers are down. I had to do it manually."

"Am I a real cop?" Kling said.

"Who knows nowadays?" the woman answered. "Here's the number. Have you got a pencil?"

He wrote down the number, thanked her for her time, and then pressed one of the receiver rest buttons on top of the phone. He released the button, got a dial tone, was about to dial, and then hesitated. What am I starting here? he wondered. I don't want to start anything here. I'm not *ready* to start anything. He put the phone back on the cradle.

THE contents of the safety-deposit box were very interesting indeed. The way Brown was finally coming to understand it, Edelman's precious-gems business was a mere avocation when compared to what appeared to be his *true* business—the accumulation of real estate in various foreign countries. The deeds to land, houses, and office buildings in such diverse countries as Italy, France, Spain, Portugal, and England were dated from as far back as five years ago to as recently as six months ago. In July of last year alone, Edelman had purchased forty thousand square meters of land in a place called Porto Santo Stefano, for 200 *million* Italian lire. Brown did not know where Porto Santo Stefano was. Neither did he know how much the Italian lira had been worth six months ago. But a look at the financial pages of the city's morning paper told him that the current exchange rate was one hundred lire for twelve cents U.S. Brown had no idea how much the exchange rate had fluctuated during the past six months. But basing the purchase price on *today's* money market, Edelman would have spent something like $240,000 for the land he'd bought.

All well and good, Brown thought. A man wants to buy himself a big olive grove in Italy, fine; there was no law against that. But where was the canceled check, in either U.S. dollars *or* Italian lire, for the deal Edelman had closed in Rome on the eighth day of

July last year? $240,000—more than that, when you figured in the legal fees and closing costs and taxes listed on the Italian closing statement—had exchanged hands last July.

Where had the $240,000 come from?

KLING kept pacing the room. He owed her an apology, didn't he? Or did he? What the hell, he thought, and went back to the phone and dialed her number.

"Hello?" she said. Her voice sounded very small and a trifle sniffly.

"This is Bert," he said.

"Hello," she said. The same small sniffly voice.

"Bert Kling," he said.

"I know," she said.

"I'm sorry," he said. "I didn't mean to yell at you."

"That's okay," she said.

"Really, I'm sorry."

"That's okay," she said again.

There was a long silence on the line.

"So . . . how are you?" he said.

"Fine, I guess," she said.

There was another long silence.

"Is your apartment cold?" she asked.

"No, it's fine. Nice and warm."

"I'm freezing to death here," she said. "I'm going to call the Ombudsman's Office first thing tomorrow morning. They're not supposed to turn off the heat so early, are they?"

"Eleven o'clock, I thought."

"Is it eleven already?"

"It's almost midnight."

"Another day, another dollar," Eileen said, and sighed. "Anyway, they're not supposed to turn it off *entirely*, are they?"

"Sixty-two, I think."

"The radiators here are ice cold," she said. "I have *four* blankets on the bed."

"You ought to get an electric blanket," Kling said.

"I'm afraid of them. I'm afraid I'll catch on fire or something."

"No, no, they're very safe."

"Do *you* have an electric blanket?"

"No. But I'm told they're very safe."

"Or electrocuted," she said.

"Well," he said, "I just wanted to make sure you're okay. And really, I *am* sorry for—"

"Me, too." She paused. "This is the 'I'm-Sorry-You're-Sorry' scene, isn't it?" she said.

"I guess so."

"Yeah, that's what it is," she said.

Silence again.

"Well," he said, "it's late, I don't want to—"

"No, don't go," she said.

Silence again.

"Well," he said, "it's late, I don't want to—"

"No, don't go," she said. "Talk to me."

IT SEEMED evident to Brown, as he studied the purchase prices on Edelman's various real estate documents—and translated the French francs, Spanish pesetas, Portuguese escudos, and British pounds to U.S. dollars—that Edelman had been involved in cash transactions that totaled some $4 million over the past five years. His *recorded* transactions, the purchases and sales covered by his various checks and subsequent deposits, amounted to some $1,275,000 over that same period of time. That left almost three million bucks unaccounted for—*and* unaccountable to the Internal Revenue Service.

The trips to Zürich, five in the past year alone, suddenly seemed to make sense, especially in view of the fact that the only expenses he'd incurred there had been for food and lodging. Apparently, Edelman conducted no business in the city of Zürich, no *gem* business, anyway. Then why did he go there? And why had his visits there been followed invariably by side excursions to *other* cities on the Continent? His itineraries, based on the flow of checks in each city, seemed to follow a consistent pattern: Amsterdam, Zürich, Paris, London, with an occasional side trip to Lisbon. Brown guessed that Edelman's trips to Zürich were prompted not so much by a desire to visit the Alps as they were by a need to visit his money.

There was no way of finding out whether or not he had a Swiss bank account; Swiss bankers were as tight with information as hookers were with free trade. Perhaps *Mrs.* Edelman knew something more about her husband's various trips abroad and his ownership (in *his* name only, Brown noticed) of real estate in five foreign countries. Perhaps *she* knew why Zürich had been an essential stop on all of his little journeys. Or perhaps, faced with what now looked like a simple case of tax evasion, she would claim she was an "innocent spouse" who knew nothing about her husband's business activities. Perhaps she didn't.

In any case, it now looked as if they had a mildly prosperous gem merchant who kept honest books on the little baubles he bought and sold here and there, deducted his operating expenses from his small profits, and then paid the tax man whatever was due on his net income. In the meantime, this same guy was spending large sums of cash for the unreported purchase of gems abroad, selling those gems for cash here in the United States— again without reporting the transactions—and then using his huge profits to buy not only *more* gems for resale later, but real estate as well. It did not take a financial genius to recognize that a cash buyer in today's real estate market, when mortgage interest rates both here and abroad were astronomical, would be welcomed with open arms in any country on the face of the earth. Edelman had been buying like a drunken Arab; his *real* business was netting him millions of dollars, none of it reported to Uncle Sam.

Brown reached for the phone on his desk and dialed Kling's home number.

The line was busy.

SHE had asked him not to go, she had asked him to talk to her, and suddenly he could think of nothing else to say. The silence on the line lengthened. On the street outside, he heard the distinctive wail of a 911 Emergency truck and wondered which poor bastard had jumped off a bridge or got himself pinned under a subway train.

"Do you ever get scared?" she asked.

"Yes," he said.

"I mean, on the job."

"Yes."

"I'm scared," she said.

"What about?"

"Tomorrow night."

"The nurse thing?"

"Yeah."

"Well, just don't—"

"I mean, I'm always a *little* scared, but not like this time." She hesitated. "He blinded one of them," she said. "One of the nurses he raped."

"Boy," Kling said.

"Yeah."

"Well, what you have to do . . . just be careful, that's all."

"Yeah, I'm always careful," she said.

"Who's your backup on this?"

"*Two* of them. I've got two of them."

"Well, that's good."

"Abrahams and McCann. Do you know them?"

"No."

"They're out of the Chinatown Precinct."

"I don't know them."

"They seem okay, but . . . well, a backup can't stay *glued* to you, you know. Otherwise he'll scare off the guy you're trying to catch."

"Yeah, but they'll be there if you need them."

"I guess."

"Sure, they will."

"How long does it take to put out somebody's eyes?" she asked.

"I wouldn't worry about that, really. That's not going to help, worrying about it. Just make sure you've got your hand on your gun, that's all."

"In my bag, yeah."

"Wherever you carry it."

"That's where I carry it."

"Make sure it's in your hand. And keep your finger inside the trigger guard."

"Yeah, I always do."

"It wouldn't hurt to carry a spare, either."

"Where would I carry a spare?"

"Strap it to your ankle. Wear slacks. Nurses are allowed to wear slacks, aren't they?"

"Oh, sure. But they like a leg show, you see. I'll be wearing the uniform, you know, like a dress. The white uniform."

"Who do you mean? Rank? They told you to wear a dress?"

"I'm sorry, what—"

"You said they like a leg show."

"Oh. I meant the lunatics out there. They like a little leg, a little ass. Shake your boobs, lure them out of the bushes."

"Yeah, well," Kling said.

"I'll be wearing one of those starched things, you know, with a little white cap, and white panty hose, and this big black cape. I already tried it on today. It'll be at the hospital when I check in tomorrow night."

"What time will that be?"

"When I get to the hospital, or when I go out?"

"Both."

"I'm due there at eleven. I'll be hitting the park at a little after midnight."

"Well, be careful."

"I will."

They were silent for a moment.

"Maybe I could tuck it in my bra or something. The spare."

"Yeah, get yourself one of those little guns . . ."

"Yeah, like a derringer or something."

"No, that won't help you. That's Mickey Mouse time. I'm talking about something like a Browning or a Bernardelli, those little pocket automatics, you know?"

"Yeah," she said, "tuck it in my bra."

"As a spare, you know."

"Yeah."

"You can pick one up anywhere in the city," Kling said. "Cost you something like thirty, forty dollars."

"But those are small-caliber guns, aren't they?" she asked. "Twenty-twos? Or twenty-fives?"

"That doesn't mean anything, the caliber. A gun like a twenty-two can do more damage than a thirty-eight. When Reagan got shot, everybody was saying he was lucky it was only a twenty-two the guy used, but that was wrong thinking. I was talking to this guy at Ballistics . . . Dorfsman. Do you know Dorfsman?"

"No," Eileen said.

"Anyway, he told me you have to think of the human body like a room with furniture in it. You shoot a thirty-eight or a forty-five through one wall of the room, the slug goes right out through another wall. But you shoot a twenty-two or a twenty-five into that room, it hasn't got the power to *exit,* you understand? It hits a sofa, it ricochets off and hits the television set, it ricochets off that and hits a lamp—those are all the organs inside the body, you understand? Like the heart, or the kidneys, or the lungs, the bullet just goes bouncing around inside there doing a lot of damage. So you don't have to worry about the caliber, I mean it. Those little guns can really hurt somebody."

"Yeah," Eileen said, and hesitated. "I'm *still* scared," she said.

"No, don't be. You'll be fine."

"Maybe it's because of what I told you yesterday," she said. "My fantasy, you know. I never told that to anyone in my life. Now I feel as if I'm tempting God or something. Because I said it out loud. About . . . you know, *wanting* to get raped."

"Well, you don't *really* want to get raped."

"I know I don't."

"So that's got nothing to do with it."

"Except for fun and games," she said.

"What do you mean?"

"Getting raped."

"Oh."

"You know," she said. "You tear off my panties and my bra, I struggle a little . . . like that. Pretending."

"Sure," he said.

"To spice it up a little," she said.

"Yeah."

"But not for real."

"No."

She was quiet for a long time. Then she said, "It's too bad tomorrow night is for real."

"Take the spare along," Kling said.

"Oh, I *will,* don't worry."

"Well," he said, "I guess—"

"No, don't go," she said. "Talk to me."

Suddenly, and again, he could think of nothing else to say.

"Tell me what happened," she said. "The divorce."

"I'm not sure I want to," he said.

"*Will* you tell me one day?"

"Maybe."

"Only if you want to," she said. "Bert . . ." She hesitated. "Thank you. I feel a lot better now."

"Well, good," he said. "Listen, if you *want* to . . ."

"Yes?"

"Give me a call tomorrow night. When you come in, I mean. When it's all over. Let me know how it went, okay?"

"Well, that's liable to be pretty late."

"I'm usually up late."

"Well, if you'd like me to."

"Yes, I would."

"It'll be after midnight, you know."

"That's okay."

"Maybe later, if we make the collar. Time we book him—"

"Whenever," Kling said. "Just call me whenever."

"Okay," she said. "Well," she said.

"Well, good night," he said.

"Good night, Bert," she said, and hung up.

He put the receiver back on the cradle. The phone rang again almost instantly. He picked up the receiver at once.

"Hello?" he said.

"Bert, it's Artie," Brown said. "You weren't asleep, were you?"

"No, no."

"I've been trying to get you for the past half hour. I thought maybe you took the phone off the hook. You want to hear what I've got?"

"Shoot," Kling said.

THIRTEEN

IT WAS nine o'clock in the morning, and the four detectives were gathered in the lieutenant's office, trying to make some sense of what they now knew. It had snowed six inches' worth overnight, and more snow was promised for later in the day. Byrnes wondered if it snowed this much in Alaska. He was willing to bet it didn't snow this much in Alaska. The detectives had told him what they knew, and he had taken notes while they spoke—first Meyer and Carella, and then Kling and Brown—and now he guessed he was supposed to provide the sort of leadership that would pull the entire case together for them in a wink. The last time he had pulled an entire case together in a wink was never.

"So Quadrado identified the girl, huh?" he said.

"Yes, Pete," Meyer said.

"Sally Anderson, huh?"

"Yes, Pete."

"You showed him her picture yesterday afternoon."

"*Four* pictures," Meyer said. "Hers and three we pulled from the files. All blondes."

"And he picked out the Anderson girl."

"Yes."

"And told you she used to live with Lopez and was supplying him with coke."

"Yes."

"He got this from his cousin, huh? The girl who was stabbed?"

"Only the coke part. The rest came from him."

"About Lopez and the girl living together?"

"It checks out, Pete. We located the building Lopez used to live in—right next door to the drugstore on Ainsley and Sixth—and the super confirmed that the Anderson girl was living there with him until last August sometime."

"Which is when *Fatback* went into rehearsal."

"Right."

"So there's our connection," Byrnes said.

"If we can trust it," Meyer said.

"What's not to trust?"

"Well, according to one of the dancers in the show, the Anderson girl went uptown every Sunday to *buy* coke."

"So now it looks like she went up there to *sell* it," Carella said.

"Big difference," Meyer said.

"And Quadrado got this from his cousin, huh?" Byrnes said.

"Yes."

"Reliable?"

"Maybe."

"Told him the girl went up there every Sunday to sell coke to Lopez, huh?"

"*Plus* a roll in the hay," Meyer said.

"How does that tie in with what her boyfriend said?" Byrnes asked.

"What do you mean?" Carella said.

"On one of your reports . . . Where the hell is it?" Byrnes said, and began riffling through the D.D. forms on his desk. "Didn't he mention something about a deli? About the girl picking up delicatessen on Sundays?"

"That's right, but she could've been killing two birds with—"

"Here it is," Byrnes said, and began reading out loud. " 'Moore identified word "Del" on calendar as—' "

"That's right," Carella said.

" 'Cohen's Deli, Stem and North Rogers, where she went for bagels and lox, et cetera, every Sunday.' "

"That doesn't mean she couldn't have come *farther* uptown afterward, to deliver the coke to Lopez."

"He didn't know anything about this, huh? The boyfriend?"

"The coke, do you mean? Or the fact that she was still playing around with Lopez?"

"Take your choice," Byrnes said.

"He told us there were no other men in her life, and he told us she wasn't doing anything stronger than pot."

"Reliable?" Byrnes asked.

"He was the one who tipped us off to the ice operation," Meyer said.

"Yeah, what about *that?*" Byrnes asked. "Any connection to the murders?"

"We don't think so. The Anderson girl's involvement was a one-shot deal."

"Are you moving on it?"

"No proof," Meyer said. "We've put Carter on warning."

"A lot of good *that's* gonna do," Byrnes said, and sighed. "What about Edelman?" he asked Brown. "Are you sure you read all that stuff right?"

"Checked it three times," Brown said. "He was screwing Uncle, that's for sure. And laundering a lot of cash over the past five years."

"Buying real estate overseas, huh?"

"Yes," Brown said, and nodded.

"You think that's what all that money in his safe was for?"

"For his next trip over there, right."

"Any idea when he was going?"

"His wife told us next month sometime."

"So he was stashing the money till then, is that it?"

"That's the way it looks to us," Brown said.

"Where'd he get three hundred grand all of a sudden?" Byrnes asked.

"Maybe it wasn't all of a sudden," Kling said. "Maybe it was over a period of time. Let's say he comes back from Holland with a plastic bag of diamonds stuffed up his kazoo and sells them off a little at a time, sixty grand here, fifty grand there, it adds up."

"And then goes to Zürich to put the money in a Swiss account," Brown said.

"Till he's ready to buy either more gems or more real estate," Kling said.

"Okay," Byrnes said, "a nice little racket. But how does it tie in with the other two murders?"

"Three, if you count the Quadrado girl."

"That was a cutting," Byrnes said. "Looks like a wild card to me. Let's concentrate on the ones with the same gun. Any ideas?"

"Well, that's the thing," Carella said.

"*What's* the thing?"

"We can't find any connection but the one between Lopez and the girl. And even *that* one . . ." He shook his head. "We're talking peanuts here, Pete. Lopez had a handful of customers. The girl was maybe supplying him with . . . what? An ounce a week, tops? Tack on what she was selling to the kids in the show, and it still adds up to a very small operation. So why kill her? *Or* Lopez? What's the motive?"

"Maybe it *is* a crazy, after all," Byrnes said, and sighed.

The other men said nothing.

"If it's a crazy," Byrnes said, "there's nothing we can do till he makes his next move. If he knocks off a washerwoman in Majesta or a truck driver in Riverhead, then we'll know the guy's choosing his victims at random."

"Which would make the Lopez and Anderson connection—"

"Coincidental, right," Byrnes said. "*If* the next one is a washerwoman or a truck driver."

"I don't like the idea of waiting around till the next body turns up," Meyer said.

"And *I* don't buy coincidence," Carella said. "Not with Lopez and Anderson both moving cocaine. Anything else, I'd say sure, the guy picked one victim here, another one downtown, a third one up here again, he's checkerboarding all over the city and shooting the first person he happens to run across on any given night. But not with cocaine involved. No, Pete."

"You just told me the cocaine was a lowball operation," Byrnes said.

"It's *still* cocaine," Carella said.

"Was Lopez the *only* person she was supplying?" Byrnes asked.

The men looked at him.

"Or was this a bigger operation than we know?"

The men said nothing.

"Where was the *girl* getting it?" Byrnes said. He nodded briefly. "There's something missing," he said. "Find it."

EMMA and Brother Anthony were celebrating in advance.

He had bought a bottle of expensive four-dollar wine, and they now sat drinking to their good fortune. Emma had read the letter and had come to the same conclusion he had: the man who'd written that letter to Sally Anderson was the man who was supplying her with cocaine. The letter made that entirely clear.

"He buys eight keys of cocaine," Brother Anthony said, "gives it a full hit, gets twice what he paid for it."

"Time it gets on the street," Emma said, "who knows *what* it'd be worth?"

"You got to figure they step on it all the way down the line. Time your user gets it, it'll only be ten, fifteen percent pure. The eight keys this guy bought . . . He sounds like an amateur, don't he? I mean, going in *alone?* With four hundred grand in *cash?*"

"Strictly," Emma said.

"Well, so are we, in a way," Brother Anthony said.

"You're very generous," Emma said, and smiled.

"Anyway, those eight keys, time they hit the street up here, they've already been whacked so hard you're talking maybe thirty-*two* keys for sale. Your average user buying coke doesn't know *what* he's getting. Half the rush he feels is from thinking he paid so *much* for his gram."

Emma looked at the letter again. " 'The first thing I want to do is celebrate,' " she read. " 'There's a new restaurant on top of the Freemont Building, and I'd like to go there Saturday night. Very elegant, very continental. No panties, Sally. I want you to look very elegant and demure, but no panties, okay? Like the time we ate at Mario's down in the Quarter, do you remember? Then, when we get home . . .' " Emma shrugged. "Lovey-dovey stuff," she said.

"Girl had more panties than a lingerie shop," Brother Anthony said. "Whole *drawer*ful of panties."

"So he asks her not to *wear* any!" Emma said, and shook her head.

"I'm gonna buy you one of those little things ballet dancers wear," Brother Anthony said.

"Thank you, sir," Emma said, and made a little curtsy.

"Why you think she saved that letter?" Brother Anthony asked.

" 'Cause it's a love letter," Emma said.

"Then why'd she hide it in the collar of her jacket?"

"Maybe she was married."

"No, no."

"Or had another boyfriend."

"I think it was in case she wanted to turn the screws on him," Brother Anthony said. "I think the letter was her insurance. Proof that he bought eight keys of coke. Dumb amateur," he said, and shook his head.

"Try him again," Emma said.

"Yeah, I better," Brother Anthony said. He rose ponderously, walked to the telephone, picked up the scrap of paper on which he'd scribbled the number he'd found in the directory, and then dialed.

Emma watched him.

"It's ringing," he said.

She kept watching him.

"Hello?" a voice on the other end said, and Brother Anthony immediately hung up.

"He's home," he said.

"Good," she said. "Go see the man, dear."

THE odd thing about the lunchtime skull session the boys of the Eight-Seven held in the squadroom at ten minutes past one that Thursday afternoon was that someone who wasn't even a policeman already knew the missing "something" that would have proved extremely valuable to their investigation if only *they'd* known it, which they didn't. They were *still* trying to find it, whereas Brother Anthony already knew it. Brother Anthony, as it were, happened to be a few steps ahead of them as they chewed, respectively, on their hot pastrami on rye, tuna on white, sausage and peppers on a roll, and ham on toasted whole wheat. They were drinking coffee in cardboard containers, also ordered from the diner up the street, a habit Miscolo tried to discourage because he felt it was an insult to the coffee he brewed and dispensed, gratis, in the Clerical Office. As Brother Anthony pushed his way through the subway turnstile some six blocks away and ran toward the waiting graffiti-camouflaged train, managing to squeeze himself inside the car before the doors closed, the boys of the Eight-Seven were chewing on the case (*and* their sandwiches) from the top, trying to find the missing something that would take them exactly where Brother Anthony was heading. It did not speak well for the police department.

"I think the Loot is right," Meyer said. "We should scratch the Quadrado girl."

"Except she was looking to inherit Lopez's trade," Kling said.

"That *can't* be why Lopez was killed," Carella said. "For his *trade?* We're not dealing with Colombian hotshots here, we're—"

"How do you know we're not?" Brown asked.

"Because none of that crowd would even *spit* on a two-bit gram dealer like Lopez."

"Please, not while I'm eating," Meyer said.

"Sorry," Carella said, and bit into his sausage-and-peppers sandwich.

(It was funny how things broke down ethnically in this squad-room: Meyer was eating the pastrami on rye, Kling was eating the tuna on white, and Brown was eating the ham on toasted whole wheat.)

"So okay, let's scratch the Quadrado girl for the time being," Kling said.

"And start with the Anderson girl," Meyer said. "We know more about her than any of the other victims—"

"Well, that isn't true," Brown said.

"*Relatively* more," Meyer said.

"Relatively, okay," Brown conceded. "But don't forget that three hundred G's in Edelman's safe."

"You done good work, okay, Sonny?" Meyer said. "What do you want, a medal?"

"I want Detective/First," Brown said, and grinned.

"Give him Detective/First," Meyer said to Carella.

"You got it," Carella said.

"So here's this girl—" Meyer started.

"Who are we talking about?" Kling asked. "The Quadrado girl or the Anderson girl?"

"The Anderson girl. She comes up here every Sunday after she buys her deli at Cohen's, and she hops in the sack with Lopez—"

"Well, we don't know that for sure," Carella said.

"That's not important, whether she was still sleeping with him or not," Kling said. "What's important—"

"What's important is that she came up here to sell him *coke*," Meyer said. "You think I don't know that's the important thing?"

"Which her boyfriend knew nothing about," Carella said.

"Her boyfriend doesn't know his ass from his elbow," Brown said. "He's the one who thought she was into ice full time, isn't he?"

"Yeah," Carella said.

"Sent you on a wild-goose chase," Brown said.

"It doesn't *matter* what he knew or what he didn't know," Kling said. "*We* know she was coming up here to sell dope."

"A little schtup in the hay," Meyer said, "move an ounce of cocaine at the same time, nice way to spend a Sunday afternoon."

"It's funny he didn't know anything about it," Carella said.

"Who're we talking about now?" Kling asked.

"Moore. Her boyfriend."

"That she was schtupping Lopez?"

"Or coming up here with coke. That's something she'd have told him, don't you think?"

"Yeah, but she didn't."

"Unless he was lying to us."

"For that matter, why'd he lie about the *ice?*" Kling asked.

"Who says he lied?" Brown asked. "Maybe he thought she really *was* running those tickets on a regular basis."

"Yeah, but it was a one-shot deal," Carella said. "Wouldn't he have *known* that? He was practically *living* with the girl."

"That makes *two* things he didn't know," Meyer said.

"That she was coming uptown with coke," Kling said, "and that she only ran the ice tickets once."

"*Three* things, if you count the hanky-panky with Lopez."

"Plus he didn't even know she herself was tooting."

"Said she only smoked a little grass."

"Practically living with the girl, but didn't know she was snorting coke."

"Or moving it."

"I keep remembering that a guy with three hundred thousand bucks in his safe was one of the victims," Brown said.

"Here he goes with the safe again," Meyer said.

"You're thinking cocaine numbers, am I right?" Kling asked.

"I'm thinking somebody had that kind of money to hand over to Edelman. And I'm thinking, yes, there's cocaine in this damn case, and those *are* the kind of numbers cocaine brings."

"Not in the small-time trade the Anderson girl had," Meyer said.

"Which is what we *know* about," Carella said.

"We have no reason to believe there was anything more," Meyer said. "Unless—"

"Yeah?"

"No, skip it. I just remembered—"

"Yeah, what?"

"He said they rarely spent Sundays together, didn't he? During the day, I mean. He said she was always busy on Sundays."

"Who's this?" Brown asked.

"Moore. The boyfriend."

"So what does that mean?"

"Busy doing *what?*" Meyer asked.

"Running to the deli," Kling said.

"And making it with Lopez."

"And selling him a little pile of nose candy."

"And that's what kept her busy all day long, huh?" Meyer said.

"It could keep a girl busy," Brown said. "Lopez *alone* could've kept a girl busy."

"The thing is," Meyer said, "if she was so damn *busy* all day Sunday . . ."

"Yeah, that," Carella said.

"What?"

"What the hell was she *doing* all that time? She writes *del* on her calendar each and every Sunday. Is that something important to write on your calendar? That she's coming uptown to get del-icatessen? Cohen's is terrific, I admit it, but does she have to list that on her *calendar?*"

"Steve, she listed *everything* on her calendar. Visits to her shrink, calls to Moore's mother in Miami, dance classes, meetings with her agent—so why not deli?"

"Then why didn't she just write *deli?* Do you know anybody who would write *del* for *deli?* We're talking about a single letter here, the letter *i*, the difference between *del* and *deli*. Why'd she write *del* instead of *deli?*"

"Why?" Brown asked.

"I don't *know* why. I'm just asking."

"Moore said it stood for 'deli.' "

"But Moore hasn't turned out to be so reliable, has he?" Kling said.

"First he tells us she only smoked grass, then he tells us she was involved in Carter's ice scam, then he tells us she went uptown for deli every Sunday . . ."

"Too busy to check up on her."

"Too busy with his schoolwork."

"Too busy weighing hearts and livers."

"Busy, busy."

"Everybody busy."

"Doing *what?*" Brown said.

"On Sundays, you mean?"

"The girl, yeah. On Sundays."

"Deli and coke," Kling said, and shrugged.

"And Lopez in the sack."

"Moore had no reason to be lying to us," Meyer said. "He was probably just mistaken."

"Still," Carella said, "they were close."

"Very close."

"The girl even called his mother every week."

"Nice rich widow lady in Miami."

"So if they were *that* close, how come he was *mistaken* about all these things?"

"You'd think he'd have known."

"Miami, did you say?" Brown asked.

"What?"

"Is that where his mother lives?"

"Yeah."

"Miami," Brown said again.

"What about it?"

"I keep thinking of that three hundred grand in Edelman's—"

"Forget the safe for a minute, will you?"

"But just *suppose,*" Brown said.

"Suppose what?"

"That the three hundred was coke money."

"That's a long suppose."

"Not when we're dealing with two victims who were *moving* coke."

"Okay, so suppose the money *was* coke money?"

"Well, what do you think of when you think of Miami?"

The other detectives looked at him.

"Well, sure," Meyer said.

"But that's a long stretch," Kling said.

"No, wait a minute," Carella said.

"Just because a guy's *mother* lives in Miami—"

"That doesn't mean—"

"He isn't even Hispanic," Meyer said. "If he went down there looking to buy cocaine—"

"Anyway, what *with*?" Kling asked. "We're talking three hundred in the safe. To realize that kind of money *here*, he'd have needed at least *half* that to make his buy in Miami."

"His father just died," Carella said.

"When?" Brown asked.

"Last June. He told us he inherited some money, enough to set him up in practice when he gets out of school."

"How much did he inherit?" Kling asked. "Remember the numbers we're dealing with. There was three hundred grand in cash in that safe."

"What we're saying," Meyer said, and shook his head. "Just because Moore's mother lives in Miami, we're saying he went down there and spent whatever his father left him—"

"What's wrong with that?" Brown said. "That sounds pretty damn good to me, you want to know."

"Bought however much coke," Carella said, nodding.

"A *lot* of coke," Brown said. "Enough to turn over for three hundred G's."

"Which ended up in Edelman's safe."

"Bought diamonds from Edelman, or whatever."

"No record of the transaction."

"They both come out clean. Moore launders his dope money by trading it for diamonds, and Edelman launders his cash by buying real estate in Europe."

"Very nice," Meyer said. "If you believe in Peter Rabbit."

"What's wrong with it?" Carella said.

"First, we don't even *know* how much the guy inherited. It

could've been ten, twenty thousand dollars. *If* that much. Next, we're saying a medical student could find his way around those Colombian heavies down there in Miami and make a big buy without having his head handed to him on a platter."

"It's possible," Carella said.

"Anything's possible," Meyer said. "The sun could shine at midnight, why not? We're *also* saying he made contact with a guy dealing diamonds under the table—"

"Come on," Brown said, "that's the *easiest* part. There must be hundreds of guys like Edelman in this city."

"Maybe so. But even assuming *all* of it's possible—Moore inherited a lot of money, made contact somehow in Miami, doubled his money buying pure there and selling it cut here, laundered the money buying diamonds or rubies or whatever— let's accept *all* of that for the moment, okay?"

"It doesn't sound bad," Carella said.

"No, and it would explain why he was *mistaken* about so many things," Kling said.

"Fine," Meyer said. "Then maybe you can tell me how a man can be in two places at the same time."

"What do you mean?" Carella said.

"How could he have been outside the Anderson girl's apartment, shooting her dead, and be in his own apartment at the same time, studying and listening to the radio? You talked to this Loeb guy yourself, Steve. He confirmed that there were calls going back and forth all night long, he told you Moore's radio was on, he told you—"

And just then, Detective Richard Genero walked into the squadroom with his little Japanese radio in his hand. The detectives looked at him. Genero walked to his desk, set the radio down, glanced toward the lieutenant's open door—a certain sign that Byrnes was still out to lunch—and turned on the radio full blast.

"Okay," Meyer said. "Let's go."

THERE WAS VERY LOUD MUSIC coming from inside the apartment. Brother Anthony knocked on the door again, not certain his first several knocks had been heard.

"Who is it?" a voice inside called.

"Mr. Moore?" Brother Anthony said.

"Just a second," the voice called.

The music became softer—the guy inside had lowered the volume. Brother Anthony heard footsteps approaching the door.

"Who is it?" the voice said again, just inside the door this time.

He knew that in this city, people did not open the door for strangers. Brother Anthony hesitated. He did not want to have to break down the door. "Police," he said.

"Oh."

He waited.

"Hold on a second, will you?" the voice said.

He heard the footsteps retreating. He put his ear to the wooden door. A lot of moving around in there. He debated breaking down the door, after all. He decided to wait it out. The footsteps were approaching the door again. He heard the lock being turned, the tumblers falling. The door opened.

"Mr. Moore?" he said.

Moore took one look and started closing the door. Brother Anthony heaved his full weight against it, knocking it open, the imploding door forcing Moore away from it and back into the room. Brother Anthony followed the door into the room, slammed it shut behind him, and locked it. Moore was standing several feet back from the door now, nursing his shoulder where the door had hit him, staring at Brother Anthony. Behind him, the radio was sitting on an end table, still playing softly. Brother Anthony decided he would steal it when he left.

"Anybody here with you?" he asked.

"Who the hell are *you*?" Moore said.

"I have a letter you wrote," Brother Anthony said.

"What letter? What are you talking about?"

"From Miami. To a girl named Sally Anderson. Who is now dead," Brother Anthony said, "may God rest her soul."

Moore said nothing.

"Sally was getting cocaine from you," Brother Anthony said.

"I don't know what you mean."

"She was getting cocaine from you and selling it uptown," Brother Anthony said. "To Paco Lopez."

"I don't know anybody named Paco Lopez."

"But you *do* know Sally Anderson, don't you? You wrote to her in August saying you'd made a big cocaine buy in Miami. Where's that cocaine now, Mr. Moore? The cocaine Sally was dealing uptown."

"I don't know anything about any cocaine Sally was—"

"Mr. Moore," Brother Anthony said quietly, "I don't want to hurt you. We got Sally's name from a lady named Judite Quadrado, who got hurt because she wasn't quick enough to tell us what we wanted to know."

"Who's *we?*" Moore asked.

"That's none of your business," Brother Anthony said. "Your business is telling me where the coke is. That's the only business you have to worry about right now."

Moore looked at him.

"Yes, Mr. Moore," Brother Anthony said, and nodded.

"It's all gone," Moore said.

"You bought eight keys—"

"Where'd you find that letter?" Moore said. "She told me she'd burned it!"

"Then she was lying. And so are you, Mr. Moore. If all eight keys are gone, where was she getting the stuff she sold uptown?"

"Not *all* of them," Moore said. "I sold off six."

"And the other two?"

"I gave them to Sally. She took them out of here. I don't know where they are."

"You gave away *two* kilos of cocaine? For which you paid a hundred thousand *bucks?* Mr. Moore, you are full of shit."

"I'm telling you the truth. She was my girlfriend. I gave her—"

"No," Brother Anthony said.

"Whatever *she* did with it—"

"No, you didn't give away no two keys of coke, Mr. Moore. Nobody loves *nobody* that much. So where are they?"

"Sally took them out of here. They're probably still in her apartment. Unless the police confiscated them."

"That's a possibility," Brother Anthony said. "I can tell you for sure they're not in her apartment, so maybe the police *did* take them, who knows with those thieves?" Brother Anthony smiled. "But I don't think so. I don't think you'd have let a hundred thousand bucks' worth of coke out of your sight, Mr. Moore. Not when it would've already been worth *twice* what you paid for it in Miami, nossir. So where is it?"

"I told you—"

Brother Anthony reached out suddenly. He grabbed Moore's hand in his own right hand, pulled Moore toward him, and then joined his left hand over Moore's so that the three hands together made a sort of hand sandwich, with Moore's hand caught between both Brother Anthony's. Brother Anthony began squeezing. Moore began yelling. "Shhh," Brother Anthony cautioned, and began squeezing harder. "I don't want no yelling. I don't want no people coming up here," he said, still squeezing. "All I'm going to do is break your hand if you don't tell me where the coke is. That's for starters. After that, I'll figure out what to break next."

"Please," Moore whispered. "P . . . please . . . let go."

"The coke," Brother Anthony said.

"The bed . . . the bedroom," Moore said, and Brother Anthony released his hand.

"Show me," he said. "How's your hand?" he asked pleasantly, and shoved Moore toward the open door to the bedroom. A suitcase was on the bed.

"Were you going someplace?" Brother Anthony asked.

Moore said nothing.

"Where is it?"

"In the bag," Moore said.

Brother Anthony tried the clasps. "It's locked," he said.

"I'll get the key," Moore said, and went to the dresser across the room.

"Taking a little trip, were you?" Brother Anthony asked, smiling, and then the smile froze on his face when Moore turned from the open dresser drawer with a gun in his hand. "Hey, wh—" Brother Anthony said, but that was all he ever said because Moore squeezed the trigger once, and then again, and both bullets from the .38 caught Brother Anthony in the face, one entering just below his left eye, the other shattering his teeth and upper gum. Brother Anthony reflexively clawed the air for support and then fell in a mountainous brown heap at Moore's feet.

Moore looked down at him.

"You stupid son of a bitch," he whispered, and then he tucked the gun into his belt and went out of the bedroom, through the living room, and into the kitchen. There was no time to pack anything else now—the shots would bring suspicious neighbors. He had to get out of here fast now, take the diamonds, take what was left of the coke, just get out of here as fast as he could.

He opened the door on the refrigerator's freezer compartment.

There were two ice-cube trays on a small shelf toward the rear of the freezer. He pried the tray on the left loose and turned on the sink's hot water tap. He let the water run for several minutes before putting the tray under the faucet. The ice cubes began to melt. They took forever to melt. He kept listening for sounds in the hallway outside, someone coming, anyone coming, waiting for the ice cubes to melt. At last, he turned off the tap, carefully spilled the water from the tray into the sink, and removed the plastic dividing grid from the tray. The diamonds glistened wetly on the bottom of the tray. He spread them on a dish towel on the counter top and was patting them dry when he heard the sound of wood splintering. He turned toward the living room. A voice shouted, "Moore?"

He came out of the kitchen with the gun in his hand, recognized Meyer and Carella, saw that both men were armed, saw two other armed men behind them, one white and one black, and might have put up a fight even then if Carella hadn't said, very softly, "I wouldn't."

He didn't.

FOURTEEN

THEY realized, by eleven o'clock that Thursday night, that he was going to tell them only what he wanted to tell them, and nothing more. That was why he waived his right to have an attorney present during the questioning. That was why he was flying in the face of the Miranda-Escobedo warnings, telling them whatever they wanted to know about the dope they'd found in his apartment and the letter he'd written to Sally Anderson back in August, knowing they had him cold on the dope charge but figuring he'd bluff his way out of the murders. *They* were looking for four counts—maybe five, if he'd also killed the Quadrado girl—of Murder One. He was looking for a Class A-1 Felony charge for possession of four or more ounces of a controlled substance, punishable by a minimum of fifteen to twenty-five years and a maximum of life. With a good lawyer, he could plea it down to a Class A-2 Felony, hoping for a minimum of three and expecting to get out in two. As for having shot and killed Brother Anthony, he was claiming self-defense and hoping to get off scot-free. *They* were looking for him to do consecutive time on at least four homicide raps. *He* was hoping to be out on the street again within the imminently foreseeable future. They were somewhat at odds as concerned their differing aspirations and their separate versions of what had happened over the past nine days.

"Let's hear it one more time," Carella said.

"How often do I have to tell you?" Moore said. "Maybe I *should've* asked for a lawyer."

"You still can," Carella said, making sure for the record that Moore was volunteering all this information of his own free will. They were sitting in the interrogation room, a tape recorder whirring on the table between Moore and the four detectives with him. From where Carella sat, he could see past Moore to the two-way mirror on the wall behind him. Moore's back was to the mirror. No one was in the viewing room beyond the wall.

"Why would I need a lawyer?" Moore said. "I'm admitting the cocaine. You found the cocaine. You've got me on the cocaine."

"Two keys of it," Meyer said.

"Less than that," Moore said.

"But you bought *eight* keys in Miami. The letter you wrote—"

"I never should have written that letter," Moore said.

"But you did."

"Dumb," Moore said.

"So's murder," Kling said.

"I killed a man who came into my apartment with a gun," Moore said, almost by rote now. "We struggled, I grabbed the gun from him, and shot him. It was self-defense."

"The same gun that was used in three *other* murders," Brown said.

"I don't know anything about any other murders. Anyway, this wasn't *murder*. It was self-defense."

"I thought you were a medical student," Kling said.

"What?"

"Are you also studying law?"

"I know the difference between cold-blooded murder and self-defense."

"Was it cold-blooded murder when you killed Sally Anderson?" Carella asked.

"I didn't kill Sally."

"Or Paco Lopez?"

"I don't know anybody named Paco Lopez."

"How about Marvin Edelman?"

"I never heard of him."

"Then how do you account for those diamonds we found in your kitchen?"

"I bought them with the money I realized on the sale of the six keys."

"Who'd you buy them from?"

"How is that relevant? Is it against the law to buy diamonds?"

"Only if you later kill the man you bought them from."

"I bought them from somebody whose name I never knew."

"An anonymous diamond dealer, huh?" Meyer said.

"Passing through from Amsterdam," Moore said, and nodded.

"How'd you get onto him?"

"*He* contacted *me*. He heard I had some ready cash."

"How much cash?" Carella asked.

"I bought the eight keys for four hundred thousand."

"A bargain," Brown said.

"I told you, the man was doing me a favor."

"The man in Miami."

"Yes."

"What's *his* name?"

"I don't have to tell you that. He was doing me a favor. Why should I get him in trouble?"

"Because you saved his son's life, right?" Meyer said.

"Right. The kid was choking to death. I did the Heimlich on him. The father said he wanted to do something for me in return."

"So that's how you got in the drug business, right?" Brown said.

"That's how."

"Where'd you get the four hundred thousand?"

"From my mother. The money my father left her."

"She had four hundred thousand bucks under her mattress, huh?"

"No. Some of it was in money market funds, the rest in securities. She was getting something like thirteen percent. I promised her fifteen percent in a month's time."

"Did you pay back the money?"

"Every cent."

"Plus the interest?"

"Fifteen percent."

"You gave back . . . What does that come to, Artie?"

"Fifteen percent on four hundred thousand?"

"For a month."

"It's five thousand dollars," Moore said.

"You returned the four hundred plus five, is that right?" Carella asked.

"I did."

"When?"

"At the end of September. I gave my mother the money shortly after *Fatback* opened."

"Is that how long it took you to cut and resell those eight keys?"

"Only six of them."

"What'd you get for selling off the six?"

"*Twelve*, by the time I cut them. I got sixty thousand a key."

"What does that come to, Artie?" Carella asked.

"It comes to seven hundred and twenty thousand dollars," Moore said.

"And you returned four hundred and five of that to your mother."

"Yes."

"Which left you with—"

"Three hundred and fifteen."

"Three hundred of which you spent to buy diamonds from Edelman."

"I don't know anybody named Edelman," Moore said.

"But that's how much you spent for the diamonds you bought, isn't it?"

"Close to it."

"From this Dutchman who was passing through, right?"

"Right."

"What'd you get for that kind of money?"

"About twenty-five carats. I got a break because it was a cash transaction."

"So how many stones did you buy?"

"About three dozen. Most of them quarter and half-carat stones. A few one-carat stones. Different sizes and cuts, American, European—well, you saw them."

"Just enough to fit in an ice-cube tray, huh?"

"I thought of that later."

"First place a burglar would look," Meyer said.

"I don't know anything about burglars."

"Why'd you pick diamonds?"

"A good investment. Over the past thirty years—before the bottom fell out—diamonds have gone up in value more than a thousand percent. I figured they had to start going up again."

"You're just an enterprising young businessman, right?" Brown said.

Moore said nothing.

"Where'd you sell those six keys?"

"I don't have to tell you that."

"Why'd you hang on to the other two?"

"That was Sally's idea. She figured we could get more for it by selling them off to gram dealers."

"Like Paco Lopez."

"I don't know anyone named Paco Lopez. Sally figured it might take a while longer, but over the long run we'd make maybe an extra fifty thousand on those two keys. By ouncing it out to gram dealers."

"*Another* enterprising young businessman," Brown said.

"*Woman*," Meyer said.

"*Person*," Kling said.

"So why'd you decide to kill all these people?" Carella asked casually.

"I didn't kill anyone but the man who broke into my apartment," Moore said. "And that was self-defense. The man came in with a gun, we struggled, I took the gun away from him and shot him. He was trying to hold me up. It was self-defense."

"Knew you had two keys of dope in there, huh?"

"I don't know *what* he knew. Anyway, it was less than two keys. We'd been dipping into it ever since I got back from Miami."

"Selling it here and there around town."

"Sally took care of that."

"Made her deliveries on Sundays, did she?"

"Yes."

"That's what the *del* stood for, right? Not 'delicatessen.' 'Deliveries.' "

"Deliveries, yes."

"Did Paco Lopez put her onto the *other* gram dealers she—"

"I don't know anyone named Paco Lopez."

"Why'd you kill *him* first?"

"I don't know who you're talking about."

"Why'd you kill Sally?"

"I didn't."

"And Edelman."

"I don't know who Edelman is. You've got me on the dope, so charge me with the dope. I killed an armed intruder in self-defense. I don't know what you can charge me with on *that*—"

"Try homicide," Carella said.

"If self-defense is homicide, fine. But no jury in its right mind—"

"You're an expert on the jury system, too, huh?" Meyer said.

"I'm not an expert on anything," Moore said. "I happened across a good investment, and I took advantage of it."

"And then decided to protect it by killing—"

"The only person I killed is the man who broke into my apartment."

"Did he know there'd be diamonds in there?"

"I don't know what he knew."

"Just happened to break in on you, is that it?"

"Happens all the time in this city."

"Didn't know there'd be dope, didn't know there'd be diamonds."

"I never saw him before in my life. How would I know what his motive was? He forced his way in with a gun. We struggled—"

"Yes, and you took the gun away from him and shot him."

"Yes."

"Guy built like a grizzly bear, you took the gun away from him?"

"I can handle myself," Moore said.

"Only too well," Carella said, and sighed. He looked up at the wall clock. It was ten minutes to twelve. "Okay," he said, "let's go through it one more time."

SHE felt stupid with a gun in her bra.

The gun was a .22-caliber Llama with a six-shot capacity, deadly enough, she supposed, if push came to shove. Its overall length was four and three-quarter inches, just small enough to fit cozily if uncomfortably between her breasts. It weighed only thirteen and a half ounces, but it felt like thirteen and a half *pounds* tucked there inside her bra, and besides, the metal was cold. That was because she had left the top three buttons of the uniform unfastened, in case she needed to get in there in a hurry. The wind was blowing up under the flapping black cape she was wearing, straight from the North Pole and directly into the open V-necked wedge of the uniform. Her breasts were cold, and her nipples were cold and erect besides—but maybe that was because she was scared to death.

She did not like the setup, she had told them that from the start. Even after the dry run this afternoon, she had voiced her complaints. It had taken her eight minutes to cross the park on the winding path that ran more or less diagonally through it, walking at a slightly faster than normal clip, the way a woman alone at midnight would be expected to walk through a deserted park. She had argued for a classic bookend surveillance, one of her backup men ahead of her, the other behind, at reasonably safe distances. Both of her backups were old-timers from the Chinatown Precinct, both of them Detectives/First. Abrahams ("Call me Morrie," he said back at the precinct, when they were laying out their strategy) argued that anybody walking point would scare off their rapist if he made a head-on approach. McCann ("I'm Mickey," he told her) argued that if the guy made his approach from *behind,* he'd spot the follow-up man and call it all off. Eileen could see the sense of what they were saying, but she still didn't like the way *they* were proposing to do it. What *they* wanted to do was plant one of them at either end of the path, at opposite ends of the park. That meant that if their man hit when she was midway through the park, the way he'd done on his last three outings, she'd be four minutes away from either one of them— okay, say three minutes, if they came at a gallop.

"If I'm in trouble," she said, "you won't be able to reach me in time. Why can't we put you under the trees someplace, hiding under those trees in the middle of the park? That's where he hit the last three times. If you're under the trees there, we won't have four minutes separating us."

"Three minutes," Abrahams said.

"That's where he hit the last three times," she said again.

"Suppose he scouts the area this time?" McCann said.

"And spots two guys hiding under the trees there?" Abrahams said.

"He'll call it off," McCann said.

"You'll have the transmitter in your bag," Abrahams said.

"A lot of good *that'll* do if he decides to stick an ice pick in my eye," Eileen said.

"Voice-activated," McCann said.

"Terrific," Eileen said. "Will that get you there any faster? I could yell bloody murder, and it'll still take you three minutes— *minimum*—to get from either end of that park. In three minutes, I can be a statistic."

Abrahams laughed.

"Very funny," Eileen said. "Only it's *my* ass we're talking about here."

"I dig this broad," Abrahams said, laughing.

"That radio can pick up a whisper from twenty-five feet away," McCann said.

"So what?" Eileen said. "It'll *still* take you three minutes to reach me from where you guys want to plant yourselves. Look, Morrie, why don't *you* go in? How about you, Mickey? Either one of you in drag, how does that sound? *I'll* sit outside the park, listening to the radio, okay?"

"I really dig this broad," Abrahams said, laughing.

"So what do you want to do?" McCann asked her.

"I told you. The trees. We hide you under the trees."

"Be pointless. The guy combs the park first, he spots us, he knows we've got it staked out. That's what you want to do, we might as well forget the whole thing."

"Let him go on raping those nurses there," Abrahams said.

Both men looked at her.

So that was what it got down to at last, that was what it always got down to in the long run. You had to show them you were just as good as *they* were, willing to take the same chances *they'd* have taken in similar circumstances, prove to them you had *balls*.

"Okay," she said, and sighed.

"Better take off those earrings," McCann said.

"I'm wearing the earrings," she said.

"Nurses don't wear earrings. I never seen a nurse wearing earrings. He'll spot the earrings."

"I'm wearing the earrings," she said flatly.

So here I am, she thought, ball-less to be sure, but wearing my good-luck earrings and carrying one gun tucked in my bra and another gun in my shoulder bag alongside the battery-powered, voice-activated FM transmitter that can pick up a whisper from twenty-five feet away—according to McCann, who, by her current estimate, was now two and a half minutes away at the southeast corner of the park, with Abrahams *three* and a half minutes away at the northwest corner.

If he's going to make his move, she thought, this is where he'll make it, right here, halfway through the park, far from the streetlights. Trees on either side of the path—spruces, hemlocks, pines—snow-covered terrain beyond them. Jump out of the trees, drag me off the path the way he did with the others, this is where he hit the last three times, this is where he'll do it now. The descriptions of the man had been conflicting; they always seemed to be when the offense was rape. One of the victims had described him as being black, another as white. The girl he'd blinded had sobbingly told the investigating officer that her assailant had been short and squat, built like a gorilla. The other two nurses insisted that he'd been very tall, with the slender, muscular body of a weight lifter. He'd been variously described as wearing a business suit, a black leather jacket and blue jeans, and a jogging suit. One of the nurses said he was in his mid-forties, another said he was no older than twenty-five, the third had no opinion whatever about his age. The first nurse he'd raped said he'd been blond. The second one said he'd been wearing a peaked hat, like a baseball cap. The one he'd blinded—her hand began sweating on the butt of the .38 in her shoulder bag.

It was funny the way her hands always started sweating whenever she found herself in a tight situation. She wondered if McCann's hands were sweating. Three minutes behind her now, Abrahams equidistant at the other end of the park. She wondered if the transmitter was picking up the clicking of her boots on the asphalt path. The path was shoveled clear of snow, but there were still some patches of ice on it, and she skirted one of those now and looked into the darkness ahead, her eyes accustomed to the dark, and thought she saw something under the trees ahead, and almost stopped dead in her tracks—but that was not what a good decoy was supposed to do. A good decoy marched right into it, a good decoy allowed her man to make his move, a good decoy—

She thought at first she was hearing things.

Her hand tightened on the butt of the gun.

Somebody whistling?

What?

She kept walking, peering into the darkness ahead, past the midway point now, McCann a bit more than three and a half minutes behind her, Abrahams two and a half minutes away in the opposite direction, *still* too far away, and saw a boy on a skateboard coming up the path, whistling as he curved the board in graceful arcs back and forth across the path. He couldn't have been older than thirteen or fourteen, a hatless youngster wearing a blue ski parka and jeans, sneakered feet expertly guiding the skateboard, arms akimbo as he balanced himself, a midnight whistler enjoying the dark silence of the empty park, closer now, still whistling. She smiled, and her hand relaxed on the butt of the gun.

And then, suddenly, he swerved the board into her, bending at the knees, leaning all his weight to one side so that the board slid out from under him, the wheels coming at her, the underside slamming her across the shins. She was pulling the gun from her bag when he punched her in the face. The gun went off while it was still inside the bag, blowing out leather and cigarettes and chewing gum and Kleenex tissues—but not the radio, she hoped. Jesus, not the radio!

In the next thirty seconds—it couldn't have been longer than that—her finger tightening in reflex on the trigger again, the gun's explosion shattering the stillness of the night again, their breaths pluming brokenly from their mouths, merging, blowing away on the wind, she thought, remembered, *Force part of psychological interplay*, he punched her over the breast, *Attendant danger of being severely beaten or killed*, the gun went off a third time, his fist smashed into her mouth, *But he's just a kid*. She tasted blood, felt herself going limp, he was grabbing her right arm, turning her, behind her now, forcing her to her knees, he was going to break her arm, "Let go of it!" yanking on the arm, pulling up on it. "Let *go!*" her hand opened, the gun clattered to the asphalt.

She tried to get to her feet as he came around her, but he shoved her back onto the path, hard, knocking the wind out of her. As he started to straddle her, she kicked out at him with her booted left foot, white skirts flying, the black heel of the boot catching him on the thigh, a trifle too low for the money. She wondered how many seconds had gone by now, wondered where McCann and Abrahams were, she'd *told* them the setup was no good, she'd *told* them—he began slapping her. Straddling her, slapping her, both hands moving, the slaps somehow more painful than the punches had been, dizzying, big callused hands punishing her cheeks and her jaw, back and forth, her head flailing with each successive slap, his weight on her chest, pressing on her breasts—the gun. She remembered the gun in her bra.

She tried to twist away from him, her arms pinioned by his thighs on either side of her, tried to turn her head to avoid the incessant slaps, and idiotically noticed the nurse's cap lying white and still on the path where it had fallen. She could not free her arms or her hands, she could not get to the gun.

The slapping stopped abruptly.

There was only the darkness now and the sound of his vaporized breath coming in short, ragged bursts from his mouth. His hands reached for the front of the uniform. He grasped the fabric. He tore open the front, buttons flying, reached for her bra and her breasts—and stopped again. He had seen the gun, he must have seen the gun. His silence now was more frightening than his earlier fury had been. *One* gun might have meant a streetwise lady who knew the city's parks were dangerous. *Another* gun, this one hidden in a bra, could mean only one thing. The lady was a cop. He shifted his weight. She knew he was reaching for something in his pants pocket. She knew the something would be a weapon, and she thought, *He's going to blind me.*

In that moment, fear turned to ice. Cold, crystalline, hard. In that moment, she knew she couldn't count on the cavalry or the marines getting here in time; there was nobody here but us chickens, boss, and nobody to look after little Eileen but little Eileen herself. She took advantage of the shift of his body weight to the left, his right hand going into his pocket, the balance an uneasy one for the barest fraction of a second, enough time for her to emulate the movement of his own body, her left shoulder rising in easy symmetry with his own cant, their bodies in motion together for only a fraction of a second, movement responding to movement as though they were true lovers, and suddenly she lurched, every ounce of strength concentrated in that left shoulder, adding her own weight and momentum to his already off-center tilt—and he toppled over.

His right hand was still in his pocket as she scrambled to her feet. He rolled over onto the path, his right hand coming free of his pocket, the switchblade knife snapping open just as she pulled the Llama out of her bra. She knew she would kill him if he moved. He saw the gun in her hand, steady, leveled at his head, and perhaps he saw the look in her eyes as well, though there was no moon. She liked to think later that what happened next had nothing to do with the sound of footsteps pounding on the path from north and south, nothing to do with the approach of either Abrahams or McCann.

He dropped the knife.

First he said, "Don't hurt me."

Then he said, "Don't tell on me."

"You okay?" Abrahams asked.

She nodded. She couldn't seem to catch her breath. The gun in her hand was trembling now.

"I would've killed him," she whispered.

"What?" Abrahams said.

"A kid," she whispered.

"We better call for a meat wagon," McCann said. "It looks to me like she's—"

"I'm all *right!*" she said fiercely, and both men stared at her. "I'm all right," she said more softly, and felt suddenly faint, and hoped against hope that she wouldn't pass out in front of these two hairbags from the Chinatown Precinct, and stood there sucking in great gulps of air until the queasiness and the dizziness passed, and then she smiled weakly and said, "What kept you?"

THEY had not finished with Moore until almost a quarter past one, and Kling did not get home until two in the morning. They had got from him essentially what they'd expected to get: only what he chose to admit. In approximately eight hours, Carella and Meyer would be accompanying Moore to the complaint room at Felony Court, where a clerk would draw up a short-form complaint listing the charges against him. This so-called yellow sheet would follow him later that morning to his arraignment—and indeed become a part of his permanent record. In the meantime, there was not much anyone could do until the wheels of justice began grinding, slowly.

He was exhausted, but the first thing he did when he came into the apartment was dial Eileen's number. There was no answer. He let the phone ring a dozen times, hung up, dialed it again, slowly and carefully this time, and let it ring another dozen times. Still no answer. He thumbed through the *R*'s in his directory and found the listing for Frank Riley, a man who'd gone through the Academy with him and who was now a Detective/Second working out of the Chinatown Precinct. He dialed the precinct, told the desk sergeant who he was, and then asked if he had any information on the stakeout outside Worth Memorial earlier that night. The desk sergeant didn't know anything about any stakeout. He put Kling through to the squadroom upstairs, where he talked to a weary detective on the graveyard shift. The detective told him he heard it had gone down as scheduled, but he didn't know all the details. When Kling asked him if Detective Burke was okay, he said there was nobody by that name on the Chinatown Squad.

He was wondering who to try next when the knock sounded on his door. He went to the door.

"Who is it?" he asked.

"Me," she answered. Her voice sounded very weary and very small.

He took off the night chain, unlocked the dead bolt, and opened the door. She was wearing a navy pea jacket over blue jeans and black boots. Her long red hair was hanging loose around her face. In the dim illumination of the hallway lightbulb, he could see that her face was discolored and bruised, her lip swollen.

"Okay to come in?" she asked.

"Come in," he said, and immediately, "Are you okay?"

"Tired," she said.

He locked the door behind her and put on the night chain. When he turned from the door, she was sitting on the edge of the bed.

"How'd it go?" he asked.

"We got him," she said. "Fourteen years old," she said. "I almost killed him," she said.

Their eyes met.

"Would you mind very much making love to me?" she said.

FIFTEEN

IN SOME cities, it was called a "first appearance." In this city, it was called an "arraignment." However you sliced it and whatever you called it, it was the first time a person charged with a crime appeared in a courtroom before a judge.

They had talked over their strategy beforehand with the assistant district attorney assigned to the case. They knew Moore's attorney would advise him to plead not guilty to *all* the charges, and whereas they were certain the dope charge would stick, they were on more tenuous ground where it came to the murders. Their fear was that they'd come up against a lenient judge who might accept Moore's contention that Brother Anthony's murder was committed in self-defense, and might set what he thought to be a reasonable bail for the drug offense. Even though the ballistics tests on the Smith & Wesson would not be completed until the case was presented to a grand jury sometime next week, they decided to tack on to their complaint the three additional counts of Murder One, hoping a judge would be intimidated by quantity and weight when it came time to grant or deny bail. If the gun that had killed Brother Anthony turned out to be the same gun that had fired the fatal bullets into Paco Lopez, Sally Anderson, and Marvin Edelman, they felt there was a good chance the grand jury would hand down a true bill on all *four* murder counts. When the case later came to trial, it would then be Moore's word alone that would keep him from spending more time in prison than there were days on an eternal calendar. The important thing now was to make sure he did not walk out of that courthouse. They felt certain that if bail was granted, they would never see him again.

The judge hearing the case was Walking Wilbur Harris.

The court attendant, who was called a bridge in this city, sat before Harris's bench and read off the name of the defendant and then the charges against him. Harris looked out over his rimless spectacles and said, "Are these charges correct, officer?"

"Yes, Your Honor," Carella said.

The four of them were standing before the judge's bench, Carella with the assistant D.A., Moore with his attorney. Harris turned to Moore.

"You may have a hearing in this court," he said, "or an adjournment for purpose of obtaining a lawyer or witnesses, or waive that hearing and let the case go to a grand jury. Do you have a lawyer?"

"Yes, Your Honor," Moore said.

"Is he here present?"

"I am representing the defendant," Moore's attorney said.

"Ah, yes, Mr. Wilcox," Harris said. "Didn't recognize you."

Wilcox smiled. "Your Honor," he said, in recognition of the recognition.

"How do you plead to these charges?" Harris asked. "First count, Criminal Possession of a controlled substance in the First Degree, contrary to penal law, Section two-twenty point twenty-one."

"Not guilty, Your Honor," Moore said.

"Second, third, fourth, and fifth counts, Murder in the First

Degree, contrary to penal law, Section one-twenty-five point twenty-seven."

"Not guilty, Your Honor," Moore said.

"Pending a grand jury hearing," Wilcox said, going straight for the jugular, "may I at this time request bail for the defendant?"

"The man's been charged with *four* counts of First Degree *Murder!*" Harris said, looking surprised.

"He acted in self-defense on the first count, Your Honor, and had nothing whatever to do with the other three murders charged."

"Mr. Delmonico?" Harris said, turning to the A.D.A.

"We have good and reasonable cause to believe the same weapon was used in all four murders, Your Honor."

"What good and reasonable cause?" Harris asked.

"Detective Carella here has ballistics reports indicating the same gun was used in the murders of Paco Lopez, Sally Anderson, and Marvin Edelman."

"What about this other one?" Harris said. "Anthony Scalzo."

"The man was killed—"

"The gun is now with—"

"One at a time," Harris said.

"The man was killed in self-defense, Your Honor," Wilcox said. "He was armed when he broke into the defendant's apartment. There was a struggle during which my client disarmed him and shot him. In self-defense."

"Mr. Delmonico?"

"The gun is now with Ballistics Section, Your Honor. We should have a report sometime before the grand jury hearing next week."

"What makes you think it's the same gun?" Harris asked.

"It's a thirty-eight-caliber Smith and Wesson, Your Honor. That's the make and caliber of the gun used in the previous three murders. The same gun for all three murders."

"But you don't know if it's the same gun that was used in this *fourth* homicide."

"Not yet, Your Honor."

"Your Honor—" Wilcox said.

"Your Honor—" Delmonico said.

"Just a minute here," Harris said. "Mr. Wilcox?"

"Your Honor," Wilcox said, "there *is* no ballistics evidence that would link the gun used in the previous murders with the shooting that took place in my client's apartment yesterday. But even if there *did* exist such evidence, it's our contention that the gun belonged to Anthony Scalzo and *not* my client."

"Mr. Delmonico?"

"Your Honor," Delmonico said, "we feel such evidence will be forthcoming. In any event, given the gravity of the charges before you, I respectfully submit that the granting of bail would be inadvisable in this case."

"Yes, well, that's for *me* to decide, isn't it?" Harris said.

"Yes, Your Honor, of course."

"Bail is granted in the amount of one hundred thousand dollars," Harris said.

"We are prepared to meet that bail, Your Honor," Wilcox said.

"Very well, remand the defendant."

"May I have a few words with my client?" Wilcox asked.

"Take him aside. Next case."

As the bridge read off the name of the next defendant and the charges against him, Carella watched Wilcox in whispered conversation with Moore. Wilcox was a good lawyer; Carella knew he'd have discussed with Moore beforehand the amount of bail he thought he could meet. All they had to come up with now was $10,000 in cash and collateral for the rest, easy enough when you owned twenty-five carats of diamonds worth a cool three hundred thousand bucks. Or would Wilcox simply phone Moore's mother in Miami and ask her to wire him a mere $100,000?

Either way, Moore would spend a relaxed day in custody at either the Municipal House of Detention crosstown on Daley Street or else in the Parsons Island Jail in the middle of the river Dix. By nightfall, he'd be out on the street again. He watched as they led Moore out. He watched as Wilcox exchanged a few words with the bail bondsman. He rarely thought in Italian, but the words *La commedia è finita* crossed his mind. He walked to the back of the courtroom, where Delmonico and Meyer were waiting.

"I told you," Meyer said. "There ain't no justice in this world."

But maybe there was, after all.

THERE was hardly any packing left to do.

He had done most of his packing yesterday afternoon before he'd been interrupted by the man in the monk's habit, whose name he now knew was Anthony Scalzo. Nothing had changed. He *still* planned to get out of here as soon as possible, out of the city and the state for sure, maybe out of the country as well. The only difference now was that his mother would be out the hundred thousand dollars she'd provided for his bail, a small enough price to pay for his freedom; anyway, he planned to pay her back as soon as he got settled someplace.

As he took his toilet articles from the medicine cabinet in the bathroom, he replayed the little session with the mastermind sleuths of the 87th Precinct, four of them sitting there playing cat and mouse with him, each and every one of them knowing they didn't have a chance in hell of getting him on those three murders unless he decided to fall to his knees in confession. He was tempted—*almost*, but not quite—to forget all about running, take his chances with a jury instead. They'd buy his plea of self-defense, and he'd end up spending a little time—maybe two years—in prison on the drug charge. But he supposed there was no such thing as a *little* time in prison; *any* time in prison was a *lot* of time. Better to do it this way. Jump bail, get out of the country, use the diamonds—but, ah, what a waste. Two years of medical school, what a waste. He wondered what his father would have said if he was still alive. Well, Dad, he thought, I saw my opportunity and I grabbed it. It would've all worked out fine, I'd have had the money *and* my medical degree besides, nobody the wiser, nobody hurt, Dad, if only . . .

The one person I thought I could trust.

Sally.

Would I have written to her otherwise?

Thought I could trust her. Told me we didn't have to sell off *all* the stuff right away, we could—well, listen, who knew anything at *all* about cocaine? Babe in the woods down there in Miami, Portoles leading me by the hand, I will make you rich, *amigo*, for saving my son. Tested the stuff for me. I didn't even know enough to do that. Paying fifty thousand a key, never thought to ask if it was *real* cocaine. Cobalt thiocyanate. Blue reaction. What'd he say? The brighter the blue, the better the girl. Referring to the coke. Called it girl. Best pure you can find, he told me. Yours now. Mine. Sally's, too, sort of. Told me we could hold back two kilos, ounce them out, she knew somebody uptown who'd be interested, somebody who would put them on to other customers. Knew more about cocaine than I'll *ever* know. Said she'd been shooting it even before it got fashionable, while she was studying dance in London, used to share what she called Cocaine Fucks with an oboe player she was living with. Shared those with her friend uptown, too, but who knew that at the time? Trusted her. One thing you should *never* trust is a woman in bed. Spread any woman's legs, and secrets fly out of her like butterflies. Told him everything. Told him about our little cache, the two keys of cocaine we were milking. Our insurance, she called them. Sure.

He zipped up his toilet kit and carried it to the open suitcase in the bedroom. He stood looking down into the suitcase, as though he'd forgotten something. The gun? Funny how you became accustomed to having a gun around, accustomed to using it. Police property now, evidence tag on it, a lot of good it would do them once they realized he'd packed his tent, twenty-five carats worth of diamonds to turn into cash anywhere in the world. Still, if only . . .

If only she hadn't shared our secret with him, if only he hadn't come to me, slimy little Puerto Rican bastard, wanting a piece of the action, *demanding* a piece of the action, threatening to go to the police if I didn't cut him in on a bigger piece of the pie, those dwindling two keys, greedy little bastard. Give away a piece of what *I'd* taken the risk for? Said he knew I had diamonds hidden someplace in the apartment, said he wanted *those*, too, otherwise he'd go to the cops. Said he had proof, said he knew where he could get proof. The letter, of course. She'd kept the letter. And I'd trusted her. So what was I supposed to do? Spend time in prison because Sally had babbled to the wrong lover, Sally in the heat of passion had—God, she was good in bed! Dancers, Jesus!

Bought the gun two days after he paid me his little visit. Contacted the guy I'd sold the six keys to, told him I needed a gun. Easy, he said. Cost me two hundred dollars. Never used a gun in my life before then. Never even held one in my hand. Wanted to be a surgeon one day, good hands, steady, ah, well. Knew where he lived, hell, she used to *deliver* to him every Sunday, didn't know she was *also* delivering pussy and secrets, waited for him outside his building, followed him, shot him. Easy. Killed him.

But then, you know, you start thinking, you know, you start thinking you've got to *protect* it. Not the coke, not the diamonds, but *all* of it. The *future*. I *did* want to be a doctor, Dad, I wasn't just walking through it, you know, I was busting my *ass*, just the way you wanted me to. Doctor Timothy Moore, *that's* who I wanted to be! So it had to be *protected*, you see, and if she'd told Lopez, then she couldn't be trusted anymore, could she? And how long would it have taken her to realize that I was the one who'd

killed that greedy little spic? How long before she *herself* went to
the police? No, I had to—the radio, he thought. That's what I'm
forgetting. The radio.

He went into the living room, where the radio was still sitting
alongside the telephone, picked up the radio, held it in the palm
of his hand, and looked at it almost fondly. So simple, he thought.
No way anyone in a million years could have connected the murder of a small-time coke dealer—well, Sally of course, Sally
would have realized sooner or later. Which was why I had to, to,
to do the same thing to her, you see. But with her, they'd *find* a
connection. With her, they'd begin asking me questions—well,
they *did* ask me questions, didn't they? So I needed protection,
the radio, needed someone to say I'd been talking to him on the
phone and he'd heard my radio going, good old Karl, solid as a
rock, make a good doctor one day. Took the phone off the hook
before I left the house, called him from a phone booth, radio
going, called him twice before I killed her, waiting for her, late
as usual, called him again *after* I killed her, when I got home, *kept*
calling him, radio going each time, good old reliable Karl.

He carried the radio back into the bedroom and put it in the
open suitcase. Anything else? he wondered. Anything I'm forgetting? So easy to forget things when you're, when you, when you
start something like this, all the things you have to do to *protect* it,
keep your eye on the main goal, never mind the money, I wanted
to be a *doctor!* Almost forgot about Edelman, last link in the chain,
remembered him later. Suppose some IRS agent examined his
books, wanted to know where he'd sold those diamonds, twenty-
five carats, three hundred thousand dollars in cash, who'd you sell
them to, *who?* Tie me in with that kind of money, cops would be
around asking more questions, where'd you *get* that kind of
money, no. Had to protect myself. Had to kill him. Like the others. So I could be a doctor one day. Like my father.

He closed the suitcase.

So, he thought.

He looked around the apartment.

That's it, he thought.

He picked up the suitcase, walked out of the bedroom, and out of the apartment, and down the steps to the street.

She was waiting for him in the small dark entrance lobby downstairs.

She said only, "The opera ain't over," and he frowned and started to walk past her, taking her for a crazy bag lady or something—this city was full of lunatics—surprised when he saw the open straight razor in her hand, shocked when he realized she was coming at him with the razor, terrified when he saw his own blood pouring from the open wound in his throat. He clutched for his throat. Blood gushed onto his hands. He said, "I'm sorry," but he was dead before he could say the word "Dad."

THE call from Fort Phyllis did not come until Saturday morning. There was only one notorious homosexual cruising street in the entire precinct that surrounded Ramsey University and the neighboring Quarter, but the cops of the 5th Precinct nonetheless called their turf Fort Phyllis. The man phoning was a Detective/Third Grade named Dawson. He asked to speak to Detective Carella.

"This is Dawson," he said. "Fifth Squad."

"What can I do for you?" Carella asked.

"We caught a homicide last night, slashing in a hallway on Chelsea Place. Guy named Timothy Moore."

"What?" Carella said.

"Yeah," Dawson said. "Reason I'm calling, Charlie Nichols here was in court yesterday while you were arraigning this guy. He figured maybe you ought to know about it. Figured maybe this ties in with the homicides you were investigating. The ones you charged this guy Moore with."

"How?" Carella said.

"Well, I don't *know* how," Dawson said. "That's what I'm asking *you*."

"A slashing, you said?"

"Yeah. Ear to ear. Nice job."

He thought fleetingly of Judite Quadrado.

"Any leads?" he asked.

"None so far," Dawson said. "No witnesses, nothing. Guy had a bag of diamonds in his suitcase. Was he out on bail or something?"

"Yes," Carella said.

"Looks like he was maybe skipping, huh?"

"Looks that way," Carella said.

"So what do you want us to do about this?"

"I don't know what you mean."

"You want us to turn this over to you, or what?"

Here we go again, Carella thought.

"Well, let me see what the lieutenant thinks," he said.

"Maybe you charged the wrong guy, you know what I mean?" Dawson said. "I mean, Charlie told me it was four counts of Murder One."

"That's what it was," Carella said.

"So maybe somebody *else* did it, is all I'm saying," Dawson said. "The four murders. Maybe it wasn't this guy Moore at all."

"It was Moore," Carella said flatly.

"Anyway," Dawson said, and the line went silent.

"I'll talk to the lieutenant," Carella said.

"Sure, let me know," Dawson said, and hung up.

The squadroom was very quiet for a Saturday morning. Carella rose from his desk and walked to the water cooler. Standing near the windows streaming wintry sunlight, he sipped at the water in the paper cup and then crumpled the cup and tossed it into the wastebasket. He went to the lieutenant's door and knocked on it.

"Come!" Byrnes shouted.

He went into the lieutenant's office and closed the door behind him. He told the lieutenant that he'd just had a call from Fort Phyllis. He told the lieutenant that someone had slit Timothy Moore's throat in the hallway of his building last night, and that there were no witnesses and no leads, and the cops down there wanted to know what to do about it, whether they should turn this over to the Eight-Seven or what?

Byrnes listened very carefully. He was thoughtfully silent for a long time. Then he said, "No witnesses, huh?"

"None," Carella said.

"The Fifth Squad, huh?"

"Yes."

"We got enough headaches," Byrnes said. "Let *their* mothers worry."

ABOUT THE
AUTHOR

The two homicide detectives were burly and broad and they looked self-assured.

They framed the thin frightened man like belligerent bookends.

This passage from the opening chapter of the classic urban thriller *Ice* is a pure example of the power of its renowned author, Ed McBain. At once menacing, immediate, and visually poetic, in few words it evokes crime-scene tension with unforgettable clarity. And like all of McBain's best writing, it packs a punch. A master of the unexpected, he mixes "book power" with "cop power" for his fiction snapshot and at the same time teases unsuspecting readers into feeling a tickle of uneasiness as if they too, book in hand, might be squeezed by these brawny investigators.

Widely credited with being the inventor of the modern American police procedural, Ed McBain published his first 87th Precinct novel, *Cop Hater*, in 1956. Though he insists that Isola, the gritty city in all his Precinct novels—there are now more than fifty—is imaginary, everyone knows he is writing about his home-town: Manhattan. Not only are his police dramas based on years of primary research riding in patrol cars and visiting morgues, cop bars, and squad rooms, the authenticity of his locale is clearly a product of intense personal familiarity. It is interesting to note that Isola means "island" in Italian. Manhattan is an island, and McBain (a pseudonym) just happens to be of Italian descent.

He was born Salvatore Lombino in New York City, on October 15, 1926. His father was a letter carrier, earning eight dollars a week; his mother worked for a time in the mailroom of the Harcourt, Brace publishing house. The Great Depression hit the family hard, forcing them to move in with grandparents who lived on 120th Street in East Harlem. It was a quiet, multiethnic neigh-borhood in those days, fertile ground for an imaginative young writer. The rich city colors and sounds, street scenes and accents, would eventually become Ed McBain's fictional 87th Precinct.

The author's first career goal, however, was to be a painter. He studied art at the Art Students League and at Cooper Union. Then came a two-year stint in the U.S. Navy (1944–1946), and boredom gave rise to a new ambition. While assigned to a destroyer in the peacetime Pacific, he started submitting short stories to pulp magazines—and he hasn't stopped writing since.

Success would come early, and it would last into the twenty-first century. But it would not arrive before the author earned his B.A. at Hunter College (Phi Beta Kappa) in 1950, legally changed his name to Evan Hunter, and held various day jobs, including lobster salesman, literary agent, telephone clerk for AAA, and high school teacher. This last job, at Bronx Vocational High School, was the springboard for his first bestseller. *The Blackboard Jungle* was published in 1954, when the author was only twenty-eight. A controversial exposé of what it was really like to teach in a tough, inner-city school in the 1950s, the novel was an instant sensation that was made into a major Hollywood film starring Glenn Ford and Sidney Poitier.

Hollywood soon became a natural venue for Evan Hunter/ Ed McBain. In 1959 he wrote the screenplay for the film version of his novel *Strangers When We Meet*. A short time later Alfred Hitchcock asked him to try his hand at writing a screenplay based on a short story by Daphne du Maurier: "The Birds." (His memoir, *Me and Hitch*, is filled with amusing anecdotes about his experiences working with the great director.) Hunter went on to write other screenplays (*Fuzz* and *Walk Proud*), as well as stage plays, teleplays, and TV scripts.

In the 1950s the author wrote five novels under the name Richard Marsten. As Ed McBain, he has produced, in addition to the 87th Precinct series, a baker's dozen of mysteries about Matthew Hope, a gumshoe lawyer in Florida. He has also written stories for children and numerous short stories under numerous pen names.

No American writer is more American than the creator of the hard-boiled world of the 87th Precinct. And yet his stories travel the world with astonishing ease. He is particularly popular in England, where in 1998 he was honored as the first American to receive (in the House of Lords) the coveted Diamond Dagger, the British Crime Writers' Association's highest award. His international bestseller list reads like an ambassadors' banquet table at a White House state dinner: Brazil, Japan, France, Italy, Denmark, Greece, Holland, Switzerland, Israel, Norway. . . .

At home he received the 1986 Grand Master Award for lifetime achievement from the Mystery Writers of America. And back in Europe, in 2002, he was the winner of the Frankfurt e-Book Award for the best fiction work (*The Last Dance*) originally published in e-book form.

A nearly lifelong Manhattan resident, McBain moved to

Weston, Connecticut, in 1997 with his wife, drama coach Dragica Dimitrijevic-Hunter. He spends his mornings hard at work on the current Evan Hunter novel in progress, then changes hats to write as Ed McBain after lunch.

The author of *Ice* is indeed a man of many names (Evan Hunter, Ed McBain, Richard Marsten, Curt Cannon, Ezra Hannon, Hunt Collins, and more), but he is singular in his status as one of America's preeminent poets of crime, justice, and urban reality.

Tom Clemmons
Editor